MURDER, TEA & CRYSTALS

HUMMINGBIRD
MOONRISE

SHERRI L. DODD

Black Rose Writing | Texas

The author grants the final approval for this literary material.

First printing

This is a work of fiction. Names, characters, businesses, places, events, and incidents are either the products of the author's imagination or used in a fictitious manner. Any resemblance to actual persons, living or dead, or actual events is purely coincidental.

ISBN: 978-1-68513-658-1
LIBRARY OF CONGRESS CONTROL NUMBER: 2025935293
PUBLISHED BY BLACK ROSE WRITING
www.blackrosewriting.com

Printed in the United States of America
Suggested Retail Price (SRP) $22.95

Hummingbird Moonrise is printed in Minion Pro

*As a planet-friendly publisher, Black Rose Writing does its best to eliminate unnecessary waste to reduce paper usage and energy costs, while never compromising the reading experience. As a result, the final word count vs. page count may not meet common expectations.

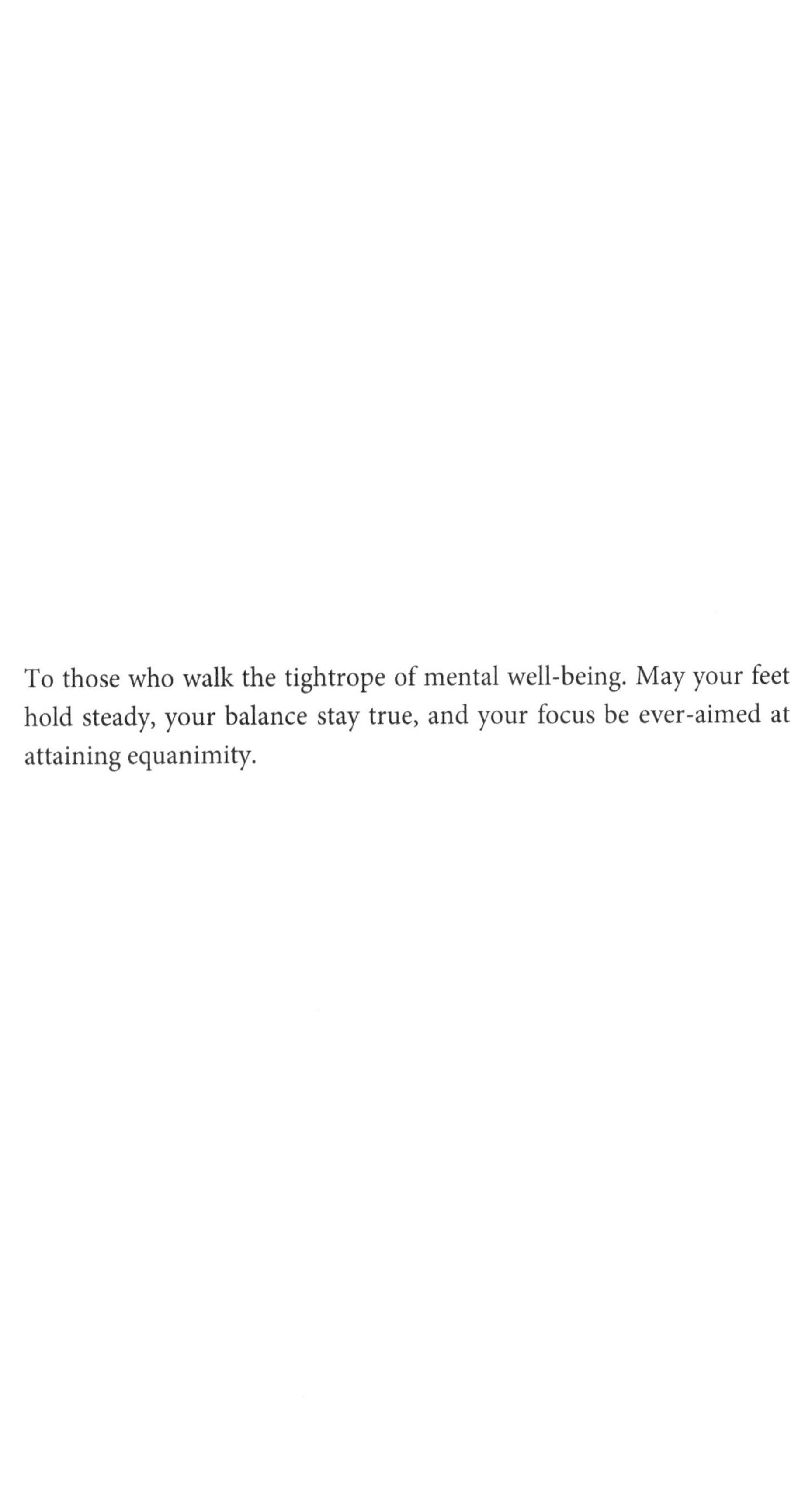

To those who walk the tightrope of mental well-being. May your feet hold steady, your balance stay true, and your focus be ever-aimed at attaining equanimity.

Praise for
Hummingbird Moonrise

"I was moved. Not just by the tragic past that hangs over the Kelly family, but by the hope that emerges through Arista's strength. This is a book for those who like their witch stories intimate, their mysteries character-driven, and their fiction laced with emotion and weirdness in equal measure. If you enjoy Alice Hoffman's *Practical Magic*, but wish it had a bit more grit and ghost stories, *Hummingbird Moonrise* might just be your cup of tea. Or maybe your crystal-infused moon water. Either way, it's worth the read."
–Literary Titan

"Dodd fuses folklore, witchcraft, and familial bonds into a mystery that's full of tension and emotional stakes. The prose is fluid and poetic, but never overindulgent. The dialogue feels
authentic, especially in the moments of warmth and wit between Arista and Auntie. The pacing is steady, picking up momentum as secrets are uncovered and choices must be made."
–Reader Views

"A nuanced, multifaceted yarn with magical machinations and real-world concerns."
–Kirkus Reviews

"The prose is so evocative, readers can almost taste Arista's homemade apple spice black tea and her Auntie's cinnamon bread, as Dodd sweeps them into a shadowy tale of magic, misfortune, and female resilience, with enough twists and time skips to drive suspense. Arista is a delightful heroine, a prophesied witch laboring under the weight of familial and personal expectations, while her Auntie is a pragmatic, mystical delight, as comfortable in her kitchen as she is fiercely safeguarding her family's "dirty little secrets.""
–Booklife, *Publisher's Weekly*

"Author Sherri L. Dodd has a brilliant sense of timing with her storytelling, knowing exactly when to drop the next breadcrumb for an engrossing paranormal mystery laced with emotion, legacy, and a uniquely feminine sense of strength."
–K.C. Finn, *Reader's Favorite*

"The paranormal activity really ramps up in this third book. Possessions, ghostly visits, new spells, and spiritual transformations—the intrigue is everywhere. You see some jaw-dropping revelations before Arista does, and it heightens the suspense greatly. Lucky for the returning reader, Dodd ties up those loose ends you've been curious about, and she does it while tackling some serious topics like grief, responsibility, and anxiety."
–Chelsey Tucker, *Independent Book Review*

"Dodd weaves a delicious tale of witchcraft, curses and missing persons that takes place in a small town among the California redwoods. The tone varies between cozy and creepy, sometimes depending on the point of view. Dodd is especially skilled at pacing and character reveal, creating a story that burns in slowly increasing intensity."
**–*BlueInk Review*

Note From the Author

This novel includes a few different accents, including Irish-American, Scottish-American, Cockney, and a Southern drawl. The words are (mis)spelled to elaborate on the annunciation. ~~ *Apologies* if it slows down your reading pace, but I love the rich texture of accents in my everyday life, and sometimes we do have to slow down to understand our fellow humans. Tips I used for writing these accents can be found in the *Reference and Inspiration* section at the back of the book!

HUMMINGBIRD
MOONRISE

PROLOGUE

~ Boulder Creek, California, 1940 ~

The scent of noble fir had already filled their cozy mountain cottage. As Barry secured the small bristly tree into its metal stand, he thought of the coming holiday—Christmas, in two days' time—and considered their lack of space. His three grown sons could tent up outside, and his daughter and her kids would do well in the spare bedroom, but that left no room for his brothers visiting from Ireland.

"Oigh!" Too much to consider, and it was Noreen's job to fret about space, anyway.

Further, he appreciated the healthy green needles. The comforting sight of them blended well with the savory aroma of the chicken and barley stew boiling in the kitchen. The warmth lulled him, and he sat down in his chair, only to scoff at his own idleness. With a man's job to be done, he arose again for chores.

"Feedin' the dogs. Oi'll be back," Barry announced, his long i's still harboring an Irish accent beneath his more recent Texas twang.

Noreen, his wife, looked up and nodded as she dutifully tended the boiling four-gallon stewpot. She flashed a look at their two grandsons waiting at the dinner table. "Dinner's ready when Grandpa returns from feeding," she said with a wink and warm smile.

He ignored the boys' cheers as he admired the hard-working woman he had met and married what seemed like a lifetime ago after emigrating from Ireland to the southeast Texas countryside. She looked as pretty now as she did then, even with her long, graying blond hair pulled up in a tight bun, her gunnysack dress covering her beautiful body, and that apron splotched with the night's upcoming dinner. Still pretty.

His oldest grandson caught his eye, staring at him with an amused expression.

"Alroight, then." He had to get to those dogs.

Barry walked out onto the porch of his self-built dwelling and peered down his dirt road of Hoot Owl Way. It was quite a jaunt into town, but the coastal redwoods had become a refuge from the bustle of the city life he had experienced back in Houston, Texas's largest city, as of the recent turn of the year—1940. Now, after ten years of southerly living, long enough to improve his English, develop a slight drawl, and pick up several southern colloquialisms, he and his family moved west to the California mountains and settled into this new life. It only took the preceding months to build his modest home and get his business of hound trading well established.

He invigorated himself with a whiff of the mountain air and readied to feed the twenty dogs he had bred and trained for hunting. Listening to their exulting howls, he chuckled, knowing his voice served as their dinner bell.

"Come on, Duke. Toime tuh go," he announced to his favorite hound. Duke was the only dog he had granted freedom to run the property and take comfort on the porch.

Duke lay motionless. But that was usual in those first few seconds while he considered rising from the old, tattered rug. A mound of gray-ticked fur with a generous black splotch on his side, Duke had floppy black velvet ears that added to his handsome look, and those relaxed jowls were always good for tugging.

"Here, boy!"

Barry nudged the mongrel's rear-end with the tip of his boot, an act of respect, considering most of his dogs would get a swift kick up the butt for not jumping to his demand.

The doom of the stillness hit Barry. He squatted down by Duke and gave his favorite dog a jostle. Instead of the usual warm plush ear, his fingers touched fur that felt stiff and lifeless.

"Níl!" he cried out.

The metal spoon clanked down on the stove within the kitchen, and Noreen's hurried steps approached.

"Níl, goddammit!"

She peered through the door. "What is it, Barry?"

"They got Duke!" He briefly massaged the dog's head, but feeling death again, he stopped. "Noreen, he was a good ol' dog." He rubbed at his own forehead and winced in anguish. "We got tuh stop this madness!"

Barry dropped his head and held back the urge to cry, forcing the sadness down deep within his gut, where it could chew at him like a coral snake on stiff boot leather. There was no use letting the little woman see his weakness. Nor would he indulge in it himself. He snuffed out the final hint of emotion and stoked his anger.

He scrutinized Duke, looking for blood, breaks, or signs of a snake bite under his ears, his neck, and upon his stomach. He found nothing.

"Third goddamn dog oi lost this month. Someone's poisoning 'em, and they're gonna pay. We're doing that Ouija!"

Noreen looked back toward their grandsons sitting at the table. They were a handful to manage with their daughter in town caring for an elderly woman for the next two days. However, the worried look in her eyes confirmed she would cooperate, and he figured she dreaded what they would discover.

"Git those kids fed and tuh bed early."

"I will," she said, and at twenty minutes past the hour, kept her word.

Once tucked, Barry bid them goodnight. A rare occasion with plenty of warning punctuated with a stern directive. "You boys stay in bed … yuh hear me?" The attention served as an implicit warning. He could not risk them getting up for even a sip of water and witnessing his and Noreen's dabbling on the witchboard.

"Don't make me git that belt out. Yuh hear me? Not a peep," he said, glaring into each set of innocent eyes with his stiff, calloused finger pointing at them.

Upon their cowering nod, he turned and shut the door.

There was no harm in putting the scare in them, and he wouldn't really beat them bloody.

·　·　·

Barry left for his mission bright and early the next morning, cold, steel shotgun in hand. His unfed barking hounds announced their concern through yips and howls while the sweet song of forest birds tweeted from the towering evergreens. But he paid no mind as adrenaline flooded his senses, stoking the energy to execute his deed of vengeance.

He jumped into his old '33 Ford Pickup, drove to the end of Hoot Owl Way, and made a left heading further up into the mountain, navigating the bumps and turns with a rickety bounce that jarred his clenched jaws. Today, Fil was going to get what he deserved. His shifty-eyed greetings in town made more sense after last night's Ouija session had exposed his guilt.

Barry came to an abrupt halt in front of his neighbor's home, grabbed his shotgun from the passenger floorboard, and flung open his door. With his dogs singing a united song of encouragement in the distance, he stalked onto the property and stopped halfway up the walkway.

"Fil! Git out here, yuh son-of-a-bitch!"

He propped his shotgun on his shoulder while watching the bustling of movement inside Fil's home.

"Fil!"

"We don't want any trouble with you, Barry," Fil's wife, Helen, said through the screen door.

"Well, trouble's here. And oi have no issue with yuh, Helen. It's that husband of yuh's. Oi wanna talk tuh him!"

Truthfully, he had never liked Helen. A repulsive woman—her long nose with the single-haired wart was framed by haggard gray hair she refused to pull back into a proper bun. No respectable woman, and she reminded him of the scariest witches he had seen in books warning against dark magick.

The screen door opened, and a weary man stepped onto the porch. His squinty eyes begged for mercy before he opened his mouth. "Barry, what are you doing here with that gun? I got the family all home for the holidays, and you're scaring every one of 'em."

Barry could hear the whispering within the house but did not care. He had a score to settle. "Yuh the one's been poisonin' moi dogs, Fil?"

Fil stood and said nothing as the distant howling persisted. After a moment of pause, his confession poured forth. "Well, Jesus, Barry, can you blame me? Listen to that!" He looked down the hill in the direction of Barry's home. "Nonstop, day in and day out."

"Those dogs are moi loivelihood, Fil. They put food on the table for moi family, and … the last one yuh took … he was a *good* dog." He shook his head, full of regret for not catching this son-of-a-bitch before he got to Duke. "Yuh got no roight."

Fil started to reach into his deep suspender pocket.

"Don't do it!" Barry warned, knowing that Fil owned a gun.

"Barry—" Fil said, grabbing the object within his pocket.

BANG!

Barry's deafening shot riddled Fil with bloody holes, sending his body into spasms before he hit the ground. Simultaneously, the house's front window shattered in a violent spray of glass, another effect of Barry's buckshot.

Helen's scream preceded her thrusting open the screen door, smashing it to the outer wall as she dashed onto the porch and fell to Fil's side, weeping over his still, bloodied body.

Barry numbed for a moment, seeing her trauma. Then he turned, feeling the strength of his justice as he marched back to his truck. He knew Fil had a gun. Had he not shot first, he'd be dead.

From behind, he heard a small child yell out from inside the house, "Grandmother, Aunt Sophie's bleeding."

Another voice yelled out. "Jimmy's hurt, too!"

Jimmy? Barry felt a twinge at the mention of others hurt, but he also believed in guilt by association. The whole family probably knew about the wrongdoing. Hell, they could have even been in on it.

Suddenly, violent squalls of hysteria from within the house joined Helen's lone, moaning cry. A chorus of dissonance that drowned out the howling song of his mongrels.

Barry plopped down on his truck seat and set his weapon back to the floorboard, picturing Jimmy, Fil's young grandson … but no! He had every right to serve this justice. Fil had brought the grief upon his own family, and he surely should not have reached for his weapon.

Forcing the stubborn clutch into gear, Barry rolled onto the street. When he saw Helen in his rearview mirror, running toward his truck, he sped up, leaving her in a wake of dust.

She shrieked out in an anger he did not know she possessed. No matter. He refused to look back, even when her message reached his hearing ears.

"Curses to you, Barry Kelly! And cursed be your family!"

•　　•　　•

Four years after Barry's buckshot took the life of Fil, Fil's daughter, Sophie, and his grandson, Jimmy, trouble brewed again. Barry paced the living area as Noreen sat teary-eyed and fretting, mending his pajama bottoms. Their two grandsons sat at the table, eating sweetbread to the wailing cries of their mother suffering from a difficult labor.

Fil's widow, Helen, had summoned the devil's work upon them when Barry was found not guilty of murder. He knew it for sure now, thinking back to how everything had unfolded. A short time after the trial, Helen sent a handwritten letter warning him that "by her soul and blood," she had cast a curse that would ensure the Kelly bloodline was wiped from the earth by the fifth generation. She signed the letter with her name and bloody thumbprint and had each surviving family member do the same. If not for the ominous subject, it would have looked like a young-un's school project.

Initially, Barry had shucked off the hoopla and tossed the written threat into the fire.

However, within weeks of Helen's foreboding announcement, Barry's eldest son ailed with influenza. After a week of sweat-soaked bedsheets, vomiting, and delirious fever-inspired rantings, he had died. The next year, while visiting, their middle son had been killed while hunting; his body found by one of Barry's own tracker dogs. The local authorities suspected a mountain lion attack based on the deep claw marks and the fact his body had been gutted like a river trout and dragged into the brush.

Barry walked over to his liquor cabinet, poured himself a stiff shot of Bushmills, threw it back, and swallowed the punishment. The burn down his gullet took away the worry. But only for a moment.

Still, his daughter cried out in pain.

Tilting the empty glass, he watched the last drop coat the base, refusing to release into his mouth. He clenched his jaw, remembering his youngest son, the one who had liked to go fishing and hang out with his daddy as a boy. The kid was a hell of a shot with the rifle, too. But he had died in June, a casualty on the beaches of Normandy. Three sons born and raised. Three sons in the grave.

He took another shot, then firmly rapped the glass on the counter, grabbing the attention of Noreen and the boys. Just as quickly, his grandsons refocused on their sweetbread.

"Mrs. Kelly," the nurse beckoned.

Noreen disappeared into the bedroom, shutting the door behind her.

Now, their only daughter, whose husband had disappeared that year during a hunting trip, faced a perilous delivery. This third grandbaby had a stubbornness—twelve hours and still it refused to emerge. He felt sure he would lose both his daughter and the baby, with Helen's curse inflicting another deathly blow.

He cleared his throat to hear just a moment of something other than her cries. Then he closed his eyes and prayed for her safety from Helen's wrath. As their only remaining child, they needed her, and he and Noreen could not raise her two boys alone.

Noreen walked back out into the hallway, her bewildered expression inviting reassurance.

"She's been through this twoice before," Barry said, taking his woman into his arms. "Don't yuh worry."

Noreen's face brightened when she saw the boys looking at her, their eyes fixed like scared bunnies hearing predatory footsteps. "Hey, boys, your mama's going to be all right. She's just having a tough time right now. Why don't we get some fresh air?"

Noreen walked them out to the porch, clearly trying her best to distract their worried minds.

Inside, the wailing continued.

He could not take much more of this.

Then, silence.

Barry absorbed the sudden settled peace, pleasing to his weary ears and mental strain. Hopefully—

The squall of a newborn baby traveled through the closed door.

"Thank the Good Lord," he said, feeling the relief of his daughter's successful delivery. He bowed his head in prayerful appreciation, then enjoyed the next few minutes of silence with a renewed faith.

"Mr. Kelly," the doctor said, coming up behind him.

Barry turned to find the doctor holding a swaddled newborn.

"You have a beautiful, healthy granddaughter." His tone sent mixed messages—happy and sad, regretful and congratulatory. He gestured for Barry to take the infant. "She asked that the child be named Bethie if that pleases you."

"Well, how's …"

The doctor lowered his head, his voice hushed. "Mr. Kelly, I'm sorry, but we could not save her."

Barry's throat dried, and his disbelief choked him. He looked out the screen door at Noreen and the boys, but the doctor placed Bethie into his arms, drawing him back.

He stifled the disappointment and looked down at his first and only granddaughter. He found a glimmer of hope in her bright pink nose, rosy cheeks, and the sprigs of wispy red hair upon her misshapen head.

"I'm sure you're aware the head takes its permanent shape in the days to come. This is simply the effect of the birth canal."

Barry smiled yet felt the urge to cry. Joy. Sadness. It did not matter because he would not release the tears, anyway. Instead, he focused on this newborn child.

"She's a real healthy spirit … real strong … good color, as you can see." The doctor pointed to Bethie's rosy cheeks. "Looks like she has your hair color, too." He kept his smile subdued.

Barry looked down at his granddaughter and held his breath. He had loved his own kids and now had lost them all. For a moment, he faced the severity of three sons and a daughter, lost to the attrition of their father's sin.

He cleared his throat and stood taller. Little Bethie offered a chance at redemption. Atonement for his awful decision that he would take back, if only possible. Her birth represented the promise of life despite Helen's deadly curse.

Bethie gave a small wriggle in his arms. She cooed and briefly opened her swollen eyes. Just as quickly, she eased them shut again.

"Is she—"

"She's fine," the doctor said. "She's just resting. However, she needs to eat. Do you have cow's milk? Or goat's? Ewe's?"

"Oi think so."

"Barry?" Noreen said, peering through the screen door. Upon seeing the baby, she burst through, joy brightening her face. Broad smiles also grew on the boys' faces as they rushed in to greet their little sister.

Barry held tight to baby Bethie, not wanting to let her go.

Noreen stroked the infant's cheek and looked at the doctor.

"I'm sorry, ma'am," he said, bowing his head.

All color left her face, and she ran toward the bedroom, her cries building as she barged through its door.

Barry felt bad for her but figured it no use wishing for something other than reality. Kneeling, he introduced the boys to their new little sister.

"Declan, it's going tuh be your job as big brother tuh take care of her."

"Yes, sir. I will," Declan assured his grandfather, his innocent eyes serious to the cause.

"I'll help too," his little brother chimed in.

"Of course, yuh will, buddy. Okay, boys. We need tuh give your granny a little toime in there, then oi want yuh tuh go say goodboi tuh yuh mama. She's gone tuh heaven." Barry motioned to the boys with a serious look. "Go … wash up, and no tears. Yuh be strong for both of 'em."

They trudged to the hallway bathroom, hesitant of their weeping granny and the sympathetic nurse by their deathly still mother.

Barry stared down at Bethie. She was such a treasure. "*A stóirín*," he said, words from his distant homeland.

He welcomed the change that washed over him. He would do right by this child. In fact, the joy she brought to his soul after so much heartache made him want to be a better man. From this day forward, he would work at being more forgiving, and not hit so hard on his whuppins. In fact, other than the dogs, maybe he would never whup again.

"*A stóirín*, Bethie," he said again, the tears finally escaping.

He would raise his grandchildren with more love than he had ever given any of his own kids. He would even try to be a little more patient with Noreen. More than anything, he would never draw a gun again, as violence no longer had a place in his world.

"Bethie, moi little treasure," he whispered to the infant, not wanting to wake her.

Still, serious work needed to be done. He and Noreen would fight fire with fire to protect what precious little family they had left.

He had always held tight to his faith, praying nightly that the widow's bane held no power against them. That her threats fell anemic to the Good Lord in Heaven. But he had gone to a darker side when he had created and then used the Ouija, and since that decision led him to kill, maybe God had forsaken them. Therefore, they would need to find other methods of protection, and since Helen had cursed his family with dark magick, they would resort to the same measure to deflect it.

CHAPTER 1
OFF TO ARIZONA

~ December 2020 ~

Fueled by caffeinated soda and lively Tejano music blaring from his pill-shaped Bluetooth speaker, Mateo pried the wood planks from the foundation of the tiny mountain house, sweating and swearing with each mashed finger. Only a dozen planks had come loose so far. It surprised him how much effort he needed to put forth in the demolition despite nearly a century of aging.

"You know, some lady killed that serial killer in here a couple months back … end of summer. Um, Henry something," Jack bellowed from the dining area, where he duplicated Mateo's de-boarding efforts. He appeared in the doorway, following his remark with narrowed eyes and booing like a ghost while wriggling his fingers.

"No way. So that's straight-up blood stains in there?" Mateo asked.

"Yep. You remember all that in the news? The showdown up here in the mountains."

"Yeah."

"When the boss assigned me the inquiry, I wondered if that's what I'd be quoting. Of course, when I got here, it sure looks like a bloody battle went down. Then, I see the owner's name—Arista Kelly—one of the stations let the name slip before it all went hush-hush. Protecting the victim, I suppose."

"Damn," Mateo commented, calculating Jack's facts.

"When her boyfriend gave me the keys, he said she'd been staying with a relative down the street."

Mateo grunted at all the new information. He had only a vague memory of their key exchange from the previous week since his attention had been on his wife's phone call.

"Now, they're off to Arizona, and I don't think they're coming back till next year. So, the boyfriend will be here end-of-week for the sign off," Jack added, eyeing Mateo's technique.

Mateo considered his work, seeing it in a new, grotesque light, and groaned. He pried at another plank and tossed it aside before picking up his rag and wiping the sweat from his face. "Rigorous," he said, wedging his crowbar into another crack.

Jack laughed. "Yeah. Careful you don't bring the dead home with you. Anyway, I'm due for a break. You wanna take thirty?" Jack asked.

"Let me get this done first so I can start fresh on the next section."

"Okay. I'll be at the truck. But seriously, this house is supposed to be haunted."

"Great," Mateo said, watching Jack head outside.

With the front door left open, the chilly December breeze crept through the house and cooled his sweat, sending shivers up his forearms. He felt the rise of goosebumps as the chill traveled across his shoulders. "Shut the door!" he hollered.

With Jack's selective hearing, the door stayed open.

Shaking off the discomfort, Mateo hastened his effort on his current board, only to see the very edge of something tucked beneath the flooring. Another board stripped, and the edge of a case became visible. Two more earnest efforts and the object sat in clear view—an antique canvas suitcase with rusty hinges.

His imagination ran wild. What if it was a cache of loot? He craned his neck, looking down the hall and out the door at Jack, reaching into his brown bag.

He got up to shut the door. "Hey, please keep this shut. You're letting all the cold in," Mateo said, with a firm slam.

Through the door's glass panes, he saw Jack nod with his mouth full of sandwich and pick up his phone.

Mateo resumed his position on the floor and pulled the case from the exposed earth. A simple click of brittle latches revealed a cache of papers and trinkets. He picked up the first page and studied the drawings of what looked to be knots, practice examples scratched out with only one traced over several times. Its appearance, darker than the rest. He flipped to the second. Now, that title caught his attention! "Vision spell, to see clear—"

"Hey, Mateo," Jack called out as he opened the front door.

Mateo nearly jumped out of his skin and froze with his back toward Jack, hoping he couldn't see him arms-deep in the client's belongings. "Yeah, man, what's up?"

"What time did we get here this morning? I forgot to clock in on the app."

"Just after nine. Like, 9:07 a.m."

"Thanks, man."

Jack shut the door.

Relief! He confirmed the heading—*Vision spell*. While he had never taken a single thing from any of their clients, this topic of vision held his highest interest since his son struggled with his own. Sure, the stuff in this suitcase leaned toward the occult, but that didn't scare him since his mother-in-law claimed to be a seer. If the supernatural helped her, like she claimed, maybe a secret method lay in this case that could help improve his son's vision. It sure wouldn't hurt to try.

Quickly, he re-stacked the papers and snapped the case shut. Since the owners were vacationing in Arizona, he would take it back to the privacy of his house to read further. Of course, he would return it.

He paused, considering the possibility of the house being haunted. He looked at the walls hovering above him and listened. Nothing to hear but the thump of his own heartbeat. The dim natural lighting overhead added a bit of eeriness, but the vibe of the house itself seemed pretty light. Empty more than anything, and he would know. His gut feelings had been well honed over the years with the help of his mother-in-law, a superstitious woman who also talked of her many successful house readings.

With the decision made, he strategized his next move. To get it to his truck without Jack knowing would take some finesse, but sneaking it back in after dark would be easy since they had a house key. Further, they hired him and Jack to tear up the floor. So, if it were that important, they would have put it elsewhere. In fact, maybe they didn't even know about it? The rust and creak of the hinges suggested no one had opened it in ages.

After checking several spots, Mateo wedged the case in a temporary holding area under the back bedroom headboard. Jack rarely came into the hall, and he had no need to root around in the farthest room.

With the treasure situated, he joined Jack for lunch, then finished the day, biding his time until they had fully prepped their respective sections for the installation on the following day.

"Alright, I got the cleanup. You can go. I know you got that dinner tonight," Mateo said in a generous offer.

"You sure?" Jack asked.

"Yep. Go for it! I'll lock up."

Mateo glimpsed out toward Jack several times before he drove away, then hustled to retrieve the case. He slid it out from under the bed and arose, handle in hand. Unexpectedly, the weak latches gave, and the lid dropped open. In a grand swoop, he saved the contents from crashing to the ground, stuffed them back into their space, and quickly slammed the case shut again. With care, he cradled it in his arms and took it to his car.

•   •   •

After his wife and son had gone to bed, Mateo snuck out into the garage and removed the old suitcase from his trunk. He took it to his workbench and flipped on the four-foot fluorescent shop light above him. Next, he unsnapped the fussy latches and opened the case.

He wiped at his runny nose before pulling out the second paper and held it up under the bright light to read the entirety of it. "Vision spell – to see clearly a path to heavenly beings and open the doors of full intuition." He groaned and scanned the page, hoping to find something about actual eyesight, but reached the bottom and accepted disappointment. "All figurative!" He flipped the sheet over—Nothing. Had he wasted all his effort for *this*?

Again, he wiped at his nagging runny nose and shuffled through the remaining materials. One paper caught his eye. With its ink still vibrant, he read the words aloud. "'*Incant … protection … may this tablet deflect the curse and send the evil back.*'" He stopped, not liking those words—curse and evil—nor their meanings. He should have never taken the case.

He had to get it back to that house. After organizing the contents, he shut the lid. It would be easy to put it back under the foundation tomorrow before they installed the new floor.

He yanked up the case by its handle, forgetting his previous error.

The lid flew open, this time sending all the contents to the ground, including a thin slab of stone that broke in half upon landing.

He flinched at the commotion. "Frickin-A!"

He set the case back on his workbench, picked up the stone halves, then the papers, and put them all back inside. For formality's sake, he snapped the useless latches.

"What are you doing out here?" Alicia, his wife, said from the door.

He jumped at the sudden voice.

Alicia laughed and said, "Feeling guilty about something?"

Deflection. "Nope, just forgot my phone on the bench." He quickly shut off the overhead light before turning around, knowing his body had blocked the view of the case from her. She'd go ballistic if she, number one, knew he had taken something from a jobsite, and number two, knew the "evil" contents that lay inside it. He barged past her. "Just got sidetracked with my new tools. Thanks again! Killer birthday present … best ever!"

"Uh-huh! Maybe I should look at your phone," she said, feigning suspicion.

"Go for it," he said, handing her the cell as they shut the old case in the garage behind them.

.   .   .

The early morning alarm came too soon and jangled Mateo's nerves. He could barely open his eyes from the stickiness that enveloped them, and his runny nose had turned into a full-blown, congested headache. With his ears plugged and his jaws stiff, he felt like a semi had hit him.

He wished Alicia had not already left for her job. Nevertheless, he dragged himself out of bed, every inch of his body aching. This did not feel like the usual head cold, and no way would he make it to work today. Still, he took the precaution and trudged to the medicine cabinet, removing the generic over-the-counter test packet for the superbug for which the governor had shut down the state.

Moments later, all became clear with the positive results. He phoned Jack and gave him the news.

"Great. Hopefully, I don't catch it," Jack said with a groan. "Anyway, hope you feel better. Enjoy your ten-day quarantine."

Mateo hung up the phone and could barely drag himself back to the sanctity of his warm covers. Now, Jack would complete the job without him, and that meant the keys would go back to the owner's boyfriend before he recovered. At this point, he had no energy to care. With any luck, the owner knew nothing of the old case, but he would keep it tucked away in his office in the event something came of its absence.

CHAPTER 2
AN OLD STONE TABLET

~ Present day – November 2021, Boulder Creek ~

Royal watched as Auntie paced the small living area, his cautious stare ping-ponging back and forth with her.

"This is off. I feel it in my aging bones," Auntie said, rubbing her forehead. "There's no way Iris would have left her favorite Lapis bracelet on the outside step like that. She would have picked it up the moment she got home, and it's been almost a week since our Samhain ritual!"

In the kitchen, Arista hummed in agreement while preparing the herbs for two cups of apple spice black tea. Unfortunately, the delightful autumn blend would likely not be enough to quell their worry.

"… and I thought the gwishin getting rid of that bloodthirsty uncle of yours was the end to all our worries … yet here we are again!"

"I know." Everything *had* felt settled and promising and looked to be on track. Now Iris had disappeared with Fergus's body. While they might be overreacting in a typical situation, in her constantly shifting, chaotic world, it meant trouble. "She talked about a friend. Could she be there?" Arista asked, setting the diffuser into steamy water.

"I'd love to dismiss the absence, but she would not leave her cats like that all week. Oh, Arista, I don't want to say it, but what if she's …?"

Arista threw a quick look in Auntie's direction. She knew what was coming next.

"We had to bring her back from the dead! What if …" Auntie grimaced with regret. "We should have taken her to the hospital."

"Maybe we should report her missing to Sheriff Michaels?"

Auntie grunted. "I really don't want him involved. That man is going to catch on soon enough." She sighed. "He cares for us, and I don't want to lose that. If we can, I'd like to keep our dirty little secrets to ourselves."

With three minutes past, Arista removed the diffuser and tossed the natural debris into the small compost bin under her sink, already half filled with apple parings, banana peels, and similar broken wads of tea potions. *Note to self, take that out to the compost pile today.*

Auntie walked over to her and took a steamy mug of tea. "I need fresh air. Good with you?"

"Sure," Arista agreed.

Auntie pulled her hand from her pocket and opened the door, inviting a gust of the brisk November morning into their midst. As she did, a tiny metal container clattered to the ground.

"Oh, shoot!" Auntie said, balancing her tea with care while reaching down for the trinket.

"What is that?" Arista asked. She had noticed the tiny pillbox a few times the past few years but never thought to question it.

Auntie burrowed it back into her skirt pocket and said, "Just a little spell I've been honing. But enough of that. I need a cold, invigorating slap to settle me down right now."

Weird that Auntie evaded spellwork talk, but this Iris dilemma had her pretty scattered.

Dressed in cozy layers, they stepped into the bright sunlight. Steadying their heated teacups, they brushed the wind-blown, sunny yellow leaves from the neighbor's quaking aspens off the chair cushions.

They sat and sipped together.

"What to do? What to do?" Auntie said, fretting while blowing on the rising aromatic steam from her cup.

"Oh shoot. I think I left her bracelet by the mandrakes."

"It should be safe there. Unless Mr. Pitch sees it."

"Yes, ravens do like shiny trinkets," Arista agreed.

"We can go back. In fact, we must. Those kitties need care."

Arista hummed in agreement while sipping. She wished she could help with Iris's disappearance. When were all the rumored, prophesied powers going to come upon her? The ones that Auntie and her friends alluded to. Promised one? Hah! So far, the only promise seemed to be that of endless trouble with her in the middle. "Changing the subject, how long did it take for Candace to develop her ability as a seer? I mean, with me supposedly being this super-gifted witch, do you think I'll be able to do that someday? I'd like to help more when we come into chaos like this."

"Hers came at quite a young age. My guess is that your visions will become stronger as you mature as well."

"I just don't know why sometimes I get detailed visions, and other times it's like grasping at nothing. Like trying to make something materialize and knowing if it does, it's just my imagination and not the universe exposing truth."

"I don't know, Arista. I've not had any visions. My intuition has always been a gnawing gut … and mostly to do with you."

Auntie dazed off, distracted by her thoughts, and froze while narrowing her eyes.

"What are you thinking?" Arista asked.

"I *think* I saw something when I peeked through Iris's living room window. While her disappearance created a major distraction, it's remained a whisper of suspicion ever since we left."

"What was it?" Arista sipped her tea, now the perfect temperature after a few minutes in the cold outdoors.

"A tablet encased in glass on her hearth. An old stone tablet … one very similar to one my grandparents had and kept hidden from us kids."

"And?" The wind whipped a strand of Arista's hair into her tea as she sipped. Now, in her mouth, she fussed at it, pawing at her cheek, and freeing it with her pinkie.

"Are you having problems, dear?" Auntie asked.

They shared the laugh.

"Anyway, it's brought back a few memories, and they aren't good," Auntie said, pursing her lips. She took her second sip of the brew and swished it within her mouth. "Such a lovely flavor."

"It is. So, what is the stone tablet, and why does it concern you?"

"As you know, our family endured tremendous hardships. I lost my mother the moment I was born. Just before that, my father never returned from a business trip, and my youngest brother died when I was only two. Thankfully, Declan, your grandpa, lived to adulthood … bless his dear soul! He was around to raise Ian, who brought me you! But even Declan left us too soon. No other family aside from long-forgotten kin from my grandfather's homeland. Sheesh." She shook her head. "There's just been so much death."

Arista touched Auntie's knee, empathizing with her sad memories that she had shared from time to time. With the recent loss of her own mother and father, never had she valued Auntie's losses so dearly.

Auntie responded with a loving tap to her hand. "Anyway, the tablet was our grandparents' curse tablet … or more of a curse *reversal* tablet, really. I don't know the full details, but over the years, I had wondered if it had something to do with our kin dropping like lemmings off a cliff and the animosity my grandfather held against Iris's grandmother." She released an ironic laugh. "Nevertheless, my intuition tells me the presence of that tablet in her house is not a good thing."

"Really?" Arista remembered her first impression of Iris—piercing eyes and leopard-like stealth in her silky loungewear. "Yeah, Iris has a certain vibe."

"I hate to admit it, but she does. While we were quite friendly in elementary school, Iris and I became a little stand-offish ever since our young adult years." She lightened her tone. "Though we have also maintained a healthy mutual respect. I was genuinely happy to see her the day I introduced you. In fact, I had never visited that house. Her family moved around quite a bit within these mountains. A very private bunch." She took a swig of her tea. "Truth is, my grandfather did not care for her, and I could never understand why. As I said, he practically hated her grandmother. Strong, I know, but he'd keep an eagle eye on *her* and a scowl on his own face anytime we'd run into them in town … with her grandmother reflecting the hostility right back at him."

"I thought your grandpa was a super nice guy?"

"He was with anyone but them."

The notion struck Arista, bringing a focused awareness with it. "Wait a minute!" She set her mug down, and her mind raced with potential reasons. "Oh … my—"

"What is it?!" Auntie asked, stunned.

"Think about it. Curse and curse reversal tablets. Scowls, glares and animosity between her grandparents and yours? Lots of relatives dying … for both of you! Didn't you tell me that Iris has very little family left on our way to her house?"

"It's possible … as she doesn't."

"What if …" Arista felt the merging facts as if she'd unfurled a lost treasure map. The words left her mouth in a flurry of enlightenment. "Did you ever wonder … if he was so nice to everyone, why he had so much anger toward their family?"

"Well, when you put it that way … that's what I'm talking about! I didn't know Iris had a tablet at all, but I sure know seeing one in her house brought back a flood of insecurities."

For Arista, the picture only became clearer. "Figure … she's a witch … may be a descendant of witches. Now I hear all this talk of animosity … curses and reversals. What if they directed all these curses and reversals towards each other? Specifically, your family against hers?" Arista paused, calculating the facts and imagining plausible scenarios. "Now I'm more worried about the tablet than where she is."

Auntie drew in her brows and narrowed her eyes, taking another sip. Her expression changed to bubbly appreciation. "Oh, I truly love this apple-y flavor."

"How can you flip the switch like that?" Arista asked, astonished by Auntie's control of her emotions. "Worry to appreciation in a nanosecond? That's a mighty magickal power in itself! I want to hone that in me."

Auntie scoffed. "Honestly, I think it's ADD, but who's to say? That diagnosis did not exist when I was a child, and by the time I became an adult … well, you just accept that people find you annoying." She dismissed her spaciness with a cackle. "Anyway, it's all speculation until we confirm it *is* a curse tablet." She took a breath, finished her last bit of tea, and set her mug on the pebbly ground. "We don't want to take advantage of this situation, but perhaps while we're helping care for her kitties and plants, we can get a better look at the tablet. But we only *peek* through the window … no breaking in!"

"Of course not. We also need to secure her bracelet before it disappears by way of Mr. Pitch's black beak."

Auntie nodded, pleased. "Let's do it a little later. For now, shall we take a pleasant autumn jaunt to my house? Aside from honing spells, I made a batch of cinnamon apple bread before we left this morning. I think it would taste marvelous with another round of your tea."

"Of course! We need the energy anyway."

CHAPTER 3
IT'S PROBABLY NOTHING

After the exhilarating walk to Auntie's and a spongy, sweet snack with tea, they hopped in Auntie's bright yellow Volvo wagon for the drive to Iris's house.

As Auntie backed her car out of the driveway, they noticed a forest green van with tinted windows idling in front of Arista's driveway just down the street.

"Do you recognize them?" Auntie asked.

"I know Maddie's friend Skylar just bought a van, but I don't know what color it is. It could be her." Arista peered at the occupants. Both passenger and driver had their heads angled toward her front door, only their profiles visible but too far away.

"Is it her?"

Arista strained her view. "I can't tell, really. Skylar changes her hair all the time. The girl looks my age. That's all I can really tell. Pale-skinned female and dark-skinned male. Hmph."

The driver noticed the attention, U-turned away from them, and drove off down the street.

Arista blew out a frustrated breath and tapped in a quick text to Maddie. "It could have been Skylar with a friend, and she didn't recognize your car."

Auntie watched the tail end of the fleeing van and twisted her mouth in contemplation.

"Let me just call her," Arista said, dialing Maddie. It went straight to voicemail. "Well, they're gone, and I can't reach her, so let's just get to Iris's. After all we've been through, I normally wouldn't blow it off, but it *is* possible that was Skylar."

They took one last look, then headed for the rustic house with needy outdoor cats.

Arista mulled over who her unknown visitors could be other than Skylar. What if Fergus's coven had come looking for him? "Auntie, I thought with Fergus dead, I'd find precious relief, but I'm suspicious of everyone now."

"Yes. I know what you mean. I'm feeling the same stress. Let's hang in there. We'll get through all of it. Other than that, how are you?" Auntie flashed her a look. "You doing okay?"

Only weeks had passed since her dad's murder, and she did not want to discuss it. She reserved processing her grief for nighttime rituals with Royal curled beside her. She didn't need the tears triggered by anyone else, even her beloved Auntie. And while her therapist said the painful memories could endure a lifetime, she felt blessed from the memorable trip to the pastoral Summerland. The beautiful setting had provided her with the reassurance of her parents' ever-living grace and togetherness. Still, at the wrong time, she could easily get sucked into a sudden bout of anxiety and sadness over it. Now was not the time. "I'm getting through it, Auntie. Thank you."

"I'm here … anytime."

"I know, and I appreciate that," Arista said with a smile.

The drive to Iris's house passed quickly while Auntie talked about a lifetime of chaotic events—such as the Bay of Pigs, the first time she remembered the animosity of conflicting international governments, and 9/11, when as an American, she felt the first heavy blow of national vulnerability. She then shifted to events that were smaller in scale but no less scary for her, personally. Two drunken, burly mountain men harassing her and Margaret in their twenties, threatening to burn them at the stake. Or the time that a potential burglar had barged into her yard.

"That was the first time I tried my Hummingbird Spell."

"Really? Let's talk about that, as you've never really given me details. All I know is some guy rushed out of here, never to be seen again, ranting about hummingbirds."

Auntie cackled with pride. "A Fergus follower. Yes, that spell proved very effective and is ever-evolving to this day."

"See?! You can do more than just feel my vibes," Arista said with a gentle razz.

"Anyway, as I was saying about my biggest scares, and speaking of Fergus followers, there was also that degenerate from last year. I felt sure that ol' Henry would be the death of me. Literally! Almost nothing worse than coming face to face with an agitated serial killer. What do you think?" Auntie said with a wry grin.

Funny remark, but a diversionary tactic. After all these years, Auntie remained vague with the details of her Hummingbird Spell. No worries. She knew she simply wanted to lighten the mood by showing that troubled times come and pass. Nevertheless, the reminder of her parents' recent deaths brought a sense of mental battery, and she looked out her window at the passing scenery to settle the angst.

Auntie reached over and patted her thigh. "I'm sorry. Too much, too soon. I just want you to keep life in perspective. I tell you of these things because I want you to see we deal with tragedy, yet life goes on. And you can deal with it in the rough, hopeless way, or you can dig in … like you are already doing, grab it by the horns, and ready yourself for the next phase." Auntie glanced at her. "Grieve. Absolutely grieve! I'm devastated by the loss of my dear nephew. He was like a son to me." She paused and sighed. "He was also the last of our kinfolk. It's just you and me now, kiddo." She paused, then perked up again. "So, while we're here, in this realm, let's work toward moving forward."

"Noted."

The warmth of Auntie's hopeful perception revived her as they pulled into Iris's driveway to embark on their new mission.

The furry feline faces peeked from the decking but stayed put while Arista tended to her self-appointed chore—heaping enough food on plates to hold the kitties for a day or two. Meanwhile, Auntie filled the dish beneath each mandrake with water for moisture at their roots.

Once finished, they set about graver concerns and walked to the front door.

Auntie gave a token knock. "Hello! Iris, are you home?"

As Auntie knocked a second time, Arista glanced at the mandrakes, then asked, "Did you get her bracelet?"

Auntie fished it from her skirt pocket and knocked once more. "Yes. In fact, tuck it in your pocket for now. I'm going to forget."

"My pockets aren't deep enough. As it is, my credit card slips out all the time."

"Well, it's me forgetting or you watching that it doesn't slip out."

Arista took the bracelet.

With no answer, Auntie looked Arista in the eye. "Let's find an open window."

"I thought you said no breaking in."

"Well, what if she's hurt?" Her eyes bugged as if an obvious fact.

Without waiting for an answer, Auntie walked straight toward the closest window and tugged. No luck.

Arista groaned. This felt precarious and the beginning of more trouble, but she followed, wanting to confirm whether this curse tablet scare held merit.

Thankfully, a window on the side of the house was free of surrounding clutter, closer to the ground, and, most importantly, cracked open.

Arista climbed atop the step ladder they had found by the mandrakes while Auntie waited nervously at her hip. She pushed at the aged glass, attempting to slide it open. When the window budged a smidgeon, the spark of success motivated her even more, and she repositioned herself for better leverage. "Is this ladder sturdy enough?" she asked Auntie.

"Don't worry. I gotcha."

Arista gently pressed and pushed until she slid the aged pane open enough to poke her head into the still and darkened house. An unwelcome feeling greeted her, and the musty smell wasn't much better. She reconsidered. But when she looked back at Auntie below her, worried and fretting despite her positive words from earlier, she found her courage and readied for full entry. "Okay, here I go," she said, overruling her nerves.

"Straight to the door, and don't get side-tracked. The sooner I'm in there with you, the better I'll feel."

"Got it." Landing on the bedroom floor, Arista bellowed, "Hello? Iris, are you here?"

The atmosphere remained deathly quiet, and she braced herself for an eerie journey through the eccentric woman's house.

Auntie stepped up the ladder and peered in to scrutinize Arista's surroundings, then she secured the screen back into place. "Straight to the front door, young lady."

"I will," Arista said while shutting the window. She watched Auntie carefully dismount, grab the ladder, and hurry off toward the front of the house.

She crept into the hallway and headed for the foyer. Not only was the musty, dusty smell unpleasant, the air felt unmoving, and old. Every step she took upon the floor made it and the walls achily pop.

To her right, she came upon a banister, the stairwell beyond it barren of family photos and ascending into utter darkness.

"Oka-yyy," she intoned to herself, imagining the idiocy of her predicament if she were on the big screen in front of a popcorn-eating audience.

The light from her entry point faded as she drew deeper into the hallway; the light strangled so much from the closed blinds and curtains that she strained to see the floor in front of her.

Onward, she walked. Slow and methodical, listening for sounds of life. She slowed her breath and looked up as a dimmed spray of outdoor light bled in through a sliver of glass by the front door.

A sudden presence!

Her stomach dropped in fear.

False alarm. The Art Nouveau-style mirror only reflected her image back to her. Its gold frame of ornate leaves around her reflection looked pretty, quickly alleviating the scare. Then, she saw a flicker of movement behind her in the mirror. She did not investigate. She just wanted Auntie in there with her … and fast!

With the front door in sight, she hastened forth and began fumbling with the latches. It seemed a challenging puzzle as nervousness overtook her efficiency from the heavy feeling closing in behind her. The ceiling creaked just as the third lock released.

Auntie's entrance brought a fraction of relief.

"What is it?" Auntie asked, noticing her anxiety. She looked around in a panic.

"Super creeped out … that's all," Arista said, releasing the eeber jeebers in a vigorous shiver.

"As you should be," Auntie said, as she led them to the living area.

Arista noticed no electric hum of appliances nor the ticking of a clock, and no outside sound penetrated the gloom. Passing the stairwell, she peered up, still feeling a heavy presence linger atop the stairs. The lump in her throat thickened. "I don't know about this, Auntie."

"We won't be here long," Auntie said, leading them to the hearth, where many vases contained brittle, dead flowers, their lead crystal vessels long empty of life-giving water. The webs surrounding these decorations hosted only the shriveled bodies of the spiders that once tended them.

Arista glanced toward the outline of the beaming sun coming from the border of the blackout blinds of the living area and fought down her urge to allow all the light in.

As they approached the glass case above the fireplace, she noticed the scent of tobacco becoming stronger. However, instead of the scent being pleasant, she felt a burn in her nose and rubbed away a sneeze.

Auntie moved in closer to peer at the tablet, while she studied a nearby floor lamp standing as tall as she, its base a worn brass faux tree trunk adorned with dozens of dark gray ostrich plumes as its branches.

The dust particles swam in the dim light around its plumage. On the table beneath it was a collection of vintage black-and-white family snapshots in small frames.

She nudged Auntie. "Family pics." Finally, an aspect of hominess. But when Arista looked closer, she saw an old woman who looked very much like your classic Grimm fairy tale witch—long, straggly hair and a sizeable wart on the end of her nose. Worse, her face hosted a joyless glower.

Auntie strained to see the tablet. "I can't quite make it out. It's too dark in here," she griped, then shot a glance at the picture. "Yes, that's her grandmother. The same one my grandfather thought ill of … and, as discussed, the *potential* creator of the curse."

Arista picked up the frame and stared into the eyes of the sullen woman. "I'm all for witches of all forms and natural beauty, but *eek*, that is one angry woman." She felt the need to quiet her voice. "…gives me a bad feeling."

Above them, the ceiling creaked again, this time grabbing both their attention.

They paused, listening.

Arista returned the picture to its place and looked into the hallway, feeling a rise in her urgency to leave. "I think we get going soon."

"Just a little longer," Auntie said, her voice reflecting frustration as she struggled to read the tablet. She stood on tiptoe, trying to better see.

Arista continued her review of the spacious living room. A huge taxidermized bat hung above the large, sooty fireplace, with fake blood-red orbs and its wings almost as wide as she stood tall.

On the wall closest to them hung a five-foot-high, hand-carved wooden wall sculpture that looked to be a rendition of *Dante's Inferno*. Close to the window, the slivers of light that infiltrated the room helped her identify nine separate levels representing the ugliness of a Christian's sins, including the drooling mouths of lust, the scowls of anger, and the hollowed eyes of greed. How incredible that a wood carving could convey such repugnance.

Behind her, Auntie mumbled to herself.

"Oh! Here!" Arista said in realization and flicked on her phone's flashlight. She handed it to Auntie. "Sorry I didn't think of it sooner. I think I'm just transfixed by all of the super creepy décor."

"A little glare-y on the glass, but surely does help!" Auntie said, illuminating the glass capsule.

While Auntie got a better look at the tablet, Arista walked over to the steampunk wall clock that measured about the size of an eatery's round table. Stuck at three o'clock, the object comprised typewriter blades, stopwatches, and monocles, as well as many other unidentifiable metal items.

Auntie gasped in shock.

"What is it?" Arista asked, rushing to her side.

Auntie maintained a look of horror and remained speechless, pointing to the tablet.

Arista took the phone and spotlighted the etched words.

"Look at it!" Auntie said in a low, demanding voice.

Arista moved in closer.

"The second line! Read it!" Auntie whispered, her voice frantic.

"'Let your castigation and deathly hand fall upon Barry … *Kelly* … and his generations to come.' That was your grandpa's name … Barry!" Accustomed to the rush of dread, the sensation washed over her in an all-consuming queasiness. Their fear of Iris's tablet being ill will proved true.

"My *many* stars! Arista, this is the tablet that cursed my family! It has never been more than a rumor. And while it explained our slow demise and was the excuse for our incessant run of bad luck … we never actually saw it!"

Arista sank into herself, knowing all along that Iris and her vibe were more than a mere threat.

"And Iris has it in her possession!" Auntie said, with a controlled volume and incredulous gape. She backed away from the case, her face frozen in anxiety.

Arista read the full script aloud. "'Dark Goddess Chthoni, Dark God Chthon, let your castigation and deathly hand fall upon Barry

Kelly and his generations to come. Mine enemy is thus bound in fire and ash, in blood, spit, and hair.'" She looked at Auntie, then finished in a somber poetic meter.

For the first generation, be it loss of pride,
The next, be it sons and a mothering bride,
For the third generation, be they taken by two,
And the fourth generation, from violence, subdued.
And the fifth generation ends it all when the last Kelly member
shall finally fall.

The sound of shattering glass startled Arista. She turned to find Auntie lying on a broken end table, groaning.

"Auntie! Are you okay?" She ran to her side as Auntie held the back of her head, struggling to open her woozy eyes and sputtering forth gibberish.

Arista rushed to the nearby kitchen. A dirty rag on the counter. A worn sponge on the sink. Yuck! Instead, she ran cold water over her hands, then rushed back to Auntie. Dabbing her cold, wet palms on Auntie's nape and rosy cheeks, she worked to keep her conscious. "You're okay." She *hoped* she was okay!

Bleary-eyed, Auntie pushed herself up against an ottoman as Arista continued gently blotting her face, shoulders, and neck with her cool, wet hands.

"What happened?"

Auntie opened her mouth to explain, then paused. "Uh-oh. Arista, my vision's gone blurry." Her voice built up in worry as she grasped at the wooden frame of the broken table to pull herself up. "Oh dear, I can't see clearly."

"Careful with your hand!"

Arista helped her stand before looking around and feeling the dark and callous spirit of the house closing in on them. "We've got to get out of here."

While there were no explicit signs that ghosts hovered, there was absolutely something happening—after another wooden pop from above, a thickness invaded the air, and Arista could swear that despite her adrenaline, the air grew colder by the moment.

"What if Iris comes home? We need to clean up this mess," Auntie said.

"We'll get it next time."

The house popped, and another round of creaking on the ceiling above them now sounded like deliberate steps.

With Auntie on her feet, Arista walked them toward the door. Upon opening it, she took one last glance at the ill-omened tablet and watched as a black, prickly spider with a fat abdomen emerged from behind it. It scuttled to the edge of the stone hearth, released a silken thread, and lowered itself down into the long-dormant fireplace.

She secured Auntie on the front porch and turned to close the door. As she did, she heard a subtle effect, looked, and saw the case holding the tablet had cracked.

CHAPTER 4
SLIPPERINESS AT HER FEET

A sudden jarring awoke Iris. Coming to, she found a bloodied straight razor in her hand. Repulsed, she thrust it to the ground while looking around her. She sat in the middle of a spacious room, unlit and quiet. Where the hell was she?

She tried to recall what had happened last. Through a muddled haze, it slowly came to her. The lonely drive to Manny's house after Arista's Samhain ritual … the struggle to stay coherent … and … the pigs. Yes! She had gotten Fergus to the pigs. The memory of that first crunch into his bones—though horrendous, necessary.

But this place? Completely unfamiliar. She squinted, trying to see the outer edges of the low-lit room.

"Hello?" she called out, her voice resounding in her own ears as it bounced between the walls, harboring sparse furnishings. Her aching head felt like a nasty hangover, yet rarely did she drink.

She called out once more, then glanced back at the stiff chair she sat on. Its dark mahogany design represented true Gothic workmanship. This perch belonged to someone obviously quite full of themselves. Which, presently, was her. She ran her fingers along its carved arms but stopped when she noticed the blood streaks on her hands. She recoiled at the gore and immediately tried to wipe it on her pants, but the stickiness had already set.

Grimacing, she carefully stood, feeling a slipperiness at her feet. The pooled substance on the floor likely matched the blood on her hands.

The scene created a horror she had not felt in some time. Sure, death by pigs could be grotesque, but only if you stood by and watched the carnage. But this! Hideous! She eyed the trail around the back of her chair to find a young man, motionless, his throat slit ear to ear.

"Oh," she said in sober awareness. "Well, that explains the blood." She studied the young man, the floor, and the entire room. "A ghastly predicament I seem to be in."

Cautious of her steps, Iris crept away from the viscid spillage. In doing so, she noted the strange fact that she was wearing her spiky black high heels. Worse still were the clothes on her body. Feeling it had become inappropriate for her age, she'd sworn never to wear this tight, black jersey jumpsuit again, which is why she had packed both shoes and ensemble into the donation bag in the back of her car. Yet here she stood, stuffed into both.

She grimaced, feeling the material bunched up within her crotch. She pulled at her pants, readjusting the discomfort, and proceeded toward the door. "For the sake of all souls, what have I gotten myself into?"

From beyond her walls came the sound of fast-approaching footsteps.

Iris saw a light switch by the door and stepped carefully toward it, readying for her meeting with the owner of noisy shoes.

The moment she flipped the switch, he appeared in the doorway. His attention became fixed on the gory mess. "Oh, damn! I'll get that cleaned up right away."

Iris stared at him—a chubby, middle-aged, man-next-door type with a pleasant smile.

"Are you okay, Iris?" he asked, studying her face. "I know I've been out a couple days, but we agreed that I'd call you Iris, right? Or do you prefer Fergus? I'm truly sorry. I don't recall."

"Iris," she drolly said, insulted by the question, but still unsure how he knew her name at all. Much more intriguing was that he thought he might call her Fergus. "What say you of Fergus?" she asked, peering down her nose at him.

The man darted his eyes and stammered. "Well … I … just wasn't sure if this was a situation like with Fallon or not."

"Fallon?"

"Oh, never mind. I'm just confusing things. I'll address you as Iris, and I'll remember next time. I promise! It's COVID. It really wrecked me this time around."

"What is this dead man doing here?" Iris asked. Her gaze swept the room, ceiling, and far windows before settling back on the man. "And where *is* here?"

"We're at the Rec Center."

She stared at the man, awaiting more information.

"Spokane."

"Washington?" she asked, flabbergasted by the possibility.

The man stifled his snicker. "That's right."

"Uh-huh." She played it cool but wondered how the hell she ended up in Spokane. In fact, tact was of the essence, and since she had this man's respect now, she would use it to her advantage. "Yes, please dispose of this body," she said, flicking her finger at the bloody corpse. "I presume you have a receiving party lined up?"

"Of course. Same guy as always."

"Great." As the man dug through the body's pants pockets, the picture became clearer. He had mentioned Fergus, so obviously, this scenario had something to do with Arista's bloodthirsty uncle. Still, she needed strategy and stealth in this most critical situation. In fact, the more she thought about it, maybe the wooziness she had experienced after Arista's ceremony had been a dire warning. One she had not heeded.

The man stood up with the victim's wallet, keys, and a phone in his hand.

She had to ask. "Your name?" She snapped the directive while looking away, feigning disinterest.

"Jameson."

"How long have I been here?"

"You mean today?"

"When did I return to Spokane?"

"You arrived by plane a week ago."

I've been here a week?! "Right. And … you picked me up?"

"No, you called me, and we met at Riverfront. I think you got a ride from the airport … or something. You didn't say." Jameson paused and gestured to the body. "You had just met Antonio, and we all came back here to the Rec. I … thought he'd be with us much longer." His demeanor livened. "We had an exceptional attendance last night. You spoke well, and people love this new you." His smile beamed. "Great work, boss!"

Jameson eyed her up and down, prompting her to remember the ill fit of the clothes she had on her body. Which begged another question—where the hell were all her belongings, other than this awful passe wardrobe someone had dressed her in?

"You don't seem yourself today. You okay?" Jameson asked.

Iris inhaled, gaining a better understanding of her situation. All the dizziness the night of Arista's ceremony to the Otherworld—by the fire and on the ride to Manny's—represented her succumbing to Fergus's control. Her short stint of falling dead, thanks to that savage little gwishin child, had probably made her even more vulnerable to his possession of her. Yes! She had even felt his presence before Bethie resuscitated her.

"Iris?"

Now, she had landed dead center of Fergus's lair. She needed a strategy for this grim situation, and distractions from his minion did not help. "Jameson, you're right about me not being myself today. I think I may need to go home."

"Are you taking the car, or should I drive you?"

"The car?"

"Your Mazzy."

"What's a Mazzy?"

"The Maserati. Your new car."

A Maserati? Well now, this could be a little more interesting than I imagined. I wonder what other tricks Fergus has hidden in his closet.

Reading her confusion, Jameson gently took her by the arm. "Let's get you cleaned up, and I'll make sure you get home nice and safe."

Jameson had her remove her shoes to better walk, helped her wash up, then led her down the hall and out into the parking lot where a sleek black beast of a luxury coupe sat quietly waiting to roar.

"Key?" Iris held out her hand while looking nonchalant in the opposite direction.

"Oops, sorry. I thought you would have grabbed it. I'll be right back."

"My cell, too!" she yelled out to him.

"Will do!"

She circled the vehicle, running an index finger along the spoiler, the rim of the door, and then down the hood toward its shiny, silver trident. When she looked at her dust-free fingertip, she also took a second look at the thick, black watch on her wrist. "Hmph." But the car! While she had traveled the world and seen many spectacular landmarks—Angkor Wat, the Pyramids, the Parthenon, and so many more—never had she driven a luxury sports car. This debacle she found herself in at least promised a few novel perks.

Jameson returned, huffing from his haste, and handed her the keys and an unfamiliar phone.

She looked at the case and flipped it over, disappointed it was not her own. "Jameson, I seem to have forgotten my passcode."

"Man, you must've gone into a frenzy in there with poor Antonio. You're definitely out of kilter. It's good I'm driving you home."

Yes, she needed him to drive her home. She did not know where Fergus lived but hoped his accommodations matched the comfort of his ride. After all, it would be half-cocked to jet back to California without fully comprehending what she had gone through over the past week. Further, disappearing now would raise a red flag to this group of—judging entirely on their disregard for the young man with the gaping neck wound—absolutely horrible people. Not that she hadn't pulled her own deviltries over the years, but the blood and brutality here were so … explicit. Pigs and poison provided a much cleaner death when necessary.

Iris left the comment about the body unaddressed. "Yes, I'd appreciate you driving me home. You have my house key?"

"I have my copy." He paused. "Oh shoot! Hang on one minute while I lock up. I'd hate to have someone stumble onto that mess."

"Truly."

This unplanned predicament proved a challenge. Here she was without her cell and its contacts, in a strange town, and with no recollection of how she got there. She needed to track down Bethie, the most reliable of her current company, and that would be difficult since she had no idea of her unlisted phone number. Most importantly, time was of the essence since Fergus could re-emerge, leading her to disappear again.

Within moments, Jameson reappeared, jingling another keyring.

"Here you go," he said, handing her the house key.

He popped the door locks, and they took their seats inside the snazzy sports car. He started the ignition.

"Whoa! Yeah! Kickstart—"

"Woo! Little loud there, boss!" Jameson said while lowering the blaring metal music.

"How lovely." Nothing like yelled vocals and raucous guitars added to her already unpleasant situation. She worked to ease her neck's tension.

The short drive across town provided a plethora of unfamiliar sights. The evidence of a recently melted snow took form in the withered plants and shrubs lining office buildings, struggling in vain to recover. They drove past an arena, its digital signs boasting hockey games and an upcoming college basketball game where the local team had a fierce bulldog for its mascot. Beneath the tall buildings of downtown Spokane, she noticed a colorful flag boasting a green hill and flowing water with a classic golden sunshine in the top right corner. "What is that flag? A hotel or spa?"

Jameson followed her gaze. "No, that's the Spokane flag. It's brand new this year."

Already on to more sights, she saw a grape-colored tram skimming the distant sky. "Where does that go?"

"It takes people over the falls … over there," Jameson said, pointing.

Their right turn prevented her from seeing the purple pod's arrival at its destination.

She studied the dreary urban streets and wondered why there weren't more people out walking in the chill.

"Here we are!" Jameson said, pulling into the parking lot of a seven-story, modern-looking building.

She stared at its attractive architecture of mixed media—multi-hued red bricks, paneled glass, and black and gray metal framing.

Jameson held out her purse. "Did you pick up your tongue drum yet?"

"The what-sy?"

"The steel tongue drum. You said you were going to pick it up from World's Wonders." He pointed to a building at the corner of the lot. "The crystal shop."

"Oh. I think we'll wait on that."

"Actually, I'll just pick it up for you now. You wanted it for the office anyway, right?"

"Yes, and how very kind of you," she said, giving him a strained, close-lipped smile.

With effort, Iris hoisted herself out of the low-profile car. She took a last look at its sleek lines before following Jameson up a small set of stairs to a double-door glass entryway.

He pointed at the steps. "Watch your footing."

"I will. So, do I have any upcoming appointments I should know about?"

"Not unless you want to. After the meeting last night, you're set for a week or two."

"Good."

The elevator opened and swallowed the pair of them before ascending to the seventh floor.

Iris had nothing more to say to this helpful fellow. She would work out a plan of getting back to Boulder Creek in the privacy of Fergus's home, which, judging by the car he drove, the lush building they currently walked through, and his yes-man's obedient behavior, would be no hardship.

"You've lived here about a year now," Jameson offered, unprompted, then stopped in front of a glossy red door. He unlocked the knob and deadbolt, then dangled the keys. "I'll leave ya to it, boss. Just holler if you need me."

"Thank you," Iris said, then entered the threshold.

The first thing she noticed was the scent of raw tobacco and the cold temperature. The scent and chill were eerily similar to her own home. She rid herself of the obligatory spiked heels—which Jameson had nicely washed off for her—and absorbed the thick, plush carpet caressing her feet.

The decorated entry hallway was long for a condo. To her right stood an antiqued wall table, over which hung a babbling wall fountain. Scattered about the tabletop were a multitude of Obsidian items—discs, obelisks, and spheres on wooden stands. Unlit black pillar candles with dried, cascading wax stood on each end, but it was the small vial that caught her attention. She picked it up. Blood, no doubt. "This Fergus fellow seems to have a bit of an obsession with blood." Disgusted, she set the vial down.

She figured the little dish with a picture of the High Priestess tarot card must be for keys. She plinked them down and proceeded into a spacious living area, knowing a sink for washing her hands must be nearby.

Despite the shut-tight shades, the windows clearly let in an abundance of natural light when given the chance. While she rather liked it dark, she walked over and reached for the nearest string to pull open the blinds. One by one, her efforts revealed a tremendous view of the rushing river below the complex and an expanded cityscape across the living room. She envisioned the overlook at night, sparkling with city lights.

"Mr. Fergus, I will say this for you … you have exceptional taste."

With a good wash the priority, she walked to the kitchen with its elegant black-and-white marble countertops and stainless-steel appliances. She soaped her hands, noting the basil-scented foam, and observed the stringent cleanliness of the countertops. After toweling off, she rummaged through the cupboards, grabbed a glass, and poured a filtered serving of water from the floating island spigot. She sipped every drop. Then, she set down her empty glass, breaking the pristine image of a model-perfect home.

"So, what other tricks have you?"

She ambled into the bedroom and found a cracked closet with its light left on. It was the only sign that someone had been in the home. As she neared, she recognized the clothing from her own donation bag hanging just inside the door. But she opened it to find a wardrobe of a most elaborate impression—glam-sequined trench coats, ritual cloaks, and fine silken men's suits—were all to the right. To the left were sateen sheath dresses of deep reds, rusts, and black. On the floor sat a plethora of shoes, both men's Italian leather loafers and boots, as well as the spikiest red-soled, patent-leather pumps and sandals made for a large foot.

She picked up a slender stiletto sandal and held it up in front of her. "Hmph. Too big. Such a pity I won't be able to wear it." She tossed it back to the floor, annoyed by the thought of its cruel clench upon her foot.

A chest of drawers stood against the back wall of the closet. Could be promising, but first, a shower. She plucked a rust-colored satin robe from the hanging surplus and headed for the bathroom.

Within moments, she returned fully refreshed and ready for more discovery within the chest. She opened each drawer and shuffled through the belongings—a disorganized mess of R-rated snapshots from elaborate parties, business cards, and phone numbers written on Post-its in the first drawer, extra-large women's lingerie of all colors in the second, and thick cashmere scarves and beanies in the third. Finally, she sat on the ground to peruse the bottom drawer.

She rifled through dull legal papers—a deed to the condo, a lease contract from a Maserati dealer, one … two … three gym memberships. She flipped through the paperwork until reaching the bottom. So far, a bunch of nothing. She lifted the last manila file folder from the drawer, removed its contents, and, one by one, looked at the papers.

At last, a surprise. "Hmph," she said aloud. "Mr. Fergus was adopted when he was eight. And he was born in Santa Cruz County. Indeed, a small world … parents deceased."

Then she froze.

Little shocked her, especially the older she got. But this!

"I don't believe it."

She read it again. All of it. From the first filled-in box to the very last signature that released an orphaned eight-year-old Fergus into state custody. In jet black ink, the signature was none other than her very own grandmother's.

She took a deep, slow breath, returning the papers to their file and organizing everything back into the drawer. Dumbfounded, she shut it, stood up, and left the closet. Numb, she hesitated by the black brocade bedding with red velvet pillows, sitting on the mattress's edge, captivated yet quite disillusioned. It was impossible to deny or ignore her role in Fergus's troubled past.

CHAPTER 5
RETURN IT!

Mateo could not breathe! He struggled to get away from the looming, unseen force, but gravity pulled him further downward into a space of absolute darkness. He felt his throat constrict but then realized in horror that he hung from his neck. He kicked and flailed, dangling by the noose above a pitch-black chasm.

Then he dropped. Plummeting into an endless void. Nothing to see. No sound, but the rushing wind receiving him unto his death.

Mateo awoke with a gasp and sprang up, shaking and panting. He wiped the sweaty film from his face and looked around his settled room.

"What?" Alicia grumbled, her face sunk deep into her pink satin pillowcase.

He absorbed the safety of his bedroom and worked to settle his pounding heart. "Sorry. Bad dream. Just go back to sleep."

She already had. Good. He looked at the clock—three a.m. Not too bad, as she gets up in an hour to ready for her hour-long commute to Silicon Valley.

Not so good for him. With his adrenaline surging, Mateo knew sleep would not return so easily—nor did he want it to. Not with that nightmare looming in his psyche.

He ambled his way to the toilet, still haunted by the sensation of his bottomless fall. Unnerving. Nothing crazy going on in his life right now. In fact, he just received his journeyman promotion, and the boss set him up with an important flooring job in a mountainside

McMansion. No more assistant jobs for him. Weird that he'd have a nightmare meant for people with problems.

He started back toward the bed but heard a rustle downstairs. Fully alert now, he grabbed his steel baton from behind the headboard and went to peer down into his entryway. He stilled and listened.

Again, the sound. Like a nylon windsock blowing in the breeze. Yet no significant wind blew through his home, only a subtle rise of heat from the floor vents.

He crept to the first floor, making a visual sweep of his living space. Seeing nothing unusual, he flopped down on the couch to let his eyes adjust to the darkness. From outside, the almost full moon shone through the uncovered arched glass above his curtained windows, allowing plenty of natural lighting into the room.

The rustle sounded again from behind him now. He shot a glance over his shoulder, seeing his oaken curio cabinet, hoping to glimpse the cause. Maybe a mouse?

Then, a flutter of movement came right in front of him. He jerked his head forward, only to see their hanging Baja blanket lightly tapping at the wall … with no heating vent below it.

His heart picked up pace again.

Rapidly, a whoosh came right at him, straight into his face. Saturating the room with a musty odor and causing him to identify what seemed to be … breath. The breath of another.

His heartbeat spiked to triple-time. Someone occupied the room with him. Like his dream, he saw nothing, but he could feel the tension.

Squeezing his eyes shut, he prayed aloud. "Our Father who art in heaven, hallowed be thy name …"

"*Tn! Nt!*" the breathy voice whispered, gruff and forced, right into his face.

Eyes kept shut, he pulled his head back from the stale air and turned his cheek, praying to his Lord. "Thy kingdom come, thy will be done—"

"*Retn Nt!*" the voice said in a forceful rasp, as if a brutish mob boss.

"Please leave me alone!" Mateo said, his volume rising. Horrified, he began his prayer again, loud and committed in his plea for divine intervention.

"Return it!" the voice said, circling around him and growing angrier by the moment.

In an instant, he knew his shortcoming—the case full of creepy occult drawings and dark art verbiage that he had found the previous December at the mountain flooring job. He never returned it!

A translucent presence materialized in front of him. Taller and thicker than himself, it looked to have once been a man of substantial bulk.

In a violent burst of activity, the visage charged through him. He felt the pummel of the energy rip through his paunch and released a loud "Oomph!" Then, a stinging sensation ripped across his cheek just as something moved at the bottom of the staircase.

The living room lights illuminated.

"What are you doing down here?" Alicia asked, standing at the foot of the stairs, blinking with sleepy eyes.

Mateo frantically looked around, then huffed out a breath and dropped back onto the couch, holding his aching stomach. With the danger gone, he buried his face in his hands.

"Mateo, what the hell are you doing?"

"Oh, my God!" He tried to calm himself, not wanting her to think him crazy.

Alicia came over and cocked her head. "What did you do to your face? You're cut."

He touched his cheek, then flinched at the rawness of the open slit. He shook his head and announced the news. "I think I'm in trouble."

Mateo recounted his find at the old Boulder Creek home. He kept vague on the occult contents, knowing if Alicia told her mother-in-law, he'd never hear the end of it … from either of them. He said he had meant to take it back but ended up sick. When Jack finished the job without him and returned the house keys, he had no clean chance of returning it. "… when I saw what was inside … how it could help vision

… I thought maybe it could help Matty, but it wasn't that kind of vision. Anyway, I thought it was a bunch of useless crap. And seriously, all has been fine until tonight."

"What makes you think it's the case?"

He sheepishly looked at her. He could *not* tell her the truth.

"What was in the case?"

"Ugh, don't be mad at me." She would not stop until he copped to it.

She glared at him, awaiting the declaration.

"There were some … a few … like, occult—"

"What?!"

"I didn't—"

"*¡Oh, Dios mío,* Mateo!! How could you do this to us?" Her face went red with anger. "How could you do this to little Matty?! He can barely see as it is! What if that thing came at him, and he couldn't defend himself?! You put all our lives at risk! *Eres un idiota!*"

"I swear it's been fine. Tonight is the first time anything happened like this."

"Where is it?!" Alicia screeched, flashing a look up the stairs. Reverent of their sleeping son, she hissed in a forced quiet, "Where?!" Not waiting for his answer, she rushed to the curio drawer and withdrew a freshwater pearl rosary, its silver cross dangling. Only a few words of prayer came out before she interrupted herself. "I can't believe you!" Her speech became angrier and more rapid. "Where is that suitcase?!"

"I don't have it anymore."

"Where is it then?"

"I sold it." Actually, he still had it and the whole damn lot of its contents, but she'd flip out even worse if she knew it sat two doors from their bedroom.

"*Como puedes ser tan estupido?* Who the hell did you sell it to?"

"The antique shop."

"Well, tomorrow you're going to that antique shop and get it back where it belongs! And you damn well better hope they haven't sold it!"

"I know, I—"

"*¡Cállate!* How am I supposed to sleep now? And what about Matty?" Her voice became choppier and more adamant. "If I hear … *one* little peep of a fright from him, I am taking him … we are going to my mother's … and NEVER coming back!"

"Yes! Of course, I want you both safe. You think I'd ever do this on purpose?" He cautiously approached her; the raging of his beloved could turn physical if he failed to play his cards right. He slowly put his hands around Alicia's waist, delicately shushing her. "Hey. Hey. I'm sorry. I'll make this right, okay? I would never put us in harm's way."

She stewed but allowed for the closeness.

"It could have just been part of my dream," Mateo said.

She tensed up and jabbed a stiff index finger into the cut on his face. "Dreams don't make you bleed!"

He ignored the soreness. "Baby, I'm sorry. I promise I'll make it up." He pulled her in for a reassuring hug.

Alicia softened. "I can't believe—"

"Shhh, I'm sorry," he said, tenderly rubbing her back, working to calm a spirit much more intimidating than an aggressive ghost.

Alicia looked away in a fussy pout before returning his hug. "We don't need this, Mateo. You know how protective I am of Matty since the accident! Nothing can ever happen—"

Mateo hugged her, remembering the heartache of their son's eye problems caused by the car accident. He rocked her in his hug, soothing her angst.

"Promise me you'll take care of it first thing tomorrow."

"I promise. It helps this new job is swing shift, so I'm available till the afternoons for the next month."

Alicia sighed and relaxed into his arms. A few more words of reassurance, and she retreated upstairs.

Mateo entered the hall bathroom to examine his stinging cut. He heard Alicia upstairs, rushing about, readying for her early-morning commute. Amused, he laughed at his reflection and visualized the pitiful scene from earlier. Afraid of a ghost, like a little child.

But when he looked into the mirror's reflection, he remembered the stale breath and dominating force of the unwelcomed presence. Quickly, he shut off the light and went upstairs.

CHAPTER 6
THE SWAGGER OF AN ELDERLY COWBOY

Sheriff Michaels stood in front of the crowd of riveted faces and gave a new government-approved spiel for grade schoolers.

"That's why you'll see an officer walking the grounds every day now. We're not here to be mean to anyone or make you feel uncomfortable. In fact, we care for every one of you, and our being here will assure your parents of your increased safety." He omitted that dreaded, rising statistic they need not know, then looked over at the smiling principal. "Now, I don't know if Ms. McKinley has told you, but once a month, a student will get to help the on-duty officer make their rounds."

The youngsters' expressions stayed unmoving and quiet, their usual exuberant energy quelled while transfixed on the man with the badge.

"… and skip a couple of classes on that day," he added.

A buzz of chatter filled the auditorium. The response he had hoped for.

"Anyway, that's about it for me. I've enjoyed talking to you all today. Remember to be kind to your teachers. And parents."

He placed the microphone back on its stand, nodded at the principal, and headed for the bleachers, delivering a few fist bumps on his way out the door. An unexpected voice of a young miss came from behind him.

"Excuse me."

He turned to find a girl with a lion's mane of auburn hair and a pair of big, brown eyes peering up at him. Beside her stood a pudgy blond with freckles and a mouthful of pre-teen braces.

"Zoelly, that's enough questions for the sheriff today," the teacher called out to her. "You girls let him get on his way."

He held up his hand to the teacher, gesturing acceptance, then addressed them. "Yes, ma'ams, how may I help you?"

"I just want to give you this." Zoelly held out a small black polished stone. "It's Black Onyx … for protection. I know your job is sometimes dangerous, so I hope it helps."

"Well, that's really nice of you." He eyed the smooth, opaque rock, rotating it, then looked back at the girls. "Thank you. I'll keep it in my cruiser."

"Good. You accepting it helps me turn over a new leaf."

He smiled. "A new leaf, huh? That's an interesting term. Who taught you that?"

"My friend Arista. She's helping me be a better person."

There was only one Arista he had ever known. "Well, I'm quite confident that you're in excellent hands."

"Okay," Zoelly said, now shying away. She and her friend whispered to one another while they made their way back to the crowd.

As the sheriff walked out the auditorium door, he turned up his radio, beckoning him to a crime scene. He responded to the dispatcher, thankful the location was far from the Kelly household for a change.

In moments, he swooped down the school's driveway and onto Highway 9, headed to Boulder Creek. Well past its downtown, he took a right on Bear Creek Road and finally onto Puma Road, eventually pulling into a driveway.

A man in denim suspenders waved him over, then waited patiently as he exited the car.

"Mornin'!"

"Mornin', Sheriff, I'm Manny Whelan. It's over here."

Manny walked with the swagger of an elderly cowboy, bowlegged and rangy. There was no doubt this man had grit in his gut—still working hard. He crackled with the energy of someone half his age.

"Nice property you have here, Mr. Whelan."

"Thank ya, Sheriff."

Manny led him to a structure where the sound of snorting pigs overtook the effect of all other natural sounds.

"My guys and I were doing some fence work, 'cause my pens are shot ta hell. Damn hogs had nudged out the wiring. And ya gotta get right on that, or they end up running amok all over creation. And I'll tell ya, they eat damn near everything!" Manny winced at his own words. "Er. Well, you'll see."

As they walked toward the backside of Manny's pen, the sheriff looked at the various footprints in the mud—cleated work boots, prints with lesser tread and one smooth print, long and narrow, out of the usual footpath.

When they reached the backside, Manny pointed into a foot-wide crevice between the pigpen and a large woodshed. "Up there! Ya see it? 'Bout eight feet in?"

The sheriff peered into the tight space.

"Ya see, my eyesight's not that good, so I guess I just missed it for God knows how long. My hogs must've nudged it out of the wiring … another darned reason we're repairing it. Anyway, my guys were working on the pen today and noticed it. I didn't move it or nothin', just left it where it was for ya to have a look-see."

He saw it, alright. The subject in question could have been mistaken for a chunk of wood … except for the fingers curled inward like claws. "Uh-huh." It appeared to be a ravaged human hand and forearm. Torn flesh still clinging to it, but mostly bone remained. "That's a tight squeeze. Any way we can access it from inside the pen? I don't think my body's going to fit."

"I hear ya." The farmer looked at his pigs and scratched his mostly bald head, tanned and leathery. "I just don't know what I'm to do with my hogs. I got no other place to put 'em. Ya mind walkin' amongst 'em?

Ya may get your uniform muddy, but otherwise, they're pretty friendly."

"We'll make it work."

When they entered the pen, the enormous, mud-spattered pigs snorted and darted around the sty that reeked of piss and dung. Alarmed by the intrusion, they clustered together and eyed the humans.

The sheriff crouched at the back wall for a better look. "Well, it sure looks like a human hand to me."

"Yep. See, I don't want to be gettin' some kind of reputation of my hogs hurtin' people, so I just want to nip this in the bud right now."

The sheriff examined the dirty, chewed-on hand, noting an especially chunky watch at the wrist. Then, from the corner of his eye, he spotted one pig coming up behind him. When he looked over his shoulder, its pink, flat, snotty nose wriggled at him in curiosity. It moved in a little closer. Giving it a side eye, he thought surely *It wouldn't*.

When he turned back to examine the hand, he felt the large, wet nose firmly nudge into his shoulder, leaving a wet impression on his thin shirt. He wanted to groan in disgust but kept his inspection on the dismembered forearm while feeling repulsion all around him.

"Git!" Mr. Whelan said with firm authority, sending the swine darting back to its crowd of friends.

To keep an accepting front for Manny's sake, he took the porcine affection in stride and tried to ignore the saturated spot on the back of his shirt, complete with its signature scent that would probably last the day. Gross. Possibly even more so than the inanimate *meat hook* laying on the ground.

"All right. The coroner will get on this. She's real helpful, discreet, and she could probably even squeeze her little tush into that narrow opening … meaning you don't have to cut it open and spend a bunch of time repairing things to accommodate my girth. But that's her call."

"Sounds good, Sheriff."

"Do you know who this may belong to?" the sheriff asked, gesturing toward the forearm.

"No, sir."

"Do you know of anyone who may use your pigs for unlawful purposes?"

"My hogs? No, sir. Not at all." Manny answered, holding an honest expression.

He seemed straightforward, but who could say this early in the investigation?

"Could you furnish me with a list of acquaintances that know the layout of your property?"

"I don't socialize much … just keep to myself. My workers know it, but that's about it."

"What about your neighbors?" He peered at Manny.

For the first time, Manny's answer came with shifty eyes.

"Does someone feed your hogs if you're sick or on vacation?"

"Just my workers. But they're real good guys … never any trouble."

"All right then. You have access to a computer?"

"I do."

The sheriff reached into his chest pocket, pulled out a business card, and handed it to the spry fellow. "You can use that email address to send me the list. Names and addresses … phone numbers are helpful if you have them."

"Will do."

"I'm going to go call it in and do some paperwork, and when my reinforcements get here, I'll be taking off."

"Whatever I can do to help."

He bid Manny a good day and set about doing his write-up in the cruiser until the investigative team arrived. He exchanged polite formalities and office small talk, then departed.

As he drove back toward town, he reflected on his morning spent reassuring school children, only to be summoned to investigate the remains of a person devoured by pigs. How drastically disturbing it could be to manage such an unbalanced career—cheerful innocence and ghastly dismemberment. A true lesson in *compare and contrast*.

Luckily, he could flip that switch at will.

CHAPTER 7
GUN-SHY OF STRANGERS

Arista hustled out of the psychologist's office, down the tree-lined walkway, and into the glaring bright autumn day. She always felt drained and no closer to resolution each time she left and wondered if the visit would ever have a measurable benefit. While helping a little with the grief of losing her mom and dad, what about all her other nagging issues? Could she talk about her gutted uncle loaded into Iris's trunk? Could she discuss the horrifying gwishin that had haunted her yard? What about a five-generation family curse that kept playing out with horrible consequences? No, all those issues she needed to work out on her own.

She checked her rearview mirror and reversed, mind aswirl with more drama—Iris and her potential shadiness despite her help with the gwishin, the load of expectation about her great powers to come, and her once-astute intuition had been MIA over the past year.

HOOOONK!!

She braked!

A couple seconds lapsed before the car she almost backed into continued on with its driver's careful eye scrutinizing her.

"Sorry," she said, giving a quick wave.

At the top of her frazzling list, sat Auntie's eyesight struggles throughout the week, especially after the fall onto Iris's glass table. When the waves of blurriness became a daily occurrence, they scheduled her an appointment, and that came later on this day.

Maddie's ringtone broke through her barrage of obsessing.

"Hey! Sorry, I'm just getting back. I see you called the other day. What's up?"

Maddie had been heavily occupied since taking up with Skylar during Arista's sabbatical to Sedona. She couldn't recall a time when her call went unacknowledged by her best friend for so long. She understood. Her own menagerie of commitments had kept her occupied, and she felt happy Maddie had a new close friend.

"No prob. Random, but I was calling to see what color Skylar's van is."

"Teal … ish."

"Like a dark green?"

"Not really," Maddie replied, her voice filled with uncertainty. "Why?"

This did not help. While teal and dark green are not close on the color chart, subjectivity was a typical question when dealing with Maddie.

"It doesn't matter. What's new? I haven't heard from you," Arista said.

"Well … I'm moving to Honolulu."

"What?! Why?"

"Skylar got a job offer for a Marine Biologist position, and she's talked me into going with her."

Arista grunted to herself. Another, for lack of better words, abandonment. She caught her selfishness and corrected. "Okay. Are you sure that's what *you* want?"

"I knew you would say that, and I love you for it. Yes, I do. I'm also sorry for springing it on you. You've been through a lot, but I *swear* … I'm only a call away if you ever need me."

"Of course! Our phone calls became invaluable when I moved to Sedona. I'm happy for you! Only the lush Hawaiian Isles could rival our ocean and redwoods."

How could she not be happy for her? With Evan and Bree always doing the couple thing and the potential of her and Shane reconnecting, she didn't want Maddie to feel excluded. Her childhood bestie had already shown signs of exasperation with both of the relationships, including the rumor she spread about Shane. But she understood.

Maddie's tone turned serious. "Arista, I have to be honest. I've been the third wheel in all my relationships for way too long. And I love you … and Evan … and I even like Shane, but it's time for me to move on. And me and Skylar …"

Arista heard Maddie gulp in air for courage, and waited for that moment, that telling moment of which she had wondered about Maddie since high school.

"Anyway, yeah. I'm really looking forward to it," Maddie said.

Not today, and that's okay.

"I totally understand. We've gotten used to talking on the phone anyway," Arista said.

"That's for sure. My turn to leave."

Arista laughed, then asked, "When are you moving?"

"Next month."

"Wow! Okay …"

"Sorry, I didn't tell you sooner."

"No worries. I haven't been as available as I would've liked."

"Not really," Maddie said, with a slight sarcasm.

They snickered at the truth in jest together, but Arista hoped her own troubles, mixed with her attention set on Shane, had not been the sole cause of the figurative distance between her and Maddie since she had returned. While the news came bittersweet, she had nothing but happiness for her old bestie. They ended the conversation with promises of getting together as Arista pulled into her driveway.

Before exiting the car, she dialed Auntie.

"Hey, I'm just back from my Psych. Do you need me to stop by or just pick you up later?"

"Later's fine. Don't worry, I'm not blind, for goodness' sake. Even at its worst, I can see. It's just blurry. And right now …" Auntie quieted except for her mouth-breathing from a stuffy nose. "Yes … it's fine for now."

"Okay, call me if you need anything. Otherwise, I'll be over in a couple hours to pick you up for your appointment."

"Sounds good."

"I presume we're feeding the cats today?"

"Yes."

"Okay, see you then."

Walking through the door, she relaxed into the feel of her cozy cottage and set about the kitchen to create a quick snack—a banana, chocolate chip, and almond butter smoothie. Plopping the ingredients into the blender, she added the almond milk and electrified the concoction, absorbing the deafening noise. Upon hitting the off button, instant relief for her ears.

Unexpectedly, a random image flashed in her mind. "Hummingbird?" she thought aloud. The ruby-throated little zippers frequented her garden. But still. "Why hummingbird? Hmph." She correlated the thought to her worry about Auntie since that was her absolute favorite animal.

Then, a realization. Her house felt a little too quiet. Where was Royal? He would have come out by now. His routine dictated this to be the time when he scanned the yard for the sparrows, wrens, and warblers, hopping about the lawn furniture, picking up tidbits, then flying off again. If the birds offered no amusement, then any sudden movement, no matter how small, would suffice for morning entertainment.

But Royal did not sit in any of the windows. In fact, the more she thought about it, the emptiness that filled her house felt completely out of kilter.

"Roooyalllll."

She checked his usual hangouts—the beanbag chair, the foot of her bed, and his post. She checked the spots he occasionally frequented when he became bored with the same old, same old—the living room window, underneath any unfolded blankets, and finally, under the second bedroom's bed.

Upon finding nothing in the back bedroom, she took to its floor, settling her back against the footboard and letting a sadness kindle inside of her. A month ago, her father had slept in this room. She looked at the framed selfie she had taken of them on that fateful night and remembered his clean scent. She allowed the strike of pain into her heart, then relieved it with fond memories. "I love you, dad."

She took a grounded breath and left the room, cat-less.

"Royal!" she called, re-engaged in her worry. Yes, he was part ninja, but it had never taken this long to find him. She re-approached the living room window, which she always opened first thing in the morning to circulate fresh air.

A fraying at the far bottom of the screen caught her attention. "No way." She touched its mesh, and it gave way, allowing for a feline's easy exit into a very big world.

Desperation! She had to find him. Barging into her shoes, then to the door, she imagined him walking into the street with a speedy oncoming car. No. What if a coyote roaming the mountain streets snatched him up and ran off with him clenched in hungry jaws? No! Or the neighbor's Pitbull in his fenced backyard. Stop it! That one had a feline brother he basked with in the sun.

Her heart raced as she hurried out into the morning chill. Midway through November, no sign of a warm day remained. Occasional drips from the eaves tapped into the small puddles from the early morning rain. The glare of the sun on the slick surfaces made it even harder to see clearly, and her lightweight jacket, chosen in haste, barely kept her body insulated.

But time was of the essence. She scoured the area—her shed, the lawn furniture, and then her shrubs and bushes. "Royal. Come on, baby. Kitty, kitty."

She walked her yard's perimeter, peering down toward the base of her hedgerow's thick foliage.

The low mumbling of a man's voice on Hoot Owl Way met her ears. With her attention caught, she peered through the hedge and saw a mid-sized white coupe parked across the street. Realizing the driver's eyes looked toward her driveway, she shrunk back into herself. Luckily, there was no way he could see her through the leafy camouflage.

Great! Another stranger gawking at her property. The paranoia crept into her psyche, and she wondered if she faced a certain danger. First, the green van, and now this guy in his white car. He was talking to someone, but she could not see through his tinted windows. Were there two of them? Hopefully, they weren't hired guns out to avenge Fergus.

An air of caution struck her when the man opened his door and walked back to his rising trunk.

She ducked backward and hustled toward her porch. Safety first! But when she reached the first step, she heard the crunch of the man's shoes on her driveway. She turned around to find him … with a suitcase?

They froze at the sight of one another. The pause swelled to an uncomfortable level.

"Can I help you?" she asked. After all, maybe it was just a delivery.

He mumbled something, then, to her bewilderment, turned in haste and jetted from view.

She heard the car door open and shut and an engine start. Then, she watched as a streak of white zoomed past.

"Great! A new stranger to add to the never-ending chaos that is my life." She snorted at the thought of it and felt a bit of relief from his alarmed departure. "Hopefully, they all go just as peacefully from here on out!"

Just as she felt the oncoming anxiety of dealing with her lost, runaway, or murdered fur baby—

Mew.

"Royal!" Joy slashed through the paranoia and doom. Happiness! He was alive and well!

She hurried over to her feline as he strolled out from the base of the hedge, a casual strut with his tail high. As she neared him, she slowed her pace, hoping not to spark an urge for him to dart in the opposite direction. She wiggled her fingers and cooed at him in a soft voice. "It's okay, my baby."

He plopped down on the sun-dried pea gravel and gave a strenuous arched stretch. His paws reached with vigor just before he tucked them back into his body and rubbed his whisker pad against the beam-warmed pebbles of her driveway.

"Aw, you love that pebble bath, don't you?"

She gave him a long stroke before gingerly scooping him up and propping him on her shoulder. Keeping her tone gentle and reassuring, she walked toward their sanctuary. Hopefully, he would not use her flesh as leverage for a quick, bounding getaway.

Luckily, he accepted his limited excursion to the outside world and found the food dish just as rewarding.

·   ·   ·

"You ready for your eye appointment?" Arista bellowed into Auntie's house.

Auntie, in a flash of orange floral, bustled out of her altar room and into the hall bath.

"Wow. You're bright today," Arista noted, humored, as Auntie now darted into her kitchen.

Her long yoked red dress had a print of pink, yellow, and orange flowers covering it. From beneath it, a khaki-green lace slip-skirt hung four inches lower and hovered above a pair of red, pebble-leather, lace up boots. Perhaps lack of clear vision played a part in the colorful ensemble.

She followed Auntie into the kitchen for another eyeful. "Like, wow! You're really dressed up today. Is that new?"

"I actually made this years ago." Auntie flipped open doors and drawers, finally finding a pumpkin barrette that she immediately clipped into the frizzed curls upon her head. For fun, she struck a pose.

"You look absolutely *marvelous*," Arista said, eyeing her up and down.

Auntie smiled before putting an acrylic lid atop her steamy travel mug full of tea.

"So, is your vision still okay? It's certainly not slowing you down right now."

Auntie walked them out the door. "Just fuzzy at times. First thing when I wake up and the night seems to get … a little worse."

That worried her—at least until she saw Auntie's outfit up against a backdrop of her bright yellow Volvo. She kept her giggle to herself, then realized she had not felt so amused in a while. The lightness coalesced inside of her as she took the passenger seat.

"I just found out Maddie's moving to Hawaii," Arista said, the words coming out easier than expected.

"She is?" Auntie responded, straightening her mirrors. "What's the occasion?"

"Skylar got a new job, and she's going with her."

"Hmph. She's been with you a very long time. Rather a shame … though inevitable that our closest friends move away," Auntie said, her expression turning to concern, before turning to Arista. "Are you okay?"

"I'll miss her, but I understand. That leaves just Shane and Evan from our old high school pack."

"The couples," Auntie said in a perky voice. Her eyes lit up. "Did you find out her friend's van color?"

The couples? That sounded encouraging. "Yes, and no. She said teal, but when I mentioned dark green, she wasn't sure."

"One person's red-violet is another person's purple."

"Precisely," Arista said, noticing Auntie still fussing with mirrors. "Are you sure you're good to drive?"

"Yes, it's all fine right now. I could even read the fine print on my Oracle card today," Auntie said, starting the car.

"Really? What'd you draw?"

Her lips quirked. "Hummingbird."

"No way. I just thought of a hummingbird for absolutely no reason earlier today."

Auntie let out an abrupt hoot as she pulled onto Hoot Owl Way. "We're in sync! Anyway, I'll miss the little buggers come late winter."

"Yeah, it's pretty incredible how far they migrate with their tiny little wings."

"Twisting and turning in turbulent winds … using their little tail feathers as a rudder," Auntie added.

The topic charmed them both, and they gushed with fondness on the drive to Scotts Valley. Farther, they wove out of the mountains, catching sight of a tree lot readying for large deliveries of fine firs.

Another uplifting thought, the festive oncoming season. With so much drama this year, Arista looked forward to the coming Winter Solstice more than ever. A time of solace and the promise of rebirth. Specifically for her, if not a lessening of chaos and an increase in understanding of her presumed powers, she at least hoped for an improvement in mental well-being. She was beginning to dwell a little bit too much on the bad *what-ifs*.

"Hmm," Auntie said, staring into her rearview mirror.

"What is it?"

"I saw the car behind us on our street twice this week."

Arista pulled down her visor to check the scene. "Yes! I just saw it, too! Royal escaped this morning, and while I was looking for him, that guy came into my yard. He had a suitcase in his arms. When he saw me, he totally froze, then took off. He was talking to someone beforehand, but it looks like it's just him now."

"Arista, don't tell me we have strange men to watch out for again," Auntie said, only half joking.

"I was hoping you could tell *me* there was nothing to worry about!"

Auntie squinted while looking into her rearview. "There's a child in the car with him."

"Really?" Arista adjusted her visor mirror to better see into the man's backseat. "Ah, got it. A little boy with glasses." She paused. "Wow! Looks like your vision *is* working well today."

The driver changed lanes as they arrived in the trendy town of Scotts Valley, with its smoothie bars, theater, and spa boutiques. Upon their turn into the doctor's office parking lot, the stranger in his white car continued on toward the highway.

Arista's eyes trailed after him.

"Well, this worked out well," Auntie said, gliding into a front space. She turned off the engine and harrumphed.

"What do you think?" Arista asked, wondering which she should worry about more—the mystery green van or the zippy white car.

"To be honest, I'm just so gun-shy of strangers by now. I'm just hoping we don't have another stalker, murderer, or dark-magick witch on our tail!" Auntie said, before she let out an exasperated laugh.

Arista laughed along but knew Auntie's statement was hardly a joke. Still, she found some comfort in keeping it lighthearted. "Well, Fergus held *my* deepest worry, and now he's dead!" She paused and felt security in the statement. "D-e-a-d."

Yes, it unsettled them that Iris had gone missing, but maybe she had left town on purpose. She seemed to involve herself with shady dealings. Including the curse tablet. Who knew what she was up to? For a second, Arista's musing brought forth a notion of Iris as Dr. Frankenstein, reanimating Fergus's corpse with a roar of maniacal laughter.

"I keep thinking of Iris. Such a mystery … in so many ways," Auntie said, a tinge of disappointment in her tone.

Funny, Auntie should bring her up. "She just crossed my mind as well."

"Oh shoot, I'm late!"

Auntie hopped out of the car, fully energized, and hustled to the door. She grabbed the handle, pulling it open for Arista. "After you," she said in her most courteous mannerism.

"Well, thank you kindly," Arista said, mirroring the exaggerated politeness while taking another gander at Auntie's very outlandish outfit.

CHAPTER 8
THE OLD BRUJA

As Mateo navigated the hairpin turn, the *thunk* from the trunk served as a reminder of unfinished business.

"Daddy, what's that noise?" Matty asked on their drive home from school.

"It's just some stuff I have in my trunk."

"Oh."

Two days earlier, he had tried and failed to leave the case at the owner's property. Since he had startled the owner as she walked up her porch steps, he felt too embarrassed to return it directly to her and left. Luckily, Alicia had let him slide … on that day! She would be unhappy to hear he still had it in his possession. Plus, he needed to rethink his approach in case he ran into the owner again. In the meantime, he should probably get it out of his trunk.

Once home, he situated his son at his bedroom desk with homework, pencils, and crayons to study his three-letter words and their matching pictures. "You got this, buddy. Remember to color in the pictures, too, and holler if you have questions."

"M-kay, dad."

Mateo hustled downstairs and out to the trunk to grab the case. Just as quickly, he went back upstairs and slinked into his office to slide the case back into the closet where it had sat since he had first taken it. In the coming days, he would try to return it again. It needed to be soon since his big flooring job neared.

"You good, buddy?" he bellowed through the hall to Matty.

"Yep."

He exhaled in relief and bounced down the stairs to park himself on the couch in order to drink his ready-made cookies and cream-flavored protein shake that would tide him over until dinner.

The sound of Alicia's footsteps on the porch came within moments of his settling. He flinched at how close her arrival was to seeing him bring the case back inside the house and brainstormed excuses for not returning it, just in case she found out.

Her heels clicked into the kitchen as she set her purse and a bagful of groceries on the table. He snuck a quick peek. From the look of the bag, she had stopped at the fruit stand for an array of farm-to-table ingredients for the night's dinner. That meant salad. Hopefully, she would serve it with chicken quesadilla strips, or he'd end up snacking all night to quiet his hunger.

The shoes clicked to the entryway behind him and stopped. He could feel her peering at the back of his head, her inquisitive eyes boring through his skull. Slowly, he turned around to face her. "Hey, beautiful."

When their eyes met, she got straight to business. "I didn't bug you about it yesterday, but did you get rid of that case yet?"

He did not want to tell her. She would get so mad. He twisted his mouth. Lie about it? He couldn't lie, even if he wanted to. "There was another problem."

She tilted her head with impatience and slapped her hand upon her cocked hip. "What? What was the problem, Mateo? You got it back from the antique shop. Why is it so difficult to just give it back to the owner?"

He should have never lied about giving it to the shop. "I tried, but I ran into the owner again, so I had to split." Dammit, another lie slipping out of his mouth. Truthfully, he did not go today at all. After getting the specs from the new client, he only had enough time to pick up Matty from school and did not want to drag him into the mountains to return it.

"Aigh! You said that last time!"

"It happened last time, too," he reasoned.

"I don't care anymore! We have my mother here any minute. If she knew about all of this, she would go crazy!"

Ugh! Why a mother-in-law visit today? "Don't tell her."

Her face flushed, and she lit into her rant. "That's always your deal. Just don't say anything, and maybe it will be okay. Well, it's not okay. It's not okay!" She stomped her spiky heel on the ground, but it was not as effective as her fast-talking tirade. "And you're right! We don't have to tell her because she'll know!"

He heaved out a sigh as she stormed up the stairs. Certainly, he would keep quiet about putting the case back in the office.

The other matter concerned him, too. His mother-in-law, the old *bruja*, always got "feelings" when something was off, and her accuracy of pinpointing freaky trouble over the years had been spot on. Hopefully, she would come and go without event.

A faint murmur permeated his tension. Upstairs, Alicia had softened her angry tone for the sake of their son. The sound of his little boy's voice responding to her melted his heart. Of course, he wanted to keep them safe. Still, the timing had to be right to return the case. After all, if the owner wanted to be ruthless about it, she could press charges for him stealing it in the first place. He might if the roles were reversed.

Matty came down the stairs, holding the railing, his eyesight hindered since the car accident two years earlier. If it had to happen, he was glad it was a year before he found the case, or he would wonder if his dishonesty had caused the traumatic event.

"Sorry she's mad, Daddy," Matty said with a forgiving smile.

"He just needs to take care of his business," Alicia said, coming down behind him and heading to the kitchen to start dinner.

Mateo's eyes trailed her, and he snorted. One thing about Alicia, when she blew her top, she calmed just as quickly. He tapped his lap for his son to come sit.

Matty took a calculated run toward his father, carefully dodging the end table, ottoman, and coffee table in order to jump into his lap.

"Oomph!" Mateo grunted. His son had grown, and his jumps came with a little more weight. "Where's your glasses?"

"Mom says I don't have to wear them at home."

"Well, Mom's the boss!" he said, poking his son's nose.

Matty giggled as his dad gave him a few tickles under his arms.

"Is the case you put upstairs the *business* that mom means?"

Mateo did a double-take at his son and threw a quick glance toward the kitchen. Regardless of hindered eyesight, the little bugger caught his sneaky antic. "Ssshhhh, our little secret," he whispered. Then he snickered and stretched his arm over the back of the couch. "Yeah, that's the business." He flipped on the television to a cartoon of a little blue dog that filled the screen, capturing Matty's full attention within seconds.

The doorbell rang, sending a melodic chime through the house.

"Ugh." Mateo dropped his head back and let his tongue hang down the side of his mouth, causing Matty to laugh. Then, he braced himself for his mother-in-law's visit. He prayed there would be no mention of the case.

"Tita's here, Daddy," Matty said, jumping up.

"Yeah … yay for Tita!" Mateo said, pretending enthusiasm. "Matty."

His son stopped and looked back at him.

"Our little secret on anything to do with the *business*. Okay? Just you and me."

"Okay," he said with an earnest nod, then hurried to the front door to help his mother greet his grandmother.

Alicia went back to her cooking, and her mother walked into the living room. A fussy, apple-shaped older woman, she always wore tight-fitting clothes with red high heels and carried a designer handbag half her size. Besides her astute, self-proclaimed paranormal gifts, she thought herself quite the hottie to men half her age. Sometimes, he could swear she flirted with him.

"Hi, Tita," Mateo said, smiling, and comfortably awaited her harassment.

"You're not even going to get up to say hello?" she razzed.

He stood halfway up and gave her a one-armed hug before plopping back down on the couch.

Satisfied, she still harassed him. "You better get up. I come all the way over here, and—" She paused, a puzzled expression growing as she glanced about the room.

Matty watched and then mimicked her. "What's wrong, Tita?"

She held her hands waist-high as if bracing herself, fingers separated but said nothing. Then she cocked an ear toward the ceiling. "What is that?"

"What is what?" Mateo asked.

"That voice." She narrowed her eyes and listened. "There's a voice."

"I don't hear a voice." Mateo could not believe the efficiency of her troublemaking. This time, starting the minute she got in the door.

"I kinda hear something," Matty said, taking his grandmother's hand.

Tita's face froze, and her bottom jaw dropped. "Something's not right."

Alicia peered around the doorway from the kitchen. "What are you feeling, Mama?" She flashed a glare over at Mateo on the couch.

Mateo had hoped this time, just once, he could get something past the old gal without her knowing.

"Ooooh, there is something very unnatural in here." Her expression became a mix of awe and dread. She looked toward the stairs, sniffing at the air like a wildcat detecting the pheromones of a challenger.

Alicia came over and stood above Mateo. "What is it, Mama?" She nudged Mateo to stand up, and he complied.

Tita walked over to the stairs, Matty still holding her hand.

"Ooooh! I can see him … so clear," Matty said with wonder, looking up the stairwell. "He's smiling at me."

Tita's face grew ghostly pale, and her mouth stretched open in terror.

"… he's coming down the stairs," Matty said just before he observed his grandmother's heightening fear. In an instant, Matty's expression grew fearful, too.

Mateo watched them back up slowly, his mother-in-law's eyes round in horror.

Unexpectedly, she let out a shrill scream prompting Matty to squeal with her.

Alicia screamed and ran toward their son, with Mateo right behind her. When she grabbed at Matty, he ran to his father, so she settled for calming her mother.

Mateo looked at the stairwell but could see nothing except carpet and the wall at the top of the stairs. He scooped Matty up into his arms, trying to console his terrified son.

Suddenly, Tita's body stiffened, and she clenched at her own left arm.

"Mama!" Alicia cried out, clutching on to her mother, trying to soothe her without success.

Her mother's eyes rolled.

Reading the sign, Alicia reached out to break her fall. She guided her to the floor, then ran and grabbed the phone while her emotions poured forth in worried Spanish profanity.

Matty continued to scream, his eyes still fixed on the stairs, bucking in his father's arms as he attempted to get away. "No, Papa!"

"What do you see, Matty?" Mateo asked, still seeing nothing but smelling the staleness of the air, similar to the night of his own ghostly encounter.

"The old man. He says he wants it back!" Matty pointed at the stairs, then screamed again, digging his feet into his father's side, trying to get away from … nothing.

Mateo moved them back toward the couch, clutching onto his wildly agitated child.

Alicia came back to her mother, and sat down on the floor beside her, stroking her hair, but kept her eyes on Matty. "What old man, Matty? Tell him to go away! Go away!!" she screamed toward the stairs.

Matty's head burrowed deep into his father's neck, the tears soaking his collar.

At last, when he glanced back at the stairs, Matty's tension eased.

"It's okay, son." Mateo put his palm on the back of Matty's head and bounced him, thinking of the case and Matty's announcement about the old man wanting it back.

The thought of a coming ambulance did little to settle his guilt. He looked at Alicia by her mother's still body. He prayed his mother-in-law would be okay. Then, he looked at a teary-eyed Matty and remembered his petrified screeches. What in the world had their legally blind little boy and his mother-in-law just witnessed?

His responsibility for the chaos pricked at his conscience. It was all his fault for not getting rid of that evil case!

CHAPTER 9
THE HOOKUP

Mike gazed out through the sliding glass door of his temporary crash pad. The Santa Cruz yacht harbor lay just across the way, full of sailboats of unique designs and statures. Beyond them, three pelicans flew against the backdrop of a blue horizon, awaiting the arrival of the distant, thick fog.

It had been a few weeks since some old battle-axe knocked him out with her shovel at the job Fergus was supposed to pay him for. No money came, and now Fergus was ignoring his call … again. In fact, the last time Mike saw him was the same night as that unpaid job. The condescending flake had been in an unconscious heap on his niece's porch, but there was no way he could remember how to get back to that house. He did not know the mountain nor its creepy, windy roads. Anyways, Fergus always wriggled out of trouble. He figured the sneak lurked somewhere and would probably call soon enough with another favor to ask.

Until then, his ex-girlfriend Katie had this posh condo and a soft spot for little girls.

Stroking Soonsil's sleek hair, he looked down at her, napping on the pillow in his lap. He had to figure out a plan. She had been with him for over a month now—from the time he had found her in his neighborhood graveyard in San Francisco. Still, no one had come forth to claim the child or report her missing, but it was time to find her a home, elsewhere.

Soonsil looked up at him as if aware of his quandary.

"Hey, you about ready to get up? You've been sleeping for a couple hours, and the movie is long over." He laughed at the ridiculousness of him coddling a child for that long. That had to stop, too.

She readjusted her head to keep sleeping.

Mike let out a frustrated sigh. She had to go.

Soonsil sprang up, rigidly walked to the bathroom, and slammed the door.

"Jeesh," Mike muttered, surprised by the outburst but relieved to stand up and stretch his legs. He walked to the sliding doors to better observe the scenery. He liked Soonsil. He really did. But he had to find her a home because this parenting stuff was not his gig. Yes, most of his friends were already starting families, but he was not ready to settle down, especially with someone else's kid. Even worse, he hadn't gone out on a single date since he found her.

A generic ringtone interrupted his enjoyment of the oceanic view. Probably no one important. All the better, since the bathroom door reopened and his little protégé walked back into the room.

"You okay? Are you hungry?"

"No." Her answer came sharp and precise.

"Wow! A true answer. Feeling more comfortable to talk to me now?"

"No."

"Okay."

As Soonsil sat down and impatiently threw her head back on the pillow with no lap, Mike walked over to his phone. As soon as he saw the number, memories of a swelled cleavage and a tight, low-cut dress flooded his mind. "Hot damn!" It was the chick he had met at the club on the night he had found a blood-soaked Soonsil and dodged drunken street thugs.

'Hey hottie 🐾 Kept waiting for your call, but no such luck. HMU Friday!'

He felt a flush of arousal, followed by an immediate feeling of hindrance with his current responsibility … who now sat up and stared directly at him.

When their eyes met, Soonsil held her gaze for a moment, then fell back to her pillow.

He turned away from her to answer the invitation. No way would he miss out on this hookup. He finished his affirmative text, then walked to the sofa, seeing Soonsil whimpering into her pillow.

"You want to watch another movie?" he asked.

Her small, shuddering shoulders stilled, and she looked up at him with glistening, saddened eyes.

It hurt. He did not mean to feel so jaded, and looking at her, he softened his previous inner threats of giving her the boot.

"What do you want to watch this time?"

Soonsil sighed.

Katie's selection of kid flicks was pretty limited, but at least she owned the classics. "We've got Finding Nemo … Monsters, Inc … My Neighbor Totoro … a couple more. Any of those?" Mike asked. "Or we can watch TV."

After many minutes of prying a decision from her stubborn will, Soonsil's head was back atop the pillow in his lap, watching a teal monster with purple spots vie for Top Scarer. And he played the parent again.

CHAPTER 10
A SPECIAL PLACE IN HER HEART

After nearly a month of luxury living—fine dining and mall trips with Fergus's credit cards and lounging in his classy pad—Iris readied herself for a speech meant to impress. To date, she had only made one appearance to the unsuspecting coven, but Jameson kept the pressure on for her next leadership talk, so she decided to make these last words, ones for them to remember.

But she wanted to look good while doing it.

Anticipating many eyes upon her, she perused the abundant designer clothing in the closet. She had found most of the outfits too uncomfortable for her body. No telling why Fergus had so many women's clothes, but they held an unfortunate fit for her.

She narrowed her selection down to two items while reminiscing about her adventure over the past month. Slipping on outfit number one, she recalled her visits to Manito Park with its manicured lawns and Japanese gardens representing a picturesque Shangri-La in autumn technicolor. Twice, she had accidentally crashed a wedding by walking through at inopportune times. She would miss that lovely park.

As she slid into outfit number two, she remembered Bowl & Pitcher and its turbulent river rushing beneath the bouncy suspension bridge. What a treat. She had not known that she could find such a natural thrill without associated ancient history, redwoods, or a nearby ocean. But that gloomy day, blended with the river's reckless energy, filled her with the threat of imminent danger. And danger and misfortune held a special place in her heart, although whether that was due to visualizations of her own death or the necromancy she dabbled in, she couldn't say.

She scrutinized her reflection in the mirror, studying the style of outfit number two. Without another moment's consideration, the fashionable decision held, and she fully dressed into a pair of wide-legged navy pants to go along with the long, light blue kimono-style wrap with raised black-velvet tiger striping. Truly, she loved animal prints, and blended with the silky fabric, its faux lace print, and ball fringe on the hemline, she felt the glorious mélange an appropriate fitting for her swan song. She wore it atop the black long-sleeved turtleneck that she had worn the night of Arista's melee … when Fergus had so rudely hijacked her body.

She took a last objective look in the mirror, front and back, and liked what she saw. Frankly, she would miss this lifestyle, but she had to get back to her family. And even though there had been nothing but indulgent novelty since she awoke in Spokane, void of signs that Fergus still possessed her, she looked forward to the coming Beltane, when she would drive him out like cattle to the field. Or better, next Samhain when she could expel him to the Otherworld, for good. Though quiet, she knew the degenerate still lingered.

Without warning, an ill feeling swept through her. She felt faint, weak in the knees, and steadied herself by the wall. The same feeling as the notorious night when she had disappeared altogether. The timing could not have been more ironic. She thought that maybe murder had played a factor in Fergus succeeding in possession—taking her over at his own death and her reemerging at Antonio's—but this bout of ill equilibrium proved he could come at any moment.

Feeling his presence sweeping through her, she remembered his disrespectful words—*"Oh wait, I don't care"*—regarding her name at their first introduction. How dare he talk to his elder like that! It did not matter he probably had not an inkling as to who she truly was.

'Iris,' he said, pricking at her compromised psyche, his voice heard between her very own ears. *'I own you.'*

Her stubbornness reared. He did not *own* her. She was a strong, well-seasoned witch who would be damned if she ever gave him control again.

Woozy and light-headed, she brought forth a vision of her grandmother, the stronghold of power within her magickal heritage. She implored the old hag to protect her in this weakened state.

'*Iris.*' Fergus's voice rang little more than a whisper. He was a foreign entity within her, waiting for her slightest error in self-control.

Staving off her dizziness, she spoke, ever determined and aloud to her possessor. "I know you, Fergus. You are not welcome here." She focused on her grandmother's thick mop of black-and-gray hair and pictured her long, bony fingers, blackened at the tips and swirling in authority. "By the matriarch of our lineage, I bid you be gone. I cast you back to darkness and see that you fade like the last withering rose petal of winter." She rubbed at her temples and behind her jawline, taking slow, methodical breaths and envisioning only her grandmother's stern face of authority. "Be gone!"

In a gradual release, her steadiness returned.

It had worked … this time. She released a heavy breath and went back to her primping with renewed confidence.

"Little twit. I acknowledge your prowess, but that does not mean I accept it." She jutted her chin and modeled her image into the mirror before her—*her* body, *her* face, and her stunning outfit. All hers! She stood strong as that had always been her way.

She walked toward the bathroom vanity and ran gel through her hair to develop a nice spiky do. She pursed her lips as she preened, proud of staying strong through his attempted reemergence. Now, she could really relish in the hijinks she planned to release upon his congregation.

She sashayed out of the bedroom, grabbed her wallet and keys, and left for the parking lot. Once outside, she disarmed *her* Maserati alarm twice so that all within earshot would hear the beep. In an awkward move, she plummeted into its cockpit. She glanced around and felt relief that no one saw her clumsy entry.

The engine started with an intense snarl, and off she went. Past the plump, purple sky tram full of gawking eyes, through the bustling downtown area with die-hard joggers running past life-size metal sculptures of die-hard joggers, and up over the bridge with its colorful, artsy metal fish.

When she arrived at the rec center, she puckered her lips, added another coat of clear gloss with the help of the mirror, and headed into the building to create a stir. While it had been quite fun, her time in Spokane had reached its end.

As she entered the rec center's hallway, she wondered why Fergus spent so much time in such a dingy space. The walls needed paint, and the baseboards were filthy with grime and dust bunnies. And the smell … that awful, stale smell reminded her of a convalescent home, at its cleanest.

Click-clack. Click-clack.

Had any other woman ever felt this sense of power in this darkened hallway?

Click-clack. Click-clack.

"Silly, silly man," she said, arriving in the sterile dressing room. She set her effects upon the vanity. Family curse or not, Fergus did not have a lick of sense in his head and would have ended up dead in a ditch, one way or another. That such an idiot had gained control of her body irritated her to no end.

Jameson burst into the room, a satisfied glow on his round, cheerful face. "Iris! So good to see you. Okay, so as you instructed, there's no food this afternoon. No music and really no frills at all. I presume you have an important announcement." With an encouraging smile, he invited a hint of her content.

"Pretty much, Jameson, and we will not keep these people here for more than … I'd say … fifteen minutes."

His smile dropped in disappointment. "Sounds good, boss. They're waiting."

"Oh! They're already here? It's so quiet."

"I think they're anxious to hear what you have to say."

"Well, let's not keep them waiting any longer."

She glided into the hall, Jameson trailing behind her. She thrust open the auditorium door herself and entered the room without looking at anyone.

The whispers as she passed merited no thought. Upon the stage, she took her place behind the lectern and stared out into the well-lit room, aware of every rapt face. She raised her eyebrows and began.

"You have all been lied to."

The room's silence held, all eyes riveted on her words.

She looked over at Jameson. "Jameson, you're the right-hand man. Are you not?"

Jameson responded with a nervous grin.

"Well, are you?" she barked.

"Yes, Iris," he said with an attentive nod.

She grunted. "Oh, come on. You can be more convincing than that." She glared at him. "Oh, never mind. Seriously, you've *all* been deceived. Even Jameson was deceived. I've been reviewing what this coven has accomplished, notes about what they taught, and ..." she snorted and shook her head, "it's all rubbish. I mean seriously." She focused on a young man in the front with long black hair and matching eyeliner. "Are you satisfied?"

He stared at her like a deer in Xenon headlights.

"Are you happy here?" she asked a woman and her friend standing next to him, who looked like your average suburban soccer moms. "They suck down your money month after month, feed you, maybe, twice within that period, throw in a little dance night or two, and *that* placates you? What kind of club is this?"

"We're a coven. Witches," a woman asserted, followed by a couple of chuckles. Her tone combative.

"Oh, you are? What is your power?" Iris narrowed in on the stalky person with black-framed glasses, bushy eyebrows, and blue-dyed hair braids. "It's definitely not style."

"Intuition," another called out.

"Really? What lay in store for you? You certainly didn't read this sham correctly." She looked around the room. "Who *ever* told you this was the place to be … or the group to join?"

"Fallon!" yelled a voice from the audience.

"Fergus!" hollered another.

Iris grunted with disdain. "And there it is. You cannot even agree as to who runs this ship."

Sporadic murmurs bubbled around her.

"I'll tell you this … right now, I run this ship." She glared at anyone daring to dispute her. Then she grabbed the mic and strolled the length of the stage. "Here's a story about a ninth-century Buddhist monk Linji Yixuan … pronounced Eeee-Schwinn … similar to the bicycle."

Silence.

"Yixuan gave his pupils precise instructions on what to do if they ever met the Buddha on the roadside. What were they to do?" The silence held as she awaited an answer, scanning her audience for a glimmer of insight. "Oh, come on. Just throw out some guesses."

"We're witches, not Buddhists."

Her crowd grew impatient, which fell exactly into her plans. "Are you so single-minded that you would refuse knowledge from other valuable teachers?"

"Venerate," a random voice answered. "Venerate the Buddha."

"No." Though her answer came out curt, the engagement satisfied her.

"Give him food and water," offered a squeaky voice.

"No." They may not know the story, but at least they were trying.

The crowd quieted, their quiver of arrows almost depleted.

"Pray with him."

"No, again," Iris answered with a sigh.

"Kill him," said an older man amid the audience. He had short gray hair and a salt-and-pepper beard. Instead of cocky, his answer had come out pleasant and unintrusive.

"Ah, yes!" Iris stretched out her arm toward him. "Now, dear man, if you know this, why do you bide your time in this group? What brought you here?"

"Camaraderie … companionship of like-minded individuals. Maybe the food … when we have it," he added with a wry smile.

Iris chuckled at his audacity. When the audience joined her, she interrupted, "So *why* do we kill the Buddha when we see him?"

The room stayed silent.

Again, the older man spoke. "Because when you find Buddha, it is never the true Buddha and anyone who claims to be him is a liar."

She gave a respectful nod. "And as a koan explanation, that will suffice. None of us has the answer. And when you find someone who claims they have all the answers—that the greatest teachers have spoken to them directly—Run! They are liars." Her gaze swept the room. "So, you may see why, when I read all these notes about what you have been told in your one-on-ones with a madman and an equally crazy wo-man, I scratch my head and wonder why the hell you would fall for such folly."

The crowd stood speechless. Utterly stunned.

"Spirituality is impossible to define. So, when you think you have found the one who can tell you what it is, or furthermore, when you think you can teach it to others … when we all speak in such different love languages with different meanings and different histories—scars, baggage, warts, and all—and our lives and aims are so, so very different—"

"We have to *at least* try."

Iris stopped, insulted by the gray-haired man's interruption during her rant. She studied him then felt a calm wash over her. "'We *have to at least try*.' My good man, what is your name?"

"Eli."

"Eli, you seem to have all the answers today. Please come join me on stage."

Eli dismissed her request with a subtle wave of his hand.

"Eli, don't make me ask twice," she said firmly. No one would get away with defying her today. Or ever, really.

The crowd watched as Eli carefully navigated up the steps and walked into the spotlight. He offered Iris his hand for a congenial shake.

She eyed his hand and put her arm around his shoulders. Thanks to her new acceptance of high heels, she stood several inches above him.

"My good people, there is no more Fergus. Nor is there a Fallon. Both are dead," she said, smirking and wondering if Fergus could hear her. If he were ever to intrude upon her again, he would find an effective strike had been dealt to his position of authority.

"As of today, there will be no more me." She stood taller and cocked her head at Eli. "If you feel you must be led to understanding and hand fed truth, then you have Eli here. After only minutes, I truly believe he is probably the wisest man in this room." She smiled, exposing her teeth.

"What about the wisest woman?" a voice yelled out.

Iris scanned the room, looking for the satisfied smirk of the one who delivered the clever quip. Ah! There she was—dressed in a lace corset two sizes too small with a quaint crown of rosebuds around her long, flowing locks. "The wisest man—and definitely wiser than you think *you* are."

The young woman sunk into her gloat and turned to her friend for reassurance, who remained riveted to Iris's words.

"Yes. Eli is the new leader of this coven. Jameson, please make sure that he is outfitted appropriately. I have nothing further to say to any of you apart from *goodbye*."

With her spiel complete, Iris gave Eli a firm pat on the back, handed him the microphone, and left him standing at the lectern. She walked past a crowd full of confusion, irritation, and apathy aimed at her quick exit.

Jameson hurried to catch her in the hall. "Iris! What are you doing?"

"Jameson, it has been quite lovely to have your loyalty, courtesy, and ass-kissing, but I must get back to my real home. I am quite confident that Eli will make an exceptional leader. However, if you want to throw your hat in the ring, you'd probably beat him in an arm wrestle."

Jameson stopped in his tracks. "Iris—"

She looked him in the eyes. "The bank account is rich in funds. I'm sure you'll make it work."

Jameson's annoying voice faded behind her as she pulled out her new cell phone and called Manny, her neighbor and owner of body-ridding pigs.

"Hello?"

"Manny," she said when she reached her car. "It's Iris. For the life of me, I don't know why yours is the only number I finally remembered."

"Yeah, well, Iris, I've been tryin' to reach ya. We have a problem. I had some work done on my pens, and the workers found a token of your last drop. I had to report it, or they'd wonder why the hell I didn't. Ya know, I can't have that sort of trouble."

Iris put her hand on the car's door handle, causing the lock to release. She lowered into her ride, shut the door, and sat in the isolated silence amidst the sweet, earthy scent of leather. This was not good news.

"Iris?"

"Yes, yes, Manny. And what did you tell them?"

"I told them I found it and didn't want some bad rep … that I wasn't that kind of person. So, no more of that. Okay?"

"Of course, Manny."

"I tried callin' ya—"

"Yes, I know. I had to get a new phone."

"Are ya in town? I haven't seen ya … went by your house a few times—"

"Oh, heavens, did you feed my cats?"

"I didn't need to. Someone else is doin' it."

"Really?" Maybe Bethie had come back, figuring they were chummy after working together on Samhain. "Well, that's good, Manny. I'll be in Boulder Creek tomorrow night as long as I can get a flight. Let's get together … end of week. We need to catch up."

"Sure. Where ya comin' from?"

"I'm up north," she said, guarded, considering he had just ratted out their arrangement to the law.

"Oh, like Sacramento?"

"I'll talk with you soon."

"Okay—"

She disconnected, feeling unnerved and exposed.

At least the design of the dashboard provided a pleasant distraction. She ran her fingertips along its supple leather before strapping herself into the body-hugging seat, which would soon warm her tush. She would miss this aerodynamic chariot. But she had to leave all the frivolity and fine luxuries behind her. Nothing was more important than getting back to the spirits within her own home in Boulder Creek.

CHAPTER 11
A CADRE OF ISSUES

Arista could not remember the last time she had taken a bath in her century-old tub, usually opting for the hall shower and its quick and easy wash. Difficult to take a serene, carefree soak when her visions had warned of a serial killer lurking on her street.

But for now, the ambiance brought serenity. Three stout vanilla-mint candles gave the room a heavenly, warm glow and subtle, sweet scent. Around the base of each, she had sprinkled Quartz crystal pieces that further set the mood with a melodic tinkle. It was her version of Candace's *throwing the bones,* though she did not read them.

Her tub hugged her body as if an orthopedic chaise lounge, but even better, the hot water within it filled the air with an essence of roses, thanks to the salts and floating magenta, soap petals. With one cup of almond milk added to benefit skin health, she felt as if she were soaking in a delightful cup of tea.

She hummed, allowing every bit of tension to leave her body as she sank deeper into the water. She could not think of anywhere she would rather be.

Her father seeped into her mind, and she allowed a moment of remembrance. She told him she loved him, then focused on the shiny chrome spigot of the tub to come present.

A sudden movement at the door grabbed her attention.

"Hi, Royal," she murmured, peering over the rim as her curious cat walked into the room.

In a blink, two black paws, a black nose, and a spray of white whiskers arose at the edge. He peered over, scrutinizing her unusual activity.

"Hey, pretty." She softly stroked him with wet fingers, focusing on the bald patch in front of his ear, rubbing it as if a mother cleaning her kitten.

Royal pulled away and dropped toward the floor.

She snickered, then sunk every part of herself beneath the water, until only the very front of her face floated above its surface. In the solitude of the aquatic barrier, she focused on her breath, pulse, and heartbeat. She lingered in the quiet self. The silence from the water in her ears snuffing out all but what she put forth. Breathing in … then out … mindfulness.

She shut her eyes and allowed the fade-in of a vision. A hummingbird flitting about at her kitchen window. In an urgency, it flew off, headed to Auntie's—

A flurry of struggle brought her back to reality, with Royal teetering on the tub's rim, his eyes wide, and his tail flailing in circles.

Into the water with an impressive *SPLASH*!

His efficient hind claws checked her immediate compassion, leveraging his escape against her bare torso.

She sprang up, giving him momentum to bolt.

After a wild *Scooby Doo* scramble at the door, he disappeared down the hallway, leaving only a trail of water.

"Ow! That was a total *Wally* move!" She looked down at her torn flesh. "Owie," she groused to herself while tapping at the bright pink welts already forming under the water. They sat just above her age-old scar, a memento from her diabolical uncle. "Why always my stomach? Jeez!" She placed her palm over the scratches and winced at their sting. "I was totally having a vision, Royal. I can't believe you did that," she whined.

She reached for the soap, rubbed it with two fingers, and gently wiped her scratched skin. Then she agitated a swirl of water to rinse it.

Despite the lovely ambiance, she abandoned the thought of further relaxation. Somewhere in the house was a soaking wet furball, who probably sat cowering in a dreadful chill from the early December nip. She could not let him suffer like that.

Arista rose from the tub and toweled off her body. After sweeping her hair up into an exaggerated turban and donning her robe, she wiped up the watery mess. She could take a bath anytime, especially now that she remembered how lovely it felt.

She absorbed, then wiped up the splotched puddles leading a path out of the bathroom. In a thoughtful circular motion, she resolved this was a perfect opportunity to turn the fiasco into a clean floor and a ritual of good intention.

Deosil, these splotches dry,
Deosil, delight,
Deosil, bring love and fortune back into my nights.
So may this be.

She needed all the good luck she could conjure.

The wetness trailed all the way into the living room.

"Kinda cool. I just had my first vision in a while," she said cheerfully, knowing a feline audience sat listening.

After tidying the hallway, she arrived in the living room and peered behind the couch. Here is where she found her wet lump of cat with slick globs of fur spiking up his back, forehead, and tail, his eyes blinking in humiliated slits.

"Aw, come here, my baby."

She pried the bedraggled feline out and wrapped him in the towel taken from her head. Then she scooped him up like a swaddled newborn infant and dabbed at his wet fur with the dry corners.

"That hummingbird keeps coming to mind. Twice now. I thought of it a couple of days back, too. I'll have to let Auntie know that this solid new vision involves her favorite sprite."

At the same time, she could not overlook it as an important message. Despite Fergus being gone, she still felt wary. She thought of the green van and the white car. Could either of those have something to do with the vision?

"Or maybe it involves the curse tablet dilemma. Wouldn't be surprised. At least it's not Fergus." She felt the relief of her statement.

With one last quick rub to Royal's forehead, she set him to the ground, ruffling at his fur with the damp towel.

Dingledeedoo. Dingledeedoo.

Her stomach tightened at the sound of Shane's ringtone. Yes, they had broken the ice, but the thought of being close to him again still brought insecurity. Their romance came from a time of carefree, ignorance-is-bliss days, and right now, that seemed like a lifetime ago. How could it ever work?

Again, Shane's ringtone invited a response.

How could she not answer?

"Hey, I want to talk to you, but Royal just fell into the tub. Can I call you back in a few?" she asked in a cheery, yet rushed, tone.

"Sure," Shane said without hesitation. "Poor kitty."

"Aww, I'll let him know you said that. Call ya back!"

She quickly disconnected and caught her breath. She'd done it! Answered the phone, talked with him, and felt fine. He was the same thoughtful Shane, and it was nice to have his friendship again. Still, buying herself a little extra time felt right.

After readying for bed, she put the wet towels in the laundry hamper—washing the damp load a must come morning! Thereafter, she considered her promise to return the call. First, she wanted to see his image again.

She grabbed her phone, opened Photos, and stared at the plethora of captured memories. The last picture was the one she and Shane had taken together in Sedona—a selfie on Auntie's couch, her cuddled within his arms after blissful sex, her naked body out of view. In fact, it was the last time they made love. She giggled, remembering how Auntie had barged through the door only minutes after they had dressed. A prime memory.

She sighed. There was a reason she held off on dating Dakota. She still loved Shane.

"Hey, Riss," he said as soon as he picked up.

"Hey, how's it going?" How odd that the relationship felt fresh as butterflies fluttered within her.

"Good. How's Royal kitty?"

"That was crazy! But he's all good and dry now." She held the phone away and released a huff of tension. There was nothing to feel anxious about. Shane's story had checked out, and he had not cheated on her, which was the only hesitation that she had about him.

"So, another tea date this week?" he asked.

"Yes."

"Great! What day?"

"I work every day except Thursday." She enjoyed the collaboration of planning with him—three weeks now, one date a week. If taking it slow was the recipe for success, they were off to a great start.

"Okay, Thursday's good. Is the afternoon okay for you? I can get there pretty soon after teaching."

"Sure. Where are we going?"

"Ladies pick."

"Hmm. Let's talk more about it in a couple days?" She wondered what other cafés had opened in her year-long absence and looked forward to the research.

"Alright. Everything else good?" Shane asked.

"Yep, good here. You?"

"Yeah, real good here, too."

The thaw had begun, but it was still too soon for overt celebration.

"Okay, I should get to sleep, but I look forward to our tea date," Arista said.

"Alright, thanks for taking my call. I'm looking forward to it, too."

Afterward, she snickered, finding the charm in their mutual awkward cordiality. Then she dropped her phone on the bed, walked to her altar, and prepped for a bedtime appreciation ritual to celebrate the little joys returning to her life.

CHAPTER 12
FERGUS'S SEVERED HAND

"Hey, Jo, how's it going?" Sheriff Michaels asked as he got up and closed the door. He'd had a few complaints about his loud voice disclosing confidential information throughout the hallway.

"Well, Sheriff, your little murder mystery is solved. Kind of came full circle."

"Oh, yeah?"

"The DNA samples from this severed hand have revealed the culprit!"

"Yeah?"

"Yep, you'll be shocked to know … the pigs did it!" Jo chuckled.

To his surprise, she didn't wait for his reaction.

"Hey, did you check out the watch on this paw?"

"I could see it had a watch, but between the muck and the palm-up position … no. What about it?"

"It's a goddamn Rolex."

In an instant, he recalled Fergus's wristwatch during their impromptu interview at the hotel. "Was it black?" *That's a long shot.*

"It *is* black! The sap probably paid a fortune for it. Anyway, we identified the DNA to one Fergus—"

Jo's words fell to the back of his mind. How the hell did Fergus's severed hand end up in the mountains, in a pigpen? Further, was he walking around without it somewhere? Or was he lining the sty as fertilizer?

"Anyway, Sheriff, that's the profile. Any questions?"

"Let me digest it a bit. I know this guy. I questioned him on the Wallish murder case and a couple of other matters. It's real suspect that he's missing his hand."

"I remember you questioning him, hence the full-circle comment. Also, after rinsing all the gunk off, it looks like we have half a thumbprint on the face of the watch. So, we're working to match it."

"Excellent. I look forward to hearing more. Thanks for calling, Jo."

He chewed the inside of his lip as he ended the call. "Be-thie," he intoned, wary of illegal antics. He ticked the data into his keyboard, accessed the contact information on his favorite former babysitter, and waited while the phone rang.

"Hi there, Ms. Dandelion Spiritbrite." He knew she loved to be addressed by her witchy name.

"Oh, hi, Sheriff. Could you please hold for a moment?"

"Sure." Was this a stall tactic?

Bethie began talking in a worried tone. "Sheriff, I'm sorry, but my vision is so blurry right now. I thought you were Arista returning my call."

Her desperation sounded authentic. "You okay?"

"I honestly don't know. It's been happening quite a lot. Do you mind if I call you back?"

"Of course, you need an ambulance?"

"No, it usually passes, but I gotta tell you, it's most concerning."

"I'm sure it is. You go ahead and call your niece again."

"I will. Thank you."

Her distress sounded genuine, and he could let her know of Fergus's possible demise later. He'd hate to think she already knew. Nah … she couldn't have anything to do with it.

•   •   •

After her distressed call to Arista, Bethie felt her way toward the kitchen sink and splashed her eyes with cool, refreshing water. Despite the invigorating sensation, her vision remained blurred.

She found it telling that this episode, like the other times, had occurred right after her latest efforts at honing the potency of her Hummingbird Spell. At onset, she could have sworn that hitting her head on Iris's table had caused the reaction, but it became more evident each time she concocted then suffered the effect.

Rarely used, her Hummingbird Spell remained the only effective bit of her witchcraft. The one she could truly *hang her hat upon*—other than intuiting trouble for Arista, of course. Further interesting, she had felt no danger coming Arista's way since Fergus's death, in spite of strangers loitering outside of her house.

She let out an exasperated huff. "We can only hope!"

Bethie sat down to calm herself, willing her vision clear, and mentally went over the recent replacement she had made to her enchanting concoction. "Out with the snakeweed and in with Datura wrightii root. Perhaps I'll call it daddyroot," she said, adding humor to ease her vulnerability of eyesight woes. "The question is, why the poor effect? The amount is so very small."

Perhaps she took it too lightly. Even unperfected, her Hummingbird Spell had served her well over the years. It was a combination of focused will, a hard stare, and a mixture of dried and crushed bee balm, spruce wasp abdomens, leafhoppers, saliva mixed with a teaspoon of raw cane sugar and three drops of fresh rainwater from the first winter storm. The timing of the blessing ritual also mattered, with successful batches created on a Super Blue Moon. Currently, only a generous teaspoonful remained from her last Super Blue Moon batch, made a decade earlier—as Super Blue Moons can be very rare—and she kept it in her tin for the direst emergency. For all other in-between's, she used batches from a Black Moon—more common, as they can occur every three years. While not as potent, they still served as a temporary distraction to haranguers.

The trick was to get close enough to blow the pulverized dust into an offender's face. She would have used it on that awful serial killer had she not already tucked it into her car's darned ashtray that day!

To date, she had performed the Super Blue Moon spell three times—on a reckless female driver who had sideswiped her car, then angrily came at her with raised fists; against a deranged man flailing a tire iron and cursing at frightened children and their mothers at Felton Covered Bridge Park; and, most notably, on the associate of Fergus, who had wandered into their town searching for Arista while she was still a teen. Even before she saw the telltale pentagram tattoo on his palm, she had felt it in her gut that his prowling around their neighborhood meant trouble.

Arista burst through the door, causing her to jump.

"Are you okay?!" Arista asked, rushing over to sit beside her on the chenille loveseat.

"I'm so sorry to worry you," Bethie said.

"We're going to figure this out. Let's get you to the eye doctor today."

"I guess if they have an appointment available. I hate to be such a bother. It usually goes away after a bit. Though I admit it's hanging on a little longer this time. I held off calling you to see if it would pass."

Arista squeezed her shoulder. "Let's call the doctor."

Bethie blinked, rubbed her eyes, then leaned back on the sofa. She refused to become a needy inconvenience for her grandniece. Possible spellwork or not, she felt the sting of her aging and dreaded the loss of independence. Distraction time! "I was watching my little hummingbirds. They were so busy today, flitting around and bickering with one another. Then the sheriff called. I can only imagine what *he* has to say. I'm supposed to call him back. Oh … wait a minute …" She sat up and widened her eyes. "Yes, here it comes now." She saw Arista's face peering at her, sharpening by the moment. "Whew! That was a long one." She patted Arista's cheek.

"We need to find out why this is happening. Do you get dizzy, too?"

"No, no dizziness," Bethie said, considering her spellwork. From here forward, she would be more careful, but for now, she would keep this potential rookie mishap to herself. What kind of role modeling would it serve to Arista? After some time, if she found it caused her eyesight issues, she would offer a lesson in proper vs. improper experimentation.

"I say we still call your doctor. Maybe you should come stay with me until we solve all this. Or me with you?"

"I don't think so. They're just minor spells. So long as they keep passing, I'll be fine." She handed her phone to Arista. "I do like your idea of scheduling another appointment."

"Of course."

Upon Arista's call, they received surprising news.

"Ms. Kelly was actually on my list to call today," the nurse said. "We have your test results back, and the doctor would like to review them with you."

Thankfully, they had already reserved a time slot for her, and she only needed to wait one more day for a professional explanation.

CHAPTER 13
ABRACADABRA ... ISSUE GONE

Katie felt shocked that Mike had come back into her life with an adorable child in tow. Ironic, since the only reason they had ended their five-year relationship was his disinterest in having children. Now, he seemed completely invested in this little girl, and she had to admit, she was quite the jewel with her superb manners and no-fuss obedience. Weirdest of all, she had turned Mike into a grounded, responsible guy. She figured his vagueness on the child's story had everything to do with a prior relationship.

Two thick foam pads lay stacked by the work center in Katie's second bedroom. Surrounded by whirring fans from her resting computer and Wi-Fi equipment, small red lights lit up the room. Good for a child. As was the extra nightlight. And the white noise helped drown out actions by her and Mike beyond the door.

As she tucked Soonsil into the pearlescent sheets and plush red blanket, the child gazed into her eyes. "Aw, you're beginning to like me, huh," Katie said, feeling her heart melt. She stroked Soonsil's hair, then tucked a wisp of it behind her ear to better look into the sweet child's eyes. "Are you ready for a story?"

Soonsil nodded and snuggled further under her blanket.

"Okay, we're at the end, too."

She appreciated the acceptance even more since Soonsil had wanted nothing to do with her upon arrival. However, over the past couple of days, the tables had turned as Mike sought more distance from the child, leading her to latch on to Katie.

Over the next twenty minutes, Katie read aloud the book they had selected together at the local bookstore. A story about Meg Murray and the underlying theme of love's power.

With each passing page, Soonsil's eyelids grew heavier, each time holding closed a little longer until Katie reached the end of the captivating tale.

"*… a gust of wind, and they were gone,*" she said in little more than a whisper.

She closed the book with gentle care and tucked its bookmark back to the first page. As she reached for the light, Soonsil's eyes opened.

"Love," Soonsil said.

Katie smiled and whispered, "Yes. Love saved him … saved them all, really."

"I love you," Soonsil said in a soft voice.

"Awww, sweetheart. I love you, too," she whispered, stroking Soonsil's cheek. "Sweet dreams."

An hour passed before Katie heard Mike's steps trudging up the outside staircase. She struck a sexy pose on the couch.

"Hey," he said, barging in. "Soonie asleep?"

"Yes. About an hour now."

"Good." He shook his head. "I've done a lot of thinking, and I'm not cut out for this. I feel bad saying it, but seriously, I don't need the responsibility of feeling guilty every time I miss her bedtime. Or whatever."

"It's okay. I got her to bed with a story, and she was fine." *Uh-oh. Sounds like the old Mike.*

"Yeah, I just can't …"

Katie walked over to him and gave him a hug. "I think we're a good team. She's beginning to take to me, so the load won't just fall on you." Maybe if he saw the child would not come between them, he'd feel better about it. She seductively lifted his shirt.

Mike raised his eyebrows, liking where this conversation headed.

•   •   •

While the optometrist's small reception area felt cramped, at least the stark white setting and bright, lime-green benches created a crisp sense of cleanliness. Arista found it reminiscent of a Pippen apple, like those upon her Silver Bough used during the Samhain ritual.

After checking in with the office staff, the ladies took a seat, and Arista eyed the lovely orchid on the counter. Another reminder of her Silver Bough—its tall arched spike held one small, tight bud, two larger buds exposing scant floral pizazz, and three showy, blushed flowers with dark pink lips.

"Oh shoot, I still haven't gotten back to the sheriff," Auntie blurted with a repenting snap of her fingers.

"Well, you told him of your eye troubles. Hopefully, he'll be patient," Arista said, while she watched a white car pull to the outside curb. It looked like the sedan that she and Auntie had seen a few times. When the driver flung open his door, she recognized the same man who had walked into her yard.

With the car still running, the man helped his thick-spectacled little boy out of the car seat while a slim, professionally dressed woman exited the passenger side. She led them up to the door.

"Good morning, Matty," the receptionist greeted when the family entered.

"We're here for his eleven o'clock," his mother said before the two took a seat next to Auntie.

When the presumed father saw Arista, he turned to avoid eye contact. After a low-voiced disclosure of "errands to run" to his wife, he left, but not before looking back once more at Arista. This time, their eyes locked just before the door shut.

If there had been doubt, it no longer existed. He recognized her, too.

Arista nudged Auntie with her leg and whispered into her frizzy hair, "That's the guy from my house the other day … white car."

Auntie looked but gave a stern nudge back. After all, the man's wife and child were sitting right next to her.

Arista looked at the little boy, his eyes magnified by thick bottle-lensed glasses that sat upon his cute, round face. The perfect representation of a Latin Harry Potter.

Matty looked up at Auntie after studying her colorful clothes. "Hello."

Surprised, Auntie looked down at him. "Well, hello there, young man. How are you today?"

"I'm good."

Matty's mother shot a quick glance at Auntie, then continued pecking out a text.

"Does your eyes not see good?" he asked.

"I'm having a little trouble. How about you?"

"My vision is blurry. But I can see ghosts now—even *without* my glasses."

"Matty," his mother gently warned without looking up from her phone.

"You can?!" Auntie animated with enthusiasm. "Ghosts, huh? I've seen a ghost or two in my life, too. Was yours scary or friendly?"

The little boy lowered his chin. "Mine looked friendly, but my tita got really scared and had a heart attack."

"Matty," his mother said, her voice hosting compassion this time, as she pulled him in for a side hug.

Arista considered the facts—a nervous man who came to her house, his son talking about ghosts—seemed too strange to be coincidental. Maybe the hummingbird vision was coming clearer.

"Matty, that's enough for now. We can talk more about it in the car. Okay?" his mother said, loving but firm, before looking at Auntie. "I'm sorry, but it was very traumatic for him."

"Oh, I'm so sorry," Auntie responded.

"We consider ourselves very blessed that she is recovering," the mother said.

"Thank goodness," Auntie said, then looked back at Matty, who was peering up at her.

Arista kept quiet. She had been down this road before and recognized the sense of oncoming turmoil from the building evidence.

"Ms. Kelly?" beckoned the pretty assistant with huge sparkling eyes fanned by false, sweeping lashes.

Within moments, they sat before the eye doctor in the examination room, enduring his unaffected manner while giving the diagnosis. "Mrs. Kelly—"

"Ms.," Auntie corrected.

"Ms. Kelly, there are a few possibilities for us to consider. Primarily, I believe this is a development of cortical blindness or traumatic optic neuropathy. You mentioned that you have had a couple of blows to the back of your head." He glanced at his pad. "One in August of last year, and another more recently. It is my thought that the first violent blow was enough to damage the occipital cortex, which is the control center for sight. However, this would have been a significant delay. A short time ago, you had another fall and hit the back of your head again."

"Yes, but she was having sight problems before this recent fall," Arista interjected.

Auntie had been complaining of her vision while they lived in Sedona. It had just never blurred out completely. She hated to think the serial killer's assault had caused the affliction. If so, she was glad Great-Great offed him.

The doctor paused and considered Arista's words. "The second blow is close enough to the first incident that it may have exacerbated an existing condition. Therefore, it's possible that you are experiencing results from those injuries combined. Add to the fact—and I say this with all due respect—we all age and do not have the eyesight of a twenty-something-year-old. My professional opinion … this is progressing, and it's likely to become chronic." He flipped open the file and noted the data. "Another possibility is typical age-related macular degeneration."

Arista felt irritated by the flippant responses but cooled, remembering he's just delivering the news, not responsible for its cause.

The doctor quieted for a moment, perhaps awaiting questions, or maybe letting the worst-case scenarios soak in.

When they said nothing, he continued, "With that said, I believe that things will not go completely dark for you. We can fit you for glasses that will help with the loss of clarity. If you would like a specialist's opinion, I can also give you a referral."

"Hoo! Well, that's a lot to swallow," Auntie said with a hint of humored courage.

"If you work with the glasses, you can use a more powerful lens during periods of blurriness, and when they pass, revert to your regular prescription."

"Well, I suppose that's not so bad." She nervously glanced at Arista.

"The trick is finding the right prescription. Since the spells are short-lived, it will help if you can come in while one is occurring."

Once the session wrapped, they thanked the doctor, paid for the bad news, and entered the confines of Auntie's yellow Volvo, still cozy from the ride over.

Auntie sat in a daze, pursing her lips. "Hmm."

Arista waited for her to elaborate on her worries about eyesight or even possible theories about the anxious man who had left his wife and child in the lobby.

"Oh, Arista, I'm going to end up an invalid pain in your butt," she blurted out in a troubled fret.

"No, you're not. Not at all!" Arista responded, realizing now was not the time to consider any other matter, aside from Auntie's worrisome news.

•   •   •

This was the perfect time to deliver the case. With its owner occupied in the optometrist's office, Mateo's heart pounded as he barreled toward Boulder Creek. Luckily, he had already put the case back in his trunk since the unfortunate episode with his mother-in-law. He could not waste any more time, not with his son afraid to go upstairs because the *scary old man* had hurt his grandmother.

Mateo maneuvered the twists and turns of Highway 9, keeping a close eye for animals and pedestrians. All progress halted as he became part of a line of slow-paced cars. It did not settle his inner turmoil, his heart racing as if he had slammed two energy drinks.

One by one, the cars cleared, and he zoomed onward past the Highlands Park entry toward the road's hazardous bend. With the recent rain, he tapped the brakes to slow his speed, but it was too late. The wheels caught a slick patch of roadway, and his car shimmied.

He over-corrected left and skidded toward the cliff's edge.

Quickly, he spun his steering wheel hard right.

SCREEEEEEECH!

He glided into the wrong lane just as he hit the nasty blind curve. With all his might, he stomped hard on the brakes and held firm. The car made a loud thunking noise. Its metal body, his teeth, and all his senses shuddered before everything came to an abrupt stop.

Now, *he'd* almost had a heart attack. He forced an exhale, his hands still death-gripping the wheel.

Cognitive awareness struck. He had survived the skid-out and needed to keep going.

An oncoming car slowed to a patient wait as he righted his vehicle. He motioned gratitude for their kindness and proceeded with a renewed measure of safety.

Moments later, he arrived and turned onto Hoot Owl Way. He pulled up to the driveway's entrance, jumped out of the car, and rushed to his opening trunk. There it lay—the old, unassuming case of terror. Hoisting it up, he hurried onto the young woman's property and saw a Siamese cat bolt from the house's interior windowsill. If he were lucky, after today, he would never have to see this case or place again.

Where to leave it? He looked around the yard, anxious of time. The porch would be fine. Wait! What if someone stole it before she came home? Around back. What if she didn't see it? He wished he could just stuff it back in the foundation, but that option had long passed.

Mateo pictured the women on their way back, and the awareness of his limited time clouded his judgment. The porch would do fine. As he placed the case on the top step, he heard a rumbling engine enter the driveway.

He turned to find the driver's eyes locked on him and froze, contemplating his story or next move.

"Hey, man, what's up?" the young man asked, getting out of his truck with a bouquet of red roses.

Already full of guilt, Mateo freaked and bolted past the flower-carrying man toward his car. He had to get away!

The athletic young man gave chase. "Hey!"

Mateo struggled with his car handle, trying to enter, but the party crasher was upon him. He turned around and swung in defense, missing.

"Hey! Hey!" the young man said, holding his palms open. "Whoa, dude, I'm just wondering what you're doing at my girl's house. It's cool!" He cautiously lowered his hands. "You worked on the floors, right? I dealt with you guys while my girlfriend was gone. Last December. Remember? You were sick when your partner returned the key."

Mateo looked at him and remembered the young man. In an involuntary wave, the honesty rushed out of him. "Yes! I'm sorry. I was just returning something I found when we replaced the floor. I … I took it by mistake."

"Alright, that's cool. No need to freak out over returning something."

Mateo rubbed at his sweaty forehead and pointed toward the porch. "It's that old suitcase. I found it under the old floor." He shook his head, feeling the emotional toll of all his ghostly encounters. "It's got some kind of evil inside it, and I just want to give it back and go. I swear, I didn't mean any harm."

The young man's eyebrows shot up at the mention of "evil," but before he could respond, the slow crawl of a cruiser coming down Hoot Owl Way distracted them.

Pulling up beside them, the lawman rolled down his window. He sized up Mateo, then looked at the young man. "Mr. Stoddard. Is there an issue here?"

•   •   •

With a complicated vision diagnosis to consider, Arista had decided that a comforting, warm treat was in order. They sipped their velvety peppermint mochas from the quick stop at Raven's Latte as the street sign for Hoot Owl Way came into view.

"Well, at least it's all clear now," Arista said, belatedly second-guessing her choice of words. "Not only your vision but *the why* of its issue."

Auntie slurped her beverage. "Hmph. Not what I'm used to … very rich! Anyway, yes, I know these age-y things are going to hit me now and again. I just don't like it all at once. Cataracts would have been nice. A round of LASIK and *abracadabra*, issue gone! I don't know, Arista." She sighed. "I was even beginning to think it may be my spellwork, but his medical explanation seems to apply."

"What kind of spellwork?" Arista asked, navigating the sunny yellow Volvo onto her street.

The conversation stalled upon seeing a gathering of familiar faces—Shane, the sheriff, and the notorious stranger, with a frazzled look on his face. All of them gathered at her driveway's entrance.

"Well, I can definitely *see* all that!" Auntie said, gawking.

"Yeah," Arista said, bypassing Auntie's home.

Arista scanned the small crowd, reading each of their expressions while pulling into her driveway. Getting out of the car, she looked at Shane first, and despite the brewing problem, the sight of him comforted her. Next, she looked at the sheriff with his hitched eyebrow, staring at the stranger. Then, her eyes met the stranger's.

"I'm sorry, ma'am," the stranger said. "I took something that didn't belong to me, and I hope you will please forgive me."

Within moments, everyone heard the story of the haunted case, Mateo's and his son's supernatural visits, and the mother-in-law's unfortunate medical emergency. Arista felt a sense of validation from her earlier intuition on matters.

The stranger continued, "I don't care how ridiculous it all sounds. I just want my conscience clear, and I'll do whatever you need me to do." He turned to Arista. "If you want my number, I can give it to you, and you can call me with any questions. I didn't mean any harm. Really! I'm so sorry."

The sheriff pulled Arista aside. "It's your call. Technically speaking, we have theft, trespassing—"

"No, that's unnecessary. He seems sincere enough. Don't you think?" she asked, looking up at him. Her question was rhetorical, as the thought of Mateo and his family seemed a far cry from the criminals to which she had become accustomed.

Sheriff Michaels led them back to the group. "As long as Ms. Kelly is amenable, you're free to go," he said, looking at Arista.

She waved her hands, dismissing the idea. "Of course. Thank you for returning it." Poor Mateo looked like he had not slept in months, and his effort at risking legal consequences took a lot of courage. As far as the supernatural stuff, she really wanted to say *welcome to my world*.

"Thank you so much," Mateo said with weary eyes. "Just be careful."

The sound effect came before the visual, distracting her from Mateo's appreciation. When she looked to see what vehicle's engine made the high-pitched, whining noise, the green van rolled past her hedge. Arista saw the female driver gawking at her before it disappeared. That was not Maddie's friend Skylar, as she had hoped. Thankfully, she had the law, her boyfriend, and even Mateo, who looked like he could hold his own in an MMA bout, all present. Hopefully, these prowling van people realized she had plenty of friends.

Still, the new sighting brought on that old, familiar looming threat.

"… and she claims to be a bruja—how you can mix that with Catholic, I don't know—but she sensed the spirit in my upstairs office. She could hear a voice. She and my son both saw something that my wife and I could not. So, please, just be careful."

Catching the tail end of Mateo's comments, Arista felt an odd comfort that she and Auntie were not the only ones in their community with such supernatural dynamics. This made her world just a little smaller. "We'll be careful. Also, your son? I think we met him in the doctor's office a little earlier."

"Yes, Matty is my son," Mateo said, his shoulders easing.

"He's so cute!"

"Thank you. Thank you for everything." Mateo gave an appreciative nod, then walked toward his car.

Shane went to his truck, reached into the window, and raised a bouquet of deep red roses. "The element of surprise is blown, but I had intended to leave these on your porch. Mateo and his suitcase beat me to it."

Arista laughed. Ominous trouble, green vans, and now … red roses. Emotional roller coaster at its finest. The feeling from the sight of the sweet gift from her loving guy rose to her lips. She smiled, knowing she could worry about everything else later. She gave him a hug and thanked him for not only his thoughtful gift but his attentiveness to invading strangers.

"Anyway, this was supposed to be a short stopover. I've got to get going." Making sure she felt settled, Shane departed, too.

Standing in the crunchy pea gravel, only Auntie and Sheriff Michaels remained.

"Sheriff, I apologize for not getting back to you. I'm having a real go with my vision, and it's caused major distractions for me lately."

"No worries. The reason I was calling is that … as morbid as it is … I thought you should know that we found Fergus's severed forearm at a property up Bear Creek." He quieted, awaiting their reactions.

"Really?" The word barged out of Arista's mouth. What a horrific discovery. It sounded worse than a de-livered Fergus on her porch, but at least his body was intact when they loaded it in the trunk. Kind of. But dismemberment? Had Iris literally fed him to pigs?!

Auntie released a breath, and her gaping mouth snapped shut. "You know, Sheriff, it has been one chaotic thing after another for too long now. Maybe stress is causing my blindness."

He kept his chuckle brief. "Sorry to hear about your eyesight. I know you two have had a rough go."

"I honestly hope that man is dead. I do!" Auntie said, nodding.

"Well, we cannot prove that, but he has a hell of an injury if he isn't."

Arista held her breath and casually looked at the ground. She knew too much and was glad the sheriff's attention was not on her.

"Ms. Kelly."

Crapola. She looked at him. "That's awful. I just want to thank you for being here to help Shane. It means so much to me and Auntie." She waited. *Did the deflection work?*

"You bet. Okay, ladies, just keeping you updated. I'm sure you want to dig into that mysterious suitcase. Shall I take the first look to make sure all is okay?"

Whew!

Auntie cackled. "That won't be necessary. I'm sure it's just old papers and photos. I wouldn't think they left a pile of money underneath the floor. My granddad believed in banks. So, I'm thinking poor Mateo worked the bugs out for us already."

The sheriff gave a wink. "Sounds good. You two have a good day. Bethie, you take care of those pretty eyes of yours."

"Oh, Sheriff," Auntie said, thwapping her hand toward his uncharacteristic, cheeky grin.

With the chaos dispersed, they looked over at the porch and wondered what familial mysteries lay in wait.

CHAPTER 14
SURVIVOR OF HER BLOODKIN

Iris sashayed past the five-foot rolling assistant with its red-and-white painted dress. The bowling pin shaped robot had a monitor face showing a smiling young, animated miss. Above her, thousands of strung glass tiles hung from the ceiling, fluctuating from clear to opaque, representing the outside weather and its abundant rolling clouds. This place came straight out of the space age.

She had not flown into the San Jose Mineta International Airport except once before, in the 80s, always opting to fly International out of SFO. Now, its modernistic upgrades created an impressive change. Fitting, as she had also changed a bit during her past few weeks of luxurious living in Spokane. Whether her changes would stick remained to be seen, but she had packed a substantial amount of items into her two appropriated Louis Vuitton brown roller bags, also borrowed indefinitely as mementos. However, she found the copious number of L's and V's stamped upon the leather a bit too garish.

With her curbside ride already waiting, she introduced herself and let the driver take care of the heavy lifting. Watching the scrawny man suffer the chore, she felt she may have been more capable. She unzipped her overcoat, finding San Jose much less frigid than Spokane, and buckled in. In the night, the equally futuristic exterior of the airport, which ran beyond her line of vision, looked like a giant spaceship awaiting lift-off.

She sat quietly as the driver took his place at the wheel, rounded the complex exit lanes, and eventually merged, cars whizzing past them, onto the ten-lane expressway. Downtown San Jose's high-rise buildings created a thriving night-time ambiance, and while she normally resisted urban environments, now it reminded her of her Spokane adventure. After her stint of experiencing Fergus's posh lifestyle, she realized a bucket list item she never knew existed—wealth.

She glanced down at her wrist. There sat her favorite find from his closet—a gold-tone watch with a leopard-print face and strap. So utterly brash, yet irresistible to own. Which reminded her … she should have taken the watch off Fergus's wrist when she left him with Manny. Sure, pigs ate everything, but doubtfully they ate metal, and even if they did, it could come out in the end. She twisted her mouth, experiencing a moment of unsureness. Too bad this homecoming brought forth a certain reality of recent events. Hopefully, they would not come back to haunt her.

But the watch dazzled her. She loved the leopard spots, and that little gold crown added the *chef's kiss*. Right now, anyway. In all probability, it would end up in her jewelry box, unused, in no time. Where would she wear it? To the grocery store? Gardening? Utterly ridiculous.

A swirl of nausea shut down her appreciation. Immediately, she identified it. Another attempt from Fergus to overtake her. She braced for the episode.

'*Iris.*' His essence taunted her from within. '*You can't hold out forever.*'

She felt her energy wane, as a tinge of black creeped into her line of sight, obstructing her view. She tried to lower the window. It stayed put.

"The window," she gasped, not able to get the words out loud enough.

The driver's eyes cut right into the rearview mirror, but he soon refocused on the road.

With no relief, she journeyed within to bring forth her grandmother's image—the wizened crone's scowl, the one who knew no fear and embraced the gravest sorrows. Iris's grandmother remained her greatest source of strength over the years and, as of late, a deterrence during each of Fergus's attempts to repeat the possession. Nothing surpassed the wickedness of the ageless woman, and Iris found solace in her presence. She focused, keeping her breath steady, then softly closed her eyes. *Grandmother.*

"Ma'am, you need some fresh air?" the driver asked, his concerned eyes peering in the rearview mirror again.

When she nodded, he lowered the window, and an immediate blast of brisk December air crashed into her face. She took deep breaths, hanging on to her grandmother's visage.

"Sorry about that. I forgot to turn the child lock off. You okay?"

Iris shucked her hand at him, then closed her eyes again, and thrice more mentally repeated the internal syllabic chant—*Grand-mother, Grand-mother, Grand-mother.* After regaining equilibrium and feeling no further sign of Fergus, she rolled up the window, leaving only an inch gap.

Each invasion Fergus dealt came a little stronger and lasted a little longer. Ironic that a month ago, she had worked with Arista on a possession only to now find herself dealing with one. Irksome, but no true threat. As a seasoned witch, she would not allow him to take control of her ever again! He held no power against her, especially now that she knew what he was capable of if she dropped her guard. In fact, his audacity to fly her off to Spokane in the first place still rankled her, regardless of the grand adventure.

Stable again, she looked down at her pilfered watch and dismissed the notion of him. "Moron."

"Excuse me?" The driver's earnest eyes aimed to please.

"Not a thing for you to worry about. Just looking forward to getting home."

Passing the mountain-hugging stretch of a roadside restaurant out of Los Gatos, she noted the regally magnificent white-stone lynx statues guarding its entrance. How could she stand guard? She had to ensure that Fergus stayed in the deepest depths of her psyche until the liminal times of year when she could banish him. Not only did he intrude in her life, but Bethie and her grandniece were his constant obsession. She could see why now. He shared in the family curse toward the Kellys. She wondered if he knew his drive had come from the curse.

It mattered not. While Bethie had not been her favorite person over the years, because of that same curse and its deflected repercussions, she had come to like the companionship of a witch almost equal in substance to her own prowess. Plus, her dingy quirks were a joy to be around.

"Be damned that another Kelly pointlessly falls. Especially by my hand."

"Ma'am?"

"Nothing. Nothing, again," she said.

Iris looked to her left as they passed the large reservoir marked with sporadic red lights, its liquid presence glistening in the moonlit night.

As far as she knew, there were only two Kelly members left—Bethie and Arista. That did not bode well for her own status as the lone survivor of her blood-kin. Unless the unruly wandering soul of Fergus counted, which it most certainly did not. The Kellys had already won in the sense that only Arista held the ability to extend any lineage. Yes, Iris held utmost respect for her grandmother, but any further action played futile. Surely under the circumstances, her grandmother would agree.

Now she needed a plan. It would need to be the most complicated, sophisticated, and especially designated spell she had ever conjured, and she would cast it upon herself. She needed the best-lain path, a guide at the crossroads, and a light to guide her way. Therefore, she would call upon the darkest and wisest goddess, the first and eldest of all witches from her grandmother's homeland. Judging by the verbiage of her relic tablet at home, she was likely one of the deities conjured at the onset of the destructive curse.

Once more, fate called Iris forth. As she discovered in Spokane, Fergus had been her burden to bear long before now. She just did not realize it, dodging appointing the first time around when her niece and nephew were put up for adoption because of the loss of their parents to carbon monoxide poisoning. Surely a deflection of her family's curse upon the Kellys. Her bedridden father had begged her to take the remaining boy child, now identified as Fergus, after a loving family promptly adopted his little sister, Keira. Iris had rebuffed the constraint of responsibility. Too busy traveling the world and feeling the energy of her lustful young adulthood, she had also turned a blind eye when all the rumors of the boy's abusive foster homes came at her again and again. Could her rearing Fergus have created a better outcome? No use contemplating it now. She only knew that destiny had brought them together again.

This time, she accepted the burden. How could she not? If any ritual to cast him out failed, she would opt to keep his soul confined within her own for the rest of days. At the helm of her family's remaining destiny, which had lost its footing when the enemy, Ian Kelly, married Keira—her newly discovered niece—her grandmother's curse would finally die with her.

CHAPTER 15
A BIT OF A MOOD

They eyed it from a distance—the mysterious piece of haunted luggage sitting on the top step of the porch. Arista led the way.

"I have no idea," Auntie said, hands raised in surrender.

"I want to believe this is just a case with no intrinsic issues," Arista said, then laughed at her own desperation. "… and really, Mateo's just mistaken about it being haunted."

Auntie stroked the mysterious artifact's material, then grabbed the handle to lift it.

"Wait! It's not stable. Remember?" Arista said, pointing at the latches. "I'll get it." She hoisted it up and walked up the steps with Auntie behind her.

Inside, Auntie cleared the Ouija dining table, allowing Arista to set the case down, front and center. A relic sitting atop a relic.

"Here we go," Auntie said, unlatching the closures and opening the lid.

While the items were tossed like a fresh garden salad, likely from its many road trips, Arista saw immediate signs of witchcraft—an aged parshell made from shaved redwood sticks and hemp twine; an antique version of The Sun tarot card; a knotted piece of rope with six medium-sized brass bells; and a short, wide mason jar with a single rusted nail, sand, and crispy brown herbs long past their shelf life. Surprisingly, the jar had endured all the manhandling without breaking.

"Well, that's a good sign the spell worked," Auntie said, holding up the stout jar. She perused the contents and then handed them to Arista.

"How's that?" Arista asked as she began an orderly pile.

"Because as banged up as everything is, the jar is intact."

"Got it. So, what's the nail for? I've seen these before but never knew."

"It's some sort of protection thing. Margaret used to say it protected the caster from faeries, but I don't remember any faerie talk from my childhood."

"Do you need protection from faeries? They're so cute."

"Hah! In cartoons, maybe. Think about it. Even Tinkerbell goes into a mood sometimes. Subject matter for another time."

Auntie eyed a small stack of pictures twined within yellowed cellophane. She unwrapped the package and announced the images, one by one, passing them over to Arista. "My mother as a teen … her brothers as kids. Definitely our family stuff, so I'm thinking this belonged to my grandparents. Well, would you look at that!" She held up an aged sepia photo showing a toddler with wispy, pert braids in a white dress and a big white bow atop her head. The child's beaming smile countered the expression of the two young boys on either side of her with grumpy frowns. "There's a little me with my brothers." She hummed in sentimental approval. "Declan and my other brother, Peter. I'm around two here."

Auntie sat the picture down to her left and handed Arista the rest. Next, she flipped through papers of scratchy handwriting and doodles. "Hmph. Runes … knots … spellwork. Well, look at this!" She gave an amused cackle and handed Arista the drawing.

"The athame? So, he forged it himself?! That's crazy!"

"Looks like he did. I should have known because I've never seen another one like it."

Arista handed the drawing back to her. "No wonder he used it so efficiently with the serial killer."

"Indeed. I'd give it to you now, but this case seems to have been a safe haven for preservation. We'll keep it all together, and you can consider it yours, whether it's at my house or not."

Once through the papers, Auntie handed them all to her for the orderly stack.

At the bottom of the suitcase lay the heaviest item, a thin-stoned tablet broken into two large, even pieces.

Arista stared at the damage and considered the correlation to the halved Rose Quartz of Trini's love spell, Auntie's broken spoon rest, and the flagstone she had noticed on their trip to meet her father. Perhaps this new discovery is what it had all been leading up to. She let the meaning go when Auntie spoke.

"This, my dear … is a curse tablet. Albeit, a rather lightweight and flimsy rendition of what we found in Iris's house." Auntie shoved the suitcase away from her and set the pieces down, side by side.

"Why stone?" Arista calculated the years in her head. "This is the forties era, right? I mean, it's not like ancient Greece or something."

"Maybe they believed stone to be symbolic of endurance, and … I don't know, better at enticing the ancient deities?" She cackled. "Ironically, it's broken. Perhaps they should have considered wood."

They shared the humor, then looked closer, trying to decipher the illegible, etched verbiage.

"Hand me those papers again, please."

Arista complied.

Auntie flipped through, then withdrew a page and handed the rest back to her. "This looks to be the one they used. See?" She used her finger to compare the number of words within the verses on the tablet to the inked paper version and read it aloud.

Woe to us all, the widow's bane unjust,
Strike it down, smite it, deflect it to dust.
So, may this Sun shine its light on those dear,
And protect us through reversal, year after year,
For if they but one of our kin make fall,

Reprisal for the one, swift vengeance shall call.

Auntie raised her eyebrows and harrumphed. "I'm impressed. Pretty clever wording, and it explains The Sun card."

Arista lifted the vintage tarot card and studied its artwork. "So, they used it as a divination tool for the spell? I wondered where the rest of the deck went. So, Sun for … optimism? I'm surprised they didn't use the Star or maybe The Empress."

"The Sun is the most powerful force in our universe. It warms us, brings light upon the world, and *rises* above all else. I'm thinking they believed the light would banish the darkness brought upon them."

"True. Very insightful."

"And the picture becomes clearer." Auntie paused. "It also sheds full light on my relationship with Iris all these years. I guess I can't judge her too harshly for a curse tablet when I have one myself. Unbelievable. So many strained interactions between our grandparents. Even the two of us, at times." She shook her head with regret. "For what, and why? Those are my biggest questions. I know our grandfathers had a fight, and hers was on the losing end. But all of this … from that?"

Arista pulled the chairs out so that they could have a sit, and said, "Iris must realize all this. Your last name is Kelly."

"It has never been too overt, but the mutual murmurs and jeers of our families showed the animosity. I truly believe that our generation broke the barrier of hatred—Era of Love, you know. Her and I got along fine in the younger school years, and I may have mentioned, everyone knew she liked my big brother, your grandpa, Declan. She tried so hard to be his soulmate, but your grandmother had him smitten."

"Have you ever gotten a bad vibe, like a watch-your-back kind of thing, from being around her? Cause I have to say, I felt something the day I first met her. I just figured her a catty witch and ignored it for the sake of your friendship."

"Never on a critical level." Auntie momentarily second-guessed herself, then dismissed the notion. "No. Not at all. And it's been tested multiple times, including during our Samhain ritual. We all had our eyes closed. If she meant us harm, it would have been so easy. For that matter, she could have pushed me toward the gwishin, but she pushed me to safety instead and kept the gwishin's attention on her. Which, by the way, cost her her life!" Auntie pondered a moment. "Also, if we stop and think about it, I'm just finding this out myself. Other than the tablet, maybe Iris doesn't know the complete story either. Just has it displayed as a family keepsake?" Auntie shrugged.

"Could be," Arista bit at her lip, doubtful.

Royal strolled into the kitchen, stopped, looked at the witches' eyes upon him, then settled at the food dish, which disappeared behind his girth.

"I may need to start him on a diet."

Auntie looked at the feline's rounded rear end and laughed. "Maybe so. Anyway, I wonder how things would have gone if Iris and Declan had gotten together." She studied the stone tablet. "What's amusing is that we always honored our grandparents' Catholic faith for their benefit." She flippantly flapped the spell sheet. "But it looks like we were all just fooling one another."

"Who do you think wrote that?"

"I'm not sure. My grandfather? Grandmother? Maybe if I scour old documents, I could piece it together with handwriting samples, but I don't suppose it matters. They were quite the team, and I have no doubt they did it together."

Arista felt the sudden rub of Royal's shoulder against her lower leg just before he jumped up on the table.

"Shoo!" Auntie swatted the air in front of him.

He jumped down, looked back whilst twitching his tail, and strolled out of the kitchen in a huff.

I'll have to make that up to him. "Too bad it's broken," Arista said. "I wonder when that happened."

Suddenly, Auntie's eyes bulged in alarm.

"What?" Arista asked, nervously looking at the pieces.

"Call him!"

"Who?"

"Call Matty!"

"You mean Matty's dad? Mateo?"

"Yes! Yes! Call him, quick!"

Arista grabbed her phone, dialed, and held it up for Auntie to talk.

"Yes, this is Bethie, and I'm here with Arista … you just left us."

"Yes. Hello," Mateo said, a slight inflection from their unexpected call.

"A very important question for you—was this tablet broken when you found it?"

An uncomfortable silence followed.

Arista interjected, understanding Auntie's hunch. "You're not in trouble or anything. We just need to know *when* it broke."

"The case fell open, and the tablet fell out," Mateo mumbled. "I'm so sorry."

"No worries, young man," Auntie said, refusing to meet Arista's questioning gaze. "Was that when you first found it, or more recently?"

"The case broke open when I first found it last December. The tablet fell and broke. Again, I'm so sorry."

"No worries. That's all we needed to know. Thank you again for returning it. You have a good day."

Arista understood the connotations. "Do you think this is the reason Fergus came at us so hard after so many years? How he almost found us in Arizona and then here?"

Auntie looked her dead in the eye. "Close to two decades without problems. This tablet breaks and within *months*, he almost found us in Sedona … and again he tracks us right here to Boulder Creek! Sure, Stevie blabbed, but everything falls into the sequential timeline of the breaking of this curse reversal tablet."

"Okay. But how does Iris's family curse and our reversal relate to Fergus?"

"A magnificent question. There are benefits to Iris being away." The wild, bugged-eyed look on Auntie's face felt hazardous. "We need to go back! I think we may find more answers. For now, tuck this someplace safe. After we work everything out, I'll safely store it. Or maybe I'll encase it and put it on my living room bookshelf." Auntie chuckled with a hint of spite as she began re-stacking the items in the case. She released a large breath. "As much as I'd like to barge over there now, I'm pooped from all this activity. Let's go first thing tomorrow."

Arista paused and considered the possibilities. "You know, poor Mateo may not be used to our family ghost, but knowing it's probably Great-Great, I kinda hope this case means *he's* back too."

"Well, he's not possessing you, and his suitcase is back home. So, the odds are in your favor."

CHAPTER 16
TO BATTLE A BOSS

Shane's mother, Magda, sat at her desktop computer, her blond hair in a perky ponytail situated atop the rim of her light blue Adidas visor. Her computer glasses neared the tip of her nose as she tapped away at the keys, her face focused on the results.

"Hey," Shane greeted, plopping down on the emerald-green velour chair in his mother's home office. He tucked a giraffe-print pillow beneath his arm and stared at the oil painting on the far wall that she had done of him and his little sister years earlier.

She stopped and looked over her shoulder with a toothy smile. "Hey, sweetie, what's goin' on?" Her body language held tight to her project.

"I've been thinking of making some changes."

"Well, you *did* just start working full time. That's quite a change."

"Yeah, but I'm thinking of getting a place with a friend."

"Really?" she said, her interest rising. She pushed her glasses into place, swiveled her chair around, and rolled closer to him. "When did all this come about?"

"I'm mid-twenties, and I think I'm the only teacher who still lives at home with his parents."

She smiled. "Well, maybe in that school. But Shane, this is an expensive state to live in, and our area is even pricier than most. Are you sure you're ready for that kind of responsibility? I mean, you just started your permanent job. Can you afford it?"

He shrugged. "I've done the math, and it looks good on paper." He knew he would get this resistance from his overprotective mother. "The monthly expenses will be an easy split between the two of us, and—"

"Who are you moving in with?"

"A cohort from school."

"Job school or your time in school?"

"Job school. Dom—he's already got his teaching credentials and is a full-time English instructor at the high school."

"Oh." His mother pursed her lips. "I thought you were going to say Arista."

Shane chuckled. "Not yet, but hopefully, someday. In fact, it's another reason I want to step up and become more independent."

"Aww, my responsible young man. Well, good luck, sweetie."

"I think I'm ready to go back to school, too."

She held up her French-manicured hand in confusion. "Wait a minute. You're moving out, *and* you want to go back to school?" She exaggerated the incredulousness with a low hung jaw.

Why did she have to act like he was a complete idiot?

"One at a time. Okay? Your dad and I would love for you to finish graduate school, and we've waited for this day. How about you take that route first, recalibrate, *then* increase your monthly budget?" She looked pretty sure of herself. "Whadaya say?"

He numbed his previous enthusiasm and fiddled with the small reindeer figurine sitting on the side table. "Um …" He calculated his estimates and wondered if he had truly missed anything.

She removed her glasses and peered at him. "Don't rush everything at once. As you said, you *are* in your mid-twenties. From my point of view, that's still very young. Enjoy this bit of freedom and all-expenses-paid lifestyle while you can. Have you talked with your dad about this?"

"No."

"Good. He'd jump at the chance. But I want you to take baby steps into independent living. That way, you avoid moving back home because you made a false start." She stared at him, awaiting a response. When none came, she filled the space with more parental advice. "If you're still hanging around here in your thirties, I'll be more concerned. But that's a ways away from now."

"Mom! My leotard's not in my drawer," Shane's teenage sister yelled from upstairs.

Her gaze stayed fixed on him, and her words came out in a compassionate whine, "Okay, sweetie?" She followed up the gentle touch with a bellow in his face back to his sister. "What d'ya say?"

Already irritated with her shutting him down, Shane stood up and retreated to the drawing board of his bedroom between the hollering voices talking about laundered dance wear.

"Shane, was that all?" his mother called after him.

"Yeah."

"K."

He heard her chair swivel and roll back into its slot before she recommenced her key-pecking.

As he entered his bedroom, he felt the same sense of insecurity that had beleaguered him throughout his life, especially when he had a differing opinion from his folks. For instance, when he wanted to stay at his public high school in the mountains. Often, his mother reminded him that prep school would better prepare him for college and that he needed to consider his future. He hated to admit it, but she was right. She also had a point about them living in an expensive area. He had heard that from several people. And he had just started his full-time, permanent job at the school.

He sat down in front of his computer and numbed while dazing into the dark, inactive screen.

In an unusual turn, the thought of Arista's cheerful, genuine smile overrode the dominance of his mother. He imagined stroking her cheek, running his fingers through her hair, and loving her.

He sat with the images.

A resurgence of confidence filled him. He wanted to be with her more than anything. He truly loved her! All his past unease with her witchy ways no longer mattered. Her spirit, her character, and the joy of being around her meant everything to him.

He expelled the former heaviness. Perhaps moments like these would be much easier without his hovering mother under the same roof, instilling her doubt into everything.

He let his plan materialize. Thinking about it, he did not need an MBA to teach at the high school. His mom was right about one thing—he needed a good plan to move out. He would commit to Dom on the roommate situation next time he saw him, then if life went according to his unspoken plans, he and Arista would move in together sometime thereafter. If she accepted. He hoped she accepted.

Self-actualization washed over him, and he felt solidified in his decision. He grabbed his phone, selected Favorites, and dialed Evan.

"Hey, Shane, what's up?" said his long-time friend.

"Hey, can you help me out with something?"

"What?"

"Something big, and I think you'll give good advice since you and Bree are doing well in full-time couple mode."

"Right on."

"I want to get Riss jewelry for Christmas."

"Of course. First bit of advice—frame it as a Yule gift."

"Yes! See? You've already helped me! I'll read more about Yule. Anyway, give me another week to stack up funds. Then we'll go."

"Sure, just give me a heads up beforehand so I can let Bree know. She'll want to make her own plans."

"Deal."

"Sounds good."

Shane hung up, high on his dopamine rush. Confidence surged through him at making this right decision. He flipped through his photos and stared at a snapshot of Arista at Quail Hollow Park amongst the purple patches of lupins. Then, another of her at the Highland Games beside a burly and bearded man in a kilt, complete with its sporran, dagger, and embossed-buckled belt. Yes, this was the right move.

He'd strategize more later. For now, a little free time. He flipped his desktop switch, igniting a colorful light show of spinning disks amongst the snaking black cables within his glass tower. The fans engaged, and on popped a screen of mythological graphics—a flashy fire dragon, tail swishing, ready for action. He assumed his on-screen identity, selected his *Worgen,* and began an arduous journey to battle a boss.

CHAPTER 17
RUMOR MIXED WITH HORRIBLE LUCK

With her long-missed morning chore of cat feeding complete, Iris readied for Manny's visit by heating a kettle of water and collecting her grandmother's fine Grecian white China teacups with gilded edges. While the elegance was wasted on Manny, her hospitality mattered to her during such an important meeting.

A knock on the door announced her guest.

"Good morning, Manny. Please come in."

Iris welcomed her accomplice into her darkened living room with a sweeping hand gesture. She had cleaned up the shattered glass from the broken end table found upon her homecoming. While she had experienced her house spirits' antics over the years, the mess was quite sizeable, more of a human-caused mishap.

"Thank ya, Iris. In all the years I've known ya, I don't think I've ever set foot in your house." He looked around the room like a child entering a tech museum.

"Yes, shame on me for being such an inconsiderate neighbor."

"Ya like it dark in here, huh?" he said, his eyes shifty.

"Oh, I'm sorry about that. Let me raise a couple more blinds for you." She reached for her remote. Pressing the number one and the green button, she peered at Manny while the blinds ascended. Then she selected number two on the remote and, again, pressed the green button, watching as the glaring sunbeams of morning poured through the window and flooded Manny's face.

He released a nervous titter, flinching. "Oops, that's quite a glare … almost like a spotlight. Heh-heh. Maybe I should've kept my mouth shut."

"That's alright, Manny. I aim for your comfort."

"No harm, no foul. I'm fine either way." He walked to her wall clock. "This is some contraption ya got here."

"Yes, I picked that up at an antique store in San Francisco. Chinatown, to be specific," she said as she walked to the kitchen to grab the prepared tray of China cups and readied tea. The steam rose from the cups and the teapot's spout, wafting up beyond her.

As she carried the tray into the living room, Manny turned, and his eyes lit up as he sighted the offering. "Oh, that's nice, but no need."

"Join me for some tea, Manny. It's the least I can do since I've been so lacking in hospitality over the years."

"Iris, ya know I didn't mean to slight ya or nothing like that." Manny blinked. After a moment's hesitation, he conceded, taking a seat in the chair across from her. "Okay, then."

She could almost hear his nerves rattle as he folded his hands, sat up straight, and cleared his throat. "So are we meeting to sync stories or …"

"Well, I think that's a good start. Don't you?" She handed him his little white teacup, so dainty in his rugged, sun-damaged hand. "Now, you said you did *not* mention my name to the officer, right?"

He shook his head. "No. Not at all. But worst-case scenario, if they search my phone, look at my computer, or have surveillance from someone's home-cam along these streets, they're gonna know we've known each other a long time."

Iris took the small ceramic spoon from the cup's built-in holder and stirred her tea, each stroke creating a sweet tinkling of melody. "Would you like some honey for your tea, Manny?"

"Nah, I'm good." Manny inhaled the aroma. "You and your teas." He took a sip and recoiled. "Damn! Scorched my dang mouth."

She winced at his pain. "Oh dear. Careful." She got down to business. "So, your handyman saw the hand, and you decided it best to call the sheriff?"

"Right."

"No matter if it blows your cover and now puts you in full spotlight."

"Well …" Manny sighed and searched for the right verbiage. "Look, Iris, I couldn't let my workers think I'm okay with a severed hand in my pen. Ya know?"

"That's a logical excuse," she said. She sipped her tea and flicked her eyes at him beyond the rim. Setting down the cup, she offered him a tight, closed smile.

Manny blew his tea, creating an agitated cloud of steam. He took a small sip. "That's a little better."

"Manny, what on earth will we do with you?"

"What do ya mean?"

"You have put yourself in a most compromising position." Again, she sipped, staring at him throughout the motion.

He mimicked her swig. "Ya keep pointin' at me. What about you? Why say I'm the only one in a *compromising position*?"

"Well, recapping, you did not keep a very responsible watch as to what was happening—or shall I say, *not* happening—in your own yard. Why let that evidence go unchecked?" She sipped again. "Then you blew our cover by talking to the sheriff. Now, most worrisome to me is that you keep saying my name. How am I to know that you're not going to just hand my name over to the sheriff and you get off scot-free?"

"Now, Iris, I wouldn't do that."

She drew in a long inhalation through her nose, paused, and released it before taking another sip.

"Look, we'll be just fine," he insisted.

"Manny, finish your tea. Our meeting is almost over."

Manny furrowed his brow, irritated, but took a generous swig. "That's good for me. Thank ya." He set the cup down on the end table.

"Look, Iris, you're being real salty about this … uh …" Manny cleared his throat. "And—" *Cough.*

Iris set down her cup, sat back in her chair, and watched Manny. "My goodness, Manny."

Manny covered his mouth and coughed harder.

"Tsk-tsk. Poor, poor Manny. Drink the tea. It will help clear the tickle."

He reached for the cup and downed the fluid, but the coughing only increased. When he realized the condition had worsened, he stared at her with most desperate eyes.

She sat forward. "Cough it up, Manny. My goodness." She watched him in his uncomfortable state of violent bronchospasms, then eased back into her chair to take another sip of her tea, peering at the poor sap from above the rim.

Manny grabbed at his stomach, the wince indicative of the sharp pains he felt, which she knew of well.

"Does it feel like your insides are exploding?" she asked, setting down her cup. She stood up and walked over to him as he collapsed to the floor, clutching at his stomach and throat.

He contracted forward, attempting to pull his knees to his chest, but the couch created the barrier.

Iris lifted the phone that had fallen from his pocket and stepped back just as he went to grab her leg. "Our final problem is, who's going to chop up the pieces for your pigs tonight? That was always your job. But the position is now vacant."

Manny hacked and groaned as a bubbly white froth accumulated at the corners of his mouth. With his body in spasms, his eyes rolled backward into their sockets. Slowly, the gagging and jerking ceased.

Peering down upon him, she bent over to pick up his cup and sniffed the remaining drops of her concocted poison. "A little bitter. I'll need to work on that." She placed the cup upside down on the tray and reseated herself before pouring a freshener into her cup from the teapot. After a quick inhale of her imported herbal Sideritis, she took a sip. "Perfect temperature—hot enough to warm the body, yet not scorching on my tongue."

She sighed. Now she needed to dirty her hands. Literally. Sure, she had quieted Manny's blabbing mouth, but the effort to get him processed and back to his pigs would be grueling work.

A sudden sensation cringed within her stomach, emitting a mighty gurgle. Caught by surprise, the nausea quickly dissipated as she sunk deep into the darkest chasm within her mind. Plummeting, she felt Fergus's essence sweep past her. Angered at his audacity, she held focus to the farthest end of her space, where the only light remained. She knew from her last trip within that this was her way out.

She struggled with all her mental might; her gaze concentrated on the distant portal back to present. She had to reach it, attentive to this aim until she felt the throb of it swelling in her chest. A bubble rising to the surface, propelling her back in charge of her body.

In a sudden thrust of sheer intention, she came to and found herself walking up her staircase. Within her, Fergus's scoff of indignation faded into nothingness.

Canceling any further thought of Fergus, she froze, gasped for breath, and put her hands on her stomach. Was she real? Was she here? Seconds lapsed as she grounded. Yes, she was back. Down her stairwell, she took each careful step before turning the corner back into her living room. Manny still lay on her floor. Again, she thought about these circumstances, intrigued that each time she and Fergus successfully transformed, a dead body lay close by. It started with his own death, then Antonio's at the rec center, and now poor, dear Manny, who could not keep his mouth shut.

The sound of an approaching car beckoned from outside her door.

She clapped three times, hearing the echo ring through her house, grounding herself. Her heart held a strong beat, but her throat felt tight. She adjusted. Her throat, supple. And her eyes. Her eyes could only see Manny, her biggest problem, in all his frothy glory.

She straightened herself upright, exhaled sharply, and headed for the door to see who had invaded her space at this most inopportune time.

. . .

Auntie finished discussing their agenda as they reached the house of oddities and turned into Iris's driveway. "We won't be here long. Let's just—"

Iris walked out her front door, attracting her variety of cats to her ankles and shocking the hell out of the adventurous witches.

"Oh, my ..." Auntie said with her mouth agape. With Iris's eyes upon her, she drew it up into a quick, friendly smile, followed by a tinkling wave of her fingers.

Iris waved at them, her silky black caftan—abundant in graphics of koi, splashes of light blue water, and lotus flowers—blowing in the breeze.

"Oh wow, what do we do? Or say?" Arista said under her breath, while smiling and waving at Iris.

"Just be yourself. We're only here to help ... to water plats and cants. I mean, cats and plants!"

"I'm not good at *fake*."

"Apply yourself."

They exited the car in unison, and as directed, Arista offered a forced smile and contrived greeting, two of her biggest pet peeves. But most appropriate in this case.

Auntie marched toward Iris. "Heavens be, Iris! We've been worried sick about you!"

Iris gave Auntie an ample hug.

Just act natural. "Auntie's right. We came to check on you a couple of days after the ritual and noticed you weren't at home. Otherwise, you would have picked up your bracelet." Arista froze. Where had she put the bracelet? She had not seen it since the day they went into Iris's house. "We took really good care of all your babies—kitties and plants."

It relieved Arista to be back in honest territory. Then she realized, seldom did she say so much around Iris. Too much nervous talking!

"You seem to be full of chatter today, Arista," Iris said. "I don't think I've ever heard you utter so many words in one visit."

She noticed. Arista tightened her smile. "I'll just … go water the kitties now," she said, letting her voice trail off.

"No need. Thank you both so much for tending to my children—flora and feline."

"Sure! It's nothing after all you've done for us," Auntie responded.

"I also found my bracelet … *in* my house."

Inside?! It must have fallen out of my pocket. Arista felt herself shrink into insecurity.

"Next to my broken glass end table," Iris added.

Oh, good goddess! Can it get any worse? Just let Auntie do the talking. Arista looked at Auntie, curious about her strategy.

"You had no involvement in that … did you?" Iris's tone came out wry, but not altogether accusatory.

Auntie looked at Arista, then Iris.

With the conversation suspended, Iris changed the subject. "So, what do I owe the pleasure of your company today? Just stopping by for another watering session?"

"Indeed," Auntie said.

"Well, thank you. But I'm home now, and I apologize for my rudeness, but I've got an appointment to get to. Once again, thank you for all your help and for coming by today."

For all the drama they went through with the gwishin, Auntie saving her life, and the genuine concern they had over this woman's welfare after her disappearance, only a cold stone wall remained. Arista could not help but think more lay beneath the surface of Iris's false appreciation and pleasantries, especially with the discovery of the tablet. She was glad they found it. It's helpful to know who your enemy is.

As Iris started toward her door, a stark, cantankerous look covered Auntie's face. "Iris, what are you doing with a curse tablet that has *my* family's name on it in *your* living room?"

Arista could not believe her ears, nor the look of anger on Auntie's face.

With her back still toward them, Iris stopped. She looked up at the looming circular window of her second story. "So, you *did* go into my house."

Auntie stayed the course. "We saw it from the window when we were making sure you hadn't fallen, passed out … or something worse! We were worried about you!"

"We *were* worried," Arista said with a nod. *Just follow Auntie's lead.*

Iris looked over at the front window. "It's awfully dark to see in that far, and I keep the front window locked. Tightly."

Auntie dropped her excuses. "Well, what say you? That tablet is an *affront* to me, Iris. And to Arista!" Her tone had grown sharper.

Iris sighed, her shoulders relenting in surrender. "Bethie, you were always kind to me." She turned around and re-approached them.

Wow. She's going to explain it.

"You know I adored Declan. Truly, I did. But you must have been aware of our families' animosity toward one another."

"I knew of it, yes," Auntie said, easing a tad.

"Word is, the Kellys had their own tablet," Iris prompted.

Auntie's eyes shifted, but she kept quiet.

"Its counter-offensive proved very effective." Iris paused and changed her tone. "But I never bought into the curse. I felt awful when I heard how my grandfather killed your grandfather's dogs. While I prefer cats, I love all animals, and that was just so … unkind. However, the resulting loss of my grandfather, my aunt, and my youngest brother, who was but a child, devastated all of us."

"What do you mean? My grandfather just beat him up. And him alone! He didn't kill anybody."

"Bethie, your grandfather shot my grandfather dead in front of all of us that day, and the spray of bullets from his gun shattered our window, killing my aunt and little brother. Your grandfather killed three of my kin in one punitive blow. Further, because my grandfather made a move to grab, unbeknownst to your grandfather, his pipe as well as the initial wrong-doing toward the dogs, the jury sided with your grandfather, and he was released and fully exonerated. As you can imagine, this sent my grandmother over the sheer cliff of insanity."

Arista felt the shock immobilize her. Could she believe it? The hunting dog incident was the first noted set of initials and numbers on the Ouija table, but this sounded nothing like the story Auntie had told her. In fact, Auntie had even giggled when she revealed her grandfather had beaten the neighbor senselessly over poisoning his dogs. To hear that he killed the man and his family members went against their entire core system. Despite wishing it only more of Iris's trickery, she felt the truth of it in her bones. The soul wound still existed within her.

Auntie stood speechless, then narrowed her eyes. "That can't be true."

"After that dreadful day, I saw that vengeance only brings heartache and more death. So, I refused to put stock in it, vowing I would do nothing to help my grandmother's aim. I actually pined for the enemy. Your grandmother was a salt-of-the-earth woman … so friendly to me and helpful to our community. I remember her organizing meal runs for mothers who could not prepare their family dinners because of pregnancy or illness. A woman of kindness and warmth." Iris stared into the distance. "My grandmother and my mother hated her and often talked awful about her. So much so that when I innocently asked why, it brought great shame upon me. Even more so when I fell for your brother, hoping he would choose me as his bride." Iris looked down at her fire-point Siamese, Rupert, peering at her from beneath the nearby table. "But he chose another."

"Why didn't you ever say anything? I had hoped all the talk was just rumor mixed with … horrible luck! The version I heard of my grandfather's wrongdoing was nothing like this." Auntie shook her head, making her red curls bounce. Then she jabbed an index finger toward Iris. "You say all of this, yet I find you have the living proof of the curse against my family on your mantle!"

"Out of sight, out of mind."

"It's your living room showpiece! How is that *out of sight*?"

"When I inherited the relic, I wanted it as a constant reminder that spite and retaliation have no place amongst us magick folk. If I were to lose sight of its tragedy, perhaps I would become vindictive in my own way. For me, out of sight is not an option. I want to remember the senselessness. There are so few of us, why kill off anymore? And our most foundational belief is to not bring harm to another witch—or anyone, for that matter. Though I suppose our kin did not start out as witches."

Auntie shook her head in disbelief. Or maybe, denial.

Iris took Auntie's hand into her own. "Bethie, I care for you and have never entertained an intention of hurting you. This I swear."

Auntie gave Iris's hand a small squeeze, then released it. She exhaled a breath. "I need to think about this." She walked a tight, oblong pattern and exhaled again. Her demeanor changed to worry. "Where have you been? We were so worried about you."

"That's trickier to explain, so my disclosure must wait for another time. Honestly, I have an urgent matter to attend to. In fact, I've talked too long already. Won't you please excuse me for this day, and we'll discuss my adventures some other time? Later this week, perhaps. Or next?"

Auntie nodded, her frizzy curls bobbing. "Of course." She gazed at Iris. "Iris, I, too, have always appreciated our friendship. I know we never truly connected with one another, but … I believe you. I do. As far as harm, there have been too many instances where you could have easily accomplished it."

"I am so glad you see that, Bethie."

As they shared a genuine goodbye hug, Arista felt compelled to hug her, too. With so much sadness and loss in Iris's younger life, she found her compassion for this odd woman, regardless of her problematic decor.

Satisfied for now, they walked to the car. Yet, when Arista glanced back, she caught Iris with a guarded side-eye aimed at Auntie. The cat-like stealth remained, and with it, a rush of suspicion returned. She did not know what to believe. Iris's usual demeanor was smug and shrewd, and her deeds questionable. Ever since that first meeting up to their arrival today, Iris's vibe felt edgy. Not counting the ritual, but still. Again, Arista glanced back as Iris walked into her house. She remembered its dark, suffocating ambiance and heavy presence. This whole charade felt off. Could they truly trust her defense of shunning the curse?

"Those were *not* the answers I expected," Auntie said once behind the wheel.

"I know. I couldn't believe you just blurted it out like that. You looked *so* mad." If Auntie wanted to discuss accusations of her grandfather being a murderer, she would let her initiate the topic.

"I didn't even mean to! It kind of just flew out of my mouth," Auntie said, humored by her own boldness. "Uh-oh." She slowed the car.

"What is it?"

Auntie fluttered her eyes. "It's happening again."

"Pull over." Arista pressed the hazard lights button as Auntie pulled to the bumpy shoulder of the narrow two-lane country road.

Arista helped her over to the passenger side and ensured she buckled in. Once settled, she drove with a new mission. "We're going to Scotts Valley right now! The doctor said to come in when it happened again."

"That's fine," Auntie said, shutting her eyes and sinking into the seat. "Arista. I have a bad feeling this is not going to end well."

"Don't worry, Auntie. Just try to relax. We'll be there soon."

CHAPTER 18
POMPOUSNESS AND POISE

"Copy. On my way. Over and out."

Sheriff Michaels glanced at the wide-eyed high schooler finishing her full day's ride-along for community service hours. She'd been quiet for the duration, asking only a handful of questions while he talked most of the day. His throat felt dry, and he took a drink.

"I've got another water if you need it," he offered.

"No, thank you," she said.

The kid had manners, and he appreciated the resemblance. She looked just like her father, a former officer out of Santa Cruz in early retirement because of an injury on the job. It was the least he could do.

"To prepare you, this call is disorderly conduct," he explained. "When we arrive on scene, we've got to be open-minded as people get pushed out of shape easily these days. What one person may think of as disorder may just be their own subjective experience."

The high schooler diligently nodded.

Idling, he waited as the SUV with a bushy noble fir twined to its roof buzzed past, then made his left into the shopping center that hosted the problem. At the far-right storefront, he saw waving arms hailing his attention.

"You ready for the holidays?" he asked the student, making small talk.

"My mom always has our tree up the day after Thanksgiving," she said, laughing.

"Yeah. That's the way my folks did it, too." He pulled to a stop. "We'll get you back to the station after this. I'm sure you've had your fill for today, huh?"

She smiled as he opened his door.

As he put one foot out, a middle-aged woman hustled over from her newer-model BMW. She lit into her complaint through artificially inflated lips, her body blocking his door from fully opening.

He looked back at the student. "You think she realizes I need to exit the car first?" A rhetorical question. He turned back to the woman. "Ma'am, will you please step away from the vehicle?"

"I'm sorry," she said, her voice more audible as he exited.

He had missed the first part of her rambling.

"He almost ran me over in those skates! Meanwhile, my son is seeing this stuff. It's not right. That person's not right!"

"She's exaggerating, Sheriff," Rossy said.

The sheriff knew Rossy and his antics well. An avid rollerblader, he usually accompanied his skates with tight white or pink shorts that allowed his butt cheeks to peek out just below their hemline. Today, a pair of sheer white fairy wings accompanied his shorties sprinkled with silver glitter. The rest of his cherubic thirtysomething face was clean-shaven and rosy-cheeked from the nip in the air.

The sheriff held up an index finger. "I'll talk with you in a moment."

"Officer, he's a danger to the shoppers," the woman said. "He almost hit me and my son when we went into the store, and just now, as we came out!"

The sheriff observed the woman's tween in the front seat of her car. His bangs hung over his eyes, which were glued to his screen, attempting to hide from the attention his mother had brought upon him.

"Okay, ma'am. Thank you. I'm going to go talk with the gentleman—"

"Hah! He's no *gentle* man."

The sheriff flashed a look at his ride-along passenger and raised his eyebrows.

She stuck up her thumb. She was fine.

He strolled over to Rossy, who spun in little circles before breaking into a free skate.

Unexpectedly, a woman with spiky hair came out of the store. Rossy's immediate collision with her sent the contents of her bag scattering to the ground.

"See?!" the irate woman bellowed from beside her Beamer. "That's what I'm talking about."

Rossy showered the spiky-haired woman in profuse apologies as he and the sheriff gathered the Ajax, half-gallon of bleach, gloves, sponges, and toothbrushes to put back into her bag.

She stood erect above them, peering down with an unamused stare.

After handing her the bleach, Rossy made little prayer hands. "So, so sorry."

"He almost ran into me, too!"

"I got it!" the sheriff said, raising his voice to the Beamer woman, who grated on his nerves, so far more than any of them. With all other products collected, he stood up while noticing the spiky-haired woman's long, narrow, smooth-soled shoes. Interesting that it appeared to be the same type of shoe that created the prints at Manny's house.

He placed the stringent cleaning supplies back into the woman's bag and let his imagination run wild on the chances of her involvement. It'd come out if credible. But for now, Rossy's reckless skating took precedence.

"Looks like you're causing all sorts of trouble today," the sheriff told his flamboyant skater, followed by an acknowledging nod to the tall, spiky-haired woman. "You okay, Ma'am?"

"Quite okay. Thank you and … Tinkerbell … for your concerted efforts."

She walked off without another word, head held high, toting her groceries. Rather, her cleaning supplies. Her pompousness and poise reminded him of Fergus—the above-average height, the articulate sense of language, and the pretentious attitude. How ironic the shoes on this woman and her attitude brought thought of the open case involving him. He dismissed the notion with a snort. Back to business. He turned his sights on Rossy.

"Okay, wait." Rossy held his hands up. "First off, you know that was a *total* accident. Regarding the hussy by her Beamer, I was just practicing my 360s, and she happened to come out the door both times I was mid-spin. Total fluke! I swear it." He put his hand over his heart and lowered his head in reverence.

The sheriff attempted his authoritative stare, but Rossy began skating around him and would not stay still. "Rossy. Stop the skating."

He glided right up to the sheriff, braking with his little rubber nub. "Yes?"

"Don't do this by the door. There's a whole parking lot." He gave a widespread motion with his arm toward the back of the lot.

"That part is so nasty. Too many holes and lots of gravel. Sheriff, does it look like I can afford to fall?" Rossy gave a graceful sweep up and down his nearly naked body.

The sheriff snorted, humored by the gall. "It's December. Winter is nearing. Aren't you cold?" He, himself, felt the nip fully dressed.

"Not an ounce."

"Have you been drinking?"

"A little, but there's no law that says you can't drink and skate."

"Mmm-hmm. It falls under, *drunk in public.*"

"Well, Sheriff, I am far from drunk. I could do your little sobriety test in my skates if needed. Backward, frontward, you just watch me."

The sheriff wanted to laugh, if not for breaking up his own tension. He looked over at the unhappy woman with her hand on her hip and back to Rossy. "Don't skate near the door. Period. Aside from the two people you've already affected, we have elders in the community who cannot dodge you at all. Think about what could have happened with someone less mobile?"

"I would have noticed a golden oldie."

The sheriff cinched his mouth. "Enough."

"I'll be more careful," Rossy said, reading his impatience.

"Be sure that you are."

Rossy kissed his first two fingers and placed them over his heart. "Promise."

"Would you consider apologizing to her?" the sheriff asked, gesturing toward the hostile woman.

Rossy grunted with disdain and rolled his glassy hazel eyes. He skated within talking distance of the woman and wriggled his fingers. "Apologies, angry lady." He looked at the tween in the car. "Sorry, angry lady's son."

The woman's mouth dropped open in insult. "Is that all you're going to do, Officer?"

"Ma'am, I think he's sorry, and he's taking his skating elsewhere."

The lady shook her head, still miffed, and got into her car, glaring at the retreating skater.

As the sheriff started his walk toward the cruiser, Rossy glided past him, his nose held high, his fairy wings flapping, and his wheeling, athletic agility on full display.

"Okay, let's get you back," Sheriff Michaels said to the teen, whose eyes stayed fixed on the departing skater.

"No problem. That was something you don't see every day," she said, her daylong compliant expression replaced with a humored smirk.

The dispatcher's call crackled on the radio, prompting a go-ahead from the sheriff.

"Sheriff, letting you know the video surveillance came in. Telling you just in case you wanted to come in before your weekend."

"I'm headed there now. Returning my ride-along," he said, giving the student a wink.

Making good time back to the station, the student handed over her community service sheet, whereupon he scribbled out his neatest *John Hancock*.

"Thank you. I really enjoyed it, and I'll tell my dad you said *hi*," she said, getting into her mother's waiting car.

He was burnt, but the temptation to check out the surveillance footage of Manny's road dictated his choice. With all day-shift employees gone, once inside, he could hear only the sweeping of the janitor. He grabbed a mini plastic water bottle from the kitchen fridge and ambled to his office.

His chair creaked at his weight as he awoke his computer to peruse the mentioned email. Within it, he found the zip drive containing several files. Suffering the slow downloading process, he tended to his ravenous appetite. He slung open his bottom desk drawer and rifled through the pill containers, packs of gum, and snack packages before settling on a purple bag of cheddar crackers shaped like bunnies.

After a couple of nuggets of processed wheat, he tapped on the clips secured by Manny's nearest neighbor on the main road. While it would not identify Manny's specific visitors, it could hold a clue as to who had driven up the road prior to the discovery.

"Doubt the Amazon driver is the culprit." He fast-forwarded. "Bobcat?" He snorted while fast-forwarding again. "His neighbor … another neighbor … and another neighbor. All already verified through their plates and registration," he said, mumbling to himself.

Wait! He rewound and zoomed in on the last driver. Though a little grainy, he could swear she was the same woman Rossy had collided with at the store. "Hunh. Interesting." He made a mental note and let the video advance until the workers' truck appeared, its bed loaded with rolls of chicken wire and metal poles. "There's the fencing guys."

He flung himself back in his chair, dug into the bottom of his cracker packet, secured the last two crunchies, and tossed them into his mouth. He chewed, watching the video progress to nothing more than risk-prone squirrels and an occasional raven flyby. "Looks like a neighbor may have done it." Flippant for now, but if the picture proved to be that tall, spiky-haired lady, his gut feeling that he had learned to entertain over the years dictated she could have a role to play in the investigation.

He'd match up the data later. He shut down his computer, tossed his empty packet into the garbage, and grabbed his keys. Enough for tonight. With low blood sugar, his cheesy bunny appetizers fell way short of a true meal.

Chapter 19
Fulfill the Curse

The December night closed in on Iris's home like a tomb lid clamping down upon a dying soul's last breath. With cloudy skies and no glowing moon, the range of view beyond her property fell short of clear. Glancing at her perimeter, she poured kibble into little metal cat dishes, creating a tinkling effect in the quiet night. While the other felines milled about, Rupert cautiously darted his eyes toward the forest.

She gave a quick pat to his forehead, feeling his ruggedly coarse outdoor fur, before walking over to her terra cotta planters. With her mandrake roots harvested earlier that day, nothing needed tending. Still, she grabbed her cultivator and dug at the dirt within each pot. Come the weekend, she would sow more seeds. Keeping a fresh supply not only provided income from eager customers, but it also held a prominent role in her specialty—poison.

Wiping at her dewy nose, she glimpsed a pair of floating red orbs lurking at the forest line. From the height and pace, she figured them to belong to the county's roaming tuft-eared bobcat or gray tree-climbing fox. While no concern for her, she looked down at Rupert and his friends enjoying their dinner. "Best be extra careful tonight, my lovelies. Eat quickly and take shelter."

She lingered for as long as it took Rupert to sate his appetite. When he began licking his paw and rubbing his face, she left the outdoors behind and stepped inside to slightly warmer conditions. The comforting stillness of her home welcomed her, as did the simple tapered candle, which kept her otherwise outrageous electrical bill economically just. She felt the drastic contrast to her spoiled excursion in Spokane, but the frivolity of such poshness should always be temporary. This, the darkness and isolation, the withered senescence of her home, endured as her reality.

She walked over to the curse tablet. With evidence clear that Bethie had entered her premise, the crack had probably come from her carelessness. She wondered if it had been deliberate. Staring at the damning words, who could blame her? She remembered Bethie's anger from its discovery. Experiencing it as if through her old friend's eyes, she cleared her throat and read it aloud. Word by word, slow and deliberate. With this applied purpose, she had never felt the threatening meaning as she did on this night. An awareness churned within her.

"All this time. Why now?"

Her words circulated energy within the deadness of the room and a tinge of shame filled her, thinking of Bethie's disappointment. And Declan, Bethie's brother ... at least her first love was not alive to bear witness and know the truth.

A frigid breeze blew past her, causing her to shiver. She looked back at the door, shut tight and the locks latched. When the air grew colder, as if the outside night had seeped up through the vents of her floor, she recognized the unfolding event.

Behind her, a sweep of movement reflected on the tablet's glass case.

She flinched but remained unafraid.

Elaborate encounters such as this had always been reserved for Samhain. Otherwise, communing with her deceased loved ones came through her invitational means only. Never had they come uninvited like now.

A refreshed chill embraced every inch of her body. The sharp sensation of its iciness could only be one ancestor.

"Grandmother?"

At least, she hoped it was her grandmother. She had visited with the matriarch several times throughout her life—asking for guidance and sharing exotic tales from her international paranormal excursions. The old crone's presence unmistakably inhabited the house.

Another icy breeze softly caressed her cheek. As uncomfortable as it felt, it contained an intention of tenderness.

"I am here, Grandmother."

It is time.

She heard the message within her and attempted to swallow down the rising lump in her throat. She dreaded what burden these words necessitated.

It is time … for you.

The declaration became a breathy hiss, and a foul odor followed. The breath of a haggard woman long dead.

The rising wind outside rattled her front door, and the windows vibrated. From her darkened yard came a deathly squall. A wild animal's victory meant one less mouth to feed. Pained, she closed her eyes, hoping that Rupert would show up for his morning feeding.

A loud pop from the walls brought her back, and she caught the apparition out of the corner of her eye. Warily, she turned in its direction but saw only her coat rack of eccentric jackets, hats, and umbrellas.

'Fulfill the curse.'

The voice encircled her.

"I hear you, Grandmother."

She wanted to please her grandmother, but it just rang so trite and senseless. Especially after she had already been called for the duty once before. After spending her entire young life traveling and staying gone, hoping to avoid the trips to town and casual sightings of Declan and his new wife's marital bliss, her wanderlust slowed in middle-age. It was then that her deceased grandmother came to her through ritual and urged a single spell of lethal misfortune for Declan Kelly and his wife. Iris gave in to the matriarch's whim, its dire consequence taking the life of her only lover, along with that of her competition. However, instead of reveling in the end of them, she sank into despair and regret. Even more so when her own family met with the avenging counter effect. Soon, out of all her kin, she stood alone.

"Grandmother, must it be this way?"

The icy air brushed her shoulder. She turned to find nothing but darkened shadows of her own furnishings. The feathers upon her artsy palm tree waved, proving the encounter real.

'Fulfill the curse, or I will see that Fergus does it for you.'

Iris deflated as the sobering reality smacked her. Grandmother knew *all* from her vantage in the Otherworld—the initial possession, the frequent battles of keeping Fergus's soul suppressed, and the sickness she endured during each of his attempts. No doubt remained that she would succumb to his possession with their matriarch backing him.

She relented, as there was no use arguing with the supernatural world. "Yes, Grandmother."

A pulling motion drew the chill from around her, sending the current sweeping up the staircase. She watched the breeze blow past her dried table arrangement atop the stairs. Once more, she stood in isolated loneliness.

She turned and gazed at the tablet, then went to carefully remove its cracked casing. She lifted the etched stone from its stand and reverently held it upon her open palm. Accompanied by her red ceramic candle holder with its tall, tapered candle, she walked to the stairs. The flickering flame illuminated the plentiful dark pockets along her path. With devotion, she trudged up to her ritual room.

Given the low light of the waning crescent moon phase, the second story's large circular window allowed in more outside light than expected. She walked over and peered down upon her deck, remembering the day Bethie and her grandniece came for the Silver Bough well over a month ago. This watch tower allowed observation of all who occupied her property and currently enabled her to see Rupert tucked up on the eaves, safe from predators. A second of relief before duty called.

She placed her candle and the tablet upon her altar, then glanced around at the precious ancestral mementos of those lost to tragedies—their antique clothes, old handbags, men's hats and wallets, and clunky shoes.

The owners of these items sat present as well.

Four upholstered wingback chairs held skeletons long rotted of their flesh, positioned as if the occupants were about to hold an important meeting.

In her altar mirror, Iris stared at the reflection of her grandmother's bones. Her skeleton had spent the longest time in the macabre state. The tradition started when the family's grand matriarch succumbed to a flesh-eating disease in the early fifties. Thanks to the era when the bodies of loved ones stayed in the family home before burial, her family chose not to complete the process. From middle school through her late teens, Iris's mother had put her in charge of wiping her grandmother's decomposing tissue from the bone, grooming her long, gray straw-like hair, and kissing her skull's temple goodnight. Every night. When her own mother died, Iris placed her to the left of her grandmother. The grooming and affection portion of the upkeep she had long abandoned, but as she kept their bodies near, her grandmother had always been the biggest reminder of their family's solemn vow.

Iris took her modest, black-handled athame and held it skyward. She chanted in solemn intention and then sliced an inch-long cut on her palm, watching it seep her lifeblood onto the tablet. As it saturated the crevices of the carved text, she envisioned the tactics she would use. She could not disappoint her grandmother any longer. Her life depended upon it.

CHAPTER 20
SHORT OF THE USUAL TAINT

"Hey, gorgeous! At last, we meet again."

With Katie out of town at a sales conference, Mike held the door and watched his hook-up's squishy butt as she entered the apartment in a tight black catsuit. Her long platinum-blond hair cascaded down in salon-fresh straightness, and her red patent leather boots were doing amazing things for her legs. Different, yet equally fine, from the night they met at the San Francisco bar.

She turned to face him with a huge, crimson-painted smile and flicked her tongue ring. "Nice place. I thought you lived in the city."

"Yeah, I'm here for a while. I'm staying with my sister and watching my niece. So," he walked over, sliding his hands around her waist, "I have to ask that we keep it down a little. Babysitting comes with the territory."

"Wow, so we got a G-rated audience, huh? No biggie." She dropped her head to the side, exposing her neck and letting his lips nibble at her flesh. "Starting where we left off? Mmmm."

A mouthful of her neck muffled Mike's confirmation.

"Oh," she said. "I think your niece is up."

Mike stopped and looked toward Katie's office to see Soonsil at the cracked door, peering out at them.

"Hang on," he said, feeling beleaguered.

"No, no, Soonsil," he said with contrived patience. At the door, he grabbed her upper arm with a firm hand and steered her back inside, shutting the door behind him.

"You need to get to sleep. It's way past your bedtime."

"Katie," Soonsil said, her voice soft.

"Katie will be back tomorrow."

Back in bed, he squatted down beside her. "Look. I'm going to be honest with you. We need to find your family." He snorted and shook his head. "I think you're a real sweet kid, but I'm not a fatherly type. You know?"

A somberness washed across Soonsil's face, and she cast her eyes up to the framed photo of Katie holding up a sales award. She held the gaze.

He felt a creep of guilt. "Really, you're a cool kid, but I have a friend here. So, *please* … just stay in your bed. You hear me?"

"Katie," Soonsil said, her voice now firm. She faced him with a stern expression.

"As I said, Katie will be back tomorrow."

Soonsil looked at the door and knitted her eyebrows.

Mike rose to standing. "Remember, my friend and I need alone time." He walked to the door. "Stay in that bed." He looked directly into her eyes and pointed at her. "Bed."

Mike shut the door to Soonsil's room. What had he gotten himself into? He thought he could handle a kid. Instead, he only felt annoyed by her buzzkill. As he turned the corner, his devilish smile returned when he saw the night's delicacy looking especially buxom on the couch. "Where were we?"

"Mike?" Soonsil called from behind the door.

"She'll give up in a while. My nephew does this too," the chick said, bored with the charade.

Mike pulled her closer.

"Mike?" Soonsil called again.

"Just ignore her," the woman said, nuzzling into him.

The foreplay had already played out in texts and a few phone calls. Time to get down to business. Mike found the catsuit's zipper and began its long journey down her back.

"I think she's back, and she's kinda creeping me out," the chick whispered.

Too many interruptions! To avoid appearing like a total jerk, he arose with forced calm and turned toward Soonsil. He had to agree with the chick. He had seen that look on Soonsil's face just once, and that was when she met Fergus. Now her death stare—eyes locked and angry—aimed in his direction.

Soonsil ducked back into the room before he arrived.

Again, he shut them in the closed quarters. He picked her up and gently tossed her onto the makeshift bed. No more Mr. Nice Guy! Maybe a little coercion. He did not need her seeing him sexing the slut, and since Katie kept a camera in her bedroom, they couldn't go in there.

Though controlled in volume, his words came out harsh. "Listen to me! No more! Keep your little butt in here!"

Her shoulders dropped. She gazed at Katie's photo and whimpered. "Katie loves."

An abrupt laugh escaped his mouth. "Maybe so, but Katie's not here! She's gone, and you're in serious trouble if you come out again!" He grabbed her chin and looked her in the eye. "You hear me?! Plus, she doesn't love you as much as I do." He had to give her something of substance, feeling a little guilty.

A single tear trailed down her cheek, murky as if it had blended with black eyeliner. Weird. Of course, she didn't wear makeup. Anyway, he needed to be firm, or she'd just keep repeating the behavior. "No more!"

As he closed the door, he heard the words, "Mike doesn't love."

He hastened back to his sure bet.

"We could have done this some other time if I'd known you were *babysitting*," the chick said, verbally dragging out the chore.

Her sarcasm ate at him. He barely knew her. Was she really worth the hurt feelings he just caused Soonsil?

She rubbed her arms. "Brr! Did you open a window?"

Mike looked around. "Nope." He felt the chill but turned off the table lamp and pawed at luscious breasts. Her moans tantalized him.

She pulled away. "No, seriously. It's, like, freezing in here. Look at my breath." She huffed out a cloud of steam.

"I'll heat your body up," Mike said, unbuttoning his pants and grinding up against her.

"Oh shit! Who's that?" The chick pulled away, peering around him.

At his wit's end, Mike stood up, ready to rage at the little pain-in-the-butt who refused to listen. But before he could turn around, a blood-curdling scream blared out of the chick's mouth.

He turned to see a petite woman dressed in white with jet-black hair, growing longer by the second, floating toward them.

"Mike, no love," the woman said, her voice reminiscent of Soonsil's yet scratchy.

Her clothes saturated in blood before his very eyes.

"Fergus, no love."

Her voice deepened, and her long black hair grew straggly and dripping wet.

"Mr. Kutch, no love."

As she came upon him, the words strained from her throat, and her face turned ashen white.

"All, like Papa, with … no … loooove …"

Her voice withered to a graveled hiss before her mouth altogether vanished. Then, her hair swept forward, hiding any semblance of a face.

The screams of his date faded into the background as Mike watched a long, serrated appendage rise from behind the ghoulish woman. A flash of Fergus's unexplained bloodied body at Arista's house and the dead man in the park where he had originally found her came all too clear.

.   .   .

The taste of the woman satisfied, but Mike's flavor fell short of the usual taint of her victims. She had jumped to conclusions this time. However, she had already felt his affection fleeting. Eventually, he would have become another disappointment, lacking the tender love she craved.

Only something had changed after consuming him. She could no longer thrive on the cruelty of her bloodthirsty vengeance. Yet fate had left her here to roam for an eternity.

CHAPTER 21
MUCH HIGHER BIREFRINGENCE

Given the madness swirling about her, Arista's shift at Earth & Ocean helping customers and talking with Analina felt like it could be the best kind of distraction. She bicycled along Hoot Owl Way and mulled over Auntie's eyesight issue. At least the doctor had witnessed the incident firsthand and given his referral. He did not seem too worried about it and stood by his initial "manageable" remark.

Iris still played on her mind, too. The devastating story behind the curse tablet had inspired both regret and suspicion. For her part, Arista felt the need to atone for iniquities that happened generations before her time, but she also felt appreciation for her great-great-grandfather saving her life. How could she honor him without condoning his cold-blooded murder?

Her convoluted thoughts ceased when she heard the whining engine come from behind her. She looked over her shoulder and saw the dark green van, the driver and passenger, staring at her.

The fear struck hard. She picked up speed toward Highway 9, just ahead of her. With everything else brewing, she had dropped her guard on watching out for this lingering duo, but between their repeated visits, gawking stares, and the shadiness of their presence, it had become obvious. They were here for her!

She hit the main strip at full speed, her heart exploding in her chest with anxiety.

Beep. Beep.

Already jumpy, she startled.

The sight of Evan, her dear friend, in a brand-new black Lexus coupe brought her a sliver of relief. She glanced behind her and watched the van take a turn, disappearing down a side street. She eased her pedaling to give her heart a reprieve.

Evan honked again and waved. 'My new car!' he mouthed through the window, then gave her a thumbs-up.

Relieved the van had turned, she waved back to him. She really missed Evan.

But the van! She looked back at the street where it had just turned and waited.

No sign of its return.

She released the final bit of tension and watched as Evan picked up pace with the traffic. He and Bree were so lucky to have each other.

A final worried look all around her, making sure the van had not returned.

Then, a very welcome sight! Margaret emerged from the corner market carrying a bag of groceries. The humanity of this bewitched character charmed her. In all of her Margaret sightings, she could not recall ever seeing her carry anything. Her anxiety completely disappeared with such novelty just as she rolled in front of Earth & Ocean. She secured her bike and walked inside fully settled.

Analina flashed her a quick smile while talking with a grizzled man with a tray of stones.

She had seen these modern-day-prospector caricatures before, their rugged attire and excitable demeanor straight out of the gold rush era.

The miner talked in rapid spurts, his eyes bouncing from Analina to his product. "You see, I mined these here myself. So, I have some wiggle room as far as price, but it's a worthy stone. Very rare and real big beauties. Just look at 'em."

Arista slinked past them, knowing that Analina had her hands full in negotiation.

In the backroom, she got right to work unloading the new merchandise—a variety of Bast figurines, Quartz Crystal singing bowls with their equally lovely strikers, and a dozen new-release books from two of the shop's favorite publishers, LouEllen and BRW. She drowned out worries by reminiscing about the not-so-distant days of kind Mr. Tessay and Albert coming into Cosmic Prisms in Sedona with rose-wrapped sage kits. Without Mr. Tessay, she had no one to practice her sign language with, and she missed it. And Stevie, her former co-worker who possessed unending sass. She really needed to touch base with him, as they had not talked since she left. Hopefully, he did not still blame himself for blurting out their location to Fergus.

"Arista, can I see you for a minute?"

"Sure!"

She walked out front, where Analina and her potential new vendor stood waiting.

"Mr. Coucher, this is Arista. She's very good with crystals, and I'd like her to take a look at your inventory, if you don't mind?"

"Well, surely!"

His breath was a mixture of tobacco and coffee, but his friendly demeanor and positive energy overshadowed the sourness.

Analina pointed to the stones. "What do you think?"

She didn't quite know where this was going. Analina had never brought her into negotiations with the vendors. She waited for some kind of prompt about what to do next, but none came.

"These are beautiful stones, Mr. Coucher. Sapphires?" she asked.

"No, ma'am. This is Benitoite. Sapphires are harder on the MOHS scale than these here. They both have overlapping refractive indices …"

Say what?

"… but Benitoite has a much higher birefringence, including the blink."

"Wow, that's really cool." *What the heck did he just say? Note to self: look up 'bifringent.'*

"Yes, ma'am, I mined these out of San Benito County, where I live. And I've been tellin' Analina here that a carat of Benitoite can run about five grand. Sapphires are a little more unpredictable. I mean, there are a few of pure quality that'll run up past ten grand, but mostly, you can get yourself a low-quality, one-carat Sapphire for 'bout twenty-five bucks." He nodded, sure of his data.

Arista pinky-touched a specimen.

"Aw, don't worry about it. You can pick 'em up. Just be gentle."

His pricing swirled in her mind. Five grand? Why did Analina think she qualified for this? Perusing the stones, one struck her, and she picked it up—a solid white rock dotted with spears of translucent knobby blue crystals. As she held it, her rush of thoughts slowed. She inhaled an inner peace, feeling an airy release. She felt herself pulled into the crystal's beauty, forgetting for a moment that two humans stood beside her awaiting input.

"Okay, Mr. Coucher. I see your stones have my expert mesmerized. So, you have yourself a deal."

Analina's announcement grounded her, but it surprised her to have succumbed to such serenity in their presence, and her boss was absolutely right about the mesmerizing aspect. She smiled at Mr. Coucher and handed him back his beautiful and effective crystal.

"Oh, no, ma'am! No need for me to take it. It's yours now to gander all day if you want," he said, pulling his hands away.

"Thank you, Arista."

That served as Analina's cue. Arista placed the crystal back in its blue velvet cubby and returned to the back room.

After wishing the gentleman well, Analina came to the back with her new consignment goodie box full of Benitoite nuggets.

"Okay, Arista, I have a job for you." She opened the case, exposing all the sizeable samples of the rare mineral. "I want you to look these over and choose one to take home and study. I want to know how it affects you. With this knowledge, we can better sell the product."

"Oh wow. I'd love to."

"They *are* very pricey. Some will go for thousands. In fact, I wasn't sure I wanted the liability of carrying such an expensive stone."

Arista looked at the samples, each with their intricate designs—similar to snowflakes, but un-melting upon the white rock formation.

"There's no rush to choose now. Go through them during the day and find a piece that calls to you. By day's end, take it home."

"Sounds exciting."

Analina gave her upper arm a warm squeeze. "Arista, I know you mentioned dreams and all, but I really appreciate you helping me with my wildly spirited daughter and her fondness for *snake conjuring*."

They shared a subtle chuckle.

"I pulled my own shenanigans growing up," Arista admitted.

"Well, she's using that term you taught her—*turning a new leaf*."

"Aww," Arista responded, feeling flattered as a teacher.

"I pride myself on being an attuned mom, so I'd rather have caught the behavior myself. After resolving that insecurity, I realized that there would be no other person who I would trust more to address the matter than you. Your intuition and your … beautiful spirit continue to be a blessing to us. Thank you."

Arista felt her chest expand from the sudden gratitude. With all her heartache of the recent past and the trouble that brewed even now, the kind words held significant weight. "I love you guys and just want to help any way I can."

"And you did."

The front door chimed.

"Business calls," Analina said, perking up to address the customer.

Arista stayed with the feeling. To receive this compliment from a woman she respected felt an invaluable gift. She gazed down at the array of rocks. All so desirable, it felt like selecting a fine chocolate. She picked up a specimen, eyed it, and set it back in its cubby. Then she lifted another, rotated it, and returned it as well. Where was that first one she picked up? Ah! There it was. She held it up and treasured the familiarity. This would be fun.

CHAPTER 22
RELIEVED OF LURKING VANS

"Knock-knock," Arista announced, coming through Auntie's door fresh from work, only to see Auntie on the couch with a warm compress over her eyes.

The joy of her workday sank in her gut. "Are you having a spell?"

"Not really. Just staving one off, I think."

"Do you want some tea?"

"Sure."

She hustled into Auntie's kitchen and fussed about—selecting herbs, concocting the mixture, and stuffing it in the infuser to steep an aromatic peppermint tea in Auntie's glass pitcher. "I'm making you my Yule peppermint bark tea. Okay?"

"Sounds delicious," Auntie answered.

She pulled out a glass flip-jar, popped it open, and added a spoonful of powdered raw cacao to two mugs. The raw sugar dish allowed for a generous pinch of granules, after which she stirred the blend. While the tea steeped, she walked to the linen closet. "I'm grabbing you a blanket. It's a bit chilly in here."

"Thank you," Auntie replied.

With the tea ready, she removed the diffuser, poured the tea, and stirred in the mixture. Ready to serve.

"Lovely, dear, thank you," Auntie said, sitting up with cupped hands to accept the tea. She inhaled the steam and hummed in appreciation.

Arista flapped out the teddy-bear-soft blanket with its design of a lanky gray hare amidst a midnight-blue scene of moonlight and fallen snow. "What else can I get you? Are you hungry?"

"No, and for goodness' sake, I love you to pieces, and I appreciate everything, but will you *please* just sit down a minute? I'm fine."

No doubt her fussiness came from the frustration of her failing eyesight. Or maybe Arista had become too overbearing lately. After losing her mother, her father, and almost Auntie from the serial killer's blow to her head … and the gwishin … she wanted to ensure no chance of further loss. She sat down on the floor beside Auntie and sipped her own tea. "Auntie, should we move you to my house? Temporarily?"

Auntie scoffed. "I can see, just not clearly. I know my way around my house."

"Aunt—"

"Nhhh!" Auntie pretended to zip her lips shut and tossed the 'key' for good measure. When she saw compliance, she let out a relenting breath. "I'm just tired, Arista. That's all. You have to realize I'm getting older … mid-seventies. Pesky matters with my health are going to arise."

"I just don't understand why … all of a sudden, you have this problem."

"Two bumps on my ol' noggin. That's why! According to the doctor. Agh! I'll be fine. I promise. We are going to take these lemons and make lemon lavender shortbread. My eyesight may be failing, but all my smarts are fully operational."

Arista sighed, prompting Auntie to relax, sit back, and sip her sweetened hot tea. She did likewise and enjoyed her own cup, with its wafting hint of peppermint and chocolate, invigorating her sinuses.

Auntie smacked her lips. "Well, this is mighty delicious. You made this for me last year. I remember now."

The customary diversionary tactic did not work this time. "At least let me stay here with you tonight. I'll run to my house, tuck Royal in, and make sure everything's locked."

"Very well. Take my car. I notice the time change has done a number with our daylight. Have you seen that green van again?"

Arista considered withholding the information. Auntie had enough to worry about. "Yes, but it was closer to the main strip, so they may have family in our neighborhood or something. Anyway, I'm keeping a safe lookout." The reminder of them unsettled her. She would need to be careful.

"I remember a Mr. Someone who used to accompany you everywhere, and it helped me worry a lot less. You need to let that young man back into your life. He's making all the right moves, including taking that nasty rumor spread against him pretty well."

Arista stood up and gave an elongated stretch. "I'm thinking about it. We've had tea a few times now, so …" Auntie had not given her blessing before now, and hearing that her great aunt's intuition felt okay about the reunion further encouraged her own positive feelings.

Auntie kept her poker face at the news of tea dates, and shimmied down deeper into her cushions, her tea propped atop her throw. Arista knew that cozy body language meant she appreciated the love life update. And even better, liked the promising future in it.

"Okay, I'll be back. I want to tell you about my new assignment from Analina."

Arista started her quick jaunt home but paused at Auntie's entrance when a high-pitched whine announced the oncoming dark green van. Slowly turning onto Hoot Owl Way, she eyed the vehicle as it crept past Auntie's driveway without noticing her.

Her heartbeat picked up pace. Keeping her presence discreet, she rolled to Auntie's hedge to peek around as the vehicle slowed to a crawl at her distant driveway. There, it stopped.

"What are you two doing?" she murmured, exasperated that she must face yet another stalker.

Not wanting to upset Auntie, especially after she had just asked about the van, she called Shane.

"Hey!" Shane answered. It's true you can tell a smiling person from the sound of their voice through the phone.

"Hey. I hope this isn't a bad time, but go figure, I've got some van in front of my house, and—"

"I'll be there."

"Wait! Hold on." She watched the passenger hang out of his window, steady himself, and snap a picture … and another before the driver picked up speed and drove on toward the street's end. They turned and disappeared from view.

Arista groaned.

"What?" Shane asked, alarmed.

"It looks like they're gone now, but they totally just took pictures of my house."

"I'm coming over right now."

"No, no, no. Honestly, it's okay. I'm staying with Auntie tonight, anyway. I just need to tuck Royal in."

"At least stay on the phone with me until you're back at Auntie's."

Relieved, she appreciated the invitation and what a perfect excuse to call him. With a cautious eye, she chatted with him as she biked down to her cottage. They talked about his job at the school, her work at Earth & Ocean, and her worry about Auntie's failing eyesight. Still gabbing away with him as she walked through her door, double-bolted it, and went through her mental checklist—grabbing robe and toothbrush, straightening her counter of miscellaneous food items, and pouring a thin layer of kibble in the cat dish in case Royal got hungry in the night. After taking a quick peek out of her window to make sure no van loitered, she talked with him about the oncoming holidays. With Yule and Christmas so close together, it seemed as if they were speaking of the same festive holiday. She exhaled her heaviness to allow for a giddiness of the season rising within her. Now, sharing it with her true love felt possible. Her rekindling the relationship with Shane had to be the most enlivening aspect of her life right now.

"Hang on, I've got to kiss Royal goodnight." She gave her sleepy feline, already cozied into the folded blanket on her bed, a loud smooch. A little reminder to Shane of how important her kisses were.

"When do I get one of those again?"

Yep, that worked. She kept her cool. "We'll see."

Her task list completed, a quick jaunt travelled with watchful eyes, and she arrived back at Auntie's front porch. "I'm here. Thank you for being there for me."

"Okay, I'll be waiting for that kiss."

She gave a happy sigh at the comforting ease of their talk.

But as she grabbed Auntie's doorknob, a sense of malintent tainted her enjoyment. A cognizant reminder of her repeated visions of the hummingbird, Auntie's self-proclaimed totem animal, zipping around at her kitchen window, then beyond her hedge. She felt the crushing urgency of what it could represent, and the hounding from the green van only added more weight. She had to get to Auntie!

She burst through the door and rushed to the living room.

Auntie bolted upright, shock on her face. "Sakes alive, Arista! You scared the bejeebers out of me!"

Arista scanned the room, her heart pounding.

"What on earth is wrong?" Auntie asked, her expression going from shock to worry as she followed Arista's eyes around the room. "Is it the green van again?"

Arista relented. "No! No, it's okay. I'm sorry. I just had this …" *Choose your words carefully.* Auntie had enough problems with her eyesight and the whole Iris debacle. "I thought I heard you calling me, and I kinda just … freaked." She calmed her inner turmoil and eased for show. "Sorry about that."

"Well, go close that pneumonia hole. My vision is back, and I see and *feel* you letting December's coldest into the house."

"Okay, I'll be right back. You need anything?"

"I'm fine. Thank you," Auntie said, a little peeved.

The minute she went beyond Auntie's view, she felt the deflation of any remaining energy left from the day. Right back into the midst of her dread, her head and shoulders felt heavy as she trod through the hall. She laid her items on the guest bedroom bed, knowing the hummingbird vision was not for this night. Still, the ambiguity nagged at her. One thing was for sure—consistency in its reminders could only mean an oncoming reality, and that van with its photo-taking occupants had something to do with it.

The insecurity of losing her mentor scared her. Thinking of her mom and her dad, she knew it could happen. She squeezed her eyes shut, resisting the belief she could lose Auntie, too. Never could she bear that loss. Never!

She forced an air of positivity upon herself as she approached the living room. Turning the corner, she brightened her eyes. "So, I want to tell you all about the project Analina gave me! But first, more tea?"

"I've had enough. Thank you. Let's hear about your project."

No sooner had their conversation begun when a small tapping gave them pause. They quieted and waited for it to duplicate.

Tap. Tap. Tap.

Someone knocked upon the door. Horrible timing with all her troubled thoughts. Arista worried it might be something truly dreadful upon them.

"I'll get it. You stay here," Auntie said, arising. She called to the door. "Who is it?"

"Who is it?" Arista asked in a strong voice, finding her courage to protect them both. When no one answered, she nudged past Auntie and peeked out the window. "Oh, wow!" she whispered in shock. She stepped back, firmly pulling Auntie with her. "It's Soonsil."

"Really?!" Auntie mouthed, her eyes bulging.

"In her child form … mostly," Arista said with hesitation. She knew how much worse it could get from the gwishin's ghastly introduction a little less than two months ago. "What do we do?"

Tap. Tap. Tap.

Auntie took a peek. "The Mike fella is not with her, and she's not *entirely* human right now."

"I saw that."

Auntie took a deep breath, bracing herself, and opened the door.

At the sight of them, Soonsil dropped her head into her hands, sobbing. The hems of her white pants hung saturated in deep red, as if she had waded through a river of blood. While she stood before them the height of a human child, her hair maintained some of the straggle of her gwishin form.

Arista remembered the hideousness of Soonsil's full ghoul image, but she could not turn away from her now. There had to be a reason she stood crying before them. She knelt down before her and reached out with caution to take the child's soggy hand.

Murky gray tears streamed down Soonsil's ashen, purple-veined cheeks. When she looked up, Arista saw the inside of her inky black mouth, her teeth still razor sharp. Through her weeping, only two words, "No love."

CHAPTER 23
LOVE

Arista watched as Iris hastened up onto the porch with her tote bag slung over her shoulder. With Soonsil's reappearance, they promptly phoned the maven despite the tension that lingered from the curse tablet.

"Little time for questions, though I'm quite curious how this came about?" Iris commented, entering the cottage as poised as ever.

They all looked over at the unassuming little girl on the couch, lying in fetal position.

"She showed up just before we called you," Auntie responded. "No explanation. Occasionally, she repeats the same phrase—No love."

"Not extraordinary, since a gwishin becomes such from being killed … usually by a man, and possibly her relative," Iris said with confidence. "We need to get on with it. This New Moon plays suitably in our … well, *her* favor. No Silver Bough, though." She paused and eyed Soonsil, whose cheeks and mouth had settled back to her child-like flesh and color. "Though I don't believe this is a Celtic matter, anyway?"

All bundled for the December elements, Iris led them outside while Arista wondered what the sly woman had planned. "What kind of ritual are we doing?" She wanted to trust her but could not entirely. Regardless of her helping them, for the second time, with an organ-eating gwishin.

"This will be a freeing ritual that leads her on to the next phase … whatever that may be. I suspect this one will do better without a fire." Iris walked to the dead center of Arista's driveway and looked up to where the moon would be if illuminated. She searched her tote bag, while Soonsil stood at an obedient attention holding Arista's hand.

When Arista glanced down, she saw that Soonsil's hair had shortened back to its healthy black sheen. Happy their care and consideration must have settled the gwishin's inner turmoil, Arista felt a small comfort in their aim.

Soonsil looked up at her. "I tried."

"What did you try, Soonsil?" Arista asked, stooping over to better hear her.

Soonsil did not answer and returned her gaze to Iris.

Iris dipped a cloth into a container of water, then handed it to Arista. "When she lays down, please cleanse all skin that is showing— face, hands and feet."

Arista looked at Soonsil's feet, barefoot and crusted in blood and dirt from her mysterious journey. She wondered if the cloth would be enough.

"Bethie, if you will please help me?" Iris asked as she thwapped out a large white satin coverlet. Its pearlescent material shimmered in the night, catching the shine from their nearest streetlight.

Auntie helped her straighten the corners before Iris spread out another sizeable coverlet of white lace atop it. Together, they fussed at perfection.

Iris nodded encouragement to Arista, who had Soonsil lay down on the bedding. Gently, she wiped Soonsil's angelic face. With loving care, she raised each hand and focused on her dainty fingernails, still holding traces of dried blood. Finally, she cleansed her feet, ridding them of the crusty debris from wading in certain carnage and dirty streets. Oddly, the cloth proved effective in the full cleansing.

"*Love*," Soonsil said, like a cat purring. She stared straight up at the heavens as her stomach rose and fell in calming breaths, soothed by Arista's tender touch.

"Bethie, please bring me some pebbles from the area where Soonsil had her way with me. It will have her essence upon it, and I think that would be most auspicious for something that is associated with her." From the side of her mouth, she added, "No telling the reaction I'd get if I yanked out a strand of her hair."

Soonsil looked at Iris, then returned her gaze skyward.

Finished, Arista traded the soiled cloth for two cotton balls that Iris handed her with instruction to place them in Soonsil's ears. Task completed, she pushed herself back into a lotus position and awaited next steps.

Auntie hurried back with pebbles from the area where the gwishin had strangled Iris during the Samhain ritual, while Iris removed a narrow container from her bag. She opened it to reveal a long-stemmed, dried black rose.

Arista sat dying to ask questions but remained the silent student. She could learn the meanings later. While the black rose was not the Silver Bough, its preserved nature looked elegant and meaningful.

Suddenly, the revelation struck in grand awareness. *The Silver Bough!* She had not caught the association when Iris mentioned it before, but now she remembered offering Soonsil the Silver Bough in order to pass on to her afterlife. Of course, the child had left with Mike instead. But this is why she had returned tonight! She had come back to them in reverent cooperation, knowing they could help her. She *wanted* to cross over. Arista felt contented satisfaction flush through her.

Iris noticed Arista's inner revelation with a raised eyebrow, but returned her focus to receive Auntie's pebbles into her hands. She arranged them into a mound at Soonsil's head before placing one thick, black beeswax candle—six inches tall—atop it. She lit the wick.

Auntie sat cross-legged opposite Arista as Iris offered a last implement to the child—two weathered tokens.

"These are for you, child. To pay the toll," she said, tucking the coins beneath Soonsil's folded hands upon her stomach. With gentle ease, she slid the rose's long, thornless stem down from beneath Soonsil's hands, its pert black bud resting inches from the child's thumbs. "Eternal love be with you."

"I love," Soonsil said, trance-like and her unbroken gaze skyward.

"Okay, ladies. No protective circle, as this is not witchcraft. This is death, pure and simple. Further, we must keep our eyes closed, trust the process, and believe we are safe. This will ensure the child's well-being during the crossover. Arms upward." Iris thrust her arms up in a vee.

Here they were, putting their trust in Iris again. Arista hesitated, but let it go to join Auntie in following Iris's lead. When Auntie closed her eyes, Arista gave Soonsil one last smile, seeing her only as a child in need of love, and headed for her truest peace.

Soonsil turned her head toward her. "Arista loves," she whispered with tenderness, looking into Arista's eyes. Then she looked skyward again and closed her eyes.

Although the wintry December night enveloped them, Arista felt a fulfilling warmth that she had reached this child. Soonsil had impacted her, too. She did love! Auntie. Shane. Royal and life! Regardless of the carnage and horror that Soonsil had brought upon them only weeks ago, she realized she even loved her. And this would be the last time she ever saw her.

After a moment of silence, Iris uttered the beginning of a prayer, but her voice fell to the background within mere seconds. A frigid gust rushed them, its force like a blizzard from the high north. The wind whipped at Arista's hair, causing it to lash at her cheeks. Light, wet specks began to strike at her face as if faerie kisses. She wanted to see what caused the sensation, but kept her eyes closed as Iris had instructed. More than anything, she longed for Soonsil's successful transition to her version of the Summerland. Mostly, she kept her eyes closed because she may not have liked what she saw with them open.

The fury of the storm strengthened, causing the chill to set into her bones. The frigid, howling wind brought lightweight items clattering to the ground, some breaking. A clay pot. A glass windchime.

"Hold steady, witches," Iris said in a stern warning, her voice and chant barely audible through the powerful gusts.

Arista grounded in her position, sinking into her posture, and focused on the heaviness of her bodyweight. She wanted to reach out to Auntie, ensuring her great-aunt still sat across from her, but her temptation to peek eased as the blustery conditions died down as quickly as they had started.

Upon the last caressing arctic breeze, they sat in the returned silence as Iris finished her chant.

At last, all became quiet.

"It is done," Iris said with solemn reverence.

Not sure what to expect, Arista slowly opened her eyes, catching sight of Auntie doing the same. The second thing she noticed were the snowflakes falling in a tranquil serenity all around them. And, where Soonsil had once lain, only a mound of fresh powdery snow remained. From its center rose a patch of light green sprigs with a prominent stalk jutting upward and a single down-turned flower of six white petals. So dainty. Like Soonsil, at her best.

Arista felt the relief of victory. After all her awful circumstances, this was a true win, not just for Soonsil, but also for her. She saw that her previous efforts of yesterday—offering Soonsil the Silver Bough— had created a clear path for this night, inspiring the gwishin back to her door, knowing she would help her find a peaceful end.

"What flower is that?" Auntie asked.

Iris scrutinized it. "Looks to be Galanthus. Snowdrops, if you will." Iris looked at Arista. "Perhaps a parting gift for you."

She and Auntie looked to Iris for next steps.

Iris hesitated, a bemused expression crossing her face. "Admittedly, this was a novel experience for me, but I'd say it went quite well." She looked at Auntie with a seldom-seen perkiness.

"We make a great team," Auntie said with a satisfied smile.

"I agree, Bethie," Iris said, replicating the gesture. "We certainly do."

Out of all contact, this had been the best behavior Arista had seen and felt from Auntie's debatable friend. Still, every time she dropped her guard or turned optimistic, Iris would shoot a catty look in Auntie's direction. So, she spent the next few minutes discreetly watching the interaction of the frenemies, waiting for that fatal flaw that would keep Iris in a suspicious light. However, by the close of their night, she had to admit the warm and relatable conversation that ensued between Auntie and Iris and the hugs that followed as a parting farewell validated a potential for their healing friendship.

CHAPTER 24
UNIVERSAL ANGELS

With a light chattering from nearby tables, the server clarified their order and finished jotting down refinements. "Great, we'll have it out to you in a few."

From the window seat of Trigoso Fish House on the wharf, Arista and Shane watched as a dapper white and gray seagull flapped down on the ledge outside the glass. With the stiffest upright stance, he peered at them, swiveling his head like an avian robot.

"Mine!" Shane wisecracked.

Arista burst out laughing, more so from how Shane sounded than the joke itself. "I love that movie!" she said, remembering the oceanic CGI masterpiece. "Remember when they projected it out in the field in 8th grade?"

"Classic!" Shane agreed.

"Such good times … before you headed off to high school," she said as a harmless jab.

Shane snorted. "I ended up having a pretty good time in high school, *but* it wasn't the same without my Riss to see every day."

"Hah! Only because there were no other girls to see at your all-boys school."

"It wouldn't have mattered, as I had, nor do I have, eyes for anyone but my Riss." He reached across the table to hold her hands.

"Aww," she said, flattered. She held her focus solely on this moment, not thinking of a single issue. Both of them deserved her full attention.

Shane broke the seriousness, and playfully asked her, "So, can I tell my folks you're my girl again? They keep asking, and I really, really just want to say yes."

The way he talked like a middle school valley girl humored her. "I think so."

"You think so?"

"Well, I don't know. Am I your girlfriend? You're responsible for that answer as much as I am."

He squeezed her hands. "That's a resounding yes from my camp. What about yours?"

If there had ever been a time to air the grievances, it was now. "What about all my irksome, witchy business?"

"Not a problem," he said without hesitation.

"How 'bout my Ouija table décor?"

"Been there, done that."

"What about the fact that I'm a basket case from the amount of stress I've been under and may come unhinged at a moment's notice?" Sadly, this was no joke.

A compassion set into his eyes. "Listen, Riss. As I've told you, I *want* to be there for you. All the time. Just know, even in your darkest days, you still shine brighter than anyone I've ever known."

His sweet remark instantly eased her tension, created from simply talking about her issues.

"Remember, I never wanted the breakup. I only wanted you back home. Not trying to rub it in or anything, but you pretty much left me."

She twisted her mouth in contemplation. She kind of wished she had never left. Sure, she felt appreciation for the time with her mom and dad, but it truly stifled their budding love story. And oh, how she ached, thinking about when she heard Maddie's rumor and thought she had lost him for good.

"When I thought I had lost you, it seriously hurt me," Shane said.

She released a subtle snort at their similar thoughts, though the look of hurt that crossed his face served as a reminder that she had not verbalized hers. "No, no. I'm not laughing at what you said. I'm laughing because just before you said it, I was thinking the *exact* same thing. Like when Maddie told me I had lost you …"

He nodded. "So, we give it another full-on go?" His earnest expression awaited her answer.

"Oh yeah. For sure."

They sat in a comfortable silence, holding hands and gazing out to sea. Amidst the sparkling ocean reflecting the sky's blue spectrum upon its dancing irregular waves, two bright-colored surfboards skimmed its surface, heading out to deeper waters.

"Fried zucchini," the server said, barging into their quiet space to set down an enticing platter of lightly battered, golden-fried spears with crumbles of parmesan cheese.

•   •   •

The bustle of holiday activity flourished as Shane's truck crawled along with the other patient drivers back up the Santa Cruz Wharf. Dressed for the chilled salty air, their heavy coats and knit beanies allowed for their windows down, making them privy to fresh air and all the oceanside sounds—breaking waves, barking sea lions, and the shrill screech of overhead seagulls.

As they neared the exit, they saw the work crews had finished preparing the twenty-foot Christmas tree for the annual lighting later in the night. Its branches were full of sparkling silver snowflakes, jumbo, white-glittered starfish, and huge, pearlescent, teal-colored orbs. Cascading down from the unlit silver star, wrapped a wide sea-foam-green garland, creating a swirl reminiscent of a seaside candy cane.

"I've really got to get my tree. With all my drama, I've neglected my winter theme," Arista said, feeling as though she had finally awoken from her autumn nightmares. Making light of her darkness helped reconcile the pain. In truth, she knew she still had far to go. She also considered Shane. He knew about her parents' deaths, but could she ever disclose all the other craziness? A gwishin. The gwishin gutting Fergus. Her knowledge of Fergus's end in a pigpen?

"No one would blame you for that. But we're in my truck. You want to find a lot?" His stare volleyed between the road and studying her face.

Finding a tree … how fun and *normal* that sounded! "Yes!" Dropping all thoughts of devastation, she pondered the frivolity and felt her smile emerge.

"Okay, let's do it," Shane said, jumping at the chance. He turned on his satellite radio. "Set the mood with some jolly holly music?" He broke out in song with Mariah. *"All I want for Christmas ..."*

"... is you, baayy-beeee!" Arista sang along with the radio, her eyes closed, head back, and pipes ringing. She had to admit, it felt a little fake. But in this instance, pretending to enjoy the song and sing in this voice brought light-hearted fun. And that felt great!

Immediately relieved of their dorkiness, they settled into the ride. Through the congested stop signs of the coastal seaside city, down River Street with its glimpse of an uninhabited clock tower, now free of spaced-out loiterers, and on to Highway 9. Entering the mountain from the crossroads, they passed the Old Tannery with its rust-red buildings housing a world of abstract creativity within them. Finally, they left the salty air and ocean behind and headed for firs and redwoods.

Today, they branched even further into the mountains, past Iris's house and on, weaving down Bear Creek Road into territory Arista had rarely seen. Some hair-pinned turns so exaggerated that her body strained against the pull, straight-aways lined with piles of fallen orange and red leaves, and the trees above them brown branched, naked of their delicate covers.

Soon, a life-size wooden snowman—plump, smiling and vibrantly painted—directed them toward Frosty's Tree Lot. Another mile, another snowman. And another, spurring them on their journey. Finally, rounding a bend, the vast spread of a tree farm came into view. The lot sat below the road in a large clearing, allowing a bird's-eye perspective of organized rows of nature's finest, coiffed into coned shapes, inviting embellishment.

Shane pulled into the lot and parked. Exiting the car, they became engulfed in the scent of fresh pine. Arista inhaled nature and envisioned her Yule tree. At home, she had plenty of homemade ornaments left over from the previous years—cinnamon sticks bundled in red-ribboned stacks, dried orange slices, and a garland of small pinecones handpicked from her yard. The latter of which she would re-sprinkle with clove and cinnamon oils.

Shane trailed behind her as she perused the first aisle of trees, futzing with a few before finding one that caught her eye.

"This one!" she said, her breath sending a blast of steam into the brisk mountain air.

"You like the size?"

The tree's pointy top came to Shane's nose.

"Yes, it's perfect," she said, walking around it. "Wait." She bent over and examined the sparse foliage. "It's okay. I can put that side against the window, and the lights will cover it, anyway."

Shane peered at her with a stunned look on his face.

"What?"

"Seriously? You're done?" He looked at the tree.

"*Yeees*?" She drew out her answer while looking at the lovely evergreen.

"Good Lord, you make this so easy! I'm always carting my mom's twelve-footer to the truck, and that's only after covering the entire lot and a dozen different *maybes*."

"Glad to help!" *So that's where you get that occasional perfectionist streak from.*

After the cutting process, Shane picked up the tree and walked it over to the counter, where hot cocoa added to the aromatic blend of sweet kettle corn and cinnamon wreaths.

"Anything else? By the way, my treat," he said.

"You don't have to do that because Auntie needs a little tree, too." She eyed the tiny trees by the cashier booth and picked up a two-foot replica of her larger choice. She placed it on the counter and said, "This will look adorable on her countertop."

"I got it," Shane said and dug for his wallet.

About to oppose his offer again, a family walked up behind them, prompting her to turn and face them.

Mateo's eyes bugged when he saw her.

Shane must have felt her energy because he spun around and wasted no time in quelling the awkwardness. "Hey Mateo. How's it going?" He held out his hand for a friendly shake.

That was cool! They could get through this brief encounter without issue.

While Shane and Mateo shook hands, Arista smiled at the mother and then talked to Matty. "Hey there, Matty! We met in the eye doctor's office. Do you remember me?"

Matty shied into his mother's hip, nodding slowly.

"Are you ready for Christmas?" Rather presumptuous of her, but it seemed a safe bet.

Matty smiled, nodded again, and emerged from his mother's grasp. "I want a turtle. I asked Santa for a turtle."

That sure hit a nerve. "You did? Very cool! I hope you get a turtle."

The cashier beckoned, and Shane took care of the transaction.

Seeing Matty's mother's unease, Arista wondered if she had been too forward with the boy. She gave her a friendly smile and turned back toward the counter.

"Your grandma has bad eyes like me, huh?" Matty said from behind her.

Arista put two fifties on the counter, then turned back. "She's actually my great aunt, but yes, she's having a little eye trouble." She felt Shane shove the bills into her satchel and snickered at his sneakiness.

"She sees ghosts like me, too, huh?" Matty said.

Unlike before, his mother did not interfere this time, and simply smiled down upon him with her hand cupping his shoulder.

"She has, and I have, too. I think lots of people do." She feigned a lowered voice and said, "They just don't talk about it."

Shane beckoned, his voice further away than she expected. As he toted the trees toward the truck, he gave a final goodbye holler to Mateo and his family.

Arista smiled at the parents. "He's really adorable! I hope you guys have a great Christmas! Bye, Matty!"

"You too!" Mateo and his wife said simultaneously as Matty waved goodbye.

"You need any help?" she asked, jogging up behind Shane.

Shane unlocked his doors with a click. "I got it. Just get your sexy butt in the truck."

She settled into the seat and, within moments, Shane got in and turned the engine, sending a blast of warm air onto their chilled faces. She yanked off her gloves and beanie and scratched at her itchy head.

"What kind of magickal ideas were you weaving into that little guy's head?"

"No weaving at all. If he has the gift, great! You don't want the little guy feeling like a freak because he thinks he's the only one who sees ghosts. You know … so, he doesn't feel alone in the world."

Shane gazed at her. He reached out his hand and cupped her cheek. "I've missed you."

"Me too," she said, moving in for an amorous taste of his kiss.

•   •   •

The drive back to Boulder Creek glowed with an orange tint from the vibrant setting sun. It cast an artistic spray of color upon the last patch of clear sky behind them, as they drove further beneath the slate gray nimbostratus. A sign of the approaching winter storm.

By the time they arrived in downtown Boulder Creek, the early darkness had set in, exacerbated by the brooding clouds. Still, the spirit of the season shined bright amongst their town shops. Presented as twinkling, colored lights and strings of cool-white-lit icicles, many of the eaves provided an oasis of festive cheer. Analina's Yule tree sat in the front window of Earth & Ocean, adorned with blinks of green and blue lights—the elements of her sun and moon signs.

The plentiful foot traffic this late in the day meant locals and visitors shopped to support the merchants leading up to the merry gift-giving holidays—Christmas, Hannukah, Kwanzaa, and Yule.

Finally, they pulled onto Hoot Owl Way, and an abundant fulfillment percolated within her from the day. "Thank you for our late lunch and for taking me to the lot today. I really had a great time."

"Of course." He reached for her hand.

She squeezed his hand and wondered if she felt the energy and freedom to re-embrace intimacy with him tonight. It would make for the perfect day.

Upon arriving at her cottage, Shane hoisted her six-foot tree onto his shoulder and brought it indoors, placing it in the prepared space by her front window. Perhaps she had intuited their date would lead to a tree.

Royal, knowing full well what Yuletide meant—natural scents brought indoors, dangling new toys and wads of tinsel to romp in—put himself in the center of festivities. While they fussed with placement of the tree, and dug into the box of ornaments, he sniffed individual branches and rubbed his upper lip with great enthusiasm. His territory.

"Oops! Sorry, Royal," Shane blurted when his man-foot biffed Royal's behind.

Realizing the risk of a good trampling, Royal disappeared under the branches.

The humans kept busy.

"Oh! I forgot about these!" Arista said, holding up thin wooden snowflakes. She placed them aside. Further, she rummaged. "Oooh! I *love* these!" She held up miniature besoms strung with a skinny red velvet ribbon and a small pentacle charm. "We didn't use our ornaments last year because we were in Sedona, so I've forgotten all about these newer ones."

Shane snickered at her giddiness while wrapping the tree in multi-colored lights.

"Uh-oh." She held up the pitiful remains of her hardened orange slices, shriveled and crumbling. "A little past their prime." She set those aside for discarding, then held up a garland of little pinecones. She sniffed them. Not an iota of spice remained from two years prior. "I'll oil these later, but we can put them on the tree now."

The decorating took some time. At last, she lifted the lid from the last box and pulled out an angel dressed in white satin with elegant, feathered wings and a metallic gold halo.

"An angel tree topper, huh?" Shane remarked.

"Yes. We always had an angel on top. Funny enough, angels are universal. For Catholic boys *and* witchy girls."

She held the emblem of grace, benevolence, and protection out to him.

"Me?"

"Yes, you add the finishing touch. Just be careful you don't step on Royal. He's still under there." She hunched over and caught sight of his spunky eyes peering from beneath the lowest branch.

Mew.

"Got it!" Shane said, gently setting the angel on the pointy tip of the adorned noble fir.

Once placed, they both stepped back and took in the finished product.

"Very nice!"

"Agreed!" Arista said, then turned to him for a quick kiss. When she felt the softness of his lips upon hers, she melted into his arms. Dearly, she had missed this passion. They tightened into each other's grasp. But something caused her to hesitate.

Shane sensed it, gave her a quick peck, and released her. "Okay, let's get this place tidied up." He started grabbing the tissue paper that had housed her ornaments and stuffed it all back into the box. "Where does this go?"

She felt a tinge of guilt for her hesitation. But *him* letting go first? Didn't he want her? *Play it off.* "This way."

She led him to her guest bedroom closet, avoided looking at her dad's picture, then back to the front room. With no sign of disappointment from him, she relaxed and plopped down on the couch. *Maybe now.* She gave a flirty smile and bit at her bottom lip.

Shane, still standing, announced, "So, I've had the perfect day, ending with that awesome reminder of your perfect kisses. I finally got *my* kiss, Royal." He peeked toward the bottom of the tree, prompting Arista to laugh. "But seriously, I know you're tired, and I've got to get home. We're holding a party for the kids tomorrow, and I have three projects to get done tonight. I hadn't planned to be gone so long." His eyes widened. "Don't get me wrong, I'm glad to be running behind." He pulled her up into his embrace.

Another round of sensuous kissing, and she considered enticing him to stay. Though, after he had just elaborated on his time constraints for the night, it could put him in an awkward position. Instead, she flashed him a wicked grin, nuzzled into his chest, and ran a solid stroke along his zipper, acknowledging his rising fantasies.

He chuckled.

She giggled.

Then he left.

CHAPTER 25
REACHING IN BLINDNESS

With an hour past Shane's departure, Arista sat with Royal in her lap and a cup of cardamon and spearmint tea in hand. She sipped the minty elixir and felt a rising calm in front of the colorful glow of twinkling lights. Settled comfort. She looked down at Royal, resting in a regal position, with his upper body on her thigh and the rest of his body tucked into the cushion.

Sensing her gaze, he peered up.

Mew.

Fitting effect on cue.

She closed her eyes and sunk into the memory of her day. Walking hand-in-hand along the wharf, the drive, the laughter, and the kisses. So many kisses. She felt a tinge of arousal. Should she? She giggled and tipped her cup's last sip of tea before wrapping up the night. No. She would wait for Shane and had already planned a grief ritual for tonight to cleanse her spirit. Better to schedule your release of sadness than have it attack you out of nowhere because you've paid no mind to it.

In front of her bedroom altar, Arista could smell the fir already permeating through her cottage. She lit a green candle scented with orange and tangerine and turned off all light. As she peeled off her clothes, she felt her sobering indoor temperature of sixty-three degrees. With the chill on her body, she centered herself, feeling her flesh pimple-up in response.

A little too cold. She grabbed her robe to continue. Her goddesses would understand the need for cover.

She went about her Healing Ritual. Found in Auntie's old grimoire, it talked of losing a loved one and recovery from the grief. Auntie had her share of the emotion throughout the years. The subtitle read—*After allowing an appropriate flow of tears, the time may come to break the habit of woe.*

Arista pulled forth her purple-and-white African violet, a dropper, and a small dipping bowl of moon water from November's Beaver Moon. She studied her dark-green fuzzy-leaved plant in its miniature royal-blue pot. Its emerging vibrant buds, no larger than a third of a pinkie-finger nail.

She felt the soil to ensure it could take more water. It could. With her dropper, she drew in the moon water. Then, she took a deep breath and began the tedious meditation. She envisioned the drip at the end as her own tear, a tear from her sadness at the loss of her mother. She released it to the soil, focusing on its effort to seep downward while she kept all other distracting thoughts at bay. Another drop symbolized the heartache of watching her father killed. Another drop with focus, breathing into her plant while the water journeyed into its soil. With the memory still present, again she released a drop, watching its ball at the end of the dropper free fall into the soil and dissipate.

When she first began this ritual soon after their deaths, her own tears flowed in abundance, along with the water droplets. However, over time, she wept less and less. For the past two weeks, no tears came at all, but the sadness still visited. Therefore, on it went for every sadness that came to mind. Focused. Slow. Intended. One sorrow, one drop, one breath, repeat. Concentrated effort until no water remained.

Next, she plucked three Sodalite pebbles out of a tiny plastic baggie and set them in the pot where a dozen others were already present. She would continue this until the crystals of marbled-blue, white, and black hid all signs of the dirt. Afterward, if she still felt grief, she would either re-approach it with her therapist or perform the ritual with an all-new plant.

A sense of accomplishment filled her as she slid the little pot away from the edge and tucked the pebble baggie in her drawer. Come morning, she would re-situate the plant in her kitchen, but for tonight, it would sit upon her altar.

Ready to carve love runes upon her stout, pink pillar candle, she picked up her athame and gazed into its Moonstone's iridescent blue fire.

Mew.

Royal seldom initiated conversation. She turned to see him studying her bedroom entrance with focused curiosity. Tilting his head at an unseen-to-her attraction.

A sudden startle from Royal preceded an energy that entered the room.

Her stomach dropped, and she gasped aloud, "Hello?"

She could feel the thick air. A lingering presence awaiting her acknowledgement.

It was him! Great-Great had returned. After months of no encounter, she had forgotten the intensity and creep factor.

Her alter witch bells jingled, the energy now upon her.

She felt a rising fear and just wanted the moment to pass.

Royal stared at the space directly in front of her, his eyes growing larger, his body tensing, ready to spring away from trouble.

It had to be Great-Great reestablished in her abode, especially after Mateo had returned the case. Right?!

Her candle flickered upon her altar.

"Uh—"

The flame extinguished. Utter darkness.

She squealed in a controlled high-pitch, knowing he was right there! With his energy hovering in front of her, she wanted to push him away. Then again, what if she actually touched some … *thing*?! That would freak her out even more!

With her athame in one hand, she turned and fumbled around for the lighter on her altar.

She heard Royal bound off the bed, land on the floor with a thud, and tear off down the hall.

"Great!" she barked out in defiance, mainly to show Great-Great she was not afraid of him. But she was. She really, really was!

At last, the lighter! She grabbed it and flicked it on.

SHOCK!

She stood nose-to-nose with the apparition—a wrinkled face and vacant eye sockets peering right through her.

A glorious scream left her mouth! She shoved her hands toward the visage, sending her athame and the lighter to the ground, their scattered effects clattering upon the floor. Again, she stood in utter darkness, feeling the pressure of his presence around her. She dropped to the floor and fumbled around her, again grasping in the darkness for her lighter! Had he not been in her path, the bedside lamp would be so much more comforting.

Her hand touched metal! Desperate, she flicked her lighter and barged toward the awaiting wick.

As a small glow illuminated her room, she steadied. If he had intended to kill her, take her, pulverize her, she would have been dust by now. Settling her nerves in the warm candlelight, she took a breath and braced herself for further interaction. With stuttering words, she asked him, "So …you're back, huh?"

With the wick's flame growing, she looked around her room. Nothing. Seeing the coast clear, a shudder of post-anxiety shot through her, and she vented the angst with an abrupt, throaty holler.

"Jeeeezuz!" she said, surprising herself. She looked into the hallway again and huffed out a relieving breath. "Well, now I see why people say that! It expels the terror right out of you."

She went over to her bedside table and flicked on her sunflower lamp, adding a generous splash of warm yellow to the candle's effect.

She peeked into the hallway. Stillness.

She went over to her bed. Exasperated, she dropped her butt down to her floor and leaned against the mattress. She forgot how freaked out these little encounters left her, and this had to be the scariest one of the bunch. She'd never seen him! Even worse, her tolerance for the paranormal had lowered during her sabbatical, and knowing of his murderous past didn't help either.

"Thanks, Great-Great! It's nice to have you back, but please be easy on me. I've had a lot go down since the last time we visited."

A flash of blue brilliance caught her eye. At the base of her side table, her Blue Moonstone had dislodged from her athame and sat alone. She remembered the clatter and looked under her bed to find the athame. Both stone and blade secured, she scoffed, "Great."

Easy fix, though, as Auntie and her jewelry glue would have it repaired in no time.

A tinkling sound came from the kitchen.

She listened.

Royal at the food dish.

"I'm glad you can eat at a time like this!" she hollered.

She arose, set her athame and its crystal upon her altar and heaved out another cleansing breath. Settled back into her skin, she realized *home* included these adrenalizing moments *and* the sweet happenings with Shane. Love, joy, and sudden frights—all part of her return to normal life.

CHAPTER 26
COMICAL HUMAN BODY

Sitting in the moist air of the brick-lined patio strung with illuminated globe lights, Shane took another bite of his Bourbon Burger with its bacon-caramelized onion goo, creating a savory sensation for his palate.

"Thanks for the invite. This is frickin delicious. I've never been here," Evan said, scarfing down a Prime Rib Dip with pepper jack cheese and sriracha mayo.

"Yeah, Dom and I've eaten here a few times. I'm moving in with him for a while."

"Oh, yeah?" Evan raised his eyebrows, surprised.

"Yeah, but even that's temporary, assuming things go well."

"How so?"

"I want to get a place with Riss. For all I know, she'll want to live at her house, but I can't just invite myself to move in."

Evan nodded, unable to speak with another mouth-filling bite.

"I'd ask her now, but it's not the right time."

Evan nodded, then swallowed. "Yeah, she's been through the wringer this year."

"Serious. So, are you and Bree planning to get married?"

"Don't you remember? My mom had me put a ring on that right away."

Shane gave a humored snort. Yes, he remembered and expected nothing less from Evan's mother. "*When* are you getting married?"

"Probably another year. She throws me planning questions every once in a while. Why? Are you thinking about asking Arista to marry you?" Before Shane could answer, Evan's eyes flickered toward the entrance over Shane's shoulder. "Oh wow, small world."

"What is it?"

"That blonde me and Maddie saw you with just walked in with some guy."

Shane looked over his shoulder and caught the woman's eye, prompting her to wave. He smiled and nodded back at her.

He turned back to Evan, unamused. "Marissa," he announced under his breath and took a bite of burger. He would not approach her. He refused to chance it again, uncertain if someone would perceive it the wrong way.

Evan spoke under his breath. "Have to admit, she's pretty hot. I can see why Maddie flipped out. Bree would, too."

"Maybe. I don't see it. And I'm not going anywhere near the gray zone. I'm barely back in good graces with Riss and don't need some lurking eye to misconstrue my actions."

Evan snickered before consuming another hulking bite.

Moments later, the tanned honey and her hulky boyfriend in his skin-tight, red tee containing a bulging chest and arms stood beside their table.

"Hey, guys. Hope we're not interrupting. We won't stay long. Shane, I want you to meet Zeke."

"S'up, man," Shane said, offering a fist bump. "That's Evan."

Evan nodded out of courtesy.

While Zeke reciprocated the fist bump, it came accompanied with an indifferent expression and a flex of pec.

"Shane's the one I told you about who helped me see your side of the issue," Marissa said, rubbing her guy's arm.

"Oh! Right on, man! Thanks!" he said, dropping his tough guy act and enlivening into a congenial smile.

"Yeah, no problem. I think we all wish we had that little angel on our girl's shoulder rep-ping for us when she's miffed."

A round of laughter further lightened the mood.

"And I gotta say, your girl gave me good advice, too," Shane said, then looked at Marissa. "To not give up."

"Are you guys back together, too?" Marissa asked, hinging on a positive response.

"We are," he said, unable to withhold his smile.

She squealed in delight. "Awesome! And we all lived happily ever after."

Zeke gave a goodbye nod as they ventured to their own table.

Shane watched the poster-perfect couple walk away, thankful to have good karma in the world. *Good karma?* He snickered to himself. Just another sign of Arista's influence.

Soon after they finished their meals, he and Evan headed out to find treasures for each of their beloveds.

"I'm surprised you don't want to go to San Jose. Probably better selection," Evan suggested.

"Are you kidding me? You think Arista would want me to give my business to an urban jungle over her local merchants? Especially on a gift for her?? I'm smarter than that, Evan Navarro."

"Ha! Touché!"

•   •   •

Sheriff Michaels listened to Manny's phone ring for the fifth time in two days, followed by a drop into voicemail. No need to leave a third message. He'd drive by later. He stood up and eyed the data on his whiteboard, an organizational chart of sorts with familiar names.

Scritch. Scritch. Scritch.

His blue dry-erase marker smelled like marshmallows as he jotted down the names of two neighbors who had frequented Manny's road during the two-week period prior to finding the hand. Patty had run a preliminary report on the data, noting that the camera recorded Harold Brimley's and Iris Ardino's presence during the wee hours. He knew Harold well—a big galoot full of piss and alcohol, with a past rap sheet of drunk in public, disorderly conduct, and a few drug charges. A pain in the ass, but as far as felonies, he read clean.

On paper, Iris had been a lifelong resident in Boulder Creek, and her age ran past the mid-seventies. She had a clean record, no photos on file, and … well … she was in her mid-seventies. What sort of trouble could she get into?

He lay down his marker. There had to be someone else, or they needed to go back further in time.

He reconsidered his flippant conclusion about Iris, remembering that Bethie was in her seventies, and trouble had swarmed around her for a couple of years now. He shouldn't underestimate the orneriness and go-getting attitude of his elders. In fact, with the town so small and Bethie also being native, he wondered if she knew Iris. He scanned the extended database, looking for a clear photo, found Iris's name, and selected the file.

A pixelated photo transformed into a crisp image of the same woman from the store that Rossy had bumped into, just as he had suspected when he had scanned the surveillance videos. He snorted at the irony. This seemed all too obvious, but they needed more evidence. Doubtful, he'd be lucky enough to catch the murder weapon in her hands. Can't get that when you've fed someone to pigs.

He gathered his gear and set out for a round of interviews.

"… yeah, gutted and gory!" Patty said, the tail-end of some story she relayed to her coworkers.

"What's gutted and gory?" the sheriff inquired, stoic and unflinching. He'd seen way worse in real life.

Patty whirled around. "Hey! Yeah, you may want to check in with your SCPD buddies. Sounds like they found two victims in a yacht harbor condo with their livers and hearts missing."

"Hmph. Any leads?"

"The complex's video camera only showed a solid white blur. So, pretty much, no."

"Gotcha. Well, I'm following up on the case off Bear Creek. Will be out rest of day." It surprised him that the freakish sideshow Patty spoke of happened outside his vicinity and felt relieved that the gruesome mess belonged to another agency for a change.

Buckled in his cruiser, he realized Bethie had not returned his call. *That* did not feel right—a disinterest in Fergus's whereabouts, plus his very probable demise? Such a different reaction from her former responses of an aghast expression, probing questions, and a thirst for more knowledge. Nope! Only crickets.

However, knowing of her eyesight issue, he knew health had a way of superseding other matters.

After an efficient drive on the slick highway, the sheriff made a left onto Manny's road, hitting the rain-flooded puddles along the dirt road and further along to his first stop, Harold.

Harold answered his door, and his impression of the man remained—as wily as they came. He smelled of a brewery at ten in the morning, released a subdued belch at least twice during the interview, and, post-interview, booted his raggedy canine out of the way as he walked them back toward the door.

Still, Harold gave earnest answers to all impromptu interview questions and additional insight into Manny's questionable past, including rumored mafia ties in the 70s. Further, his body language revealed nothing but forthright cooperation—clear eyes, save for the blood shot effect of alcohol, and no fidgeting. It did not put him in the clear, but neither did it deepen suspicion.

Next, he drove to the older lady's house. Pulling into her driveway, a clowder of cats scattered in all directions. He rechecked his notes. *Iris.* He'd remember that. "Like the flower."

With a light mist dampening his jacket, he walked toward the house. The home's walkway felt imposing because of the huge blacked-out circular window on her second story that loomed above him. Ignoring it, he approached and knocked. Waiting for an answer, he scanned the ground, skirting the house, noting the long, narrow shoe prints outlined in mud. They could very well be a match for the one he found at Manny's. Interesting that this shoeprint seemed to haunt him.

Though, no harm in neighbors knowing and visiting one another's house.

After a quiet minute, he knocked again. With no car in the driveway nor answer at the door, she must be running errands. Maybe the soup kitchen or Bridge Club, like his own mother. What else does your average seventy-plus-year-old woman do when they aren't home? No, Bethie did not count. She was seventy-plus going on thirty.

After tucking his business card into the doorjamb, Sheriff Michaels inspected the shoe print. About ten inches. He pulled out his cell, snapped a photo, and forwarded it to his desktop email address.

He continued his unofficial inspection, looking around her deck. Odd matchings of cushions to chairs, pieces of a broken glass end-table piled in the corner, and a large row of empty planter pots.

The pots. Yes, that caught his eye.

He strolled over to see the resulting flora, sending a gray cat scurrying for other territory. Instead of suspected marijuana rampant in this part of the country, he found a single remaining leaf left for a wintery death. He picked it up and studied the dried semblance of a mandrake plant. Bethie, during her time as his childhood babysitter, had taught him much about this particular flowering plant. Sometimes, they would sit down with colored pencils and draw them as well. She also told him that while the root could look like a comical human body, consuming the product could prove deadly.

The pots took on a different aspect, especially since the loosened soil at each of their centers proved a recent harvest had taken place. He took out another business card, folded it in half, and slid the abandoned leaf into the makeshift miniature file folder as potential evidence. He tucked it in his pocket.

This *innocent* elder sure held a certain shadiness—wore similar shoes to prints at the crime scene, had poisonous plant care as a hobby, and had repeatedly popped up. He laughed at the audacity that her spilled cleaning supplies could be proof of a crime scene clean up, but chalked that one up to mere fastidiousness. Everyone has cleaning supplies, right?

Still, not enough to act upon … yet. He turned to leave, again noticing the overhead window. Proceeding, he kept his eyes upon it, hoping—or not hoping—to catch any sudden movements. It wouldn't shock him to discover a body inside that room. "Hah."

Once at his cruiser, he paused for a generous spritz of grapefruit-scented hand sanitizer. He rubbed his hands briskly together, ridding himself of any toxic residue from the mandrake leaf in case there was such a thing.

He had one more stop—Manny Whelan.

•   •   •

The first thing the sheriff noted upon his arrival at Manny's house was the same work truck with all its fencing materials he had seen before—in the video clip from the neighbor's door camera and during the initial discovery of Fergus's forearm.

The two workers were busy shoveling in the pigpen. They threw a quick glance as he parked his car.

"Mornin'!" he barked out with authority.

While one continued his work, the other hurried over to him.

"Is Mr. Whelan around?"

"No, sir, I think he's out of town. He sent us a text that he was leaving for a while. So, we're feeding his hogs and doing chores."

"Did he say when he'd return?"

"No sir," he said, his answers coming out quick and respectful.

"When did he send that text?"

"Couple days ago, and he's not answering our calls."

"Is that so?" He looked at Manny's front door. "Excuse me."

The worker hurried back into the pen, where he mumbled to his cohort, who continued shoveling.

A measured approach was key. Manny was not a suspect. Not necessarily, but he should have stuck around during the investigation. Nothing looked more suspicious than leaving town unannounced.

The door endured his heavy knock. "Mr. Whelan?"

No answer. No sound of movement within the home. He looked through the tall, thin glass pane to the door's right.

KNOCK! KNOCK!

"Mr. Whelan, Sheriff's Department. You in there?"

He jiggled the knob. Locked.

With the prevalent snorting of pigs behind him, he looked back to find the workers staring at him. One smiled, the other nodded, then both returned to their shoveling.

He turned back to the door. Welfare check time? Manny could have fallen or hurt himself. The sheriff made a round of his house, peering in through each accessible window. It seemed odd. A settled, aged farmer who was part of an active murder investigation skips town? He had no prior issues with the law other than Harold's alleged accusations and, until his disappearance, had been superbly cooperative.

After seeing nothing of interest within the single-story home, aside from the cluttered domestic mess, he considered all clear for now. No need to bust down a door today.

Further, he walked toward the pens and searched the area where he had seen the long, narrow shoe print on his last visit. It was gone, covered by the treads of fresh work boots and wheelbarrow rubber.

For today, nothing remained to be done, so he bid adieu to the workers after noting the time and date of his visit.

While departing, he felt an uneasy pang of unfinished business. He wanted to shake it off, but no denying something stood awry. First task back at the office was to look at crime scene photos again and research Iris a little more.

Driving onward, he realized this constant gnawing of doubt had become customary ever since the whole serial killer debacle started two years ago. One problem after another had plagued his community. And its centralized plot came back to one person—Bethie's grandniece. It all started with the Holmes woman, Arista's friend, murdered by Wallish. It escalated with Arista, a victim in her own right, taking Wallish out. Fast forward past a year, and Arista's father was murdered by the hands of a goon who looked like a distorted version of your classic surfer. And now, an extremity of Arista's uncle, the goon's boss, found its resting place beside a pigpen.

Nearing his turn onto Highway 9, he imagined the rooting swine within their pen. Now, *their* owner had disappeared. The possibilities spun forth in his mind. Nothing surprised him anymore. Some far-fetched association between this mess and the heartless and liverless victims in Santa Cruz would not even surprise him.

He snorted aloud. "The shit doth deepen."

CHAPTER 27
THEIR PLANNED RETALIATION

"Welcome to Earth & Ocean," Arista greeted from behind the counter.

The pair of new customers remained huddled close together just inside the door. Around her age, something familiar rang out about them, but she did not recall ever seeing them in the store.

"Fank yuh, miss," said the male, with his strong Cockney accent.

What a friendly sounding voice from the man who looked about five-foot-ten, with dark brown skin. He scanned the shop before his female friend, the pale white yang to him, pointed to something on the bottom shelf. If Arista was correct, that would have been the individually packaged High John the Conqueror root.

His woman friend sported a boyish cut of short chestnut brown hair, complete with a splash of freckles across her nose. Her clothes were so similar to his, save the color and size, they could have easily swapped their threads and be dressed the same way—tan-knit beanie, casual white tee, flannel, and jeans.

They moved out of her line of vision at the end of the aisle, murmuring to one another.

She felt her positive impression of the man's greeting fleeting. Why were they staying practically hidden from her, discussing something, yet no longer looking at the merchandise? With her ability to aura read MIA, she softened her gaze anyway and looked in their vicinity. Nothing. Strange how abilities ebb and flow.

"We're closing out our dragon figurines this month if you two are interested," Arista announced, hoping to steer them out of her blind spot.

The woman peeked around the corner at her, then, without responding, led her guy friend to the furthest nook of the shop from the register. They wedged themselves into the book area where, again, she nor the store camera could see them in full. More mumbling.

Maybe a couple's spat?

She listened.

No, this sounded like plotting. These two had an agenda. She could feel it. So, she centered herself with a diplomatic approach and stood up to go chitchat with them.

As she left the counter, the couple noticed and hustled out of the shop, making no eye contact.

Potential shoplifters? If they had taken a book, it was a twenty-dollar loss, worst-case scenario. Unless they took more than one. She walked over to the shelves and scanned the items. Everything appeared as she had left it—solidly stacked and organized. Odd behavior.

She looked out the window and saw them in an exuberant argument, complete with demonstrative hand gestures. Couple's spat.

Wait a minute! As an inkling struck her, they disappeared down a side street. She pondered the thought while returning to the counter. Up close, she did not catch it, but seeing them further away, they sure looked like the couple who had been stalking her house.

A minute later, she watched the dark green van drive past the window. Its engine in full whine, and within it, the elusive couple, wearing their indicative tan beanies.

She let out a gasp and negated all thought of the man's friendly accent. Their stalking had escalated—first, her home, and now they had found her work. She longed for the sense of safety again, but the claws of criminality had left her with too many scars. The pursuit had heightened. She felt trapped and exposed, and because she was the only one holding the shop, all she could do was stay there and endure it.

She walked back to the register, taking deep breaths to calm herself. She closed her eyes. After a couple cycles, she found her peace, listening to the gurgling of the store's Fortuna fountain. As she was about to open her eyes, the hummingbird vision consciously popped into her mind. She recalled the urgency of her vision and the hasty pursuit toward Auntie's house.

She shook her head, frustrated by the constant prick of danger coming from all around her, seemingly all the time. She felt a lump within her chest swelling, affecting her breath. Remembering her psyche's advice to breathe through the discomfort, an effect of her stress, she tried another round of breathwork.

Still, the vision, the strangers, and all her losses from previous dangers swarmed her. "Ugh!" she vented aloud. "The serial killer was not after Auntie either, but he pile-drove through her anyway!"

The chime from a customer at the door startled her, and his look indicated he had seen her outburst. She gathered herself and applied a friendly greeting.

He relaxed, and asked, "Yeah, just wondering if you guys carry dragon's blood incense?"

"Right this way," she said, temporarily blocking the unease from the duo's relentless pursuit. She didn't want to believe it, but the only explanation that made sense was they were Fergus's followers, and their planned retaliation would soon follow.

• • •

"Iris, what a delightful surprise."

Bethie held open her screen. Without supernatural business on the line, it was a pleasant change to have Iris come by for a quick hello. After her earnest help with Soonsil's transition, the threat of the curse tablet had lessened. Instead, the amount of goodwill between them had begun to grow.

"With all our emergency get-togethers, it's becoming easier to remember your address."

Bethie chuckled. "Can I get you some tea?"

"No, I'm just stopping by. I was in town and thought you might like some apples." Iris reached into her tote and pulled out a clear plastic bag full of plump green apples. "They were my last harvest of the season. I picked them a couple weeks back, and they have kept well in my refrigerator, but I've got so many I cannot possibly finish them all myself."

"Oh, that's wonderful. Thank you! Looks like I'll be making a pie tonight."

Iris emitted a subdued cackle of appreciation.

"Would you like to sit in the garden for a spell?" Bethie asked.

"Thank you again, but I must be off. I just wanted to stop by and say *hi*." Iris drew in a breath and released it. "Bethie, we've known each other for such a long time, and I honestly hope that we can get past the ugliness of our family's wrongdoings."

"That sounds like a great idea."

Iris cast a big smile from coral-painted lips before smothering Bethie in a controlling goodbye hug that felt a lot like Pearl's.

Bethie waved until Iris had driven out of sight and carried the bag into her kitchen. She stared at the pert apples, remembering Snow White and the queen's wicked gift. But the pleasant fruity scent from the opened bag set her at ease. She laughed.

"Bethie Dandelion Spiritbrite, you are being downright paranoid. For goodness' sake, this was a kind gesture."

She washed each round, lovely-scented apple and set them on a clean white terrycloth towel. She selected a flawless specimen, sliced it in half and removed its core. After cutting six equal pieces, she held up a wedge, gave it one last scrutinizing eye, and crunched down on it.

Sweet, tart and firm. She relished the flavor and imagined the effort of making the pie. The crust would have to be homemade, too.

Just then, a subtle movement from the yard caught her attention. She glanced out the window and spotted the tail end of a large bird disappearing into the trees.

"Margaret?" she called.

Probably, but it flew off too soon to tell.

CHAPTER 28
REPEATED SHADY DRIVE-BYS

The drizzle turned to rain as Shane exited his truck. He kept his fruit-punch-soaked gym bag at arms-distance from his white Polo shirt. During PE Class, a quick refresher for an eight-year-old turned into a shower of red and sticky when the young boy tripped in his vicinity. Luckily, his bag took the brunt. He looked down at his black joggers. Not a speck to see, but it was there. He needed a shower.

"Shane!" his mother bellowed from her office.

"What?" he answered, barely stepping in the door.

"I need Arista's address."

"Give me a minute."

What was with all the yelling through their house these days?

What was that aroma?! Sticky pants, loud bellowing, and now a spicy sweet autumn scent! His stomach called dibs for attention.

He walked to the kitchen to identify the fresh baked goods that wafted through the air.

Again, Magda hollered, "Shane, I'm right in the middle of addressing the invites."

Her drop-everything demand could wait.

He confirmed his assumption of homemade treats. The spongy brown gingerbread loaf glistened in a clear glaze and had delectable, candied ginger nodules bulging from its sides. He dropped his bag to the floor, grabbed a paper towel, and helped himself. When the warm, cakey treat met his mouth, he could not help but devour the entire slice in only a few bites. He grabbed an individual milk carton from the fridge and gulped it down.

"Shane! Please!" his mother yelled again, with a building annoyance.

He grunted, cut another generous slice, and walked to her office to find it transformed into an elven workshop. Two large boxes wrapped in candy cane paper sat on the floor. On her desk sat ten presents wearing foiled red or forest green paper, tied in gold-glittered ribbons and bows. Beside her ergonomic keyboard, a disorganized pile of sturdy sealed cards hosted a small holly-printed stamp in their upper right corner. The one in question, front and center of her pen.

A thin, unamused line had taken her usual sugary smile. "Honey, I need that address," she insisted.

"Why?" he asked, swallowing his bite.

She scoffed. "Obviously, with Daddy and I throwing a Christmas party this year, I'm inviting Arista. You want her to come, right?"

"Of course!"

"Will she come?"

"I think so."

"Okay, then I need the damn address," she said, with a gritted smile, and her pen holding steady at the envelope.

After noting his data, she made her task request as predicted. "Could you please take the presents to the tree?"

"Mmm-huh." A mouthful of her homemade gingerbread neutralized his irritation at her entitlement. She was a pain in the ass, but she sure possessed delectable baking skills.

"Are you going by the post office tomorrow?" she asked, setting Arista's invitation atop the stack, then arranging the lot of them to neatness.

"I hadn't planned on it."

"Fine, I'll just mail these myself. Do you have a minute to talk?"

Oh boy, here it comes. He nodded and took another bite of gingerbread.

"Have you given any more thought to your plans you mentioned the other day? School or moving out?"

"A little."

"Shane, I hope I didn't dissuade you from your goals. Sweetie, I'd never want to crush your dreams. I just want you to think everything through."

"I will." He hoped she did not ruin her status of good will earned from the gingerbread.

"I know you're prudent, but you've been very sheltered."

Please stop. His head sagged.

"I can see I'm losing your attention."

"I'm listening," he said, peeved. What did she expect, an expression of awe at the words coming out of her mouth?

"Just make wise decisions, okay? You've been on a good track with your career. Working at the school seems to be very rewarding for you."

"It is."

"Also, as you age and take a wife … it's important you choose wisely."

"I plan to." *Is she dissing Arista?*

Her eyes stayed fixed on him, but she said nothing.

Outside, a rumble of thunder accompanied the onset of a drenching rainfall.

"Wow, it's really coming down out there," she said.

"Anything else … *Mother*?" Just in case that was a diss against Arista, calling her *mother* should convey his perturbance.

She twisted her mouth. "Oh, just go! Here's an invitation for your own reference. Please be available that night … two weeks away. And make sure your red button-down is clean. If not, drop it in the laundry."

"Got it," he said, taking the festive cardstock while biting a hunk of gingerbread.

Instead of getting mad at her, he decided that her backing off showed a rise in respect for his decisions. Finally! Arista was his girl, period. Never could, nor would, there be another. Letting her know he would move out right after the holidays was a dragon to slay on another day.

Now, about that shower.

He emptied his gym bag, dropped it in the washer, and headed for his room. As he got undressed, Arista's ringtone beckoned him.

·   ·   ·

The December rain poured heavily outside Arista's window, dousing nature with life-giving nourishment. And she loved it! So much so that she considered herself a storm witch ... amongst a variety of other types. The late afternoon's solid gray sky and the tinkling sounds of her various wind chimes added beautiful notes in the wind. Calming, with a dash of the right kind of spooky from an occasional creak within her cottage.

With her indoor temp set high for the occasion and her pre-ritual cup of warm cranberry, vanilla, and cinnamon black tea adding internal warmth, she donned a slinky forest-green silk chemise and sat comfortably upon her small bedroom rug. After procrastinating Analina's instruction too long, she finally held the borrowed Benitoite in her palm and readied herself to contemplate its energy.

Steadying her breathing, she held up the specimen, rotating it to catch dazzling flickers of reflective light on the irregular blue crystals clumped around the white host. She had never looked up that word ... what the old miner had called it. Firefringe? Whatever.

She settled into lotus pose, carefully cupped the fragile crystal, and inhaled, focusing on the weight of the gem. So lightweight, it brought the serenity of soothing, fresh-fallen rain, perfectly matching the day's audial ambiance.

Her shoulders relaxed, and she felt the stone's metaphysical vibration flow through her arms and straight into her heart. In her tranquility, she laid back on her rug, placed the soles of her feet together, and centered this newly discovered magickal source between her brows upon a small piece of blue silk, careful not to let fragments of its matrix crumble into her eyes. She brought her arms above her head on the floor and met index fingers and thumbs together, maintaining movement fluidity in order to avoid having to reposition the stone. She called it her Triple Diamond Goddess Pose. Unhurried in the process, she basked in the sensation of breath and crystal.

As she floated in quietude, familiarizing herself with the crystal's influence, a recognizable reaction followed. A hummingbird materialized before her inner eye. It flitted about her kitchen window, then flew beyond her hedge. Its urgency prompting her toward Auntie's cottage. She set out, rushing behind the little bird, with a presence catching up to her.

The stone started to slide. Aware of the valuable piece tumbling from her forehead, she caught it and quickly brought it into view. Still intact.

Royal sat at her feet. When their eyes met, he casually strolled toward the door.

"Was that amusing for you, sir?"

His only response was to turn and walk away, allowing for a full gander at his stark white butt against silky black fur.

Arista returned to lotus pose and accepted the unsettled feeling. No more serial killer. No more Fergus. Just a mysterious couple, and possibly Iris. The stone had returned her peace, and she felt more objective to her predicament. With Iris, Auntie relayed that she had put earnest effort forth to deliver deliciously ripe apples, which had proven quite delicious.

Unexpectedly, she heard the crunch of her pea gravel as someone pulled into her driveway. She could swear she heard the whine of the green van's engine. However, they killed the motor too quickly to tell.

She lifted from the floor, set her Benitoite upon her altar, and peeked out her bedroom door, down the hallway toward her yard.

Shock! Through her front door glass, she could see the strangers and their van. No longer satisfied with the street view, the couple had boldly pulled into her driveway. Home alone, she felt vulnerable and knew this ominous timing, right after her hummingbird vision, meant trouble. Fergus *had* sent them!

She rushed to her phone to call Auntie. No answer.

While throwing on sweats, she peeked through the window again.

A rumble of thunder accompanied the pouring rain as the couple exited the van wearing dark, oversized rain capes and hoods. A shocking sense came upon her—they worked with the dead! Somehow, Fergus had called upon them, and they had come for revenge!

The male reached inside the back of the vehicle and withdrew a long black case. A rifle case! He gave it to the female, and she walked toward the door while he grabbed—

Arista could not bear to look. Frightened with death upon her again, she had to get help!

When Shane answered her call, she blurted her plea. "There's people in my driveway … the stalkers … they're coming to my door. Shane, please hurry, they have a gun!" she cried. She could not go through this again.

"Call 9-1-1. I'll be right there!"

She disconnected just as the female laid the rifle case down on her patio chair and unzipped the long, sweeping zipper.

Her heart raced as she hurried to the far back bedroom.

KNOCK! KNOCK!

Royal bolted through the door to join her, seeking shelter under the bed.

His fright triggered her even more. She lost her breath, and a flush of heat came upon her, traveling through her torso, her arms, and legs. An instant sweat covered her. She gasped, trying to regain the rhythm of her breath, but hyperventilation captured her. She could only breathe in … in … in!

And hot. So, so hot! The film of sweat thickened upon her. She felt dowsed in wet heat and stripped off her sweatshirt as the ringing grew louder in her ears. The dread gripped her, as her heart felt a beat away from bursting. All would end in this moment, and she had no control over it.

Hopeless and gasping, she collapsed to the ground. Her inner battle now surpassed her fear of the lingering couple. Suffocation. Unable to breathe and fading away. Dying with no one to help. She grasped at the floor. Any measure to hold on! To stay conscious. To breathe again. The room blurred and the high pitch grew within her ears as panic and anxiety swallowed her whole.

Above her. Her dad. His picture. On the small dresser.

She focused on his face in its rustic wooden frame, as she heaved for oxygen.

He was smiling. Holding her and smiling.

With her head feeling a foot thick, Arista felt the first sign of exhalation and released a quick puff. His face. His signature pine scent. Another puff released. Her breathing slowed while studying his face. *Inhale*—the happiness in his eyes. Ex*hale*—his arm draped around her. In and out, her breath cooperated. She whimpered from his rescue, tears in her eyes.

KNOCK! KNOCK!

She heard the knock, but his picture held her. In it, she looked happy, too. Steadily, her heart slowed. Each beat a heavy yet manageable pound within her chest. A flush of tears filled her eyes from her frustration.

Slowly, she sat up and leaned in exhaustion against the wall. Exasperated from her panic attack, she sobbed into her hands, overwhelmed by the loss of self-control. How long could she go on like this?

While the initial problem remained, their knocking held no effect. She would stay right here. In the room. With her dad. She exhaled again, calmly dialed 9-1-1, and reported her invaders. All while they continued murmuring, now outside her back window.

The rain fell harder, making her unable to hear the couple strategizing with one another. She dared not look outside lest they see her. Against the wall, her knees to her chest, she rested her head in her hands. Crying without tears, she wiped away the sweat and rubbed her sticky eyes. Help would be there soon. Until then, she would focus on the invaluable ability to breathe.

Shane's truck arrived in grand form—a grumble of big-block engine and the crunching of pea gravel beneath huge, treaded tires.

The couple stopped mumbling and headed toward the front of the house.

What if they hurt Shane?!

She launched into the hall toward her bedroom, only to remember that she had taken her athame to Auntie's for repair of its cabochon. To the kitchen, she ran and grabbed a butcher knife. She could not let him get hurt.

However, when she reached the front door, she discovered a very unexpected sight. Shane was talking with the couple and kept nodding as if understanding a new subject of study. He did not look worried at all. Then he shook the guy's hand!

She stepped away from the door and struggled with a deep breath.

No, they were tricking him!

Cautiously, she peeked again to see the rain lessen to a heavy drizzle, its drips from the downpour tapping on her glass, and the strangers and Shane still in a light-hearted conversation.

Shane saw her through the window and yelled loud enough for her to hear. "Riss, it's okay. Come out."

She balked at the thought. No energy remained for socializing, and she needed to hose off from the drench of panic she had just endured.

The female saw her, too. She raised a long, thin device and said, "It's a mic. No a gun. I'm so sorry ta scare ye like that!" The words came in a Gaelic accent of some sort.

Arista held up her index finger in a gesture of delay, then walked to the back of the house to bring herself back to earth. The innocent mistake made her want to cry even more. Instead, she scoffed at her irrational meltdown and took another deep breath. What the hell was happening to her? Was she going to end up committed?

After a quick splash of water on her face and a wipe of her soft towel, she gained her courage to re-approach the door. As she walked onto the porch, she felt a slight annoyance from the nonchalance awaiting her. She almost had a heart attack, and, questionably, the panic attack was even more miserable!

Yet, it wasn't their fault. She had catastrophized an innocent situation with unsettled drama from the past two years.

"Ah'm Caitlin," the woman said in her accent with a little wave.

Arista softened her expression and walked down her steps to meet them.

Her male friend nodded with a smile.

Caitlin introduced him. "This is Gene, and we're following up oan a lead that yer house is haunted."

Gene tapped on the huge camera upon his shoulder. "Soz for de scare, Miss."

Shane put his arm around Arista and gave her a reassuring squeeze. "This is Arista. She's the owner of the house. But she's been through a lot." He looked down at her and smiled. "You up for this?"

Not really, but she appreciated the consideration. "So, what—"

Caitlin launched into her spiel. "We run a ghost-hunting podcast. We travel the world doing stories oan supernatural encounters, and we saw a story oan oor network of underground informants that mentioned Boulder Creek. So, we've tracked … er, found ye here. We weren't sure if it wis ye in the store the other day, but today we found oor courage to knock. Figured all the equipment would prove we're legit. Dae yae mind if we interview ye fur oor podcast?"

Are you kidding me?! I thought you were going to kill me! Arista wanted to be gracious and was *so* thankful it was all a big misunderstanding, but …

A red flash preceded Sheriff Michaels pulling into her driveway.

Shane took the lead and jogged over to his cruiser.

In the distance, she heard him elaborate the story. When she looked back at Caitlin, she remained riveted on the answer regarding an interview.

Arista sighed. It was too much. "I'm sorry, but I'm really—"

Caitlin persisted. "We won't take much of yer time, ah promise. And it's fur a good cause. Mainly to keep us fed oan mince and tat'ies. Work in this arena can be sparse."

Ouch.

Gene walked up beside his girl. "Please, Aristah."

Shane hastened back from his conversation. "The sheriff needs to know you're okay."

A glance of concern greeted her when she looked the lawman's way. She waved at him, hoping that was enough.

He gave a stern look and motioned her over to his car with a flick of his finger. Once she reached him, he sounded sincere. "You had me worried, Miss Kelly. You sure you're okay?"

"Yes, I'm sorry about that." She paused. "In all honesty, I think I just had a major panic attack." She felt her eyes burn, but the tears retreated. "But I'm fine now, and … yeah, I'm just trying to be a normal person again." She laughed it off but felt the defeat. "I think it may take a while."

"You need a referral for some help?"

"I have my same counselor from after the serial killer. I started seeing her again."

"Good to hear. You'll get through it. You take it easy, now."

"Thank you." Waving goodbye, she walked back toward the ghost duo. Their eyes suggested the question still stood. "How long will the interview take?"

"You sure, Riss?" Shane asked, studying her expression.

She nodded with a tired blink.

"No tae long," Caitlin said.

Arista took a deep breath, held it in, and then released it. "Okay."

CHAPTER 29
WITCHCRAFT OR SOMETHING

The interview took much longer than expected. With the privacy of her address promised and documented on a contract, Arista kept honest with many details regarding her great-great-grandfather's presence in the house without divulging the actual possession. No one needed to know the depth of her paranormal life. She also had Shane assemble the elaborate Ouija table and took pride in showing them its noted history of catching serial killers. Since she hadn't opened it since the whole Iris revelation, the first set of initials and date struck her—that notorious dog incident and the spiraling events that followed—but she moved on, keeping the information to herself.

With the informative section complete, Caitlin and Gene set up their electromagnetic equipment. The duo was ready to discover if their unintentional haranguing of Arista had been worth it. With evening setting in, the darkness added an extra element of spooky.

Gene did most of the technical talking, pointing to his gadgets and giving technical explanations. "So, dis devoice meazhaahs proximity of energy, drops in temprachaah, an' roise in barometric preshaah."

Shane sat listening, as wide-eyed as one of his students, clearly excited to learn something new.

Caitlin made her verbal introduction for the rolling camera as Gene scanned the room and zoomed in on any slight movements that caught his eye. Meanwhile, Arista and Shane sat out of frame watching what the camera recorded on a small television set.

"I never asked—are either of you gifted in witchcraft or anything like that?" Arista asked, pushing her hair out of her eyes and wondering how much longer this would take.

"Caitlin 'as a connection wiff 'ah great-great-grandfadaah … jus loike yuh," Gene whispered, before giving a subtle shake of his head, implying questions were uninvited during taping.

Caitlin crept around the dining area, pointing out that the table served as a vessel of supernatural wonder. Then, Gene narrated the gruesome death of Henry Wallish at the hands of his intended victim, Arista, and how she had been a temporary portal for her house's ghost, most likely her own great-great-grandfather.

She cringed. Would the memories always hit her this hard? Further, she had not told them about the possession, and felt uncomfortable that they knew lots about her from some "underground" source. The frustration, mixed with this trying day, exhausted her even more.

Gene alerted Caitlin of a rise in the barometric pressure, and they panned the camera to the meter's jerking needle.

Arista wondered if Great-Great would truly make an appearance.

"Dere's definitely somefin' 'appening 'ere, Caitlin," Gene said.

Arista felt a drop in her home's temperature, but it paled in comparison to the gwishin's effect.

"Ah feel it, tae, Gene," Caitlin said, her raised hand touching only air.

Inexplicably, the camera jerked.

Arista and Shane looked up at Gene to see the cause.

Gene's face held an expression of stark terror.

"What is it, Gene?" Caitlin asked, cautiously.

"It 'it me camrah! Jus now! Di' yuh see dat?" His voice rang out, incredulous.

Shane sat forward in his seat, alarmed by the announcement.

A pang of guilt arose within her. Maybe Great-Great did not want to be discovered. Now that she thought about it, he might look at this as a hostile invasion to his privacy. Her protective instincts grew as the ghost-hunting duo scrutinized her living area, shining their light in the corners and talking. So much talking.

Enough. "You guys—"

"'old dat fought, Aristah," Gene said, entranced with the view through his camera lens.

Instead of looking at the televised monitor, she watched Gene creep up behind Caitlin while still narrating their sensations.

Gene jerked his own camera.

"Dere it is again!" he announced in awe to Caitlin's overhead mic. "Dis ghost feels angry."

They had mentioned if the process went too slow, they would hurry it along to accommodate her. But it was a bit disappointing. Further, she didn't like them labeling Great-Great as angry.

"Maybe aggressive, Gene. Are we good tae go further?"

"Oi'd say, good faah now, Caitlin."

On they skulked.

While she knew Great-Great was here, he was not gullible enough to fall for amateur hour. She turned to Shane and shook her head. "I can't take any more of this." The ghost-hunting couple's narration and stalking of her far stealthier kin faded to the background as she talked with Shane. "I just want to go to bed. They're really nice, and I respect their journey, but I can't be a part of it anymore." She would explain her observation later.

Shane arose and tapped Gene's shoulder. He whispered, "Riss is beat. You guys need to wrap it up."

"Al'oight, mate. Give us toime tuh close."

She could do nothing else. Emotional exhaustion overtook her. This had been a tortuous charade, one that had followed the worst panic attack she had ever had. A boatload of information to sift through at her next counseling session.

A drastic measure was needed to end another spiral. Maybe she should abruptly stand up, tell Caitlin and Gene they were fakes, and to get the hell out! She took a breath. Or she could surrender to everything—her past trauma, her present psychosis, and her future of ambiguity. And, yes, someday soon, she would need to chase after a hummingbird with another presence closing in on her.

She looked at Shane sitting beside her, unaware of her mental meltdown. He snickered at the duo's antics, smiling when they cracked clever quips for the camera and amongst themselves. His expression brought her a little comfort, and in this minute, he was all she wanted. She tapped his leg.

He looked at her, eyebrows raised in inquiry.

She thrust into him, pressing her mouth into his with voracious, self-destructive passion. She wrapped her arms around him, inhaling his taste until all breath left her. With agility, she swung her leg up and over him to straddle his lap, fully embracing him. Tasting him. Inhaling him and swallowing his essence whole.

When all breath had left her, she pulled back and stared into his beautiful brown eyes that reflected the camera lights around them. "I love you," she said and released a laugh that would not stop as her eyes welled with tears. This felt like the border of insanity.

Shane looked flabbergasted, though his reaction was interrupted by an outside commentary.

"'Ere! 'Ere! It looks loike de spirit has leff us faah now, but dere is somefing even more magnetic fum dese two lovaahs. And dat means toime is up. Dis 'as been Gene…"

"And Caitlin …"

"An' yuh've been watching the CKGN Supernatural 'our. Join us next week, when we visit a smaw graveyawd in San Francisco where a *cheonyo gwishin* runs around loike a maimed li'le girl an' causes all sorts of 'avoc."

Even with Gene's cockney accent, she recognized the word 'gwishin.' But now the term brought a memory of peace, powdery snow, and a delicate white flower. She let Soonsil's image dissipate and felt relief that she and Shane would soon be alone.

After they closed out the show, the duo packed up their equipment. An awkwardness filled the room as they kept their conversation low and to themselves.

Shane jumped in to help them in order to expedite the departure.

Within minutes, they all walked toward the van, and Caitlin handed Arista their business card.

"Thank you again, Arista. Here's oor card. It has all oor info. Check oot the show and please call if ye remember anything else. We'd love tae come back. Also, would love tae have ye rate the episode if ye could. Every comment helps, though we really like the four and five stars."

Arista looked at the card. "Oh wow, your last name is Kelly. Are you Irish?"

"Naw, ah'm Scot'ish."

"I thought so from the accent. So, you're actually from Scotland. Is your family there?"

"Aye. Glasgow. No much family though. Just ma faither. But according tae the Chromosomes & Me website, ah'm supposed tae have a relative somewhere in SoCal. Ma great-great-grandfaither's … brother's … family. Pretty distant."

"Really?" *What are the odds?*

"Yeah, he registered when the company first started in the early 2000s, but by the time ah mailed ma sample in, there'd been nae sign 'o him fur years."

"What was his name?"

"Ian Kelly. He's—"

A chill shot through Arista. She could not hear the rest. Not right now. What could have been joyful ancestral news landed with a weighty thud. While her dad had just saved her from a suffocating panic, the grief from hearing his name now churned inside her. She just needed peace. But as she looked at cheerful Caitlin chattering away about discovering an American relative, she knew she'd reconnect with her soon.

"… and he's Irish and ah'm Scot'ish, but who knows. Those great-great-grandparents were up tae nae good."

Arista laughed at the irony—her blood relative right in front of her and the notion of the great-greats up to no good. She reached out and gave Caitlin a strong, meaningful hug, surprising the young woman.

"A might loving, ye are. Thank ye fur that! And thanks again fur letting us tape."

Shane and Gene shook hands and then the ghost-seeking couple climbed into their van and ignited the engine. Its droning whine, no longer a threat. In fact, the potential for an extended family proved the curse truly just ran down a single line of the family tree. How many other distant relatives might she have?

"Riss, sorry, I've got to get home. I promised my dad I'd help him tonight and I'm already running hella late. Are you okay?"

"I am." She smiled and draped herself against him, sagging as a heavy blanket for a humorous effect.

He laughed at her exaggeration, then disclosed, "Just to let you know … that little episode in there … I don't know where it came from, but I'm ready when you are." He grabbed her and they delighted in another prolonged kiss. Then he went to his truck and slowly backed out of the driveway.

"Hey!" she yelled from her front porch.

He rolled down his window. "What's up?"

"You taste like gingerbread!"

CHAPTER 30
A CONNIVING HAG

"There she is!" Pearl said through the video teleconference. She peered at her phone screen sitting on the table, looking down the rim of her purple cat-eye reading glasses like a snooty librarian.

"Pearl, you can set the phone at eye level if it's more comfortable," Arista said.

"I'm fine, Arista, thank you."

"Look at that!" Bethie said, pointing to her sister-witch on the tablet screen. She looked up at Arista. "How do I keep forgetting how great this is?"

"Hi, Arista," Candace said, sitting down beside Pearl.

After greeting Candace, Arista turned back to Auntie. "When you're done, click this red button."

"Will do!"

"Okay, I'm going to head back over to my place, and I'll pick up my tablet later. Please be careful on your tea date."

"Hang on one moment, Pearl," Bethie said, then pressed mute and turned toward Arista. "Pearl would have kittens if she knew I was going to tea with Iris."

Arista stepped out of the screen's line of vision. "If it weren't for the latest, I'd be the same way. But I'm trusting she's turned a corner. You two seem to be getting along really well. With that said, should you be driving?"

"First thing in the morning and evenings seem to be my troubled times, and we're almost to ten a.m."

Arista scrunched her face, unsure.

"I'll be fine!"

"Anything else from me, then?"

"Nope. I'm all set. Let me know if *you* need anything."

After hearing of Arista's panic attack inspired by innocent strangers, Bethie agreed with Arista's idea of being in even closer contact. Luckily, the green van turned out to bear familial tidings, and she looked forward to meeting Caitlin and Gene.

After Arista left, Bethie unmuted the troops and enjoyed catching up on the latest rambunctious stories of WallyCat's antics.

"I'm sorry, Bethie, but the little bugger has broken two wine glasses since you've been gone."

"I know. He's the clumsiest cat I've ever had, but his propensity to cuddle makes up for the cost."

With feline tales exhausted, next came all the details regarding the murderous reason for Iris's curse tablet and her display of the memento. At Bethie's request, they agreed to discuss her grandfather's deeds in person later, but Pearl had plenty to opine about Iris.

"I've never liked that woman, Bethie. Please be careful."

"I know. It was a wicked discovery, but after the initial shock, I realized the impotence of the situation. Iris is harmless. A bit eccentric. But harmless. As she said, she's had plenty of moments where she could have sprung a wallop on me but never has. And to make a long story short, she's been a great help to Arista and me on a few occasions now. I'd say she's become a genuine friend."

Pearl shook her head in disbelief, her grainy image glitching from their mediocre Internet connection.

Candace dazed off from the camera. "You know, Bethie, with all this new information, I think I may delve deeper if you don't mind. We won't do it right now, but I think we need to ensure your safety. Do I have your permission to research this?"

"I don't see any harm in it, but I don't believe it's necessary either."

"Understood. I just did a very cumbersome reading for a client, but in the next few days, I may be up for it. We want to think the best, but more important than anything is protection for you and Arista. You've already been through so much."

"While you're at it, can your reading determine why I'm having vision difficulties?"

Two pairs of eyes lit up the screen.

"What do you mean by that?" Pearl asked.

Bethie shared her eyesight details. Mid-story, she had to admit to herself that her vision problems needed no help from spell honing any longer. They came when they came, and only the doctor's explanation remained. She kept the spell-influenced bit to herself and ended her account with the declaration that everything would be *just fine.*

Pearl shook her head. "Bethie, there is something awry there. When are you returning to Sedona? For years, you've flown here for the winter like the seasoned snowbird you are. I take it there are reasons we don't have you this year?"

"I need to be here for Arista. She lost so much this year. Of course, her weekly counseling seems to help, but I just want her stable again. The last two years have been nothing but rough waters and heartache. She also had a panic attack a couple of days ago."

Candace's head tilted in compassion. "Oh dear. Looks like we'll have Bethie here as soon as she's able," she said to Pearl, then faced the screen. "Bethie, do you and Arista need us there for any reason?"

"I'd always love a visit, but as far as urgency, no. We're doing just fine."

"*Just fine* with a conniving hag, the onset of blindness, and a mentally unstable Arista," Pearl blurted.

Candace gave her a gentle whack on the arm. "Stop that."

"Honest, ladies, we're doing well. Healing takes time." She thought of her upcoming tea with Iris. "Just know that I'll be okay. By the way, where's our Bridget?"

"Bridget has taken her sabbatical to Italy. She'll be back in early February."

Pearl pursed her lips. "I still think that one is La Befana in disguise. Every year, it's off to Italy with suitcases of toys and all sorts of Epiphany Eve talk."

Candace cinched her mouth. "It could be she has family there."

"Or she's La Befana," Pearl sassed, with her nose and chin up in defiance.

"Oh, be quiet. She's too lovely to play such a part," Candace reasoned.

"A disguise."

Here they went again. Time to intervene. "Anyway, my sisters, I do have a tea to get to, but I just love this video thing. Let's do it again soon."

Pearl grew serious. "Bethie, honestly, do you think you'll be able to return to Sedona come the new year?"

"It will depend on Arista. When I see she's secure, I'll make my way. It's reassuring that she and Shane are dating again."

"They are?" Candace asked.

"He's working on her, and I'm supporting the notion. Even so, she's cautious and trying to sort out her feelings … which is a good thing."

"It is indeed," Candace said, watching Pearl fiddle with her phone. "Have we lost you, Pearl?"

"Sorry, ladies. Stevie is texting that he has an irate customer at the store. I've got to call him."

The check-in had been sufficient, so Bethie bid them adieu and readied for her tea with Iris.

While tidying her home, she pined for her WallyCat and decided she would bring him back with her from now on. Especially since her trips to Sedona might get disrupted without notice, as they were this time.

At the coat rack, she covered her body in layers of textiles—a thin, long-sleeved shirt, followed by a draping, burgundy chenille vest, and a nylon overcoat. She looked through the window, observed the clear blue day, and decided her umbrella of whimsical cats and dogs dropping from the sky could stay put.

Outside, with the rain at rest, the morning felt frigid. Patches of frost seized the shady spots of her front yard, and the cold stung her nose as the brisk air blew upon her. The walk to her yellow wagon felt too long, sending shivers up her arms.

Slipped beneath her windshield wiper blade, she found a business card. "CKGN Supernatural Hour?" She tucked it in her pocket to recycle later.

On the droning drive to Iris's house, she recalled finding the curse tablet. She wished Iris would have mentioned it earlier. More so, she wished Pearl would not have stirred up doubt about her again.

The drive seemed shorter than usual, as Iris greeted her with a grand hug upon arrival. "Bethie, thank you for joining me this morning."

"My pleasure. Pearl and Candace send their regards."

"Really? Pearl, too?" She looked Bethie in the eye, a sharp awareness of her fib. "I forget how close you two are." Iris turned and walked them toward the deck. "Come, I know it's chilly, but we're bundled, and the fresh air beats out the confines of my home."

"Arista and I sit outside year-round, too. By the way, thank you so much for the apples. They made an exceptional pie." Her attention turned to the awaiting platter of pastries. "Ooo, what goodies do we have today?"

"Well, we have—" Iris stopped mid-sentence as Sheriff Michaels pulled into her driveway.

Bethie felt the excitement of their meeting deflate by the minute as the sheriff exited his car. The pig dilemma must have come forefront to Iris's mind, and as Bethie thought about it, it ran a little inopportune that the sheriff see them together.

"Mornin', ladies. Bethie, fancy meeting you here," the approaching sheriff said, his eyes upon her, confirming her concern for appearances.

"Good morning, Sheriff." What else could she say? She stood up out of respect. Or maybe restlessness.

"Ms. Ardino, I left my card on your door a few days back. I see you're in good company at the moment," he noted, winking at Bethie.

"I need to speak with you about an open investigation when you're available."

"I see," Iris said, poker-faced like a pro with an unfavorable hand.

Bethie grew more nervous. "I can leave if this is urgent. Far be it from me to stand in the way of lawful matters."

"No need. I didn't mean to interrupt you, ladies." He looked Iris in her eyes, then down at her feet. "Though it is important. How about I come back this afternoon? Will that work for you?"

Iris studied his face and said, "That should be fine."

"Great. Until then ..." the sheriff said, tipping his hat and giving a last glance in Bethie's direction.

The ladies watched his departure, seeing him look left and right and all about the ground. Busy eyes. Very busy eyes.

An awkward silence remained after he left. But the elephant in the room had to be addressed. Better put, the pig in the sty.

"Iris, did you literally feed Fergus to pigs?"

Iris adjusted herself upright, and without making eye contact, said, "Bethie, I invited you over for tea and scones." She took a sip of her tea and stared directly at Bethie. "I think it's best we enjoy our treats."

Bethie pinched off the tip of her scone and popped it into her mouth. The less she knew, the better. Unfortunately, the sheriff's appearance and her mentioning of pigs had dampened Iris's hospitable mood, and her more aloof persona had returned. After finishing their cup of tea, the shallow conversation stalled, and Bethie felt it a good time to leave.

•   •   •

With two sets of eyes watching in his rearview mirror, the sheriff pulled onto the bumpy country road. He knew of Bethie's disgust of Fergus, and that she could not say his name or hear it without recoiling in repulsion. Now, he discovered her casually sipping tea with a driver from the video recording, who could have transported the body to Manny's place. Also, Rossy had run into Iris, spilling her bag full of stringent cleaning supplies. If her Ajax, bleach, and gloves weren't the epitome of a bloody mess-cleaning list, he did not know what was. Then, there were those long, narrow shoes. His gut feeling had turned into relevant evidence, all the factors adding up to a weighty sum. He damn well hoped that Bethie's presence with this potential suspect was an anomaly. But the weirdest aspect of this whole scenario was the superb likeness that Iris had to Fergus. His smug demeanor in the hotel conference room. Her smug demeanor lording over him and Rossy picking up her spilled supplies. How odd that his main suspect in the murder case had such a resemblance to the victim. "Hmph."

Nearing the end of the bumpy road, he came to Manny's place. No workers, and the pigs remained cozied up against the early-morning winter chill in their plentiful hay bedding.

With another unanswered knock and unencumbered by others' eyes, he searched again but discovered nothing new. Still, it did not bode well.

Another hunch hit him with urgency. Manny had been gone too long for his taste. The old timer did not strike him as the type to evade the law. It surely begged the question. Had something happened to him … done by the same person who had offed Fergus?

He walked to his cruiser and called dispatch. With the home already a crime scene, his request was standard protocol. After noting the address, he prompted a further investigation. "We need to get forensics out here to gather pig dung samples."

Chapter 31
Dangling Snowy Clusters

With the onset of Yule, the winter solstice clamped its frosty grip upon Arista's cottage. Though close to go time, she tapped the thermostat—once, twice—to kick up the heat. She had not been to Shane's house since their old gang went to wish him well after his snakebite ordeal, and *never* had she seen it this time of year! Surely, Magda's creative touch covered their property in extravagant pizzazz.

After applying a silver-sparkled blushed lipstick, Arista took a last glimpse in her oval bathroom vanity mirror. Stepping on tiptoe, she checked her butt. She grit her teeth at the panty lines, and quickly changed into a thong before hot-stepping out the door to her borrowed wine-colored Subaru.

Her stomach fluttered with anxiousness. She wondered if all the stress, including this eustress, was too much for well-being. She'd probably knocked ten years off her life by now.

The musings had her through the drive before she realized it. She drove up the Stoddards' sweeping Italian Cypress-lined driveway strung with an abundance of spiraling warm-white lights. At the top, she parked by the three-tiered gurgling fountain, showered in swirling colorful hues from a light projector at the fountain's base—a miniature version of Aurora Borealis.

She exited Auntie's Subaru. While it looked crisp at her house, it now seemed aged and unwashed amongst the lot of shiny Benzos, Teslas, and Rivians. At last, a relieving sight—Evan's new Lexus! Of course, Evan and his parents would be in attendance. She released an ounce of tension now that she knew more than just Shane at the party.

Along her path, a luminaria bag with starburst and glitter cutouts covered each walkway light. A tinge of insecurity crept within her as she reached the front door, guarded by two six-foot-tall gold-metal nutcrackers. The grandeur showed impressive. She knocked on one of the statue's shoulders and listened to the clang reverberate, giggling at the overdone opulence that almost brought self-doubt. It was all pretty cool, and she wondered what kind of glitz and glamour she'd find inside.

She raised her hand to knock but paused. A quick look at her shoes, her legs, then her dress. She liked what she was wearing. She stood up straight and considered the crowd beyond the maroon, dark-green, and glitter-gold garlands and jumbo-sized wreath. The boisterous joviality radiating through the solid wood door felt like it might be overwhelming, but she gathered her sense of self.

Go-time! She clanked the lion head's knocker centered within the huge fir wreath.

Shane opened the door, looking absolutely handsome in his effortless, dressy casual outfit. Seldom did he wear such a vibrant red, and his blond hair really popped against it.

"Hey, Beautiful. Come in." His eyes sparkled with authentic admiration.

He took her hand. Her heart warmed to see him, but the moment she walked through the door, all lingering guests' eyes fell briefly upon her. They were business-minded people with powerful voices and upright posture, confident women just as much so as men. Fast-talking jabber and clinking glasses filled the room. She adjusted—shoulders back, chest out—and smiled at anyone making eye contact.

A few steps forward, and she caught her full reflection in the foyer mirror. Whether it was the lighting or Magda had a magickal mirror, she didn't know, but her sheath dress of silver sequins flashed like loose diamonds under a jeweler's fluorescent lamp. Purchased from the vintage clothing store on the main strip, it hugged her figure like sugar on the cube. Seeing it full-length in such a grand venue, she loved it even more. With the silk liner caressing her curves, it fit tight enough to look flawless but also felt flexible from the poly-blend lining. Thin, silver-silk spaghetti straps held up a modest bust adorned with wisps of her own curled hair cascading down from a strategic updo, complete with mini zircon snowflake hair clips. The winter theme also extended to her ears, where she wore dangling snowy clusters.

She proceeded with renewed confidence. She looked as glamorous as any other woman at this shindig.

Shane led them into the next room, and she felt proud to be holding the hand of the prince at this winter ball.

At the bar, Magda poured herself a glass of champagne. "Oh, Arista!" She gave a glowing smile of pearl-white teeth, and her face softened, as if she had just eaten the most decadent chocolate. "You look *absolutely* gorgeous!" Her words slurred as she introduced Arista to her friend sitting on the barstool. Together, they fawned over her appearance while they sipped from their flutes.

Probably not their first glass.

"Here!" Magda said. "Have some champagne?"

"Sure." She would sip this same glass through the night because she wanted to leave sober.

"Make it two, Mom."

"Yes, yes," Magda said, grabbing two flutes already lined up on the counter. "Well, you two darlin's just have a wonderful time tonight! Ya hear me?" Her southern accent capped the directive.

After Magda poured the bubbly, two more women with equally demonstrative personalities whisked her and her friend away, the flashes of their united Christmas bling leaving a glaring wake.

"Arista!" Shane's dad said in a sudden appearance. "Glad to see you coming around. That was a close call at the bakery, huh?" He laughed with blustery abandon before pretending to wipe sweat from his brow. "Whew!"

Awkward. "Hi, Mr. Stoddard. Yes, unfortunately, Maddie gets rambunctious sometimes."

"She sure got this one in trouble," he said, elbowing Shane in the arm.

Shane sagged his head in feigned shame, then squeezed Arista's hand in a gentle reminder that this was all part of the Stoddard flair.

"You two enjoy yourselves!" Mr. Stoddard's booming voice floated on to the next group.

With some women her age, she noticed the catty stares at her dress followed by the whispering. But others looked just as lost in the fray. For the latter, she offered an inviting smile. In the event Shane got pulled away from her, maybe they would remember her friendliness.

Shane stopped them at the Christmas tree and called out a man's name.

Arista scanned the tree's wide girth, then up, up, up to its tip-top elegant angel in a deep red velvet robe and golden-feathered wings. "This is over twelve feet," she said, mouth agape as she peered upward.

"I think she went fourteen feet this year ... because of the party. Here, turn around for a minute."

Arista turned to find a camera poised and ready to shoot. "Oh."

Shane wrapped his arm around her and seemed to grow another three inches for the photo, prompting her to stand upright as well.

"Okay, ya'll smile," said the photographer with a slight southern drawl.

Must be Magda's side of the family.

Click.

"And one more."

Click. Click. Click.

That was three.

At a tap on her shoulder, she turned around to see the open arms of Maddie with Bree and Evan at her side. Arista squealed with excitement and delivered a big hug.

"I dressed for the occasion," Maddie said, sporting a wry grin, along with her red flannel with rhinestone buttons, thick, black velvet leggings, and Converse hi-tops.

"I love it!" Arista said with a warm laugh.

Bree stepped forward in her wine-red velvet midi sheath dress with an off-shoulder neckline. Pinned upon it was a large black broach shaped like a bow and embellished with smooth pearls, and the bow's matching earrings and glitter-gold ankle boots completed her ensemble.

"So pretty," Arista said, pointing to her outfit, then hugged her. She couldn't fawn too much with Maddie there, worried it could start an issue.

Next, Evan stepped in with a genuine hug for her. It was the first real embrace he had offered since getting together with Bree. *Christmastime must be okay for friendly hugs.*

The chat flowed amongst the old gang, and Maddie soon announced that she would leave for Oahu the following day. Time had passed so quickly that she and Arista had not gotten together, so they all made the most of the next hour, putting Maddie center stage, remembering her best antics, and giving her lots of encouraging well wishes. Then Maddie left, Skylar picking her up for the ride home.

The couples continued to visit for a while. The guys shared stories of football injuries and which college year proved the hardest, while the ladies made light of their sob stories, as well as added their own tales of school woes.

Too soon, Evan announced they had only planned to make an appearance since his mother was hosting her work holiday party in Felton, and they had committed to helping. A slight nervousness in his voice suggested they had already stayed too long. They all made plans for a New Year's Eve dinner and drinks, then said their merry goodbyes.

On, the night went. A whirlwind of jolly sociability, superficial conversations, and lots of glamour. After the first hour, feeling comfortable with the environment, Arista added a second glass of champagne and dished out more smiles, nods, and occasional opinions. When a discreet moment arose, Shane whisked her upstairs to his bedroom.

The madness and hoopla felt a comfortable distance away once Shane shut the door.

Arista caught her breath. "Good goddess! I could *not* do that every day." She laughed off the slurring partygoers and their commotion of trying to talk over each other. It was so *not* nature, *not* crystals, and *definitely not* peaceful. "Crazy."

Shane took an exaggerated fall onto his bed.

Arista kicked off her silver pumps, thankful for her feet to lie flat against the floor. She curled her toes into the shag throw rug on her way to the bed before pretending to wobble in agony for humor's sake. Then she slid into bed beside him and stared at his ceiling, so different from her own.

But happy. She felt truly happy!

"You okay with Maddie leaving?" Shane asked.

"I'm happy for her. I think it will be good. Plus … I have you to keep me company," she said, gazing into his eyes.

Shane wrapped his body around her, and she adjusted into him. After a moment of absorbing his comfort, she found the lover she had so missed. The one who no one could replace. She loved being in his arms, smelling him, and feeling his skin against hers. She nuzzled into his neck and her lips opened to taste him.

His hands became familiar again, rubbing her back, stroking her hair, and reaching down the length of her spine to lift the hemline enough to feel her bare skin. All thoughts diminished as they sank into that thrilling phase of reunion. Almost a year later, they were enrapt at last.

Shane paused and gave a quick, teasing lick to Arista's lips. He pushed himself up, locked his door, and turned off the light.

Arista unzipped and shimmied out of her dress before carefully laying it across his footboard.

Upon his return, he opened his bedside drawer, and the sound of a plastic wrapper tantalized her. She wanted it and imagined the pleasure as she writhed upon his bed. Then, a thought. "What if your mom or dad comes up here?"

"Door's locked," he whispered.

All thoughts vanished as Shane came down atop her. How exhilarating to hold him again. To feel the rapture of their kissing and release everything other than the sensation of their united moment. She wrapped her arms and legs around him. Deeper into the mattress, her body sank, and he deeper into—

The doorknob jiggled.

"Shaaaane. You in there?" Magda said, outside his door.

Arista tensed. She freakin' knew it!

Shane groaned but kept to his intended business.

"Shaaaane?"

Again, the doorknob jiggled, and Arista prayed the lock held strong.

"You have *got* to be kidding me," Shane grumbled in a whisper. He stilled, holding his breath.

KNOCK. KNOCK.

"Shane."

Her drunken beckoning would have been comical had they not been in the middle of sex.

The doorknob jiggled, followed by a slap of her palm on his door. "Shane!"

"She's drunk," he said, working his hips to keep matters firm.

Arista lay there, her eyes adjusting to the hall light coming up from under Shane's door and the Christmas lights from the eaves outside his window.

Magda pulled on the doorknob, causing his door to rumble.

"Hang on," Shane whispered.

Hearing his words, she looked up at the silhouette of his jawline fixated on the door, and her fret of the situation dissipated. Her own Adonis.

Just as Shane was about to disengage and appease his mother, a man's voice came up the stairwell.

"Now, now," Shane's father said. "Magda, darling."

"Whaaaaat?" she answered in the epitome of an entitled lush's whine.

Shane's body relaxed as they eavesdropped on the gentle scolding. He half-heartedly wiggled his hips.

"I bet heeez in there with Ariss-sta," Magda said, clearly insulted by his inaudible admonishment and set on her own agenda.

Mr. Stoddard continued to mumble, receiving snappy retorts from his wife as they descended the stairs. Once downstairs, their voices came alive again, cheerful to their guests.

Shane groaned. "I'm so sorry. Next time or finish the job?"

Arista chose the latter, and many minutes later, she stood to re-wrap herself in glitz and glam, freshen her hair and lip tint, and sneak down the stairs following her beau.

"Should I say goodbye to anybody?"

"Only if you want to. Just know, they're totally bombed by now," he said, rolling his eyes.

Arista grinned and shook her head. "I don't really want to. Plus, I don't think your mom likes me." She had to say it after feeling the same uncertainty that she had felt in the woman's presence since grade school.

They stepped out into the moonlight. "You know, I think she does. In all honestly, I haven't dated a lot, but what I have, she treats you better than … them."

"Really?" How bad could she get?

"Yes, really. She says nice things about you all the time."

"Like what?"

"Pretty. Cute personality. She encouraged the relationship the minute you got back. I think the big thing for her was she didn't like when we finally first got together, and you took off on me."

Arista flinched, realizing the different perspective. "Okay, that's legit. And … maybe you're just her little boy, who she doesn't want to grow up."

"Yeah, you hit that nail on the head. But enough about my *dear mother*," Shane said, then looked skyward. "I was thinking the Full Moon would be good for our first time back together, but …"

"Following the moon cycle, huh?"

"A little," he said, smirking.

"Well, this Waxing Gibbous is pretty good for growth and progress," Arista said, as they walked toward her car.

"Noted. I'd say we made outstanding *progress* tonight."

She popped open her car door and turned to face him. Her pumps made her tall enough that she did not have to stand on tiptoe. "Me too."

A kiss goodnight, and Shane walked to his door.

As she backed out, Arista saw Magda stumble out of the door and stand by Shane. She dodged any sort of eye contact with either of them as she carefully navigated her tight parking space amongst the many cars. At a discreet moment, she cracked her window to better listen.

"Why'zzzzz she leaving without saying bye-eee?" Magda asked.

"Maybe you were less than hospitable?" Shane said with a touch of irritation.

"Nooo, I like Arista!"

"Good! Because we're moving in together … sometime next year."

"Wha—?"

Upon driving away, she watched through the rearview as Shane walked into the house, leaving his mother gaping on her festive Christmas doormat.

She giggled, descending their drive. She figured Shane was joking about moving in together. Or was he? "Hmph!"

Motoring through the posh neighborhood, she rolled her window further down and absorbed the brisk winter air. She felt a tremendous amount of joy, and the rekindled love with her guy filled her heart with happiness. Perhaps it came down to her wins of late adding up. The time of year surely added to the magick.

When she reached Highway 9, she envisioned the path to Auntie's house and remembered her vision of the frantic hummingbird. Then, she let the ambiguity of its meaning pass. She refused to get sucked into naysaying doom and gloom.

Not tonight.

Tonight, she would remain happy, settled, and so much in love!

CHAPTER 32
NOT YOUR GUILT TO CARRY

The sound of the gunshot could have been deafening, but he focused on reloading his clip. Fifteen bullets. Another chest-pounding round of fire came from both sides of him. The safety earmuffs helped.

Sheriff Michaels took his power stance, raised his Glock, sighted his target, exhaled, and fired. Head shot. He dropped his support hand, sighted, and fired again. Sternum. Thirteen more bullets, only two off the mark.

He pressed the white button in his lane and waited as the pulley brought forth his riddled poster of a green-brained, red-eyed zombie. He studied his progress, folded it up, and headed to the office.

The dispatcher had good timing.

"14M14, go ahead."

"Coroner called with some urgent news and said to call her. Over."

"Affirmative. Over and out."

He dialed Jo. Her biggest project right now comprised the print on Fergus's watch and dung from Manny's pen. Damn! He really hoped she turned up something incriminating.

"Hey, Sheriff, I've got some print *news*," she said, as if waving a sugar cookie above a child's reach.

"Yeah?"

"Yep."

"Okay, great." *Why? Why always this game?*

"What's it worth to you?" She hesitated. "Nah, I'm kidding. Prints on the watch belong to the neighbor up the road."

"Brimley?" he blurted out, electrified by the news.

"Nope. Ardino."

"You're shittin' me!" he said, a little surprised by his own reaction.

"Also, unfortunate news on Mr. Whelan. The porcine excrement did indeed have his DNA in it."

"Good God, Jo. You've hit a gold mine today."

"You bet I did!"

"Alright, going for the arrest warrant. Thanks, Jo!"

Despite the excitement, he felt awful for poor Manny. He knew he wouldn't have skipped town like that. Then he pictured the poised woman, as proud as Fergus, sitting across from Bethie. He called that, too. Declined to accept it … but knew it all along. Thinking further on Bethie, a tinge of concern regarding the association between the two women flared within him, but he nipped it. Bethie's prints weren't the ones found on the murder victim.

. . .

The waiting room of her psychologist's office looked like leftovers from the mid-80s—mauve and blue slate tones, honey oak furniture, and pictures of backyard gardens set in gilded frames.

Arista grabbed *The New Yorker* from the wall-mount magazine rack, noting how rumpled and dog-eared it looked. She pressed the little white button announcing her arrival and sat down to flip through the 'zine with its witty comics while she waited.

Five minutes later, a middle-aged woman with shoulder-length white hair opened the door. "Hi, Arista."

She responded in kind and followed the woman to a private room suitable for absorbing troubles and grief.

Sitting down on the brown leather sofa, Arista put one of the oatmeal-colored throw pillows in her lap, and the session's usual small talk began. Five minutes in, Dr. Melinat asked her what she would like to talk about today.

Arista always found this a little intimidating. She wanted to take full advantage of the counseling paid for by the county because of the murderous reason she needed it. But she could never go full truth because Dr. Melinat may consider her a candidate for in-patient committal.

"There are a couple of things. First," Arista took a breath and slowly exhaled it, "my great-aunt and I were told our relative may have killed a few people back in the 40s … including an innocent child. While some of it was accidental, it's hitting me really hard." She paused and looked at her counselor. "I feel terrible about it! And I want to love him, but I'm devastated by his deed."

Dr. Melinat's brows pinched. "I'm so sorry to hear that. Finding out something like that must have been very tough."

"It was. I mean, Auntie and I are compassionate, loving people. We wouldn't hurt an insect." *Not counting the serial killer I offed, but, technically, that wasn't me.* "To hear this about someone who Auntie adored and took great care of her and her siblings,"—*and saved* my *life through possession*—"really affected both of us." She shook her head from the convolution. "I just don't know how to reconcile it."

Dr. Melinat nodded and listened with caring eyes.

"I mean, I feel a little guilt. But then, I don't, because I would've never done something like that. It's been confusing for me to deal with it. Especially right now, with my dad killed and my friends victims of violence, and I have all this swirling …" She stopped, noticing her heart rate increasing.

"Arista, I can see this is distressing you. Let's look at it together."

Arista relaxed, realizing she had come forward on the edge of the sofa, and sat back in the seat.

"Someone else's crime is not your guilt to carry, especially when it is so far removed, as in this case of your great …"

"Great-*great*-grandfather," Arista clarified.

"Right. Great-*great*-grandfather. I could elaborate on this topic if it was your grown child or a parent or if the relationship was closer in years. However, you're talking about someone you never even met." She paused. "My belief is there's no reason for you to suffer the wrongdoing in that situation."

Arista looked at the floor and twisted her lips as she pondered. *Sounds easy, but could it be that simple?*

"I've known people with similar concerns reach out to their community. Volunteering at a retirement home or soup kitchen, holding compromised newborns at the hospital. With your love of nature, you could pursue a wildlife rescue foundation. We have one here in Santa Cruz, and they work with bobcats, owls, and many other animals. Do any of those ideas interest you?"

She felt energized by the suggestion. She pictured baby bobcats romping in a sheltered enclosure. That would be fun and super cute. "Sure!"

"Now, let's look at your losses—your mother, your father … your friend, and even your sense of security. I look at the progress you've made in a general sense. Do you remember your state of mind before your Sedona sabbatical? The terror, the uncertainty … the confusion that you were experiencing." She paused and eyed Arista. "You made significant progress before you left. Then, barely two months ago … witnessing your father's death had a great emotional impact on you. You could barely get the words out to talk about it, which is very apt for such a traumatic event." She paused, awaiting commentary. "Now, observe where you are today. Even talking to me about this, while your heart may race, you are coherent … centered … and articulate without pause. Would you agree?"

Arista let out a huge breath. "I see what you're saying."

Dr. Melinat waited for elaboration, then continued, "From what you have told me, you have very effective tools—your meditation, your diet, and rest habits. Correct?"

"Yes."

"You have relived special memories of your father with me, and I encourage you to remember them when you are experiencing a moment of grief based on what you witnessed. With your father *and* your mother. Because watching a loved one die of cancer can be just as harrowing. The death of those dear to us is heart-wrenching, regardless of the *how*. In those moments, you can acknowledge the pain—experience it with tears, anger, or a solemn silence. But then, bring yourself to the present. Journal how it makes you feel. Replace the memory with a joyful moment you shared."

Arista nodded. She considered mentioning that she also burned her written feelings in her iron cauldron, but did not think it necessary.

"I know you mentioned you have your own process of—I think you called it water-weeping?—which is absolutely beautiful."

I do not remember telling her that. I am seriously losing my mind.

"Just so you know, I suggested your process to a grieving gardening client, and they really resonated to it."

"Oh, cool." Yay, that Auntie's ritual helped others, and they did not even know it came from a witch's grimoire. "Another thing. I had a *major* panic attack. I've never had one. Horrible experience! I thought I was dying. Does that mean I'm getting worse?"

Dr. Melinat invited her to elaborate and, after carefully listening, offered a solution. "Well, first, I want to commend you on taking the precise measure to ride it out. Arista, if I thought someone had a rifle in my front yard, and they were there to get me, I'd probably have been down on that floor beside you."

Arista gave a little laugh.

"And how you remedied it … the focus on your dad's photo, the detail of it, and your breathing. You calmed yourself down, and that is outstanding! Bravo!" Dr. Melinat paused, letting her praise sink in. "Now, if you feel the need, I can write a note to your doctor, and they can prescribe a medication. But I want you to consider that your reaction was not so outlandish. That was a normal fear. While your panic attack hit the higher end of a physiological response, I'm wondering, now that you know the onset, will you be better able to manage it if it were to happen again?"

Arista had thought for sure she'd leave with a referral for meds, and she fully accepted it. However, it sounded like she still had a choice.

"Let's liken the psyche and stress to our hearts and exercise. It does not matter how fit we are, our heart is going to beat strong and rapid when we run. Right?" She raised her eyebrows, inviting verbal confirmation.

"Right."

"It's going to feel uncomfortable. Fit, unfit, the effects are similar. But! The fitness of the person will determine how quickly that heart rate returns to normal."

Arista wanted to draw the comparison herself. "So, you're saying that I'm going to be stressed and maybe have a panic attack … but it's the ability to calm myself down that determines my mental fitness … kind of thing?"

"Kind of. Right now, you tell me you've had one panic attack. If you come in next week and you've had two more … and they put you in a dangerous situation, we'll re-approach medication options. But I just don't think you're ready for that path. You're doing remarkably well, especially after all you've been through." After a pause, she smiled. "With that said, it's important what *you* think?"

Arista bit her lip through a modest smile and felt her chest expand in gladness. Good goddess, she loved when people she respected noticed her efforts. She hated to admit it, but she loved the praise, too. "Thank you."

Dr. Melinat shared anecdotes of dealing with her own guilt on subjects not hers to own, followed by Arista ending with news that she and Shane were together again. The hour wrapped, and she strolled to her car feeling lighter. With no rain forecasted, the iciness of December had increased in the shadows, but as she emerged in the parking lot, the sun's vibrant warmth showered down upon her. Comfort easing the chill.

This second Yule day had brought forth the greatest gift—an abundance of clarity that her path headed in the right direction.

Chapter 33
To Kill Your Very Own

Iris sat in the stillness of her brooding home, watching the last rays of the early winter sun disappear from her deck. A despondence saturated her will. She felt the power of her darkness and isolation more than ever.

Outside, her cats loitered, awaiting kibble, but with her legs up on the small, embroidered footstool made by her grandmother, her mind played too busy to accommodate them.

Because of her inaction on the curse, she anticipated a visit from the old crone. Also, the time held notoriety with the anniversary of her grandfather's death only a day away. While Fergus had been quiet, she could attribute it to his understanding of her grandmother's ultimatum. Time neared for her choice, and the burden carried a high price.

"This will be the death of me," she said with sobering avowal.

Her issues with the external world also pended. Only days ago, the sheriff had visited. She could not deny her arrest would come soon.

"And the Kelly's," she said, dazing back out toward her hungry clowder.

Iris loved Bethie's brother, but he left her for another woman. Now she had realized she had always loved Bethie, too. Collaborating with her on urgent rituals rekindled a long-forgotten memory. One of friendship. A virtue she had disregarded over the years. Now that she had tasted it again, it served as the only sweetness in her otherwise cheerless life.

As the dusk drew in and the house popped, Iris felt the cold sweep through her. She had not moved, immobilized by her predicament. The obligation to her grandmother would change everything. But as the sheriff closed in, change was inevitable, regardless.

The chill settled upon her as she looked at her fireplace, empty without the impending tablet and its ominous message. Maybe she should have removed it from her view long ago.

"Self-pity be damned," she said with a sigh, resigning herself to reality. After all, her own murderous habits played a significant part in her undoing.

As expected, the creep settled in and behind her rose an impending presence. The effect made her want to duck, flinch, or flail her matriarch away, but that would never do. Instead, she endured it as she always had.

Not waiting to be addressed, Iris spoke.

"Grandmother, with all due respect … after all this time, surely you realize Arista is our blood. She was born of your great-granddaughter Keira. To kill her is to kill one of our very own."

The statement hung in the air.

She waited, hoping for a reprieve from duty.

The weight of a nasty temperament held behind her. She thought about turning to face her but did not. "Grandmother?"

A sharp pain at her temples preceded an invasion into her mind. Iris sank into the chair, privy to a vision the crone had shown her once before in order to validate her hand in Declan Kelly's death. The memory she knew all too well.

With Christmas two days away, their neighbor, dressed in denim suspenders, exited his truck and approached with a shotgun on his shoulder.

"To the bedroom. Quickly!" Iris's grandmother demanded, rushing the young cousins to the back of the house with Iris's older sister

accompanying them. "Jimmy, go!" she added, but returned to the front door to address the threatening intruder with Iris's grandfather.

"No, Iris, I want to stay with you. Please!" her little brother begged, clutching Iris's waist.

Aunt Sophie scooped up the three-year-old, then scolded her. "Iris, get over here! A five-year-old should not be seeing this!"

Iris peeked outside from behind the curtains, praying that her grandfather could negotiate a resolution.

Her grandmother's courage held strong. Not noticing the young onlookers, she took charge, shouting at the intruder from inside the door. "We don't want any trouble with you, Barry!"

Despite her protest, Iris's grandfather pushed his wife aside and exited the door to confront the angry man.

Iris listened to the banter, capturing only the neighbor's words as his voice projected strong and sure.

"He says Grandfather killed his dogs," Iris said, turning toward Aunt Sophie, who still held on to Jimmy. The accusation rang true, as she had overheard her grandparents' secretive conversations about the dirty deeds.

Her aunt and she stared at one another with a shameful awareness.

An ear-piercing gunshot rang out, destroying their sanctuary. Iris screamed and ducked as the window exploded in meteoric shards, striking nicks upon her back and arms. When she looked over at her little brother and Aunt Sophie, they lay on the floor, struggling for their last breaths with bloodied dots on their chests. She lunged toward them while hearing her grandmother burst out the front door, screeching. Her cousins came from the back surveying the trauma. All around her, the wailing filled her ears.

The vision faded out, leaving her staring at a dormant fireplace.

'No one tainted with the blood of Barry Kelly will ever be our kin!'

A shrill tinkling emitted from Iris's gilded mirror, and a web of splinters cracked upon it. Her grandmother's rage expressed.

Iris held her breath, never experiencing such emotion in her previous exchanges.

'It will be done. With or without you!'

The thickness and odor of the room cleared, leaving her with a sobered reality. So futile, as she had always deemed it so. But if she did not act, Grandmother would ensure that Fergus did.

CHAPTER 34
DEAD TO THE PROCESS

Bethie awoke from her afternoon nap with blurred vision. Unusual in its timing, she cursed the moment but knew it would pass. No need to trouble Arista.

Despite her affliction, she poured a tall glass of water, guzzled half, then went about her already planned dinner, starting with a packet of yeast in a warm bowl of water. Prep work for her Rosemary Potato Rolls.

She gathered all the usual bread makings—flour, eggs, milk, butter, spices, and a few key extras—leftover mashed potatoes and a quick session of chopped rosemary. With compromised vision, she used care while handling the knife and measuring proved a bit tedious. However, having baked since the age of six, almost seventy years, she knew her approximations were close enough.

She poured and heated. Stirred and kneaded. A sprinkle here and there, then—*plop!*—she dropped the large ball of dough into an appropriate-sized bowl and covered it with a clean flour sack. The latter, from a newly purchased set bought at her favorite online shop of plentiful and creative flare. Though presently, she could not quite make out its design of mortar and pestle, with snips of lilac florae atop an antique grimoire of recipes. It read, "We Make Magic in This Kitchen." She surely did.

Her frustration set in when the blurriness had not cleared thirty minutes later. That troubled her, so she heated a compress, then went to her toolbox of jewelry supplies on the kitchen table and grabbed the glue, Arista's athame and the loose Blue Moonstone cabochon. The repair, an easy fix, could be done with her eyes closed, and she had sat on this project for far too long already.

Bethie drank the rest of her water, took a seat on the couch, and, through blurry eyes, put the cabochon in its setting. She rotated it to feel the proper placement, then removed it, squeezed out a dab of glue in the athame's emptied butt, and re-secured the stone. Benign in its sheath, she shoved it upright between the cushion to let it harden. "Done!"

She smacked her lips in accomplishment and reached for the heat compress. Relaxing, she placed it over her eyes.

The sound of an unannounced visitor came from her front yard. She heard the car, its door, then footsteps upon her porch. Iris's voice followed.

"Bethie?" she beckoned upon opening the door.

"Oh! Iris. Come on in. I'm in my living room."

How nice of her to stop by after their previous teatime ended so poorly.

The creaky screen door hinges strained open, and Bethie craned her neck to see Iris's blurred silhouette toting her bag and approaching the living area. She relaxed again and replaced the compress. "To what do I owe the pleasure?" *Maybe Arista should be here.* Bethie reached into her long skirt pocket to fish out her phone.

"Oh dear. Is it your eyesight again?" Iris asked as she took Auntie's phone from her hand. "Here, let me help you with that. Who would you like to call?"

"I was going to let Arista know you're here. She enjoys your company, too."

"In time. First, can we chat? Just a short while … elder to elder."

"I don't see why not." *Seriously, I don't see, which makes me nervous.* Bethie felt her neck tensing but purposefully relaxed as she put the compress back on her eyes.

She heard Iris walk to the counter and set down her tote.

"Iris, when you come back, will you please bring my phone with you?" The behavior of seizing her cell felt controlling.

"Of course, Bethie," Iris said, rummaging through her bag. "Bethie, I have brewed you the most magickal blend of herbs. If religiously taken over a few months, I believe it will improve your eye health. I do, *so much*, want to help you get your eyesight troubles cured. I just can't help but think I had something to do with this."

"Oh! Not at all. This happened before I came to see you. So, please never think that."

"Shall we have a drink together?"

With her eyes still covered, Bethie grasped her gurgling stomach full of water. "Hoo! I just drank a full—"

"Please. I know it will help you, and there's not an ounce of caffeine in it."

"It's not the caffeine ..." *It's the fact I'll have to pee five times in the next hour.*

"I'll pour us some now."

With Iris unreceptive to her '*no,*' Bethie arose to assist her in the kitchen.

"No, no," Iris said and guided her back to the couch with a gentle touch. "I'm quite capable of finding mugs for our tea."

As Iris turned back to the kitchen, Bethie could make out her own phone on the counter, quickly grabbed it, and tapped speed-dial for Arista. She watched a blurry Iris stop and stare at her before resuming tea duties.

Arista answered.

"Hey there! Just wanted to let you know Iris has paid me a visit. If you get a chance, stop by, and say *hi*."

"Hello, Arista. Yes, if you get a chance, I would *love* to see you. But I'll be here a while, so no need to rush."

"Sure, Shane and I are in the middle of a task, but I can be there in, say ... thirty minutes?"

"That should be fine."

Bethie hung up and smiled at Iris but could not tell if she reciprocated the expression. However, her fellow witch had their tea ready, so Bethie led them to the couch.

"Here you go," Iris said, handing Bethie her favorite hummingbird mug, the plump, colorful body showing well against its white background. There was no mistaking that!

"I bet that mug is your absolute favorite," Iris said, fully engaged again, as before the sheriff's visit.

Bethie cackled and settled into their moment. Iris's herbal creation smelled enticing, and with her known prowess as a hedge witch, she hoped this promising new elixir of goodwill proved a remedy. If she could send a gwishin to the next life, surely, she could brew an herbal aide for vision. Further thinking about it, while the sheriff may have set them back, Iris had been consistently helpful up to that point.

"I used apples from my trees," Iris said. "Take a whiff."

Bethie took a full, attentive inhalation, receiving the pleasant scent of apples, cinnamon, and hints of orange, clove, and—especially prominent—licorice. Such an aroma of appealing fruit and spices. "Oh, Iris, this smells wonderful," she purred, then took a sip, swished it in her mouth, and swallowed it down. "Absolutely wonderful." In all honesty, she went a little heavy on the licorice.

"I'm so thrilled you think so. Long have I worked on this formula … perfecting it to taste. A few years now. Which could be quite hazardous, I might add, since one must not drink too much licorice."

"Why's that?"

"Hypertension … cardiac arrythmia. Didn't you know that?"

"I did not!" Bethie held her eyes as if she could see the finest detail, but still, Iris showed nothing more than a blur. "I hope you took care not to drink too much."

"I'll be just fine. But I do love the aroma of licorice. Don't you?" Iris took the tea to her lips and tilted the cup. "Mmm. So good, if I do say so myself."

Bethie focused on the sweet smell, then took another sip. The flavor did not ring as pleasant as the aroma. She likened it to cheese—delectable to taste but dirty laundry to the nose. Only reversed!

"I like the addition of the honey. Arista and I seldom sweeten our teas, but this," Bethie sipped again, "makes for a superb blend."

"Mmm-hmm," Iris intoned. "So, Bethie, I don't think I've ever told you the story of my wayward nephew."

"Uh, no. I don't believe so." Odd. Iris had always been tight-lipped about her family. Maybe airing the grandfather episode compelled her to disclose more. Was this them getting closer or another uncomfortable family taboo rearing its ugly head?

"In fact, neither of us has talked much about our kin over the years. For instance, you only found out about how your grandfather murdered my family members a short time back. I'm so sorry you had to find out that way. It alarmed you so."

An uncomfortable taboo rearing its head. Bethie did not want to be obvious and beckon Arista again, but the concern arose within her. She heard a strange undertone in Iris's voice as if a crowbar prying open an untouched stone crypt with a nasty reputation.

"I have to admit, I knew little about my extended family," Iris said. "I kept a healthy distance from them, feeling stifled by their all-consuming obsessions. I lived with free abandon … traveled to many exotic locales. The ancient pyramids had to be my favorite." She paused. "Knowing what I know now, I would have lived life exactly the same. No regrets."

Interested in Iris's exposé, Bethie sipped her tea, feeling an odd tickle in her throat. She released a subtle hack.

Iris paused her story and cleared her own throat. "There's that tickle. I don't know which herb causes it. Perhaps the combination, but I think my palate is getting used to it." She took another sip.

Bethie hacked to ease the irritation, took a sip of tea, and smiled to convey her interest. "So, your nephew …"

"Yes. The state took custody of my niece and nephew after my sister and her husband perished in an unfortunate accident. Such young children … born and raised while I was away … I didn't even know their names." Iris sighed, sat down her cup, and leaned back into the chair. "Someone from our community adopted my niece, though I never had contact with the child. I spent so much time out of the country …"

Bethie remembered her envy of Iris's travels. "Yes, you were quite the wanderlust while Margaret, Pearl, and I rarely ventured from the county." She laughed and cleared her nagging tickle again.

"A much different world without all of today's technology."

"Ain't that the truth!" Bethie said, the tickle becoming a scratch. This could not be from the tea. Right? "Please remind me of the ingredients you used in this," she asserted, wondering if the effect could be an allergic reaction.

"It turns out my niece fell in love with someone very close to you and, well, died an untimely and painful death as well."

"Oh dear. I'm sorry to hear that, Iris." Sad to hear that they shared such pain of losing so many family members. Perhaps her family's effort at reversal played more powerfully—Wait a minute! "Close to me?" Bethie asked with a hack.

"Yes, Bethie. During my recent *involuntary* journey to the Pacific Northwest, I made many wild discoveries. Digging in Fergus's luxurious closet, I unearthed more than just my new Rolex and fine luggage. I found something almost as earth-shattering as your discovery of my curse tablet."

"Fergus's closet?" Bethie's hack became a cough as the scratchiness turned into a burn. Still, she waited for the punchline of this mysterious riddle that Iris insisted on dragging out.

"It brought back the rumors of my young nephew, who was not so fortunate. While my niece received nurturing love, my poor, dear nephew's fate had another avenue to endure. Such sad occurrences that young man suffered. So many homes he cycled through. Abuse. Neglect. A wayward young soul left to wolves." She paused. "And a wolf, he became."

Bethie felt the knowledge bubble up from within her and dropped her jaw at the shock of it. At the same moment, the burning sensation tunneled from her throat into her chest. She applied a firm pressure to the area, hoping to ease the pain, and released a barrage of coughing.

"You see where I'm going with this. I can tell by your expression. Wonderful. Then I don't have to explain why my temporary death— that *you* so graciously brought me back from—made it so easy for my nephew … Fergus … to escape his body's horrifying end by a ravenous drove of pigs. Now, I'm not saying I'm a fan of the man, but it did shed a bit of light upon this whole … ancestral … curse situation we have."

A faintness swept over Bethie, and her stomach cramped. She looked at the blurry image of the hummingbird mug beside her and reached for it, but her coordination faltered, and her hand fell limp, knocking it to the floor. The handle broke off, and the scant amount that remained spilled onto the carpet. With the urge to cough still present, her body no longer could comply.

"Oh, dear," Iris said, not moving an inch to help her.

Iris's relaxed silhouette and her lack of concern could only mean one thing.

"Do you feel it, Bethie? Do you feel your death upon you?"

Bethie fell against the couch as the burning gave way to a numbing paralysis sweeping through her body. She tried to scream, but merely a peep came from her vocal cords. Then, nothing more. She could not talk; her head sagged, and her jaw slackened. Only her blurry eyes endured.

"Let me explain your experience to you. The secret ingredient I used is a high concentration of my cherished mandrakes, minced, macerated, and well disguised by the spices. And yes, licorice. That sweet licorice adds just the right distraction to mask any unpleasant scent and taste. A pinch of hemlock and snakeweed for good measure. Good grief, Bethie, couldn't you taste any bitterness? At all?"

Iris knelt beside her, clearing all items off the floor, then stopped. "There's a familiar sight." She grabbed Arista's athame from the cushion. "I quite like this piece, Bethie, and neither you nor Arista will need it any longer." She set it on the end table, then brought Bethie down and situated her flat on the floor, allowing her spell tin to tumble from her pocket. "What's this little trinket?" Iris reached over her and retrieved her precious Hummingbird Spell tin and popped it open. "Aah. A spell, no doubt. Here." She dumped it in one clump onto Bethie's mouth. "One for the road, my old friend."

Bethie could not help but inhale its concentrated debris, sending her insides into further spasms. The inner struggle felt agonizing. Mentally sharp, yet unable to control her movement or sound. And the stomach cramps. How their upheaval roiled within her.

Iris strolled to the kitchen, no worry nor haste, and removed an object from her tote. She brought it over, knelt down, and placed it upon Bethie's chest before wrapping Bethie's hands and arms in reverence across it. The cold stone and size of it came clear.

Iris further enlightened Bethie of her Spokane experience, while she fussed for perfection with Bethie's lifeless fingers, wrapping them around the tablet. With no luck at placement, she tucked them beneath it and pressed down for good measure. "There you go. Picture perfect."

The pressure of the stone added insult to the suffering that coursed through her body. Unlike her grandparents' version, Iris's tablet weighed as a true chunk of stone—sturdy and coarse, conducting its chill through her blouse.

Iris stood up. Towering above Bethie, she scanned the room before lighting a small, tied bunch of tobacco leaves. She stoked it, blowing it into a smoldering singe, and placed it atop the tablet.

As Bethie lay helpless, Iris's demeanor terrified her—dead to the process, unflinching to the damage she had inflicted, and deliberate with each move.

Iris sprinkled an oily residue upon her, creating an annoying tickle on her face, forehead, and neck.

"Surely you did not believe my story about all that undying love for your brother. Did you? I mean, it was there at first, when he and I could have broken the curse. But he chose another." She flicked another oily sprinkle into Bethie's face. "Who do you think cast the dark spell that led Declan and his *wife* to their deaths? Criminals are the easiest minds to infiltrate, and the drunkard leaving the bar that night, in the same vicinity as their cozy, little dinner date … well, it took barely any effort at all."

No! Iris had loved Declan, Bethie's big brother and protector. To find out she caused his death created a streak of vengeance, stoking her to dig further. How could she ever get out of this mess?

"In time, your nephew and my niece altered the curse. Arista's survival after the arduous labor proved that"—her voice feigned sappiness—"*love is truly the answer*. Tch. Tch. But Bethie, my grandmother's efforts are a force of resilience, and we both know how their story ended. Who's to say whether it was my grandmother's resentment or, ironically, the Kelly's reversal curse that killed Arista's mother … but the end result remains."

Iris lifted her arms skyward and chanted in a low tone. Repeatedly, she murmured the same mantra until it became audible to Bethie's ears.

"By sitting bones of dearest kin,
Their bodies, souls, and rotted skin,
Into this realm, and here within,
I bid them, rise, and walk again."

An eerie sense washed over Bethie, distracting her from the searing pain in her body. A solemn anguish permeated the room.

The reality hit her as the first one materialized—a hooded and cloaked apparition, clearly visible despite her failed eyesight. Spurred by Iris's chanting, they appeared one by one, stepping forward as thick wisps of dense fog in a methodical rhythm. The brooding figures encircled her and positioned themselves to witness Iris execute the deed.

When the last of her dead congregated, Iris whispered into Bethie's ear. "In all truth, Bethie, by my heart and soul, I don't want to do this. But if I don't, my grandmother will see Fergus brought forth from within me. I will lose my life, and you will still die. Please know this decision has been a terrible burden for me to bear.”

Iris sat down cross-legged and tucked her lap beneath Bethie's head, holding it in her hands.

“I love you, Bethie, and I always will,” she said with the soft voice of a doting mother. Her tone changed. “Now, I believe that when murder is involved, Fergus and I transition, me to him, him to me. It turns out that because of our blood link, he manifested otherworldly power after all. Though I know that gwishin's little stunt surely helped him initialize the onset.”

The frustration of her helplessness, the physical agony, and the betrayal felt too much to bear, causing a single tear to fall from the corner of Bethie's right eye.

Iris reached for Arista's athame. “Why use an old witchblade when I now own such an ornate athame?” She unsheathed the blade and scraped the tear from Bethie's cheek, then brought it to her tongue and licked its salty residue.

Bethie felt the sting of her abraded flesh. She flurried her blinks to disengage any further tears and held her eyes wide open in defiance.

“Only one tear you shed? One tear for your soul, Bethie? For your grandniece's life? You know, a famous author once wrote … *one without tears will suffer that much more.*”

Bethie squeezed her eyes shut. She would not subject herself to any further taunting, not from Iris nor the hooded figures lording over her. Instead, she focused on her heartbeat, hoping to steady its arrythmia. And a plan.

“You're dying, Bethie. After you, only one Kelly remains, and she, too, will die. By the way, all the talk about her being the promised one … with so much power … well, we all misinterpreted *that* one. My grandmother was the first to utter those words. How it blew so out of proportion, no one knows. But to create life beyond the fifth generation … well, that indeed would have been the ultimate power.”

This new information served as an analgesic. For the moment, she felt no pain. Only revelation! How could she let Arista know that the power to create new life had been the prophecy's meaning? Producing a child beyond the fifth generation was Arista's prophesied power. And hers alone. What a relief it would be to her grandniece, who had struggled with everyone's expectations for so long.

A new purpose washed through her, further subduing the pain of poison. She had to fight to save her and Arista. *For all the successful spells in my life, if I have ever had any sort of power, let this committed witch manifest it now!*

Iris uttered a new verse to her incantation, enunciating a staccato and spiteful force of indecipherable words, bringing forth a new phantom. Its presence prompted Bethie to open her eyes. Distracted from her inner strategizing and within her blurry vision, she clearly saw the oncoming spirit, its density permeating around her. The closer it came, the more the ghost's detail emerged, carrying traces of a face that existed long ago. The shadow being of a notorious, fearsome witch.

The wretched woman in Iris's family photo by her fireplace lingered at her feet, and upon her face, she saw a scowling look of anguish from a lifetime of regret mixed with her malevolent intention of Bethie's impending doom.

Bethie squeezed her eyes shut again. Knowing and feeling, this was the woman often disparaged by her grandfather. He had warned her if she ever saw her to back away whilst keeping an eye on the old hag … and to never, never trust her.

In her heart, she prayed to her grandfather first. *Dearest Grandfather, I call on you now. The woman you always warned me about is upon me. I cannot back away. I cannot run and hide. But I will work to conjure my most powerful magick if you but only help me.*

No sooner had she finished the prayer, did the idea come upon her—*The Hummingbird Spell!* With no ability to execute in the usual manner, she had to get creative. While it had put her in complete control of humans a few times, it was doubtful the same process would work on the supernatural. She had to push it further!

She had taken care with ingestion up to now, but since Iris just forced her to inhale the dust in entirety, she would explore the possibility of transformation to the limit. Her body was slowly dying, and her mortal enemies surrounded her with malintent. There was nothing left to lose.

Keeping her eyes shut, disregarding Iris's lethal resolve, and listening to her own mental recitation, she released into a trance while envisioning her garden's finest jewel. She married the vision to the treasured verses she had learned as a child.

The humming-bird! The humming-bird!
So fairy-like and bright;
It lives amongst the sunny flowers,
A creature of delight!

The icy air lowered upon her, indicating the old, wicked crone's proximity, but she kept her eyes closed. Focusing on her aims, she pushed herself further than she had ever gone within the realms of her magick. Floating in a cocoon of intention.

All crimson is her shining crown,
Like to the red, red rose;
Her wing is the changeful green and blue
That the neck of the peacock shows.

Bethie focused on her pinky finger, imagining it tapping in a light rhythm against glass. In an ease, she swept deeper into her own trance—*Tap. Tap. Tap.*—influencing her release. Within in her void, she drew out every ounce of psychic energy as the poison branched to her extremities, the inability to move heightening into tingling stumps of deadwood.

A reign of summer joyfulness
To thee, for life is given;
Thy food, the honey from the flower,
Thy drink, the dew from heaven!

Bethie became weightless within her mind without an ounce of her physical being remaining.

Thence, a tiny peck greeted her ears, reverberating as heavy as an iron knocker on a castle door. It came from her living room window, announcing the portal.

All cognition disengaged from her physical body, and a whirlwind of motion transformed her into a magnificent and energized state of being. In swift acceleration, the sensation enveloped her in an all-consuming disguise; a whirring of high-spirited wings and a heartbeat with rapid abandon, far beyond her human form. Almost too expeditious to absorb, she darted and flitted, acclimating herself to the inception of this new ability. Front, back, up, and down, without a second's hesitation. On she whizzed through her front yard in awestruck exhilaration, gathering the sights of familiar surroundings, yet experiencing them in an all-new perspective.

And the colors! The vivid colors shone with distinct clarity, adding dimension and vibrance to what once shown as mundane. All the usual greens and blues, reds and yellows, but also an explosion of brilliant hues beyond anything she had ever known, inspiring names in a vocabulary that did not exist.

But this was no novelty. Nor frivolous occasion to deliberate.

Help lived just a short flight down the street.

CHAPTER 35
GEM IN THE AFTERNOON SUN

With rumpled hair and swoony eyes, Arista ambled into the kitchen.

"Do you want tea?" she called to Shane, still in the bedroom.

"Sure. I think I'm going to up my tea game."

Arista snickered and reached for a simply prepared spearmint blend. She sprinkled it into her diffuser and added a pinch of vanilla-soaked white tea for good measure. She placed it into a small glass pot full of piping hot water and watched it agitate into a caramel-colored swirl.

A sudden hummingbird fly-by brought her attention to the window. Used to her usual ruby-throated sprites, it surprised her to see this one had a crimson-crowned head.

"Aww, that's adorable!" Her voice twinkled, thinking of Auntie. "After our tea, we need to get to Auntie's."

"Whenever," Shane said from the bedroom.

She grabbed two mugs and picked up the teapot as the dazzling little bird zipped past her window again. The top of its head and face shined like a fiery fuchsia gem in the afternoon sun. "Hate to be a pain, but you have to check out this hummingbird. I've never seen one like this. Its color is so pretty."

As she poured the tea, the hummingbird hovered. Its iridescent crown mesmerized her as it began an incessant, square flight pattern right at her window. Its needle-thin beak and tiny eyes stared at her the entire time.

Arista froze. The shock of the moment struck her as if she had dropped into the frigid coastal ocean. "We need to get to Auntie!"

The moment had come, and that Auntie announced Iris's visit meant she played a part. An awful part!

Shane appeared at the kitchen entrance, pulling on a sweatshirt with his face stark in alarm. "What is it?"

She threw on her robe and stepped into her slides while the little bird continued a relentless flurry of swoops and ascents before dropping out of sight. In seconds, it reappeared, its wings a blur of activity, yet unmoving from her view.

She grabbed a kitchen knife and bolted out the door.

No longer muted by the barrier of her cottage, the buzzing of the hummingbird's wings had the volume of a remote-controlled toy, and it chirped in a fuss that tapped at her nerves. Her vision of Auntie's most symbolic creature and its urgency came forefront.

Running through her driveway, Shane stayed close to her side. The hovering presence in her vision, this time, an ally.

The insistent little sun gem led the way, a streak of directive blazing the trail beyond Arista's hedge. Its velocity so great that it left them behind twice, returning each time to ensure the pursuit. But only one primary direction—Auntie's house in a beeline of urgency.

Out of the blue and hot on the hummingbird's tail, a great-horned owl swooped out of the trees. Margaret! For the hermitess to appear felt truly dire, and Arista prayed they would make it in time.

As they ran toward the house, Arista's speech jarred. "It's my vision. I only had it a couple of times, but … I've been down this road before … in *so* many ways …" She dug deeper into her stride. She could not lose Auntie!

Shane kept close to her side. "This is going to be something crazy, huh?"

Ahead of them, the birds flew out of sight behind Auntie's hedgerow.

When they arrived at the entrance, Shane stuck out his arm, holding back Arista. "Wait! Who's that?"

Margaret, in her human form, limped up the steps to Auntie's front door.

"It's Auntie's friend, Margaret!" She tried to push past his arm.

"Listen! If there's something going down, we don't want to *all* barge in at the same entrance and make things worse. Let Margaret distract her." He gestured to the side of the house. "Let's go with stealth." He ducked down and took the lead.

They rounded the corner as the hummingbird flew over Iris's car roof, parked by Auntie's porch. Just looking at Iris's car, Arista validated her long-felt intuition. "I knew it," she whispered, venting her anger. Then she returned her focus to rescue, while hearing Margaret banging on the door and jiggling the knob.

·　　·　　·

Bethie came to, stifled within her inanimate body, and heard Margaret's loud rapping on the door. Still drowsy, she opened her eyes to find the hag above her, grasping Iris's hands and puppeting her motions. With Arista's athame in Iris's hands, both woman and apparition raised the sharp blade high above her chest.

It all came down to this precise moment. She had done her best. So had Arista, catching the significance of her feathered journey and rushing to her aid. Even Margaret had read the winds of misfortune.

But only a fraction of time endured.

Bethie shut her eyes, knowing her life hung in the most fragile balance. The jubilation of shapeshifting, the success of capturing Arista's attention, and Margaret's timely arrival languished into the sobering reality that rescue remained out of reach.

"… as here shall end the third generation." When Iris uttered her last words, Bethie heard an echo from the hag's clicks and rasps, scratchy and coarse.

A sudden clamor traveled through the house as the athame plummeted down at full momentum.

. . .

Margaret threw a frantic look at Arista and headed for the large Serpentine rock sitting on the porch. Shane hunched closer to the cottage, leading them over to Auntie's living room window, while Arista stayed close behind him.

The sound of shattering glass caught their attention. Margaret must have broken through the glass panes of the door.

At the side slider, Shane peered into Auntie's living room and, without warning, slung open the door and charged inside.

Arista took in the scene of sheer terror. An aura of putrid yellow and slate black surrounded Iris, a tick out of sync with her actual movements, and Arista's very own athame in Iris's hands plummeted down toward Auntie's chest.

Shane launched with determination, tackling Iris and sending her tumbling to the floor with the athame flung far from them. He engaged to fight, but Iris submitted in an instant. She sat panting and immobilized as Shane leveraged his weight atop her, threatening bodily harm if she dared to move.

Margaret dashed in from outside, startling Arista. In an unexplained rage, she barged into the room and flailed about, her hands clawing into the air like a cat bent on shredding its opponent.

Arista realized the target, an aural foggy translucence encircled Auntie. She made haste to grab her athame, then back to Auntie. Without hesitation, she initiated the circle—north, east, south, west— Margaret stepped backward and disappeared from view as she finished, above and below.

Circle drawn, Arista incanted words of protection—rapid and precise. Then, with fervent intention, she sliced through the air around her and Auntie. Her blade cutting at shoulder-level, dispersing the translucent forms, while she prayed with unwavering resolve. The words pouring forth unrehearsed and effective.

The supernatural remnants attempted to reform in wisps of smoggy air.

She repeated her chant—louder, stronger—with another rotation of the circle.

In a reprieve of chaos, the haze faded to nothing.

Arista fell to the floor at Auntie's side, her athame still in hand. A moment of relief came when she saw no sign of blood or injury. She stroked Auntie's face, attempting to rouse her, calling her name, and pleading for an answer. Her relief turned to anger at Auntie's unexplained unconsciousness. She smeared the lit tobacco on the tablet, extinguishing it, then jerked the cursed stone from Auntie's chest and slung it to the wall, breaking it into chunks that showered down upon the sofa.

From behind her, Shane rattled off details to the 9-1-1 operator while still clamped down upon Iris.

Just as she thought to set down her athame, Arista noted her visible breath and the icy chill. And a foul smell, its source close.

Auntie stirred, trying to lift her fluttering lids.

Arista's tide of relief from Auntie's rousing was immediately checked by the look of pure horror that crystallized in her opening eyes.

Arista threw a glance above her own head. The putrid aura she had seen surrounding Iris lingered just within her drawn circle. Unlike the cloaked figures, this one had a face that matched the picture at Iris's house. The harbinger of their family's ill misfortune—Iris's grandmother. Facing her down felt terrifying, but her courage took immediate charge.

A scowl of hatred brimmed across the hag's otherwise obscure features. Detestable and menacing, she drew near.

A burst of dynamism shot through Arista, and she launched herself upward and spun to meet the enemy. In a streak of savage will, she slashed her athame from the spirit's right hip up to its left shoulder. Another forceful strike down its right shoulder and across to its lower left side.

The hag's spirit faltered as it moved in closer.

With sheerest intention, Arista raised her athame, secured it in both hands, arms rigidly straight, and whirled widdershins, the blade slicing through the apparition's neck.

Gasping from the exertion, she tightened her grip on the athame and readied for more fight. Arms—*en garde!* Waiting. Looking for the slightest hint of more danger to come.

A moment lapsed.

The spirit wavered.

Arista tightened her grip.

In a slow, weakened churn, the haze of Iris's grandmother diminished, leaving the air around them clear of further danger.

Arista shuddered as the iciness eased. With her blood coursing from energized ability, she darted her eyes around the room, then threw a look at Shane.

"Uhhhh, *what* was that all about?" Shane asked, his eyes stricken with uncertainty.

By the look on his face, he had not seen, possibly, her life's greatest victory. And this time, the villain fell by more than just her hand.

CHAPTER 36
IMPULSIVE MURDEROUS DEEDS

"Bethie, I'm so sorry," Iris sobbed, owning the betrayal against her friend and wearing none of her typical pride. "I didn't want to do it." She looked up at Arista. "My grandmother would have enabled Fergus's possession of me to execute it. Please, believe me. I thought it better you two fall to me than him."

Arista sat confused by the mention of Fergus's name, leading Iris to give a full disclosure of what she had revealed to Auntie about him.

Shane sat transfixed by the confession.

"What did you do to her?!" Arista asked, her anger surging.

"I poisoned her. Death is imminent." Louder, she sobbed, tears drenching her face and her nose oozing in salty slick.

Iris buckled from a sudden bout of wooziness. Her head swayed to the right, then over-corrected left.

Shane jostled her, unamused. "Knock it off."

Arista had never seen him so angry, and she appreciated his kindred spirit by her side.

"He's coming for me. He feels my weakness." Iris said and continued crying while clutching her stomach. "Arista, I'm telling you the truth. He'll win this time. I'm going to let him. I don't want to live to see the day my betrayal of my only friend since childhood leads to her death."

Arista felt a raging resentment stewing within her, hating Iris, glaring at her, and jaded to her sudden show of sentiment.

A soft song of sirens rang from Highway 9.

Arista looked down at Auntie and stroked her cheek. She could feel her pulse, though weak, and her eyes stayed shut. "Hang on, Auntie. Help is coming." As the words left her mouth, she strengthened herself with an energizing inhalation through her nose and imagined sending it to Auntie. "Just hang on."

"I'm ready to greet the Otherworld," Iris blubbered.

"Just stop your crap, lady," Shane said, jerking her.

"Listen to me! I'm warning you—" Iris said, growing hysterical.

When Shane moved to shove her down, Arista stopped him. "No … don't. We need to listen."

"In his and my battle, Fergus wins." Iris winced, doubled over, and released an affected grunt. She shook her head, then cried out in anguish. Her words sputtered out, choppy and pained. She blinked to stay coherent. "You know what this means, Arista." She pulled her hands from Shane's loosened hold and clutched her stomach.

Arista glared at her, awaiting her disclosure, while keeping a close watch on Auntie.

Iris looked at Shane, then cried out in pain. She shook it off. "You must restrain me."

"I can overpower you, no matter who you are. Awful bi—"

Iris shrieked and collapsed to the ground. The volume and strength of her voice waned to silence. Out cold, the room grew quiet.

"Quick, we should do it just in case! Zip ties! Far kitchen drawer," Arista ordered.

Shane ran and rifled through Auntie's drawer as sirens traveled through the neighborhood. He hurried back with a handful of long white zip ties. With efficiency, he doubled them up to wrap Iris's hands just before she roused.

Iris came to and cast an indignant look at Shane while fidgeting with her ties. "What have you done?" she asked, her voice deeper than usual.

Arista stared at the caricature of Auntie's old friend. Her essence had changed, and her expression no longer contained a shred of regret. This was not the true Iris.

Iris looked away from Shane, and when her eyes met Arista's, she paused. A diabolical look glimmered. A look that could come from only one person—Fergus.

A wry smile crept across Iris's face, and her voice annunciated into Fergus's familiar greeting. "Hello, Arista."

"Hey," Shane said, lording over Iris. "Hey!" he yelled when her eyes would not meet his. Shane took Iris's chin and twisted her neck up to face him. "Look at me, bro. I got you!"

Fergus snickered through Iris's lips and pitched her voice. "You shant hit an old lady."

The sirens filled Auntie's driveway—one, two, three vehicles.

Arista kept focus on the villain. With all Iris had told her, she knew she dealt only with the shell of Iris. That the odd woman had passed on relinquishing her body to Fergus and that it was only his vile statements emitting from her mouth.

"We've been through this before, only this time, Fergus," Iris said, her eyes flickering as the name left her lips, "is dead. Give it a few days and I'll be right back out on these streets."

As the words left her mouth, Iris lunged for the athame, taking it into her hands.

In a rowdy commotion, Sheriff Michaels barged through the door with paramedics behind him.

He ordered all to stand clear, leaving Iris standing alone, mid-center of the room, with her bound hands grasping the athame. When she saw the sheriff's eyes upon her, she dropped it to the floor, dislodging the Blue Moonstone again.

"She poisoned Auntie—" Arista cried out as she and Shane approached the sheriff.

"Excuse me," the sheriff said, stopping Arista in her tracks. He walked past her, straight to Iris.

Arista felt jilted and waited for Iris's sob story, remembering how Fergus had gotten out of the murder of her father. She would put up a vigorous fight over his lies this time.

The sheriff pulled a utility knife from his belt and sliced through the plastic bindings.

"Oh, officer, thank goodness you're here!" Iris whimpered, rubbing her wrists. "These people … "

The sheriff clipped the knife back on his belt and grabbed his cuffs.

Iris blinked, confused.

In a fluid move, he slipped one cuff to her wrist, wedged her arm backward, and spun her around, securing the second. "Iris Ardino, you are under the arrest for the murder of Fergus Campbell …"

Iris's eyes bulged in shock.

"… the murder of Manny Whelan, and the attempted murder of Bethie Kelly." The sheriff lowered his voice. "And you damn well better hope it's only attempted on Ms. Kelly, or your holding cell *will* be the last thing you see."

"Wha—" Iris's eyes narrowed in indignation.

The sheriff motioned Deputy Hendrickson to the athame at his feet. "Make sure this gets processed without error. Note the suspect was wielding the weapon upon our arrival, and I believe it will close a loose end in another investigation."

Arista thought of the implication. When she confiscated her athame, switching it out with her witchblade at the scene of her father's death, the weapon and her father's wound would not have matched. Now Iris's prints were all over her athame, the weapon that Conn had used at the murder scene. Long shot, but she flashed a look at the sheriff, knowing he had made the move to protect her.

He gave her a respectful nod, then Shane, before leading an argumentative Iris to the door.

Arista threw a quick glance at Auntie. Seeing her well attended to, she and Shane followed the sheriff as he walked Iris's body, full of Fergus, to his cruiser. Fergus, Iris—who cared? They were both criminals and whoever ended up the owner of that body did not matter. She was just glad to see them carted away in handcuffs.

Shane put his arm around her and pulled her into him while she clutched his waist.

Iris looked up at the sheriff with a wry expression.

The sheriff interjected while shoving the criminal into his backseat. "There is no bail nor bonds available for you *this time*." He slammed the door and turned to Arista. "Keep me posted on Miss Bethie."

Arista waved in agreement.

The sheriff paused and narrowed his focus toward the back of Auntie's house. "Is that okay?" he asked Arista.

She looked for the source of his attention. At the perimeter of Auntie's backyard, Margaret stood in full human form, glaring at Iris sitting in the sheriff's backseat.

"Yes!" Arista confirmed. "She's a dear friend of Auntie."

The sheriff nodded and soon departed.

With the last sight of Iris, Margaret saw Arista's and Shane's eyes upon her. She dropped her angry expression, stood up tall, and put her hand to her heart. Then she bowed her head in a most respectful gesture. As quickly, her classic smirk emerged, and she walked behind the house.

Arista turned to Shane. "Did you see that?"

"Total respect. Maybe she realizes that we're looking out for Auntie, too."

"Thank you, Margaret!" Arista yelled out.

Rising from the back of Auntie's cottage, a beautiful set of far-reaching, mottled-gray wings took flight.

"Good God!" Shane said, his eyes wide in bewilderment. "Are you telling me—"

"Yes. I've been meaning to tell you. But when's the right time for something like that?"

Shane gave an incredulous laugh.

"Excuse me, ma'am!" an EMT said as they pushed past, toting a gurney full of an unconscious Auntie.

"Is she going to be okay?" Arista's anger and awe returned to sheer worry. She followed the EMTs, gazing at Auntie's soft skin, sending the most sacred blessings with her.

"We're taking her to Dominican. It will take a while to get her processed, so please do not follow the ambulance."

Hearing the odd statement, she looked at Shane.

"I think it's because too many people try to follow and end up causing an accident."

That made sense.

Time slowed down thereafter.

As the crime scene crew entered Auntie's cottage, Arista and Shane set forth to leave. Arista took a quick look at the area, remembering the horrifying scene, while an agent bent over Auntie's mug and its broken handle, ready to collect it. She glanced at Iris's cup—clean and dry, without a hint of tea ever touching it.

"Evil bitch," Arista said, then looked at Shane. "We've got to get there."

"Yep."

As they left Auntie's house, she made an interesting observation. "How am I calm right now? Innocent Gene and Caitlin send me into a panic attack, but I feel total peace after …" She gave careful thought to her words since Shane had no idea of the badass moves she had just inflicted upon a horde of ghouls. "… all of *this* stuff!"

"Because you know she'll be okay! She's in the best care and a true fighter."

She and Shane jogged back to her cottage, their heated breath steaming in the briskness of the new winter. Along the way, she relished the final showdown. How she stood up to the ghouls and expelled them … or so it would seem.

"I wonder if they're gone for good," she mumbled without thinking.

"Who's gone?" Shane asked as they neared her entrance.

"Nothing. Just thinking out loud," she said as they reached her driveway. "I need to get better dressed and lock up."

"Yeah. You know we got snow up in Bonny Doon with this temperature. Go ahead, and I'll get things warmed up."

Inside, Arista hurried herself into layered, warm clothing and pushed her feet into a pair of well-worn, gray sheepskin boots. She walked to the door and observed Royal on the beanbag. Nary a worried thought in his peaceful slumber.

"Bye, my baby. I'll be back."

Her comment merited two slits. Then he tightened his paws around his face and pulled himself into a ball. The sight of his comfort brought a future task to mind—finding homes for Iris's cats.

•   •   •

As Arista shut the door, silence ensued.

Upon the beanbag, Royal's eyes popped open, and he lifted his head.

A slight movement captured his attention.

He propped up on his elbows and stared into the hallway as a gentle breeze arose within the cottage.

Alerted, he sat up tall, his pupils dilating.

As the breeze traveled the rooms, various sets of witch bells jingled. Once in the kitchen, it caused the long, healthy green fronds of Arista's hanging fern to waver and tea leaf debris to scatter around her countertop.

The airflow eddied to a rest at the table.

The ghost materialized, admiring his craftsmanship of the age-old Ouija, the initial source of this whole debacle back in 1940. A benefit for his family and the community over the years? Or the spark of generational downfall?

Royal bobbed his head, awaiting the next move of his human's patriarchal spirit.

The apparition lingered, appreciating the homey cabin he had built almost a century earlier. For so long had he served the sentence of his impulsive murderous deed. Weary, he had grown and ever so tired of his watch over the generations. So many, he had failed.

But today, the immediate release of his lingering duty greeted him. His soul liberated. At long last, the Promised One, his great-great-granddaughter, had broken the curse and slashed his mortal enemy into oblivion. He wished he could have done it himself. But that was a lifetime ago.

Now, he foresaw a certain future, the continuance of his kin.

He took a final look at his humble abode, readying for his next journey. Then he smiled and diminished into the Summerland.

CHAPTER 37
HIGH AS A WITCH ON BROOMSTICK

Sheriff Michaels flashed his badge to the reception desk. "Bethie Kelly."

The nurse looked at her team. "We just her admitted to her room. She's in serious condition and not awake."

"I won't be long," he said, already disturbed by the situation and further miffed by the nurse's resistance.

She considered the request, cinched her mouth, then stood up and led him to the fourth door. "Please do not disturb her."

As he stepped inside, he felt an insecure sadness at the sight of Bethie's wrung-out and pallid face and the needled tubing supplying her fluid management. He approached her bed and lightly touched her hand, the same hand that held his during walks through the park and downtown as a child. Upon contact, his eyes felt a strain of melancholy tears. He held them and blew off his sadness with agitation.

"Hey, Bethie. How's my favorite babysitter?" Another flush of wetness burned his eyes. "I know they just brought you in, but I had to come tell you … well, you know I always liked you better than Mavis." He knew she loved it when he favored her over former babysitting competition. He tucked his lips into a stiff hold. "You got this. You hear me?" He wiped his eyes. "I'll always remember that you were the best sitter a boy could have, and the things you taught me … plants … patience and intuition … they help me to this very day." He moved in a little closer and murmured in her ear. "Maybe you taught me a little too much. You best not be involved in any of this Manny Whelan business." He stood up again. "Though I'm thinking Iris was not someone you deemed a close friend." He paused and regained his composure.

He let the stream of warm childhood memories with his favorite babysitter saturate his mind. He remembered stopping by the hospital to check on her after her head injury from the serial killer last year. But that concussion paled in comparison to what she now faced.

"All I know is you better get well." The sheriff blew out his tension and tucked his lips into a tight smile. "Alright, then."

With one last squeeze of her hand, he turned to leave.

Two steps away, a sound effect arose.

He stopped and turned toward her.

From Bethie's bed came a rumbling fart as loud as a novelty store whoopee cushion.

Did he hear that right?

He looked at her face while she still laid sleeping. It struck him. She did not look so drawn and defeated anymore. In fact, he could swear her mouth turned slightly upward in a mischievous smirk. And her cheeks were covered in a flush of rosiness.

He turned toward the door and snickered, drinking in the notion that she would be fine.

· · ·

Bethie awoke in a sterile hospital room, sporting a thin blue cotton gown with white piped edging. Groggy, she tilted her head forward and saw the saggy neckline haphazardly covering her sun-damaged chest. "Uck."

She went to straighten it, but the number of IVs attached to her arms and the aching fatigue within her body deterred the aim. Her head plopped back onto the pillow.

She felt ill. No, that was an understatement. Her body felt as though someone had acid-washed it from within, and every sore orifice proved they used a lot of hoses.

"Pfft!" Even to scoff, hurt.

But her vision showed clearer. She made out the little blue letters on her IV bag of clear fluid, hanging like supple fruit from its metal branch. The digital readout was even more crisp, aided by its bright red digits. The blip of her monitor alerted her of her heartbeat—steady, and from the looks of it, not so bad for someone her age, especially someone who had drunk a poisonous brew.

In irony, she chuckled to herself, holding her stomach. "Well, here I lay again," she said, thinking of her hospital stay from the concussion and cut hand resulting from her ordeal with the serial killer. "Surely, no way to spend Yule. That's for sure."

She pressed the button beside her, causing the jabbering to cease at the nurse station outside of her room.

A woman with long, straight black hair dressed in burgundy scrubs entered, carrying a cheerful smile and bubbly personality. "It's good to see you awake, Ms. Kelly. My name is Theresa, and I'm one of your nurses."

"Hi, Theresa. How long have I been out?"

"This is day two for you." The nurse checked vitals and hummed in approval. "If you're ready for visitors, we can contact your grandniece. She's onsite and very much looking forward to seeing you."

"Yes, but I feel very, *very* sore."

The nurse checked her tablet. "Looks like you're due for pain medication. I'll be right back."

A flicker of memory. The sheriff had come to see her and said many nice things. The haze of it came clearer.

Reappearing after a brief phone call to Arista, Theresa placed her tray of a vial and hypodermic needle on the metal over-bed table and prepared the poke.

"Did Sheriff Michaels visit me?"

"He did," Theresa said, flicking the bubble upward within the injectable serum. Then she grinned. "You gave him a warm send-off."

She wondered what that meant but felt too tired to pursue it.

After efficient administering, the nurse went back to her station.

While raising her bed's backrest, Bethie rolled her shoulders and stretched her neck. Then she leaned back and relaxed her sore stomach. Her thoughts drifted to her last moments with Iris. How utterly disappointing that the wicked witch had tried to kill her. She understood Iris's predicament, but still. She snorted and chalked it up to another lesson learned. Then she wondered how many more lessons her body could endure, especially if they kept landing her in the hospital. She shook her head and appreciated her dear coven sisters even more. While Pearl could be a real 'B,' she sure had Iris pegged. As did Arista.

But she was alive! Bethie let the woe dissipate and counted her blessings one by one. With grateful reflections completed, she looked at the foot of her bed, enjoying that her vision seemed better than usual as she studied the sharpened line of her metal footboard.

"Auntie." Arista entered and gave her a big, gentle hug.

Bethie could not hold back the joyous laughter and winced. "Oh. It's so good to see you." She peered past Arista at Shane. "Both of you!"

Shane smiled and reached over for a momentary grasp of her hand, then backed away.

"I'm so sorry this happened to you, Auntie," Arista said. "I swear we knew that woman was trouble."

"Yes, your intuition has surpassed my own."

"Nah, I think it's just harder to believe a friend could do such a thing."

"Can't see the forest through the trees. Hah, maybe so. Or simple denial—" A wave of jubilation dawned on her! The memory of her spell came back in a splendid blast. "Arista, did you see me?! The hummingbird?!"

"I did see the hummingbird! That's what got us to you in time. It was my vision!"

"It *was* me!" Bethie tapped Arista's hand with rapid excitement, leaving her grandniece blinking in confusion.

An overflowing exuberance engulfed her fatigued and achy body. The medicine kicking in only helped the effort. She wanted to yell it from a mountaintop but worked hard to keep her excitement low-volume. "I did it. I finally did it! After all these years. Hooo!"

"What do you mean? You mean, that *was* you?" Arista's eyes lit up like a child watching fireworks.

"Yes. YES!" Bethie shook her head, feeling her ear-to-ear smile, amazed and still in awe of the experience of speedy flight and the brilliance of never-before-seen colors. "It was ME!" She giggled, squeezed her fists, and gave a controlled *whoop*.

The beeps of her monitor alerted Theresa, who promptly entered, reset a few buttons, then gave a lifted eyebrow, reminding her of limitations upon her exit.

"In all my days …" Bethie said, still amazed, but her energy quickly draining.

After the last expulsion of delight, she sank back toward her upright bed and patted her stomach. Wooziness and fatigue returned. She released a cleansing exhalation, ready to pour forth her confession.

"I never told you, but over the years, I've worked hard to progress my Hummingbird Spell. What started as inundating a random troublemaker's senses with hallucinations of my feisty little birds became my long-time dream of following the likes of Margaret and Mr. Tessay." She dropped her chin in a second of shame. "In Arizona, I had started huffing the ingredients of my Hummingbird Spell. Several times, in fact."

Arista's jaw dropped in shock, and she winced with worry. "Auntie."

"I know. I know. But it was a minuscule amount each time. Still, my vision issues started thereafter. The morning I tripped over Iris's table, I accidentally took a bit more than usual before we left for her house. I see this now. No pun intended." She chuckled. "When I realized the correlation after a few tries at it, I stopped, but … too late. The process had already set in."

"Auntie, while I want to admonish you … I have to say … I'm super impressed!" Arista said with a giddy smile.

"There's more … and this is the good part. I believe that because I had accustomed my system to it when Iris dropped the entirety of my tin onto my face, it became the ultimate step of transformation. Had I not already adapted, it could have gone terribly wrong. Especially blended with the ingredients from Iris's toxic tea. There are some potent ingredients in my own concoction. But no. Instead, it became a grand event!" She cackled, her body now free of aches. "That old biddy actually did me the greatest of favors."

"I don't know whether to smack your arm or acknowledge your greatness."

Bethie noticed Shane looking lost. "Shane, my dear, you have gotten yourself involved with quite an unusual family."

He snapped out of the awe and shrugged in surrender. "Fine by me. I'm getting used to it."

Arista smiled at him, then squeezed Auntie's forearm. "I'll go with acknowledged greatness!"

"Yes, ma'am! This ol' gal has a brand-new trick." The seriousness of the ability struck her. "But I know from experience it's not something to do often. Otherwise, I could go completely blind, and I'm quite enjoying my clear eyesight right now."

"That's awesome, Auntie."

"Oh! And many, many revelations during my time with Iris!"

As high as a witch on a broomstick crossing the moon's silhouette, Bethie felt no pain while telling Arista all about Fergus being Iris's nephew, making her distant kin of Arista. She also told of Iris's being possessed by him and taken to Spokane and the luxurious lifestyle that she had enjoyed. Then, to cap off the wild stories that left Shane flabbergasted and speechless, she disclosed the grandest discovery of all. That even though Arista had developed many fine supernatural gifts, her prophesied power came not from a surplus of fantastical abilities.

"So, instead of, as you say, shooting lightning bolts from your fingers and starting fires with your eyes …"

Arista hung on her words.

"Your ultimate power is to create the sixth generation! When you start a family, the curse is broken … moot and formally annulled!"

Arista looked up at Shane, then back to Auntie. "Are you kidding me?!"

Bethie chuckled. "I am not. It was Iris's grandmother that started the whole legend of your importance. Though, in her perspective, that is why they wanted you …"

"Dead!" Arista laughed at the irony. "It doesn't matter! Do you know how much pressure that takes off me? I mean, I've got some abilities here and there, but I had all these unmet expectations." She laughed aloud. "And I *want* to have babies! It's my dream to have a big family!" She looked at Shane.

"I'm game," he said.

Bethie chuckled again, watching the two of them acclimate to the news. She had always liked that young man—how he'd always been Arista's friend and stayed true to her even during their separation. Now, the fella had saved *her* life in a most chivalrous way. Who else could she ever want for her grandniece?

Bethie released a big raspberry-lipped puff. "I'm pooped, you two. I hope you don't mind, but this gifted crone needs some rest."

CHAPTER 38
A RELAXED SNORE

"Yuletide comes, the old years dies ..."

Arista sat mesmerized by the blinks of colorful lights on her tree while a Yuletide chant played at a low volume through her speakers. Immersed in her surrounding peace, she felt no anxiety, no dread, and no fear of further loss. The visit with Auntie in the hospital earlier in the day reassured her. So proud of her shapeshifting accomplishment, Arista shared that joy.

As far as her own life, the drastic measures she had taken out of survival only yesterday left her feeling competent, able, and fully protected.

This, despite the emptiness she felt in her home again. She was certain that breaking the tablet had released her great-great-grandfather's spirit.

Her front door opened, as Shane entered from the wintry dark night, after a quick trip to his truck.

"Are you sure you won't get in trouble for being here on Christmas Eve?" she asked.

He had no answer. With a serious expression, he walked over and stood above her.

"What?" she asked, sensing his trepidation.

"I just need to know ..." He chewed at his cheek, peering down at her.

"Yeeeees?"

"Have you ever thrown any spells on me?"

"Oh, concerned with spells after hearing Auntie's hummingbird story, huh?" She grinned, feeling the power of her position, but couldn't toy with him too long. "Of course not," she said with compassion, rising to hug him. "You and I are all natural and very real."

Shane took a breath, stepped back an arm's length, and, clutching one of her hands, knelt down on one knee. "Arista Kelly…"

No way! An immediate surge set her heart racing, and her eyes welled. "Yes?" Focused on him and feeling a grin of anticipation, she clamped down on her lips, knowing her mouth must look funny, quivering so.

From behind him, Shane revealed a little black velvet box. Once opened, it presented a precious jewel, extra sparkly from reflecting her tree's twinkling lights. The ring boasted a magnificent round solitaire, with rose gold Celtic knots hugging the stone and weaving down and around the band. Set on the black velvet backdrop, it dazzled her more than Royal's blues upon his satiny black face.

"Riss, will you marry me?" His eyes stayed fixed on her.

A warm flush of excitement washed through her, followed by the most joyful love. She looked at his face, his eyebrows twitching in insecurity and his caramel-brown eyes affixed upon her every move. The joy brimmed within her, and her grin became a wide-open smile. "Yes!"

Together, they stood and clutched into their snuggest hug ever.

He backed away and gave a relieved smile while removing the ring from its velvet slit.

"How'd you know my size?" she asked as he slid it onto her finger. She brought it up for a closer view, studying the light refraction. "Oh, Shane, I love it!" she squealed.

"You have so many rings, you didn't even miss it when I borrowed one a while back."

"Was it the three Ambers set in silver?"

"Uh … yellowy-orangish with specks inside?"

"Yes! I noticed it missing, but the next thing I knew, it was back. Sneaky!"

Following a series of hugs and kisses, Shane plopped down on the couch and deflated into the cushions, energy fully spent.

"You won't mind a hand-fasting ritual, right?" Arista said. "Maybe at the beach?"

"If you don't mind some kind of small Catholic ceremony? We could do both at the beach at the same time."

"What about …" She realized she was overthinking the moment. "Never mind."

She scooted in and nuzzled into him, gazing at the festive sight of her adorned tree. Beneath it on the white snowy skirt, Royal lounged in a regal comfort. She looked at her diamond and sighed. Happiness had found her again. At last, maybe she could settle back into that uplifting bliss that others had once mocked her for. After experiencing both sides, she liked the optimistic outlook much better.

"Hey, would you mind having a sheriff as a husband?"

What?! "I don't think so. Is that what you want to do?"

"I'm considering it. I have to say, rushing to Auntie's rescue was a major high. Plus, I know he was joking, but the sheriff said I seem to be around at opportune times."

"Our sheriff's a cool guy. I'll support whatever you want to do."

"I enjoy teaching, too. It's just a thought."

As his voice trailed off, Arista studied her tree, musing at the absurdity surrounding Fergus's murder and his own arrest for the same. For that matter, how could she keep that from Shane if he became the law? Would he have to report it if she ever let it leak? Perhaps she could keep the secret until his retirement in thirty to forty years.

Hopefully, he stayed a teacher.

"So, December's full moon is called the Cold or Oak Moon, but I'm thinking of renaming it the Hummingbird Moon. Every year, we can celebrate Auntie's victory at spellwork with the Hummingbird Moonrise." Happy with her clever idea, she turned toward him.

Shane's head laid back on the couch, his mouth gaping to allow a relaxed snore to gurgle up from his throat.

Arista laughed, "Worked yourself up quite a bit, didn't you?"

She gently shook him and rousted him to bed. Cozy and content in the chill of their night, she had immense appreciation. Auntie had survived, Shane had just proposed, and tomorrow would be a merry celebration with her addition to his family's Christmas brunch. A magnificent feast, no doubt. Thereafter, they would spend the rest of the day with Auntie.

CHAPTER 39
THE HOLLY KING
AND NATIVITY SCENES

Up early for the seasonal festivities, Arista stood by her double-paned kitchen window, watering and spritzing her lush green fern and array of African Violets. Within the hour, the sunbeams would shine upon them all, creating the humidity on which they thrived.

After refilling her pitcher, she walked to the living room and reached beneath her tall noble fir to refill its green tub. She sat back on the floor to appreciate the array of ornaments—handblown glass mushrooms with red tops speckled in white spots, tawny lions asleep by snow-white lambs, the Holly King's semblance hand-painted on a pearlescent bulb and miniature wooden nativity scenes. Soft music played in the background to ready her for the onslaught of the day's events.

Down the hall, she heard the onset of murmurings and braced herself for a barrage of requests. In no time, the sound of little, sticky bare feet on hardwood floors made their way into the living room.

"Mom, why didn't you wake us up?" griped Rowan, her oldest. Conceived two years after their beach ceremonies, her eight-year-old daughter packed the discernment of an astute debater, loved animals, and looked a carbon copy of Shane—caramel-brown eyes and honey-blond hair—currently ragged with bedhead.

"Look, Mom, I already brushed my hair," Liam said, hoping his tidiness merited favor. At five years old, his features mirrored her own, complete with strawberry-blonde hair and sparkling blue eyes.

"Well, look at that. Looks like you *are* ready to start the day," Arista said, appreciating his usual earnest efforts.

"Yeah." He hesitated. "Mom, Rowan says Jasper belongs just to her, and Summer is just yours."

"Jasper and Summer are the *family* horses and belong to all of us equally," Arista countered, giving her daughter a gentle side-eye. "Rowan knows that. Anyway, enough of that stuff. Today's a great day! Yule and Christmas and presents and cookies!"

"Are Uncle Gene, Aunt Caitlin, and Maisie still coming?" Rowan asked.

Arista thought of her distant cousin and their many fun playdates getting the kids together. She appreciated her children would grow up knowing family. "Yes! They'll be here for brunch, and they may go to Glamma and Grandpa's house with us if we can talk them into it!"

"As Glamma says ... she loves a big audience," Rowan said.

"Yes, she does," Arista confirmed, quite humored and appreciative of her mother-in-law these days.

Gurgles of baby talk traveled down the hallway. "Sounds like Chloe is awake. Tell you what ... you two go get Auntie from the studio. Straight there—no sidetracking—and help her bring Wally if she wants. When you get back, we'll have apple cider while we wait for the cranberry orange muffins, and Auntie or I will tell the legend of Hummingbird Moonrise since tonight is December's Full Moon."

"That's our bedtime story, and what if Auntie's not up yet?" Rowan asked.

"We'll probably get back past bedtime, and believe me, Auntie is up," Arista said, meriting a nod from Rowan.

"What about presents?" asked Liam.

"When Daddy gets up, we'll open today's Yule present. Then, lots of presents at Glamma and Grandpa's house! Now go get Auntie, please."

"Yes!" Liam said, pumping his fist for the gift information, while Rowan gave an annoyed roll of her eyes, realizing the chore of wrangling a cranky Auntie.

Arista watched them hustle outside and across the walkway to Auntie's door. As they knocked, she chuckled, picturing Auntie's annoyance at the rambunctiousness of children on such an exciting morning.

Now in her mid-eighties, Auntie lived in the newly-built studio at the far corner of the yard, compliments of the funds she received from the sale of her Sedona and Boulder Creek homes. Her new place included the sleek upgrades and fresh look of her former Arizona refuge but was manageable in upkeep. They had also divvied up the garden, so that each had their own space. And with three incomes, ample funds supported the comfortable heating needed for cold bones in the wintertime. The snowbird had fully nested, yet still visited her coven sisters, staying with Pearl when she traveled.

Arista ran into a sleepy-eyed Shane at the entryway. She gave him a quick hug and kiss. "Merry Christmas!" then walked toward the baby talk.

"Happy 5th Yule day," Shane said with a yawn, then garbled something about tea.

"It's on the stove! There's also cider," she bellowed behind her while walking into Chloe's room.

On the rocker cushion, an elderly Royal sat tall, knowing his favorite human would come to the baby's call. He gave a wide, whiskered yawn, then relaxed to pear pose. At seventeen, he chose lower perches for the easier jumps. While he had lost a lot of weight and slept most of the day, his energy held strong in the morning. A perfect time for breaking the fast and getting warm greetings from all his humans.

Mew.

After a quick acknowledgment of Chloe, she gave him a gentle swoop. "You will always be my first baby." She kissed his forehead and set him back in the chair with gentleness.

Stepping cribside, she softened to a giddiness that came naturally when she looked at her baby. "Good morning, little jewel."

The babe's usual greeting reflected her mother's love—a beaming smile and excited wiggle within the swaddled baby burrito.

Arista went about the waking routine, unwrapping the muslin square, untaping the night-old diaper and allowing fresh air to hit that heated baby butt.

Expecting all the usual joy, this morning brought an ill reminder. An irritating prick struck her psyche. It had been years since she had felt the intrusion, but it came with each new, blessed child at least once. She had wondered when he would try to engage her this time and felt it upon her.

Arista.

His voice came from within her. Since Iris had ceded to him, she felt sure it was their blood within her that allowed the communication. But she knew he did not see through her eyes as he did through her mother's.

Arista, gone but not forgotten.

She smiled and stroked Chloe's tummy, wondering how long she would have to ignore Fergus's mocking before it stopped. She continued through the motions—diaper rash cream, powdering Chloe's naked butt, and securing her fresh diaper. She tried to act normal—smiling at her baby, humming—but her edginess brimmed.

Iris is out in eight more years, which means I am, too. And for sticking me with the rap on everything, I will come for recompense.

A spark of protection provoked Arista to pick up her daughter and hold their bodies close. She waited in silence, holding her breath, knowing the taunting would soon pass.

Unusual in his later age, Royal made a grand gesture and jumped onto the chest by the crib.

Mew.

Her awareness of him drifted.

I know you hear me. So glad we can attune—you and I. Perhaps one day, I'll reach out to one of those kids of yours.

Never before had he mentioned her children. A rush of bad memories flooded her mind—his mocking expressions and doggedness upon her mother, riddling her with disease, and her father's fall to brutal murder at his call. Then she remembered further back, a child herself watching her father drive away, leaving her crying in Auntie's arms at eight years of age. Was this her children's future?

A-risss-ta.

Her heart raced, and her baby whimpered from her tightened grasp.

A derisive laugh echoed within her.

Then came a feeling. A remembrance of strength. Her greatest violent moment of slashing his ghoulish grand matriarch into oblivion.

She inhaled. Then let it go, relaxing her shoulders. With courage gathered, and loving care, she set Chloe back into her crib and handed her a colorful stuffed hummingbird. She stroked the length of Royal's back, letting him know she appreciated his concern, then closed her eyes, ready to engage after all these years.

Do you not realize you were nothing more than a pawn for your great-grandmother? That every evil action you did toward me was a program, not your own? She paused for an answer. *You didn't have to follow that family curse. You had free will.*

Though he stayed quiet, she felt his presence.

I actually feel sorry for you that you didn't realize before it was too late. But I will tell you … it is too late. Too late for you. Hopefully, in your possession of Iris, you realized all these supposed powers you thought you could take from me … they don't exist. My power was to break your great-grandmother's evil curse, which is exactly what I did.

She opened her eyes to peek at her daughter beneath her.

Chloe lay transfixed by her mother's strange behavior. But upon the eye contact, she squirmed and offered an amused gurgle.

Arista smiled, stroked Chloe's cheek, and again closed her eyes. She settled back into the space between.

And I know from time to time I may hear your voice. Threatening me, trying to put fear into me of what you could do to me, my family … my children! Reminding me of the horrible mess you caused in my young life. Perhaps someday, I will find a way to never hear your voice again. But maybe not. You know why?

She paused, inviting a response.

Nothing.

Because you serve as a reminder to me of how very wrong life can go when you do not make your own way. When you fall for old patterns and beliefs that are not your own.

She took a breath and stilled. Listening. Waiting.

Just know that I'll always prevail in anything having to do with you. Like I always have. And I will continue living this remarkable … adventurous … blessed life that I have. That I love!

She reabsorbed her emerging tears of passion and gratitude.

But if you truly feel driven to stalk me or terrorize my family as a ninety-something-year-old woman—which is what you will be—or even if you find some other poor soul to possess, you go ahead and try. I'll be waiting for you. And by my will and my hands, I will strike you dead!

She felt a resolve, a fierce protective authority over her children's world with a potential for the bloodiest violence she could ever release if driven to it.

But she settled into her kindness, which always felt more satisfying.

Or you can find a bit of dignity within yourself and move on to your next and, I pray for you, better life.

She listened within herself.

Waiting.

Only her thoughts remained.

She took a supremely deep breath, drawing in every last sip of oxygen. Then, with an abrupt huff, she puffed away all the distress that the encounter had brought.

Chloe startled. She scrunched her bottom lip into a quiver; her steady, building cry threatening to be a massive wail.

"Oh, bee-bee. I'm so sorry." She scooped her up into a motherly hug. She drank in the tender moment between her and her daughter.

Rawr.

From the living room, she heard Wally's obnoxious meow, followed by Auntie, Shane and the kids uniting in cheerful chatter. The sounds of a cohesive family.

She nuzzled her daughter's soft, velvety head into her neck and swayed, calming the remaining whimper to silence. She held her out in front of her with strong, capable arms before bringing their noses together for a little wiggle.

When the smile returned to Chloe's face, she made haste to her awaiting family, Royal close behind her.

THE END

I hope you enjoyed this final installment in the
Murder, Tea & Crystals Trilogy!
and Thank You so much for taking this journey with me!

For Reference and Inspiration

Air & Fire Metaphysical Shop, Boulder Creek, CA – *Hi to Emelia and Zelly!*

https://www.babipur.co.uk

https://savemountdiablo.org/blog/benitoite-the-diablo-ranges-hidden-gem/ and Benitoite Facts

BRW - Black Rose Writing - https://www.blackrosewriting.com

Blizzard Entertainment, World of Warcraft

Frosty's Christmas Tree Farm - http://www.frostyschristmastreefarm.com

Mary Botham Howitt, The Humming-Bird, https://allpoetry.com/Mary-Botham-Howitt - Excerpt and one word changed for the benefit of the story)

https://www.youtube.com/watch?v=V9NKyBiu6FM – *For Irish Vowels sounds.*

L'Engle, Madeleine, A Wrinkle in Time, Ariel Books, 1962

Learn Religions, Linji Yixuan, https://www.learnreligions.com/kill-the-buddha and https://www.youtube.com/watch?v=jg1AwxJSfJU

Lewellyn Books, www.llewellyn.com

Mariah Carey, All I Want for Christmas is You, 1994

Hayao Miyazaki, My Neighbor Totoro, 1988

https://moon.nasa.gov

Native Animal Rescue, Santa Cruz, CA,
https://www.nativeanimalrescue.org/

Nikki Sixx, Kickstart My Heart, Motley Crue, 1989

J.K. Rowling, Harry Potter, Bloomsbury, 1997

J.M. Barrie, Peter Pan, Tinkerbell, 1904

https://www.youtube.com/watch?v=1WvIwkL8oLc – *For the Cockney English Accent - This guy is hilarious!!*

Riva Fish House, Santa Cruz Wharf, https://www.rivafishhouse.com

Slayden, Donna (born and raised in Glasgow, Scotland) – *BFF and guide for an Americanized Scottish Accent!*

Stanton, Andrew, Monsters Inc./Finding Nemo, Pixar, 2001/2003

https://sphereandsundry.com/a-guide-to-dead-and-ancestral-worship-altars-offerings-and-ritual/

Walt Disney, *Private Pluto / Chip and Dale* and *Finding Nemo, 1949 / 2003*

Ware, Flora, Yuletide Comes, 2020

Warner Bros., Scooby Doo, 1969-1970

https://depts.washington.edu/uwhatc/PDF/factsheets/Coping_After_Violent_Death_Loved_One.pdf

White Witch Podcast w/Carly Rose, Spotify – *What a personality!!*

www.wikipedia.com

Wonders of the World, Spokane, WA, https://wondersoftheworldinc.com

https://www.etsy.com

https://www.thecopperkettleteabar.com/index.php/product/norwegian-yuletide-tea/

WITCHY DICTIONARY

Beltaine - Beltane is the Gaelic May Day festival, marking the beginning of summer. It is traditionally held on May 1st, or about midway between the spring equinox and summer solstice. Historically, it was widely observed in Ireland, Scotland, and the Isle of Man. The holiday celebrates spring at its peak and the coming summer.

Deosil – A clockwise motion used in a variety of rituals to bring in good luck.

Epiphany Eve - The traditional date for the feast is January 6. In Western Christianity, the feast commemorates the visit of the Magi to Baby Jesus. Eastern Christians, on the other hand, commemorate the baptism of Jesus (but it is also called Epiphany) in the Jordan River.

La Befana - In Italian folklore and folk customs, La Befana is a witch-like old woman who delivers gifts to good children—and lumps of coal to bad ones—throughout Italy on Epiphany Eve in a similar way to Santa Claus or the Three Magi. In traditional Italian iconography, she is portrayed as having ember as eyes, sharp feline teeth, a sharp and cutting tongue, and a sooty face from the chimneys through which she enters houses. Grimm described her as a misshapen fairy. She is said to wear rags and a headscarf and carries a broom and a sack or a basket in which she keeps her gifts.

Parshall – An important Celtic craft that guards against your enemies and evil spirits. Placed above the front door, it is usually made for Samhain. It is similar to Brigid's Cross and the God's Eye.

Samhain - Samhain is believed to have Celtic pagan origins, and some Neolithic passage tombs in Ireland and Britain are aligned with the sunrise at the time of Samhain. It is mentioned in the earliest Irish literature from the ninth century and is associated with many important events in Irish mythology. The early literature says great gatherings and feasts marked Samhain when the ancient burial mounds were opened as portals to the Otherworld. In the ninth century, the Western Church endorsed November 1st as All Saints' Day, and November 2nd later became All Souls' Day. It is believed that Samhain and All Saints/All Souls' influenced each other and the modern Halloween. Most American Halloween traditions were inherited from Irish and Scottish immigrants.

The Sun, Tarot Card – The Sun is the 19th Major Arcana card in most traditional tarot decks. It is generally considered positive. It is said to reflect happiness and contentment, vitality, self-confidence, and success. Sometimes referred to as the best card in tarot, it represents good things and positive outcomes to current struggles.

Yule - Yule is a twelve-day-long celebration that starts on the eve of the Winter Solstice in the Northern Hemisphere and ends with the new calendar year. This celebration was one of the most important of the year in ancient times, and it was celebrated across Europe. In essence, Yule marks the return of the sun after the long, dark nights of winter. The word "Yule" comes from the old Norse word for wheel. It reminds us of fresh starts and the cyclical nature of our planet. It's naturally a time of year when we reflect on the year passed, and our plans for the year ahead. Many Yuletide traditions are very familiar to Christmas celebrations, including singing, lighting candles, decorating homes, feasting, dancing, and sharing gifts. Many of these traditions are not fixed to a particular day. They are drawn from across Europe, being kept alive by communities through stories, song, and verse.

And Beyond...

"Oh shoot! Liam, will you run grab Chloe's teether … the banana one?"

"Mooooommmm," he said, with resistance.

"It'll only take you a moment and I promise we'll wait."

Dutifully, he hustled back into the hallway.

Amused by his excitement, she stepped halfway into the hall to observe him, drinking in the son she loved so much.

Liam stopped just outside of Chloe's bedroom and waved his index finger in a swirling design aimed at the crib. He mumbled a few words, then making a hook with his finger, jerked it back toward himself.

In an instant the small silicone banana landed in his other open hand. Mission accomplished!

Pleased with himself, he hurriedly turned but froze in his steps seeing her eyes upon him. A sheepish expression crossed his face, and he lowered his head. Without eye contact, he walked up to her, handed her the teether and bolted passed her toward the tree, excited once again.

Stunned and humored, her eyes trailed him. She would need to keep watch of this new development.

Acknowledgements

I'd like to thank the many individuals that provided support in one form or another during this entire trilogy-writing experience.

First, I recognize my husband and two adult sons that kept the encouragement flowing, yet gave me plenty of distraction showing me that my identity will always be more than an author … to my extended families that spread the word about the books and offered plenty of kudos for my efforts … for my loving friends who oohed-and-aahed at my unknown ability to create such a project … and a hearty Thank You to all the above, who lent an ear for my expressed frustrations with the process and the scrutiny that comes with putting yourself in the public eye.

I also acknowledge my Black Rose Writing family who answered my many novice questions, edited my frequent corrections, designed perfectly mystical covers, and worked with minutia such a blurbs and elevator pitches. They have been a professional force of effective representation as well as a pleasure to work with! This has all been a dream come true and it would have never been possible without receiving that first welcoming acceptance letter!

Sherri was raised in southeast Texas. Walking barefoot most days and catching crawdads as they swam the creek beds, she had a love for all things free and natural. Her childhood ran rampant with talk of ghosts, demons, and backcountry folklore. This inspired her first story for sale, about a poisonous flower that shot toxins onto children as they smelled it. Her classmate bought it for all the change in his pocket. Shortly thereafter, her mother packed the two of them up and headed to the central coast of California. Since that time, she has worked corporate, married, raised two sons, and now writes full-time creating atmospheric paranormal fiction. Her debut novel, *Murder Under Redwood Moon,* shot straight to #1 New Release on Amazon.

Final Note from Sherri L. Dodd

Word-of-mouth is crucial for any author to succeed. If you enjoyed *Hummingbird Moonrise*, please **leave a review** online—anywhere you are able. Even if it's just a sentence or two. It would make all the difference and would be very much appreciated.

Thanks!
Sherri L. Dodd

We hope you enjoyed reading this title from:

www.blackrosewriting.com

Subscribe to our mailing list – *The Rosevine* – and receive **FREE** books, daily deals, and stay current with news about upcoming releases and our hottest authors.
Scan the QR code below to sign up.

Already a subscriber? Please accept a sincere thank you for being a fan of Black Rose Writing authors.

View other Black Rose Writing titles at www.blackrosewriting.com/books and use promo code **PRINT** to receive a **20% discount** when purchasing.